THE BOY I LIKED HAS GRADUATED.

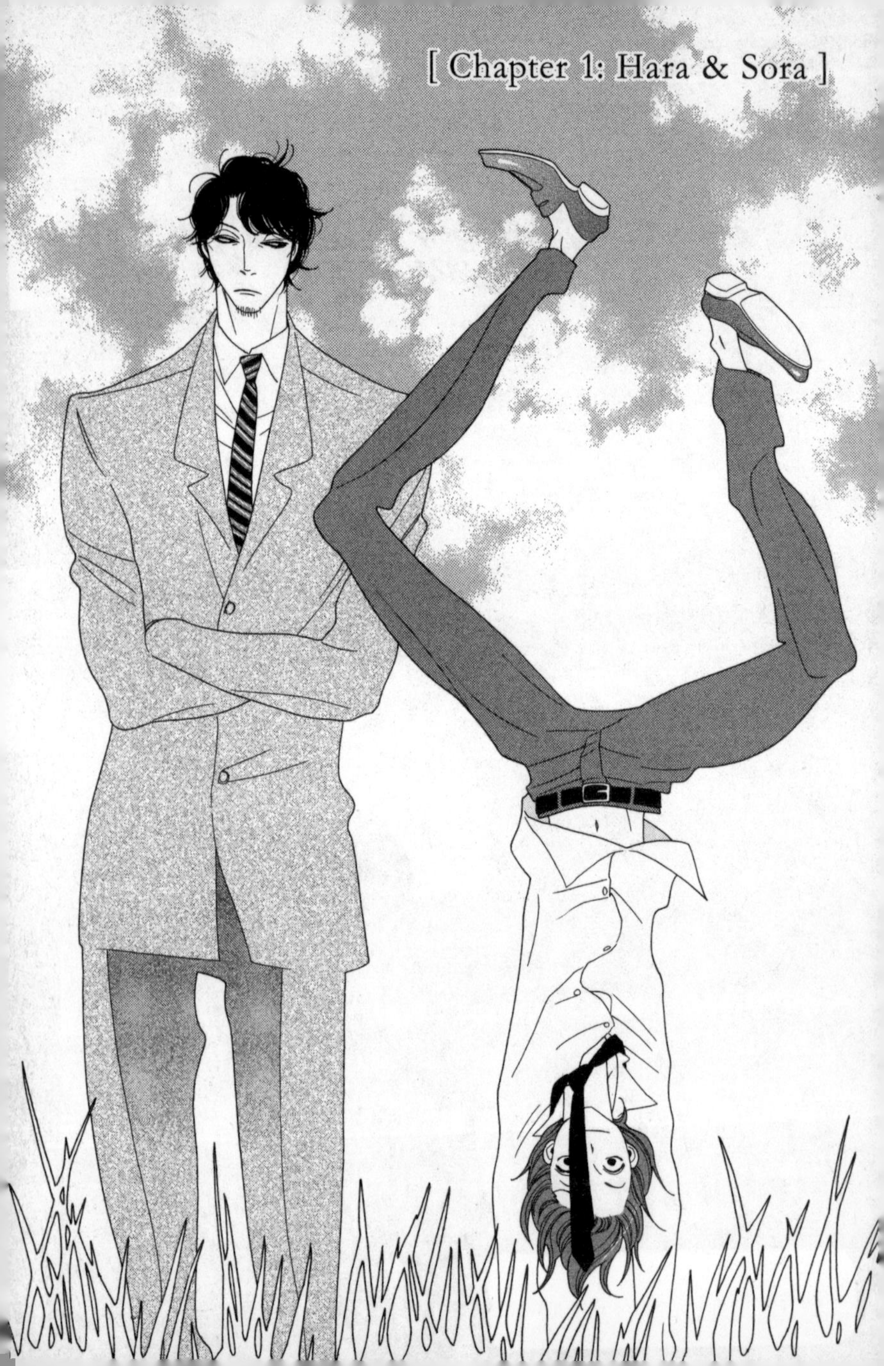
[Chapter 1: Hara & Sora]

Classmates Sora & Hara

volume four

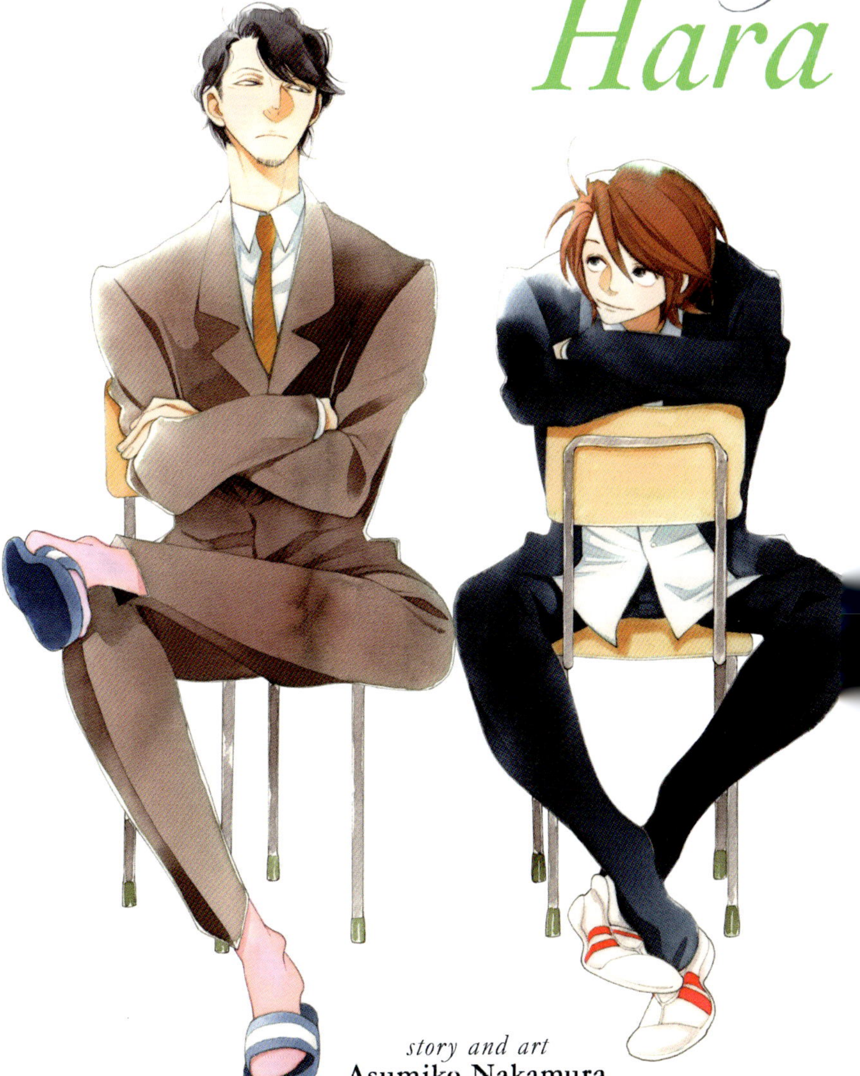

story and art

Asumiko Nakamura

CONTENTS

Chapter 1: Hara & Sora —————— 003

Chapter 2: Adult and Child —————— 035

Side Story: Undercut —————— 065

Chapter 3: Hara & Sajo —————— 079

Side Story: And...Kiss —————— 111

Chapter 4: Sorano & Fujino —————— 119

Chapter 5: Hara & Arisaka —————— 157

Chapter 6: Sora and the Drunk —————— 189

Final Chapter: Sora & Hara —————— 221

Translation note: In Japanese, "Sora" means sky and "Hara" roughly translates to field, so use of this shortened form of Sorano's name creates the title "Sora & Hara", which refers not only to the characters themselves but also invokes the image of the earth and sky.

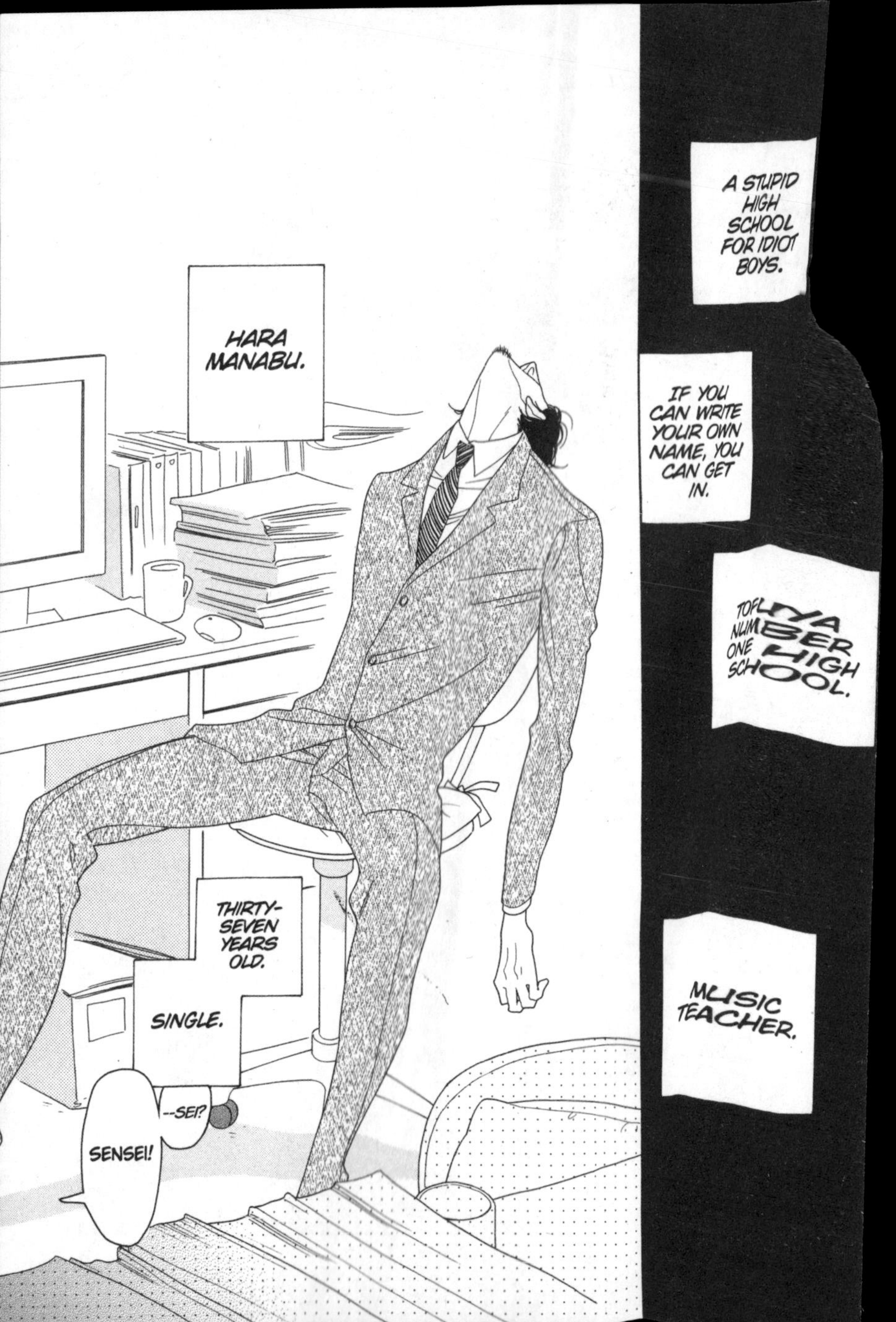
A STUPID HIGH SCHOOL FOR IDIOT BOYS.
IF YOU CAN WRITE YOUR OWN NAME, YOU CAN GET IN.
TOFUYA NUMBER ONE HIGH SCHOOL.
MUSIC TEACHER.
HARA MANABU.
THIRTY-SEVEN YEARS OLD.
SINGLE.
--SEI?
SENSEI!

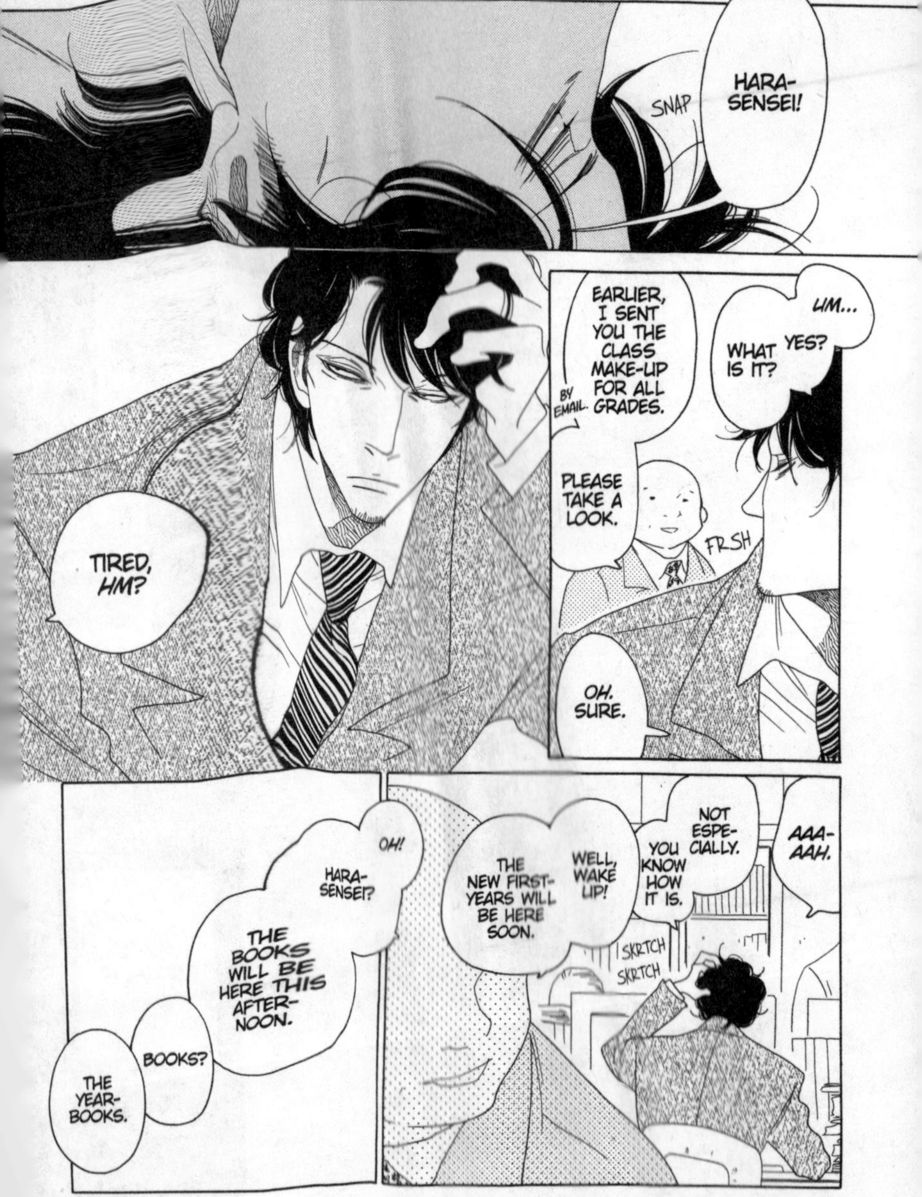
HARA-SENSEI!
SNAP
UM...
YES?
WHAT IS IT?
EARLIER, I SENT YOU THE CLASS MAKE-UP FOR ALL GRADES.
BY EMAIL.
PLEASE TAKE A LOOK.
FRSH
OH. SURE.
TIRED, HM?
AAAA-AAH.
NOT ESPE-CIALLY.
YOU KNOW HOW IT IS.
WELL, WAKE UP!
THE NEW FIRST-YEARS WILL BE HERE SOON.
SKRTCH
SKRTCH
OH!
HARA-SENSEI?
THE BOOKS WILL BE HERE THIS AFTER-NOON.
BOOKS?
THE YEAR-BOOKS.

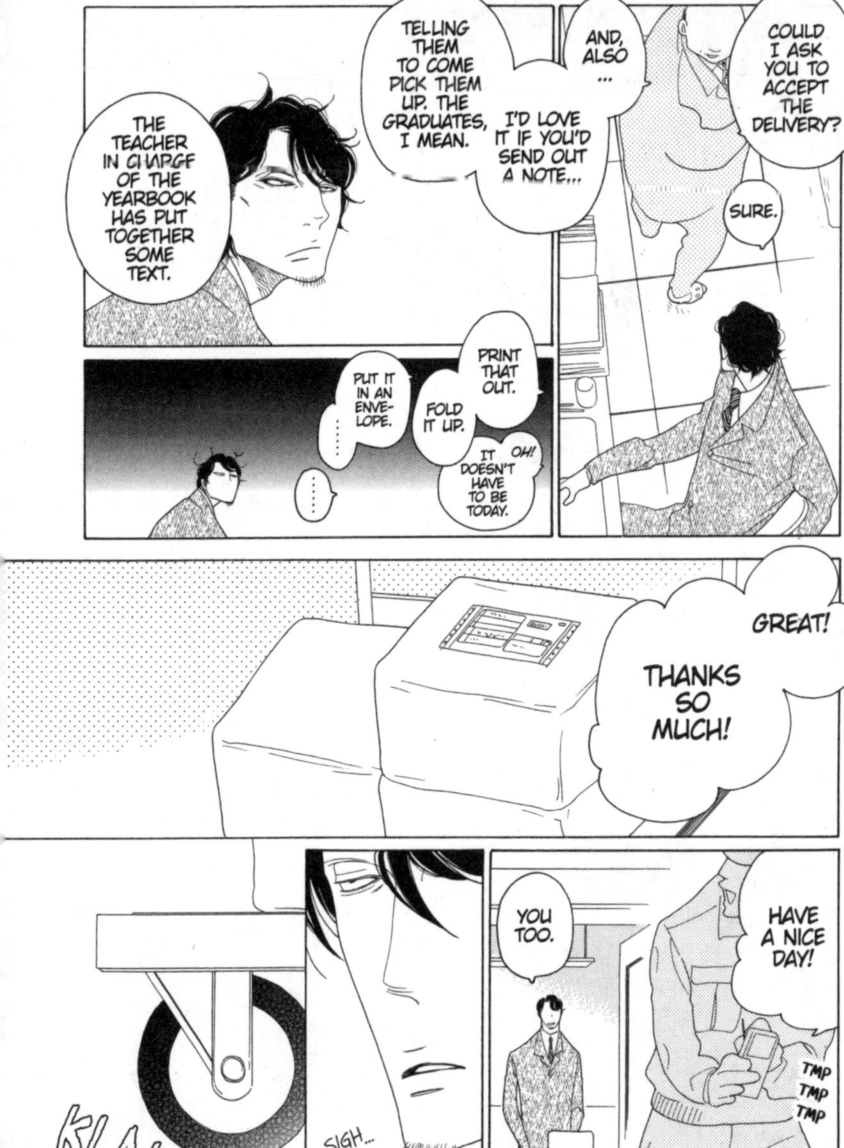
COULD I ASK YOU TO ACCEPT THE DELIVERY?
SURE.
AND, ALSO ...
I'D LOVE IT IF YOU'D SEND OUT A NOTE...
TELLING THEM TO COME PICK THEM UP. THE GRADUATES, I MEAN.
THE TEACHER IN CHARGE OF THE YEARBOOK HAS PUT TOGETHER SOME TEXT.
PRINT THAT OUT.
FOLD IT UP.
PUT IT IN AN ENVELOPE.
OH!
IT DOESN'T HAVE TO BE TODAY.
......
......
GREAT!
THANKS SO MUCH!
HAVE A NICE DAY!
TMP TMP TMP
YOU TOO.
SIGH...
KLAK

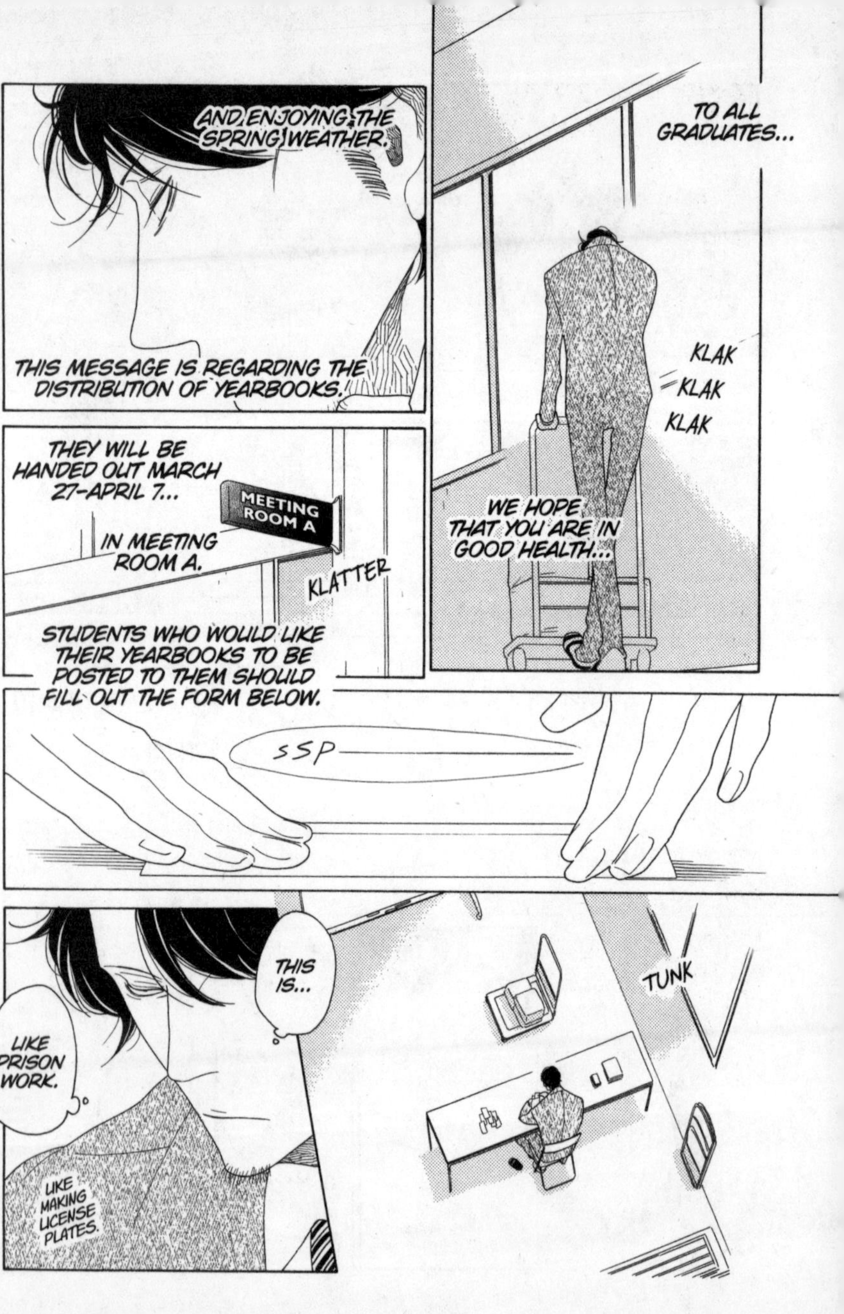
TO ALL GRADUATES...
KLAK
KLAK
KLAK
WE HOPE THAT YOU ARE IN GOOD HEALTH...
AND ENJOYING THE SPRING WEATHER.
THIS MESSAGE IS REGARDING THE DISTRIBUTION OF YEARBOOKS.
THEY WILL BE HANDED OUT MARCH 27-APRIL 7...
MEETING ROOM A
IN MEETING ROOM A.
KLATTER
STUDENTS WHO WOULD LIKE THEIR YEARBOOKS TO BE POSTED TO THEM SHOULD FILL OUT THE FORM BELOW.
SSP
TUNK
THIS IS...
LIKE PRISON WORK.
LIKE MAKING LICENSE PLATES.

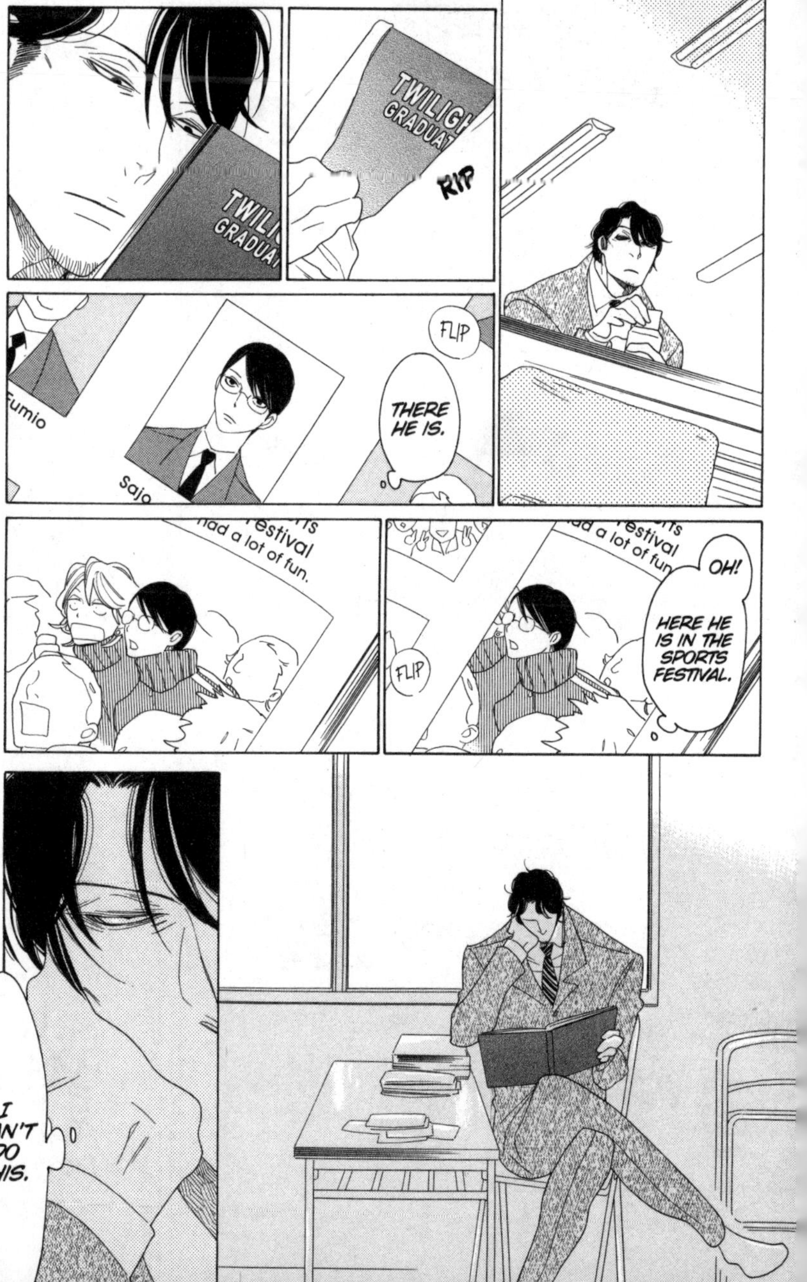
RIP
TWILIGH
GRADUAT
FLIP
THERE HE IS.
Fumio
Sajo
OH!
HERE HE IS IN THE SPORTS FESTIVAL.
FLIP
had a lot of fun.
I CAN'T DO THIS.

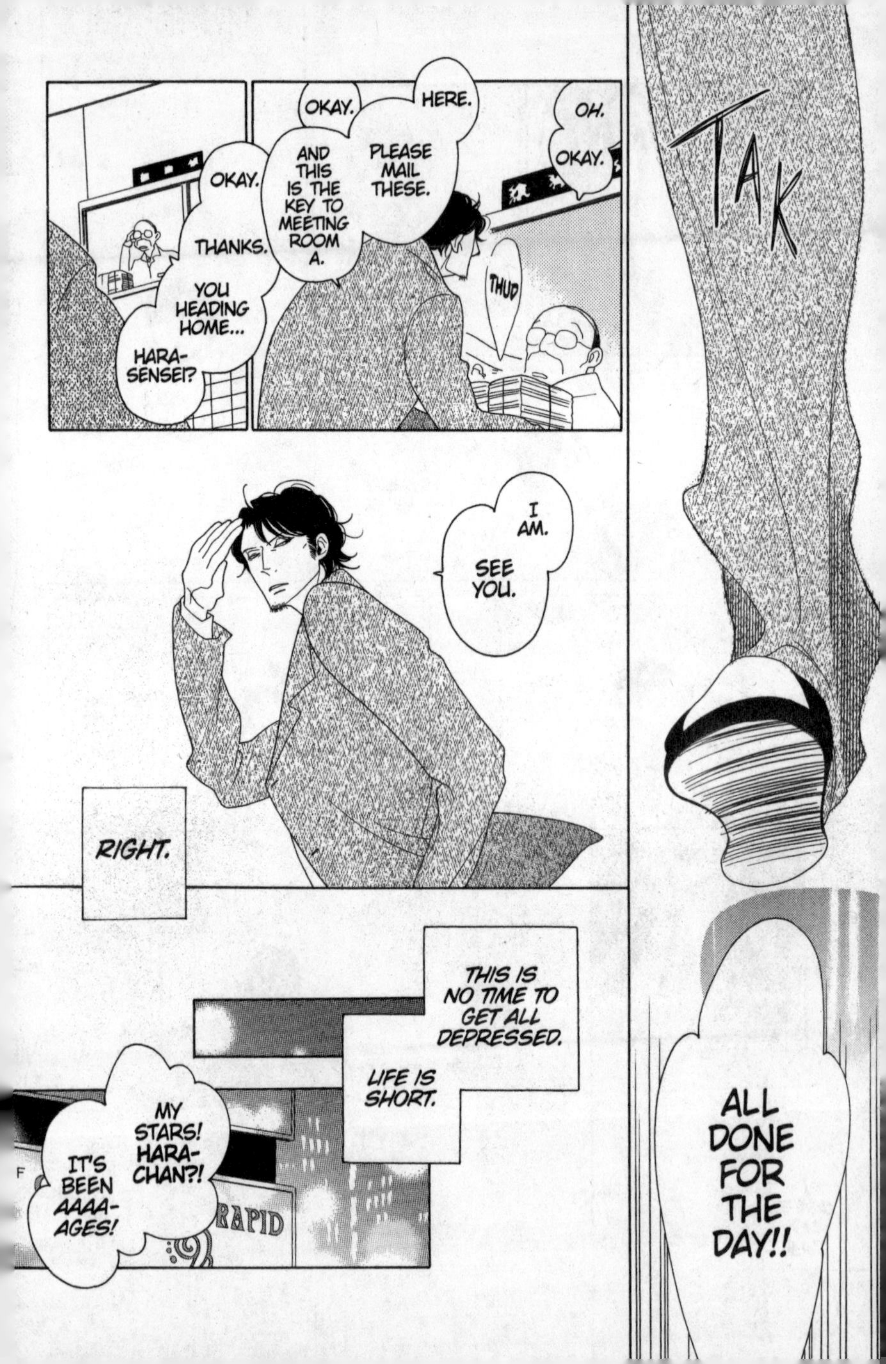
TAK
ALL DONE FOR THE DAY!!
HERE.
PLEASE MAIL THESE.
OH.
OKAY.
THUD
OKAY.
AND THIS IS THE KEY TO MEETING ROOM A.
OKAY.
THANKS.
YOU HEADING HOME...
HARA-SENSEI?
I AM.
SEE YOU.
RIGHT.
THIS IS NO TIME TO GET ALL DEPRESSED.
LIFE IS SHORT.
MY STARS! HARA-CHAN?!
IT'S BEEN AAAA-AGES!
RAPID

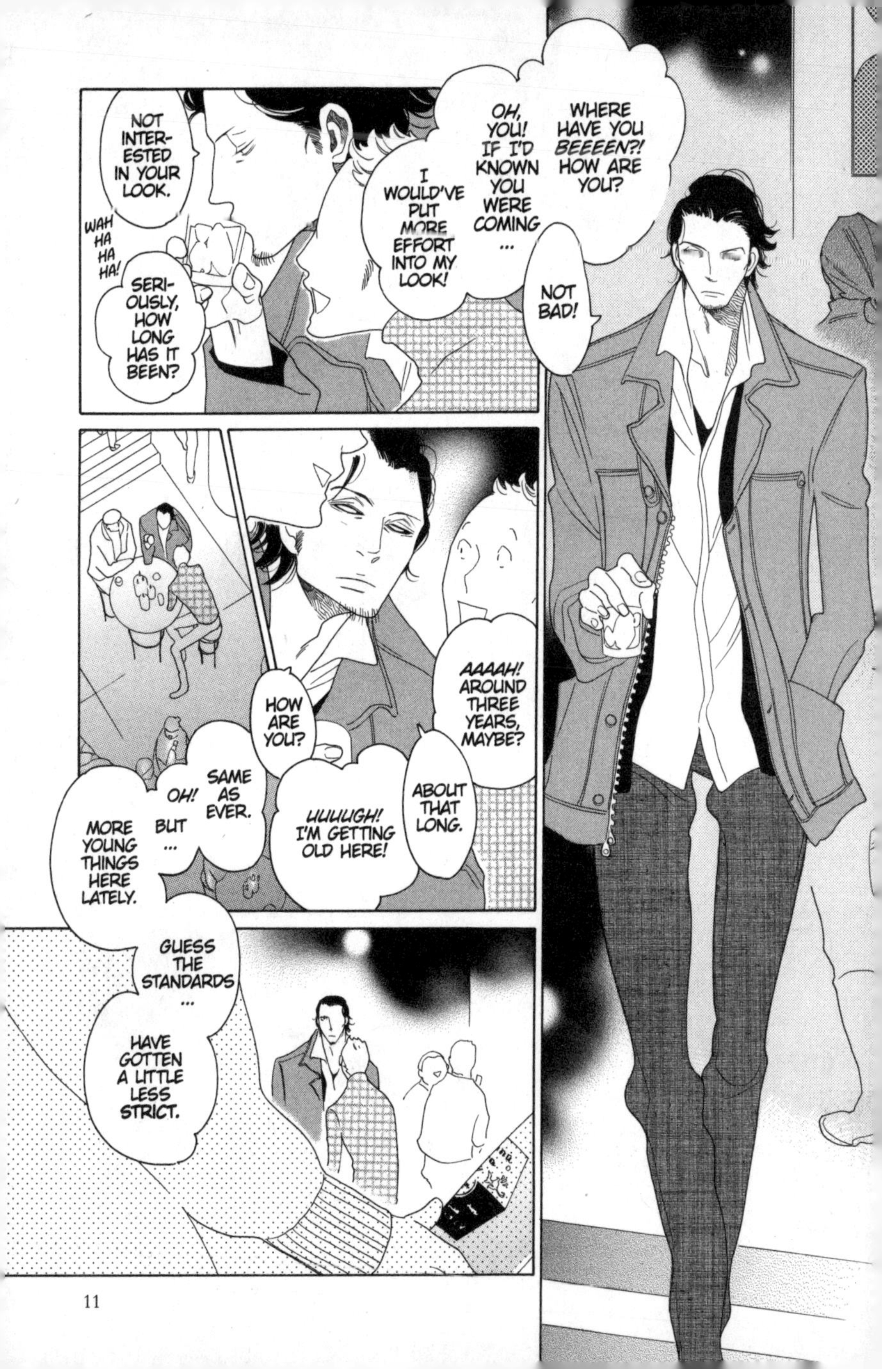
WHERE HAVE YOU BEEEEN?! HOW ARE YOU?
NOT BAD!
OH, YOU! IF I'D KNOWN YOU WERE COMING ...
I WOULD'VE PUT MORE EFFORT INTO MY LOOK!
NOT INTER-ESTED IN YOUR LOOK.
WAH HA HA HA!
SERI-OUSLY, HOW LONG HAS IT BEEN?
AAAAH! AROUND THREE YEARS, MAYBE?
HOW ARE YOU?
ABOUT THAT LONG.
UUUUGH! I'M GETTING OLD HERE!
SAME AS EVER.
OH! BUT ...
MORE YOUNG THINGS HERE LATELY.
GUESS THE STANDARDS ...
HAVE GOTTEN A LITTLE LESS STRICT.

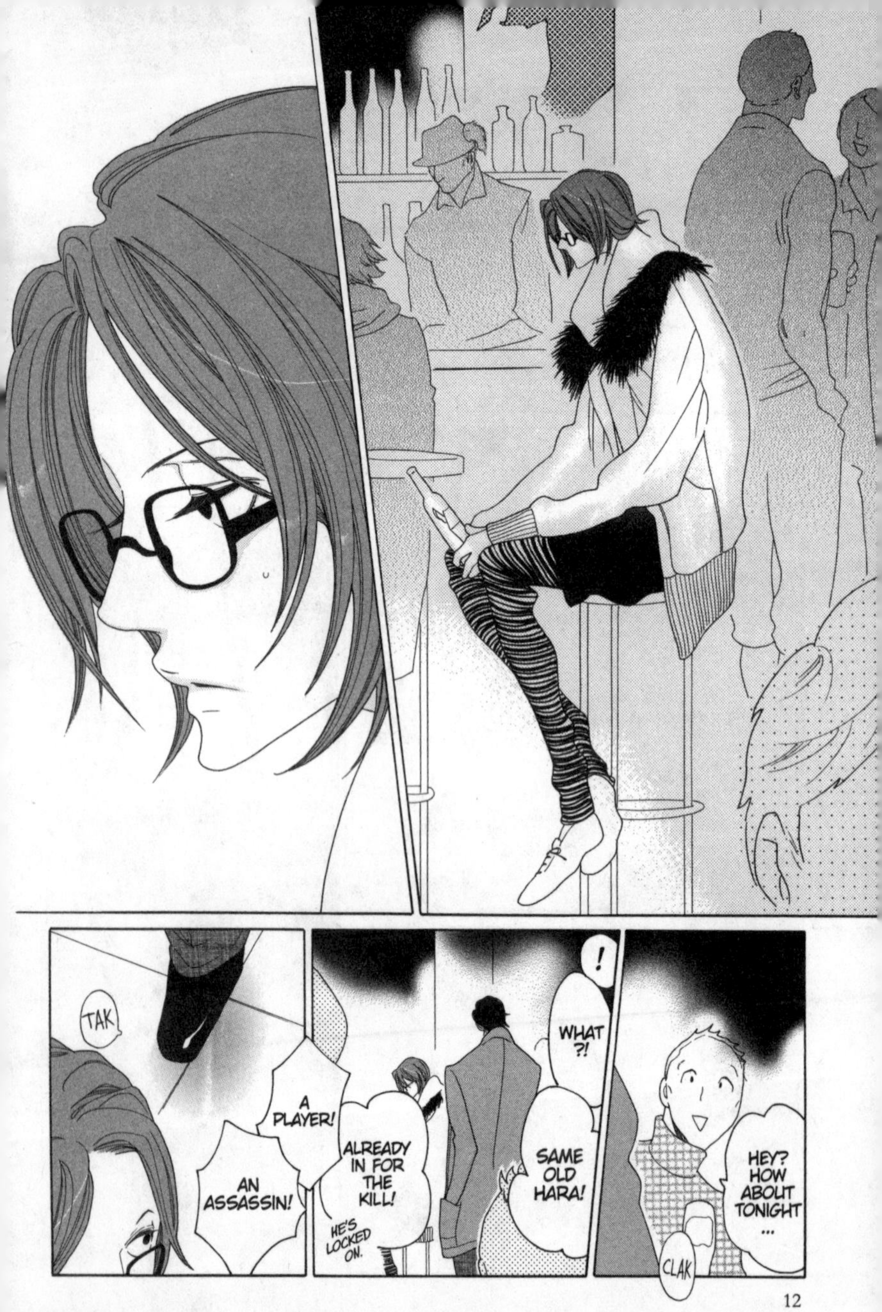
HEY? HOW ABOUT TONIGHT ...
CLAK
!
WHAT?!
SAME OLD HARA!
ALREADY IN FOR THE KILL!
HE'S LOCKED ON.
A PLAYER!
TAK
AN ASSASSIN!

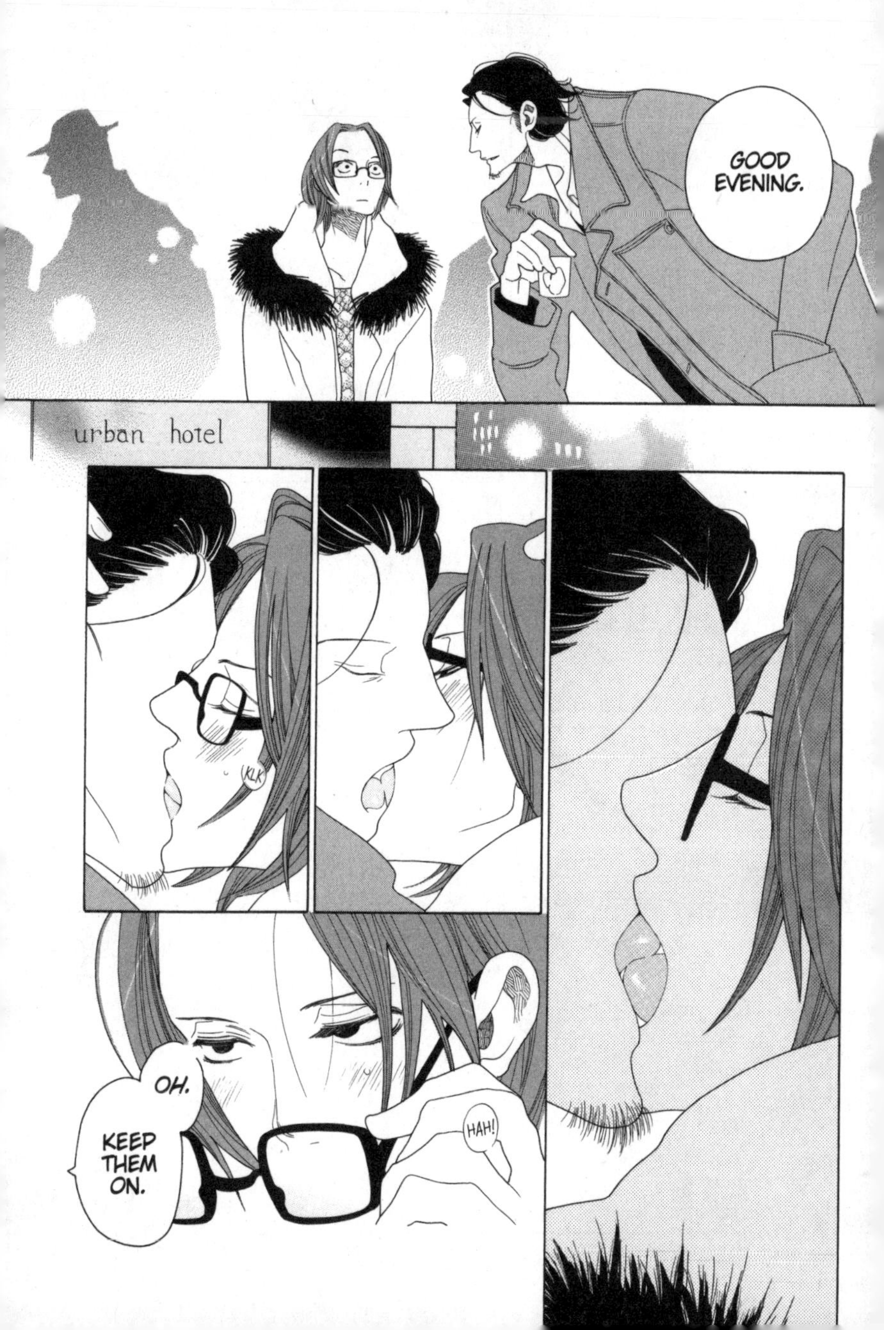
GOOD EVENING.
urban hotel
KLK
HAH!
OH.
KEEP THEM ON.

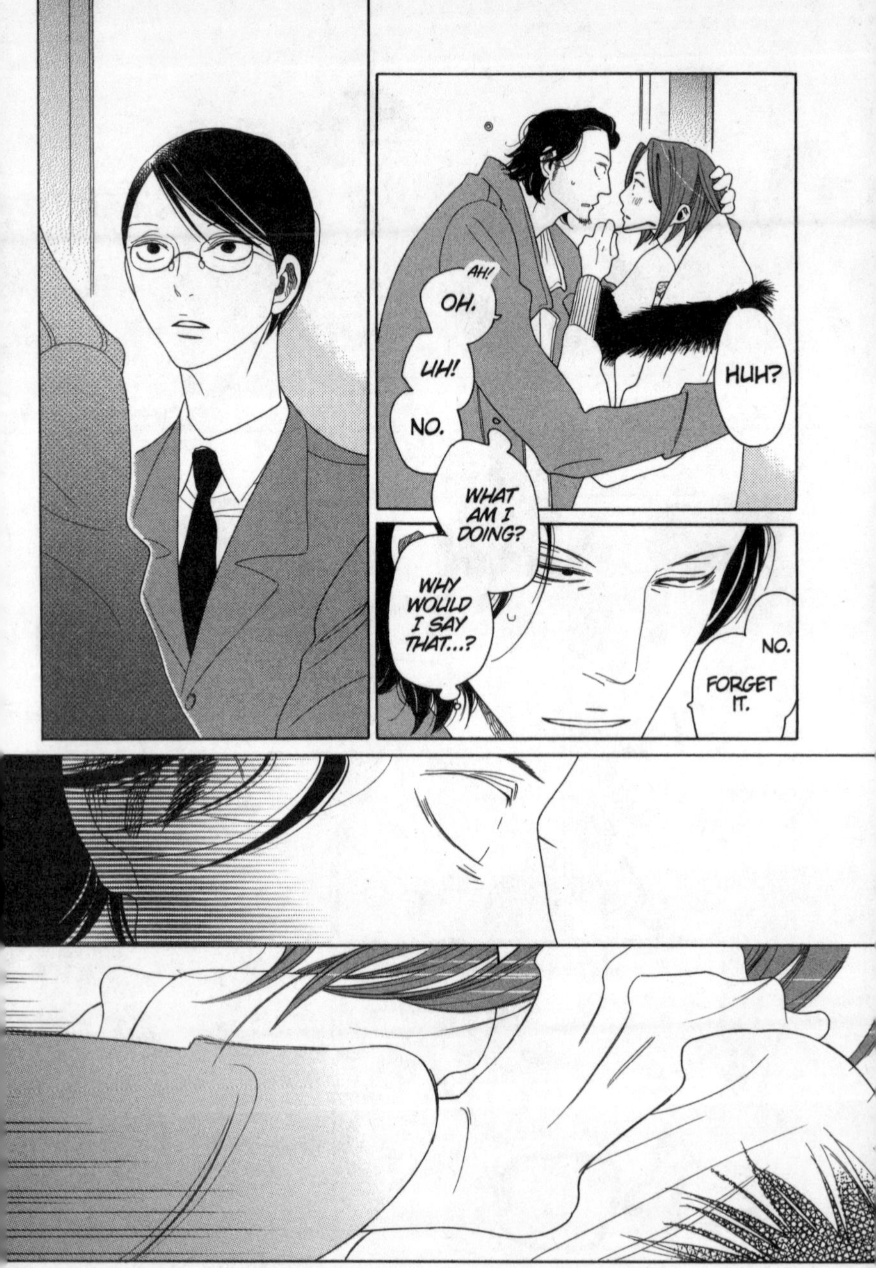
HUH?
AH!
OH.
UH!
NO.
WHAT AM I DOING?
NO.
FORGET IT.
WHY WOULD I SAY THAT...?

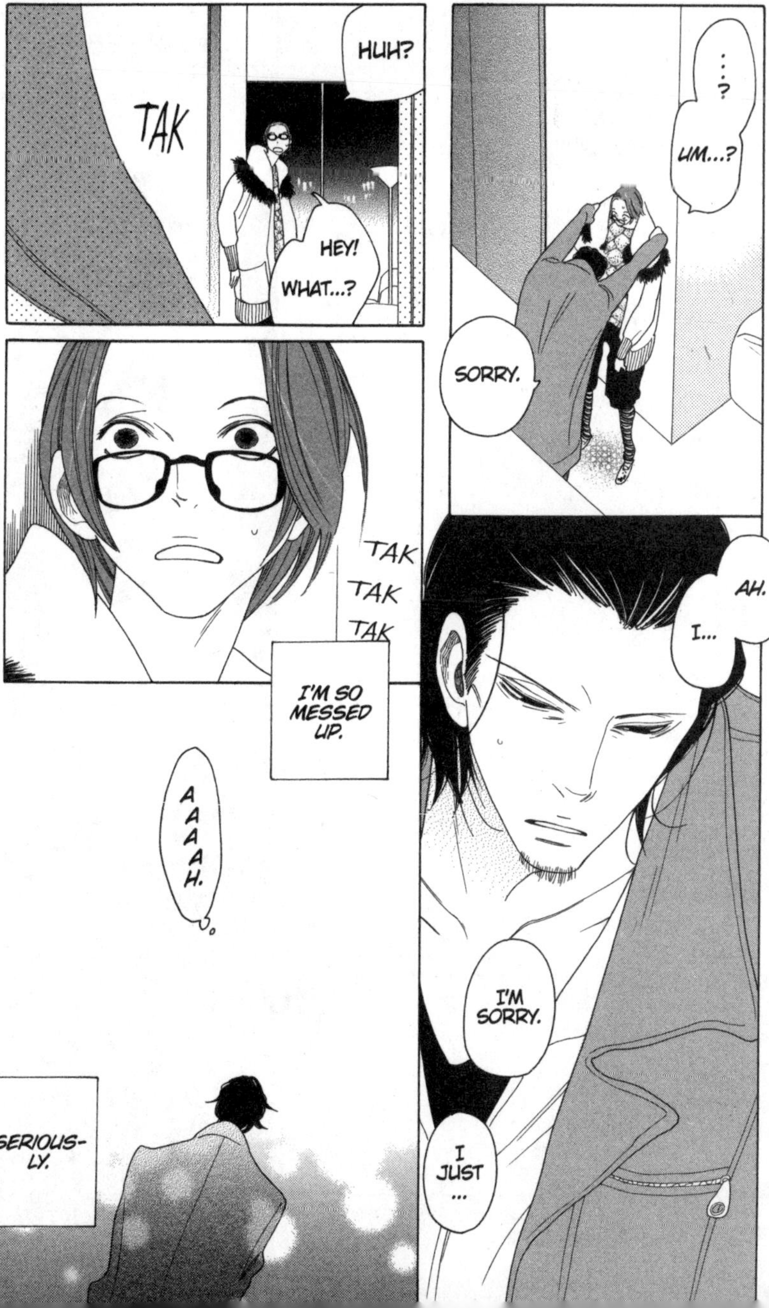
...?
UM...?
SORRY.
HUH?
TAK
HEY! WHAT...?
TAK
TAK
TAK
AH. I...
I'M SORRY.
I JUST ...
I'M SO MESSED UP.
AAAAAH.
SERIOUSLY.

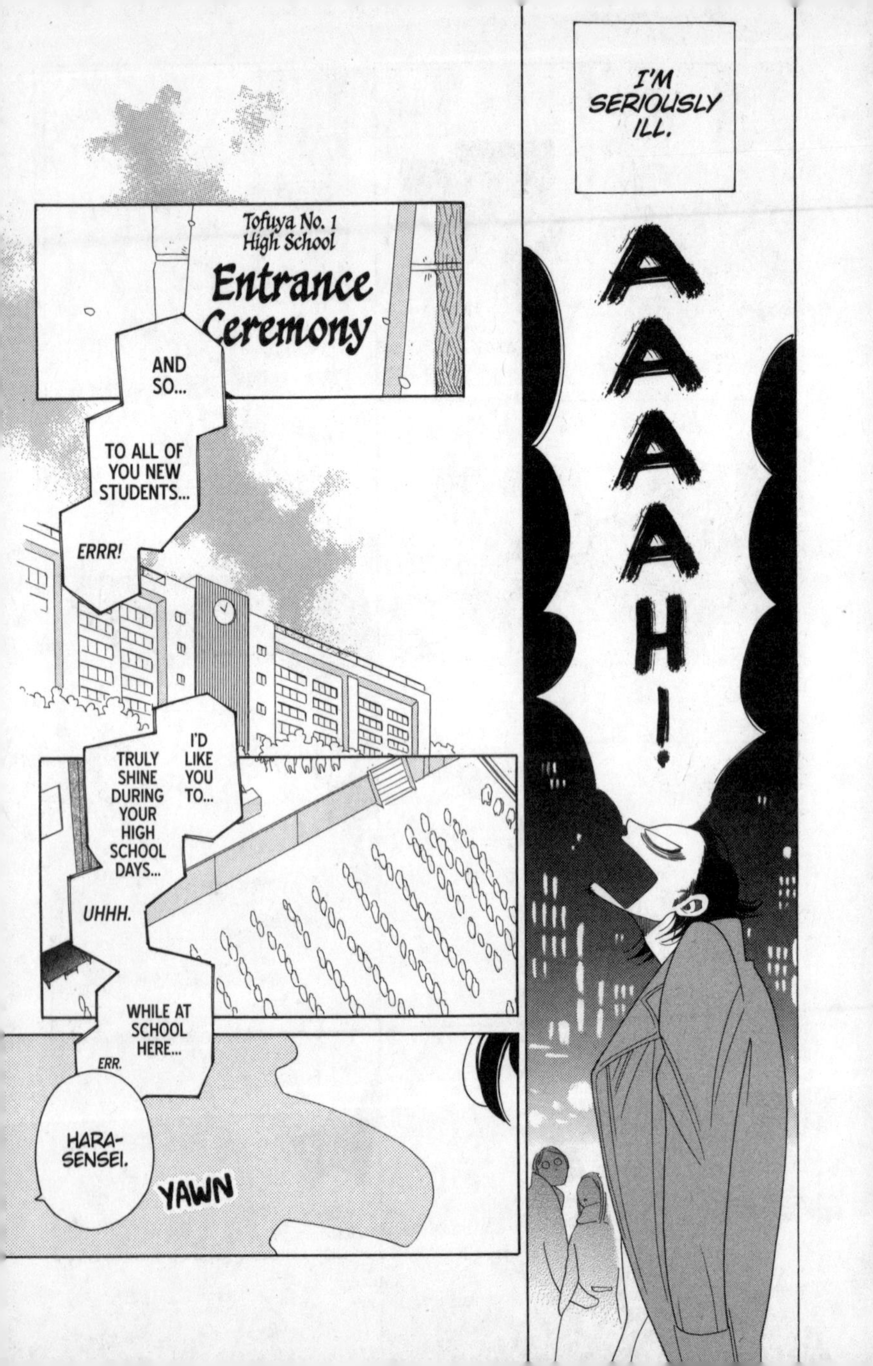
I'M SERIOUSLY ILL.
AAAAH!
Tofuya No. 1 High School
Entrance Ceremony
AND SO...
TO ALL OF YOU NEW STUDENTS...
ERRR!
I'D LIKE YOU TO...
TRULY SHINE DURING YOUR HIGH SCHOOL DAYS...
UHHH.
WHILE AT SCHOOL HERE...
ERR.
HARA-SENSEI.
YAWN

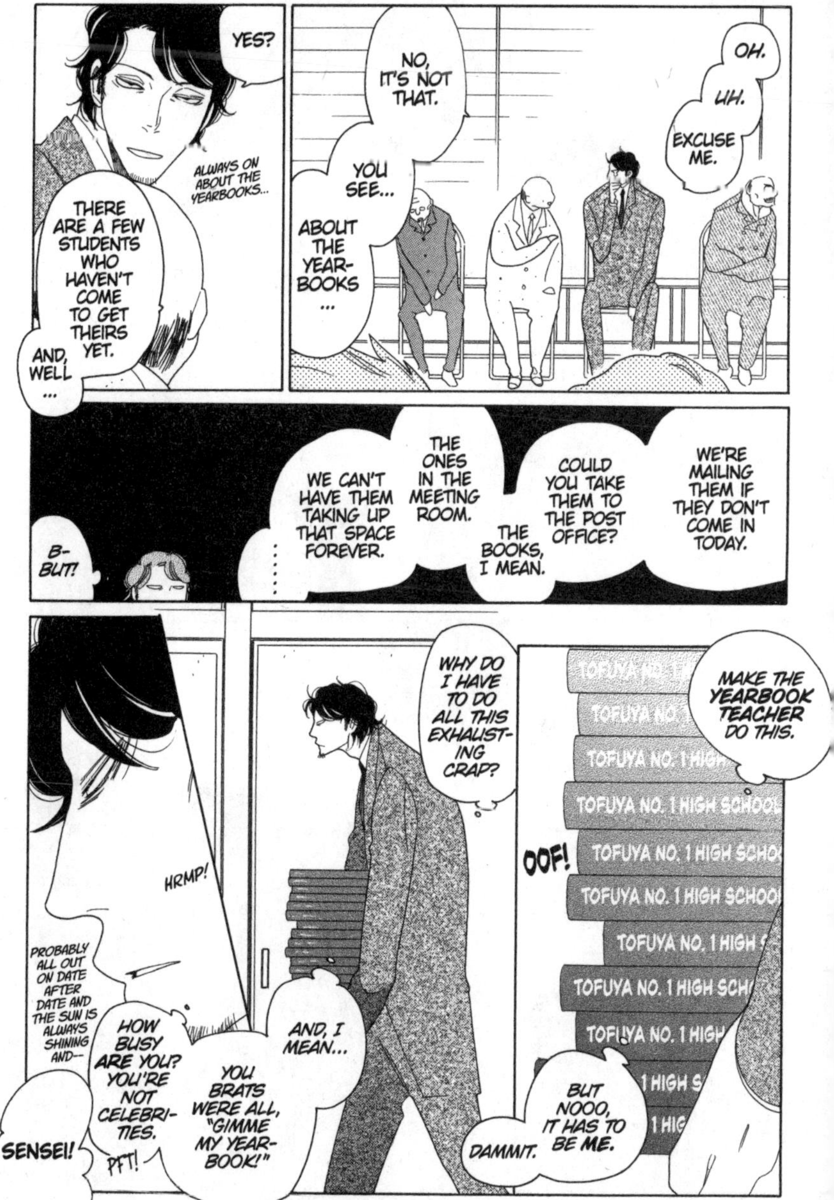
OH.
UH.
EXCUSE ME.
NO, IT'S NOT THAT.
YOU SEE...
ABOUT THE YEARBOOKS...
YES?
ALWAYS ON ABOUT THE YEARBOOKS...
THERE ARE A FEW STUDENTS WHO HAVEN'T COME TO GET THEIRS YET.
AND, WELL...
WE'RE MAILING THEM IF THEY DON'T COME IN TODAY.
COULD YOU TAKE THEM TO THE POST OFFICE?
THE BOOKS, I MEAN.
THE ONES IN THE MEETING ROOM.
WE CAN'T HAVE THEM TAKING UP THAT SPACE FOREVER.
......
B-BUT!
MAKE THE YEARBOOK TEACHER DO THIS.
TOFUYA NO. 1 HIGH SCHOOL
OOF!
BUT NOOO, IT HAS TO BE ME.
DAMMIT.
WHY DO I HAVE TO DO ALL THIS EXHAUSTING CRAP?
AND, I MEAN...
YOU BRATS WERE ALL, "GIMME MY YEARBOOK!"
HRMP!
PROBABLY ALL OUT ON DATE AFTER DATE AND THE SUN IS ALWAYS SHINING AND--
HOW BUSY ARE YOU? YOU'RE NOT CELEBRITIES.
PFT!
SENSEI!

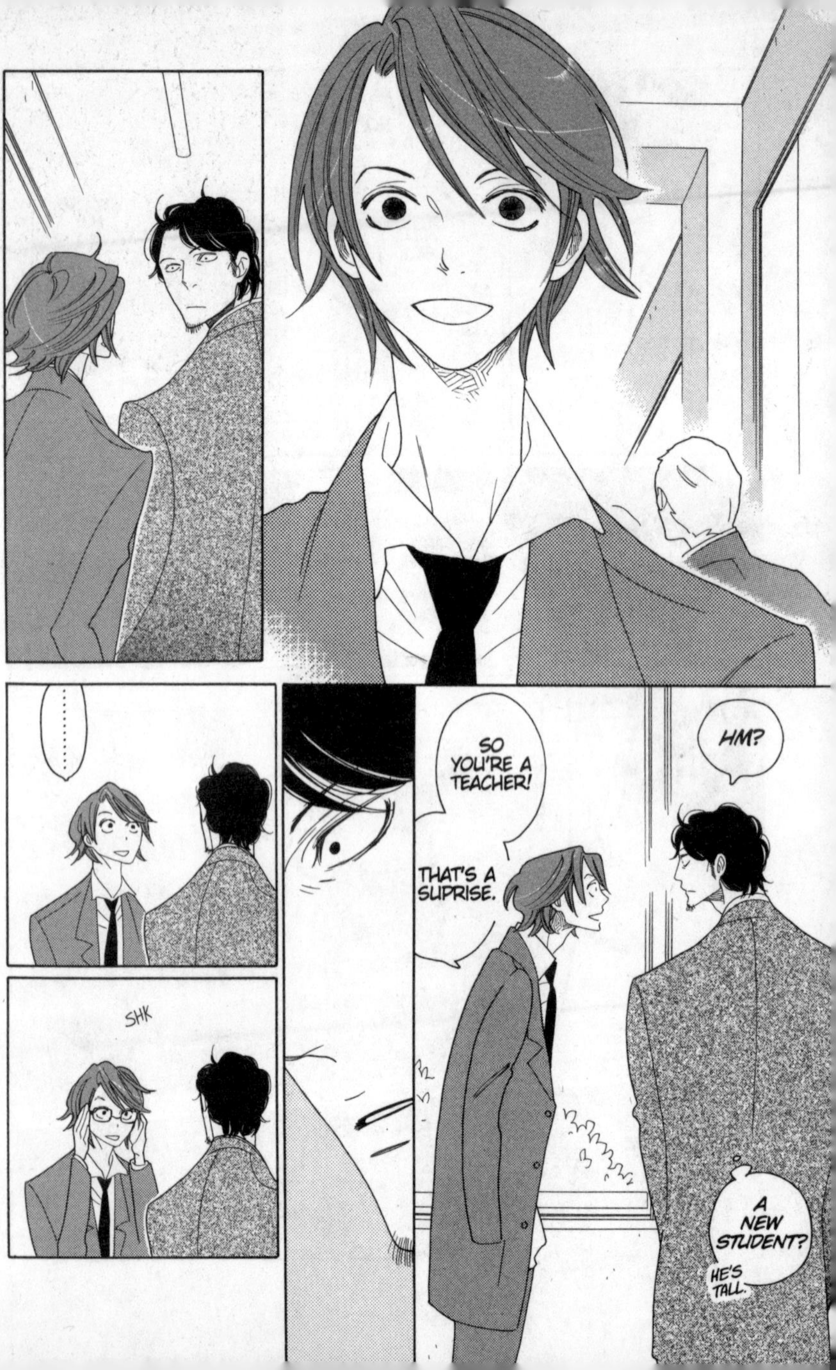
HM?
SO YOU'RE A TEACHER!
THAT'S A SUPRISE.
A NEW STUDENT?
HE'S TALL.
......
SHK

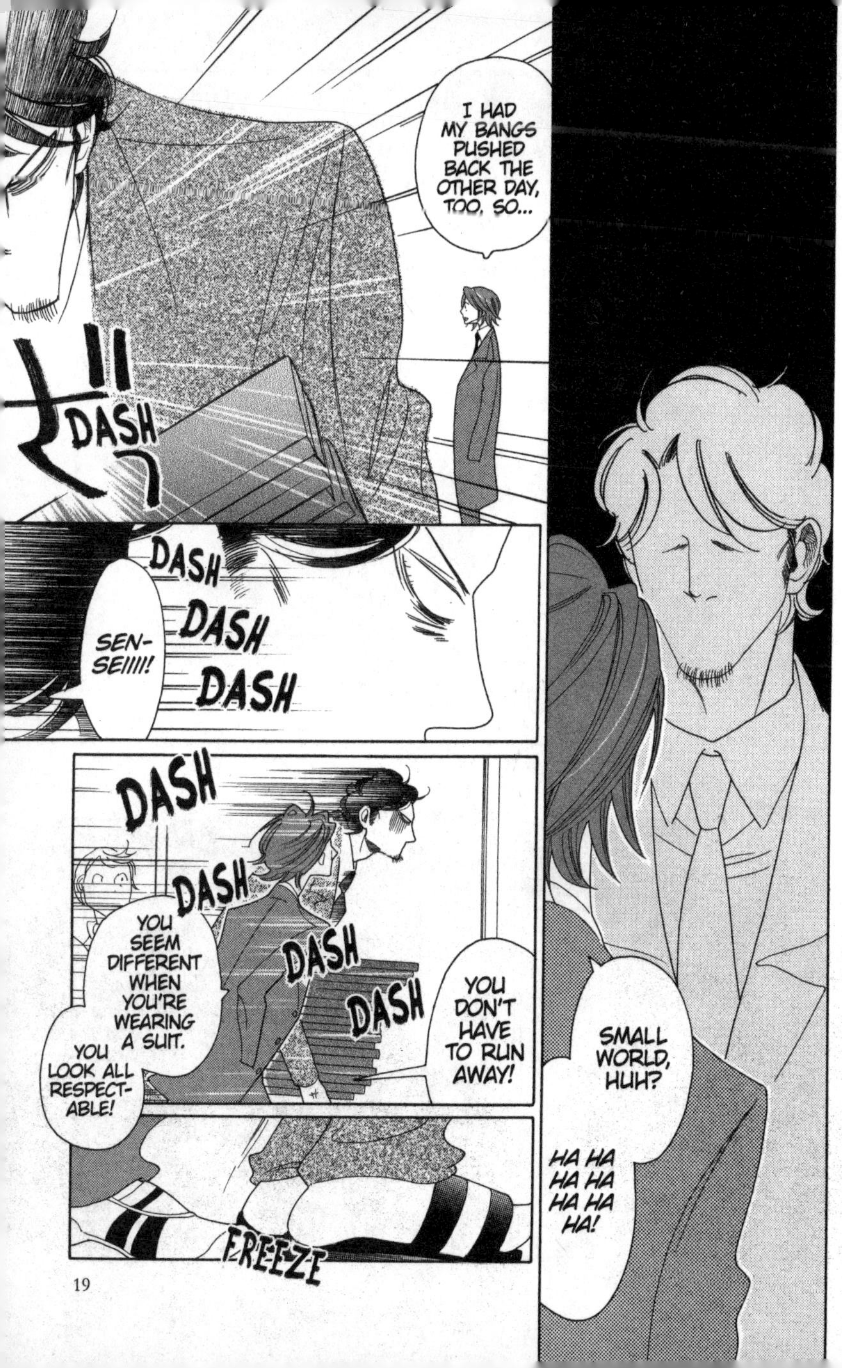
SMALL WORLD, HUH?
HA HA HA HA HA HA HA!
I HAD MY BANGS PUSHED BACK THE OTHER DAY, TOO, SO...
DASH
DASH
DASH
DASH
SEN-SEI!!!!!
DASH
DASH
DASH
DASH
YOU DON'T HAVE TO RUN AWAY!
YOU SEEM DIFFERENT WHEN YOU'RE WEARING A SUIT.
YOU LOOK ALL RESPECT-ABLE!
FREEZE

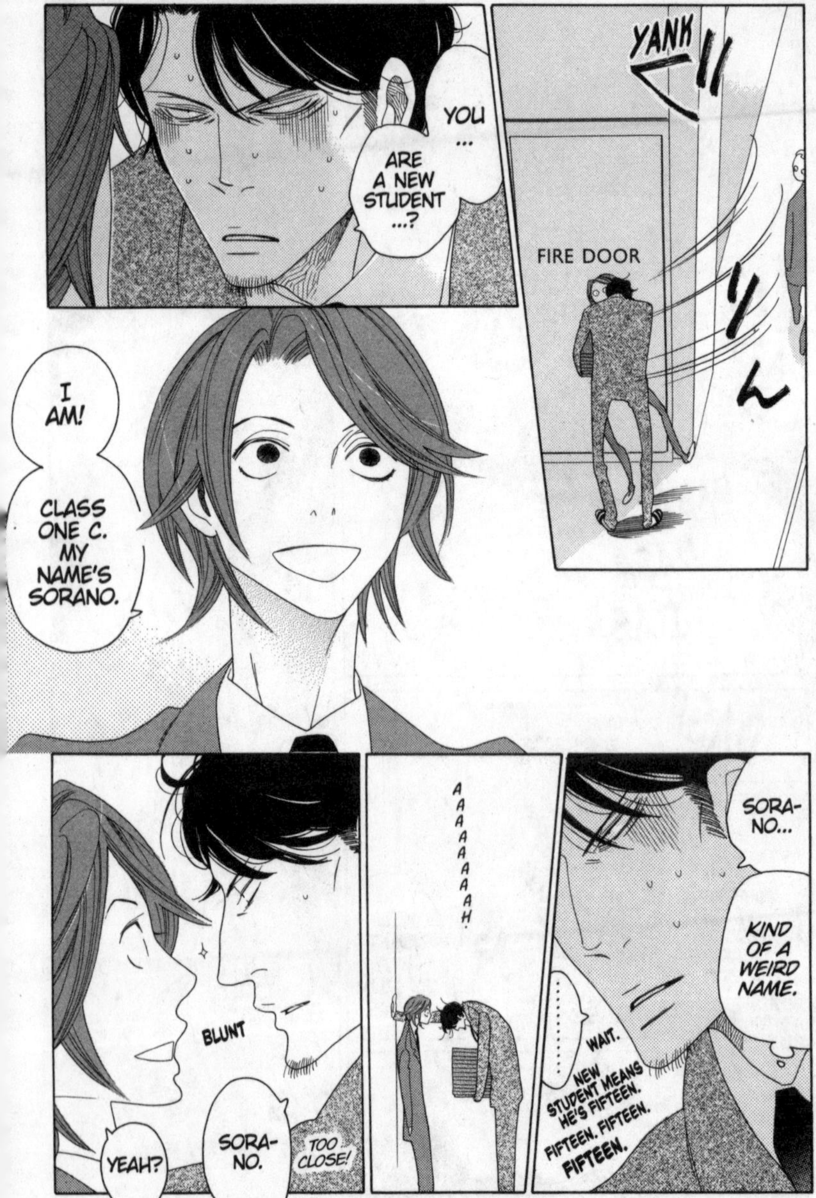
YANK
FIRE DOOR
YOU ... ARE A NEW STUDENT ...?
I AM!
CLASS ONE C. MY NAME'S SORANO.
SORA-NO...
KIND OF A WEIRD NAME.
WAIT.
NEW STUDENT MEANS HE'S FIFTEEN. FIFTEEN. FIFTEEN. FIFTEEN.
AAAAAAAAAH!
BLUNT
SORA-NO.
YEAH?
TOO CLOSE!

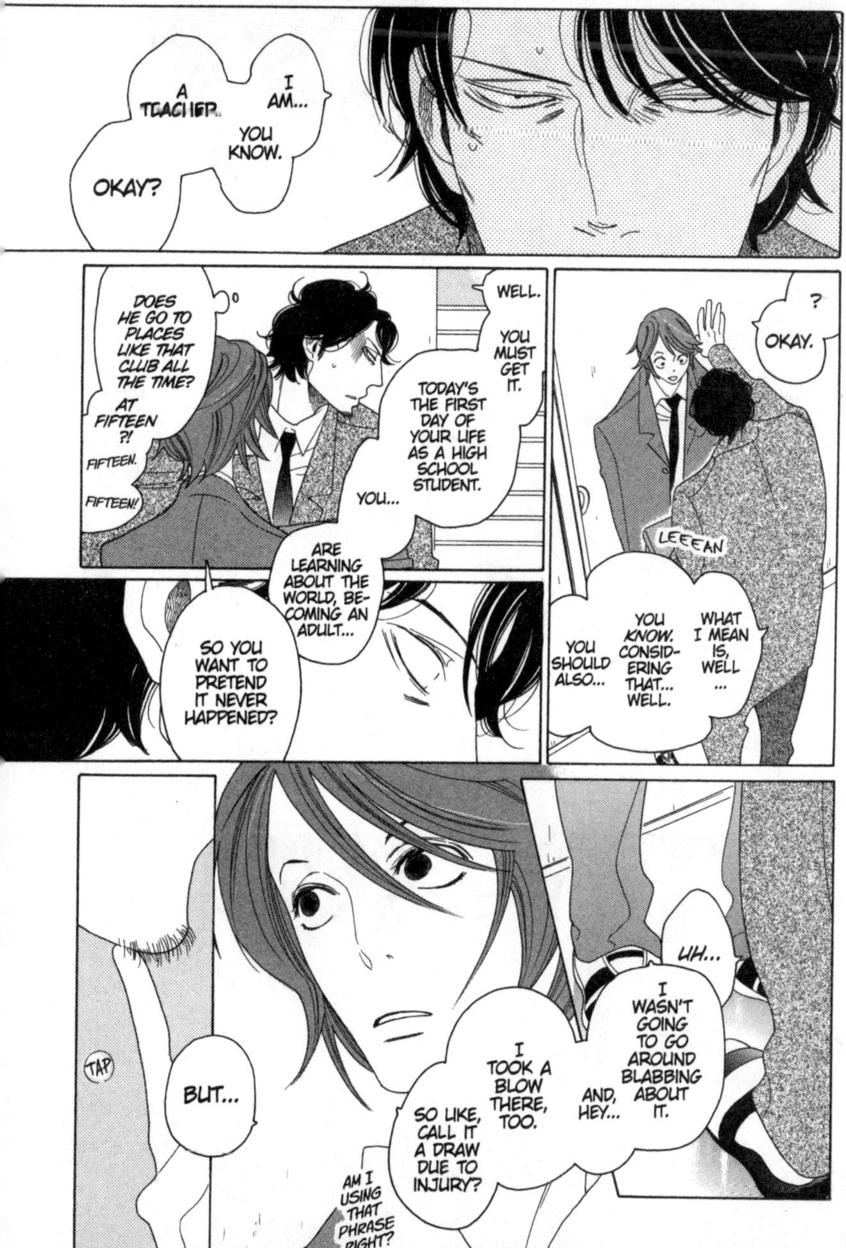
I AM...
A TEACHER.
YOU KNOW.
OKAY?
?
OKAY.
LEEEAN
WHAT I MEAN IS, WELL ...
YOU KNOW. CONSIDERING THAT... WELL.
YOU SHOULD ALSO...
WELL.
YOU MUST GET IT.
TODAY'S THE FIRST DAY OF YOUR LIFE AS A HIGH SCHOOL STUDENT.
YOU...
DOES HE GO TO PLACES LIKE THAT CLUB ALL THE TIME?
AT FIFTEEN?!
FIFTEEN.
FIFTEEN!
ARE LEARNING ABOUT THE WORLD, BECOMING AN ADULT...
SO YOU WANT TO PRETEND IT NEVER HAPPENED?
UH...
I WASN'T GOING TO GO AROUND BLABBING ABOUT IT.
AND, HEY...
I TOOK A BLOW THERE, TOO.
SO LIKE, CALL IT A DRAW DUE TO INJURY?
AM I USING THAT PHRASE RIGHT?
BUT...
TAP

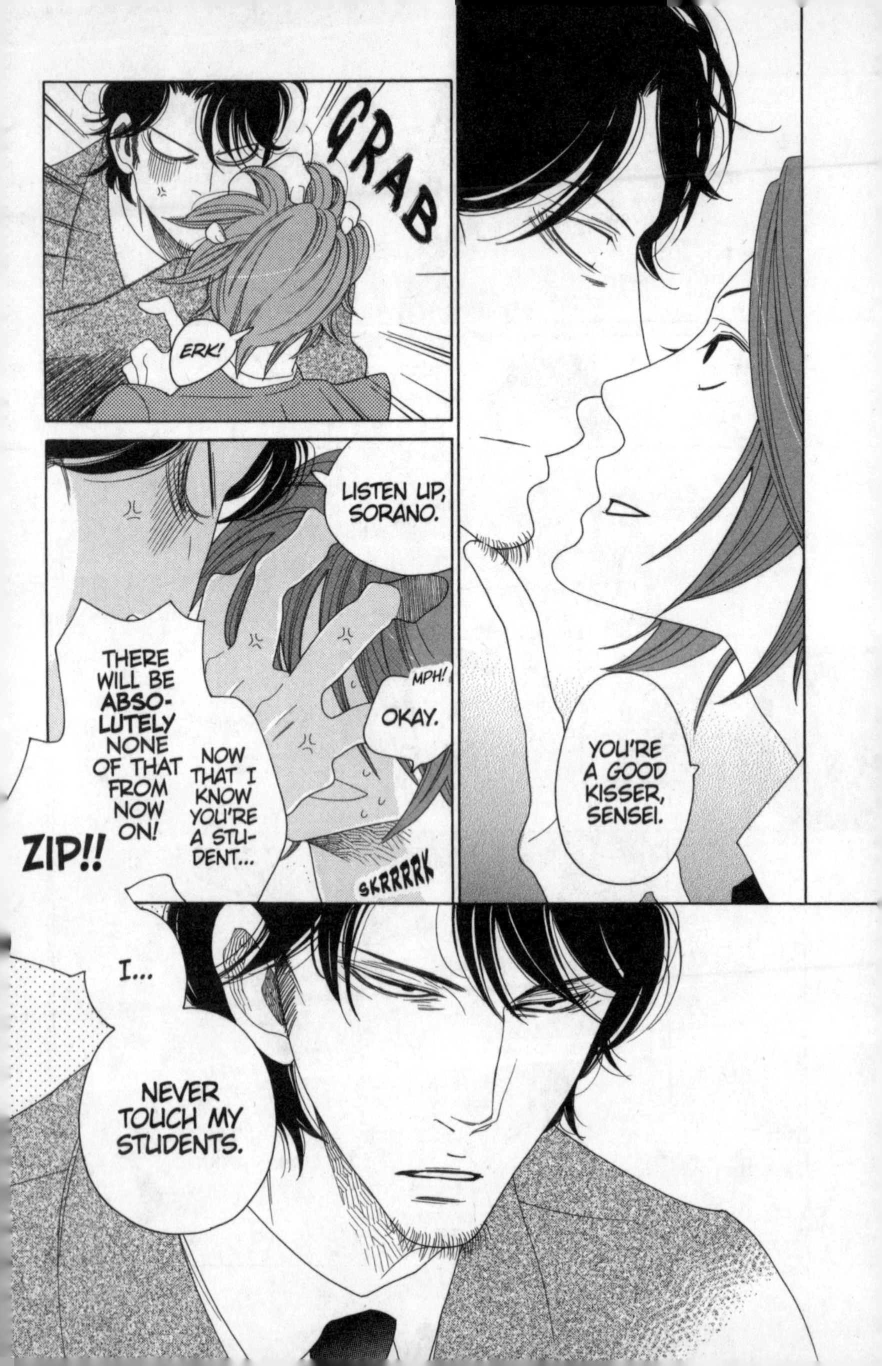
YOU'RE A GOOD KISSER, SENSEI.
GRAB
ERK!
LISTEN UP, SORANO.
MPH!
OKAY.
NOW THAT I KNOW YOU'RE A STUDENT...
THERE WILL BE ABSOLUTELY NONE OF THAT FROM NOW ON!
SKRRRRK
ZIP!!
I...
NEVER TOUCH MY STUDENTS.

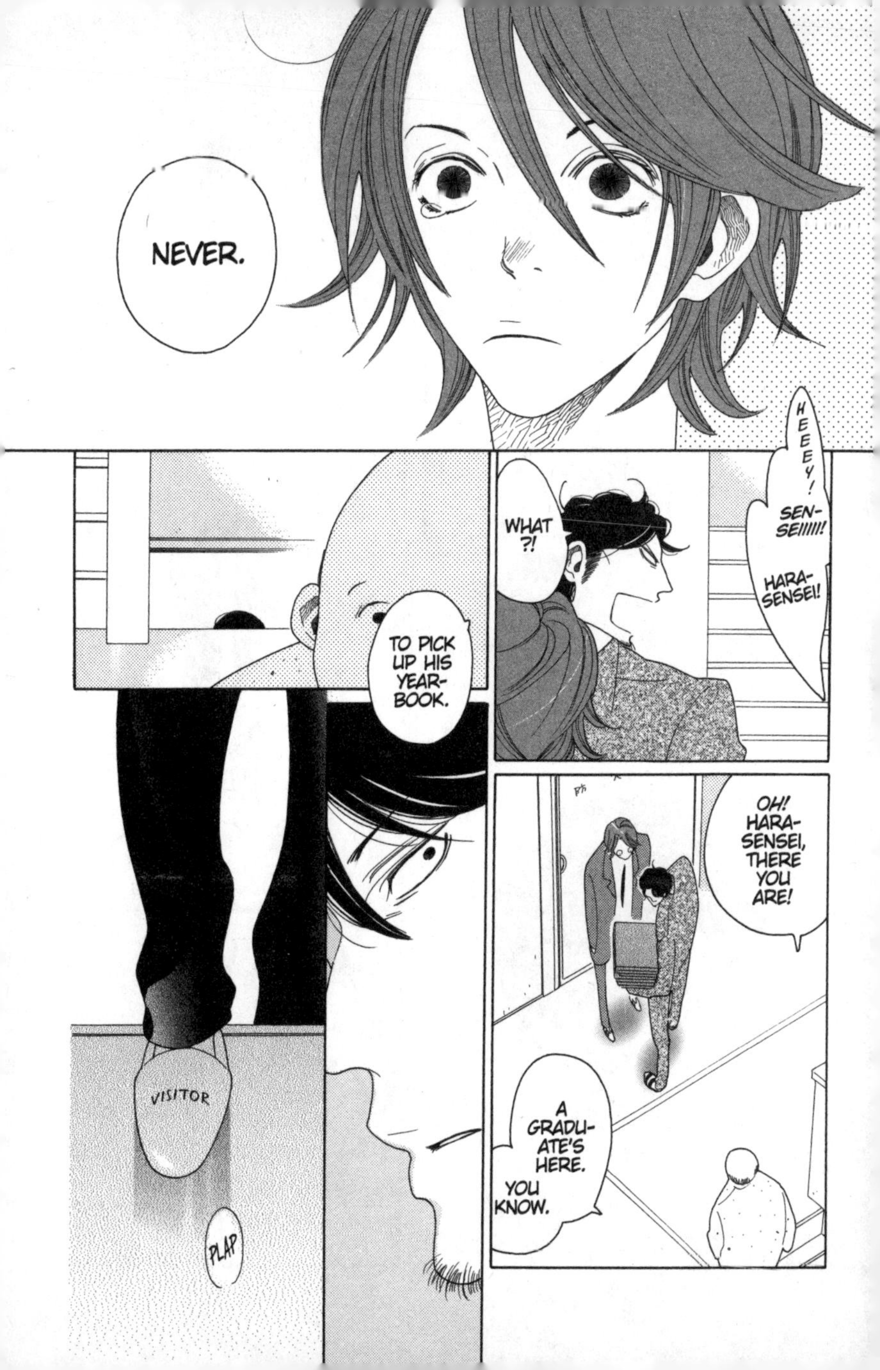
NEVER.
HEEEY! SENSEIIIII! HARA-SENSEI!
WHAT?!
OH! HARA-SENSEI, THERE YOU ARE!
A GRADUATE'S HERE. YOU KNOW.
TO PICK UP HIS YEARBOOK.
VISITOR
PLAP

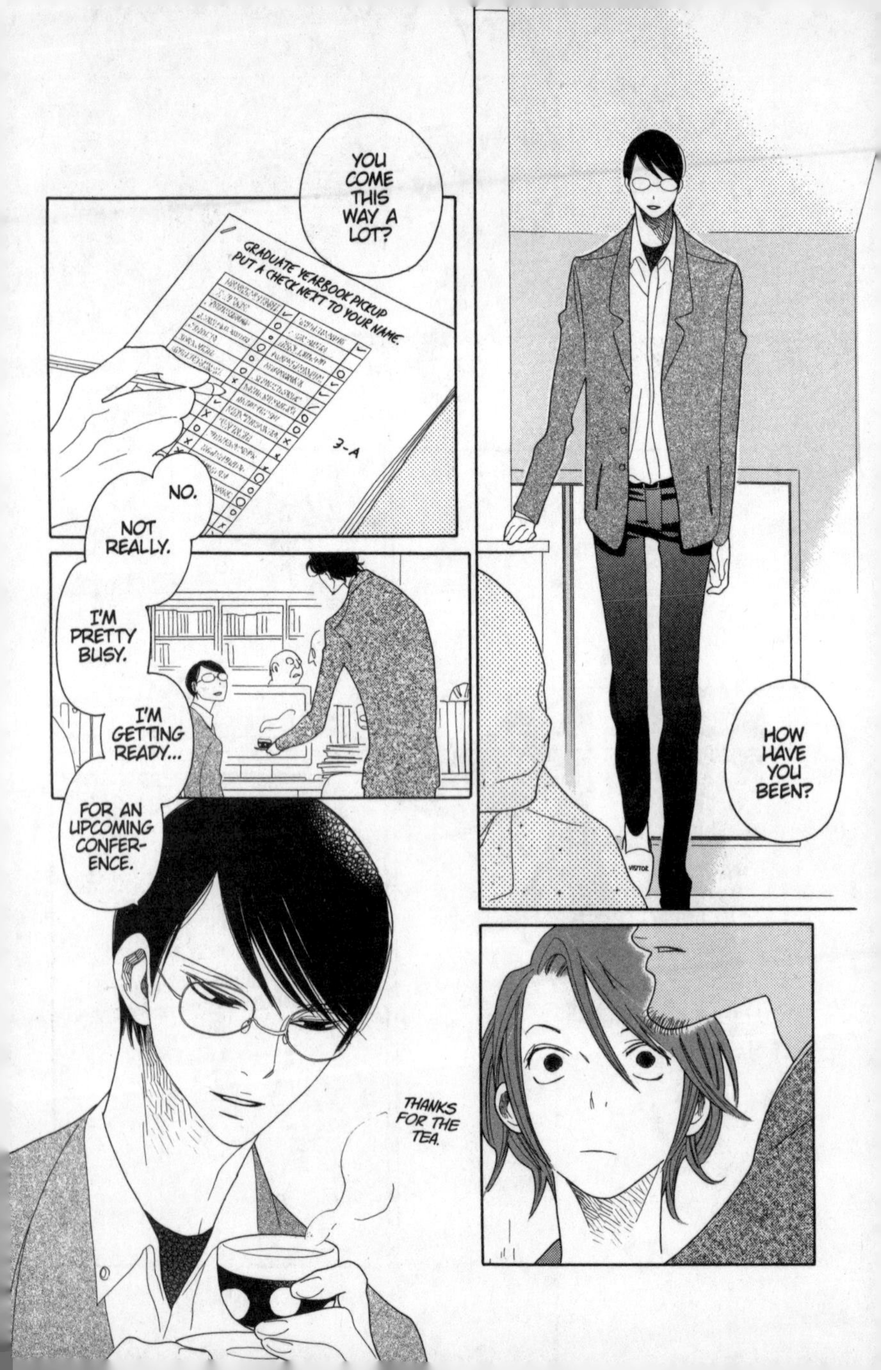
VISITOR
HOW HAVE YOU BEEN?
YOU COME THIS WAY A LOT?
GRADUATE YEARBOOK PICKUP
PUT A CHECK NEXT TO YOUR NAME.
3-A
NO.
NOT REALLY.
I'M PRETTY BUSY.
I'M GETTING READY...
FOR AN UPCOMING CONFERENCE.
THANKS FOR THE TEA.

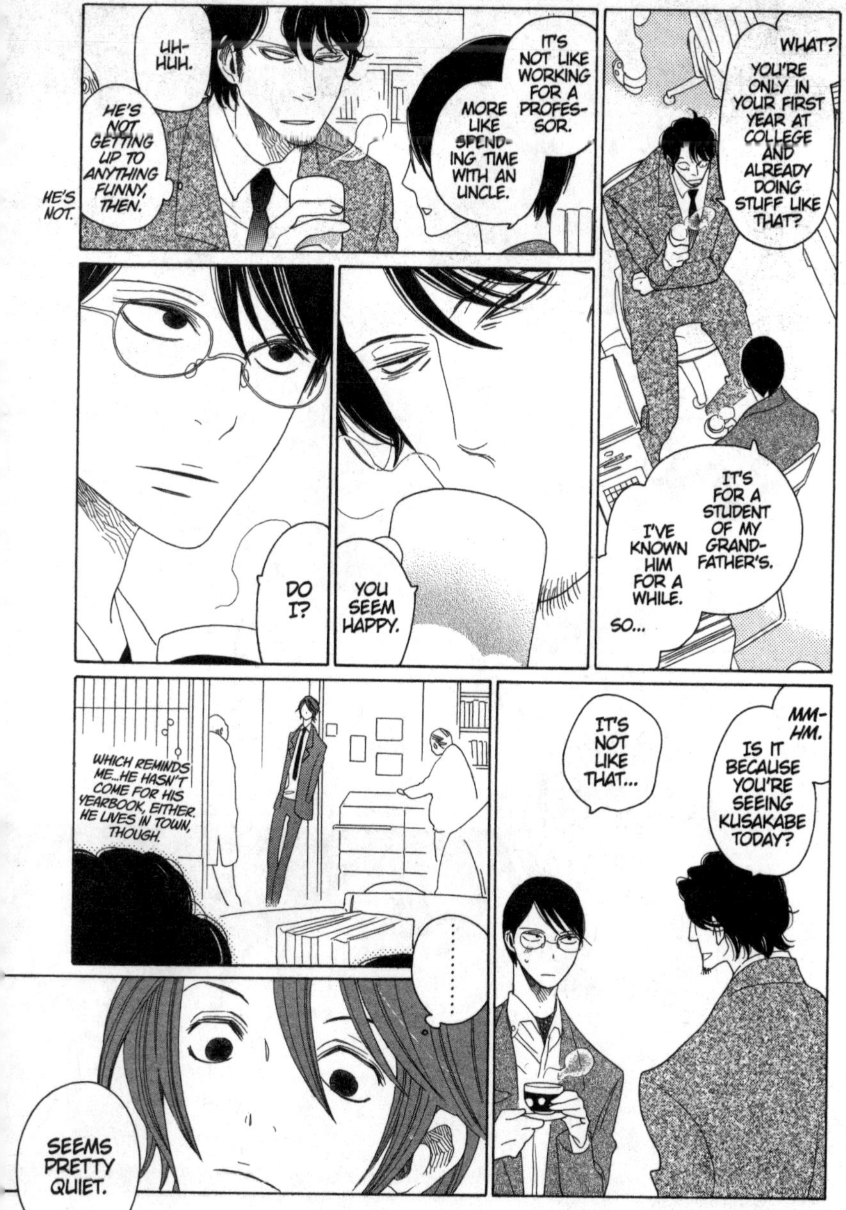
WHAT?
YOU'RE ONLY IN YOUR FIRST YEAR AT COLLEGE AND ALREADY DOING STUFF LIKE THAT?
IT'S FOR A STUDENT OF MY GRAND-FATHER'S.
I'VE KNOWN HIM FOR A WHILE.
SO...
IT'S NOT LIKE WORKING FOR A PROFES-SOR.
MORE LIKE SPEND-ING TIME WITH AN UNCLE.
UH-HUH.
HE'S NOT GETTING UP TO ANYTHING FUNNY, THEN.
HE'S NOT.
YOU SEEM HAPPY.
DO I?
MM-HM.
IS IT BECAUSE YOU'RE SEEING KUSAKABE TODAY?
IT'S NOT LIKE THAT...
WHICH REMINDS ME...HE HASN'T COME FOR HIS YEARBOOK, EITHER. HE LIVES IN TOWN, THOUGH.
......
SEEMS PRETTY QUIET.

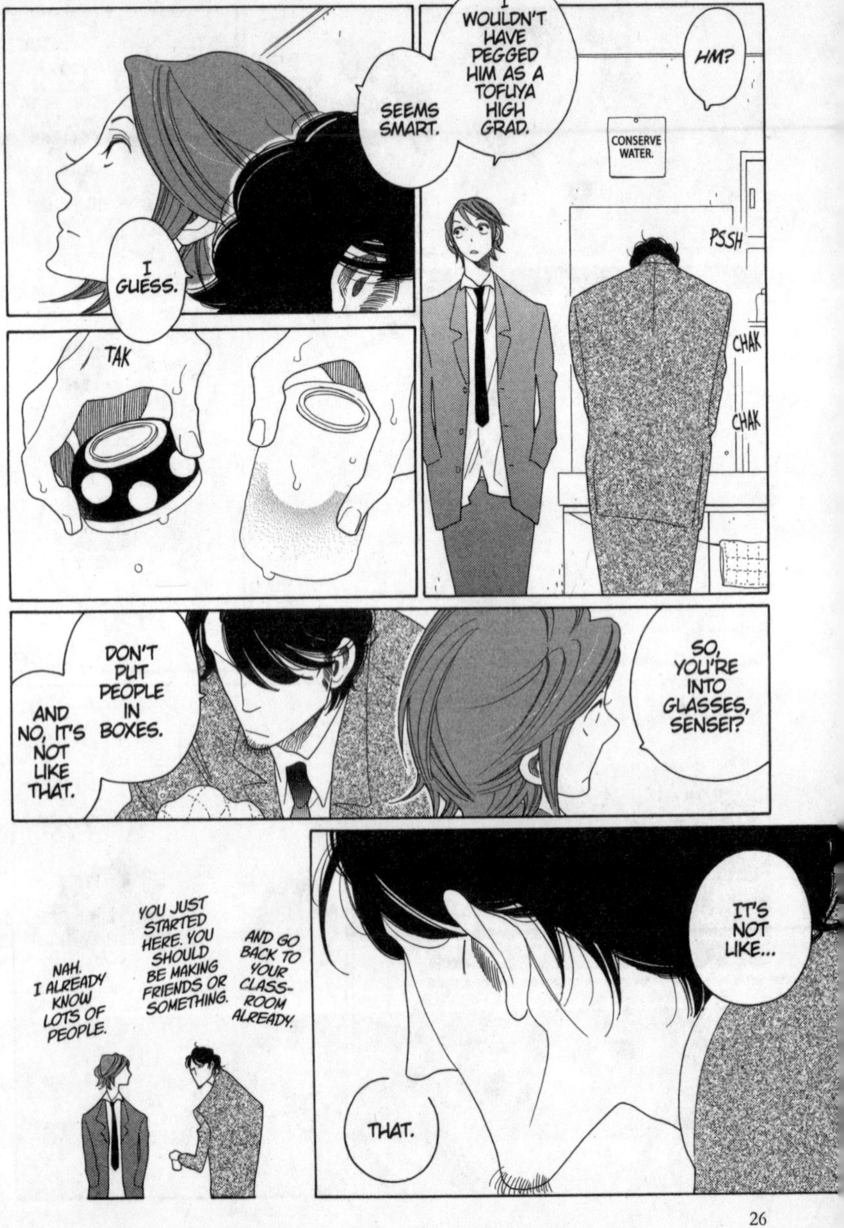
HM?
I WOULDN'T HAVE PEGGED HIM AS A TOFUYA HIGH GRAD.
SEEMS SMART.
CONSERVE WATER.
PSSH
CHAK
CHAK
I GUESS.
TAK
SO, YOU'RE INTO GLASSES, SENSEI?
DON'T PUT PEOPLE IN BOXES.
AND NO, IT'S NOT LIKE THAT.
IT'S NOT LIKE...
THAT.
AND GO BACK TO YOUR CLASS-ROOM ALREADY.
YOU JUST STARTED HERE. YOU SHOULD BE MAKING FRIENDS OR SOMETHING.
NAH. I ALREADY KNOW LOTS OF PEOPLE.

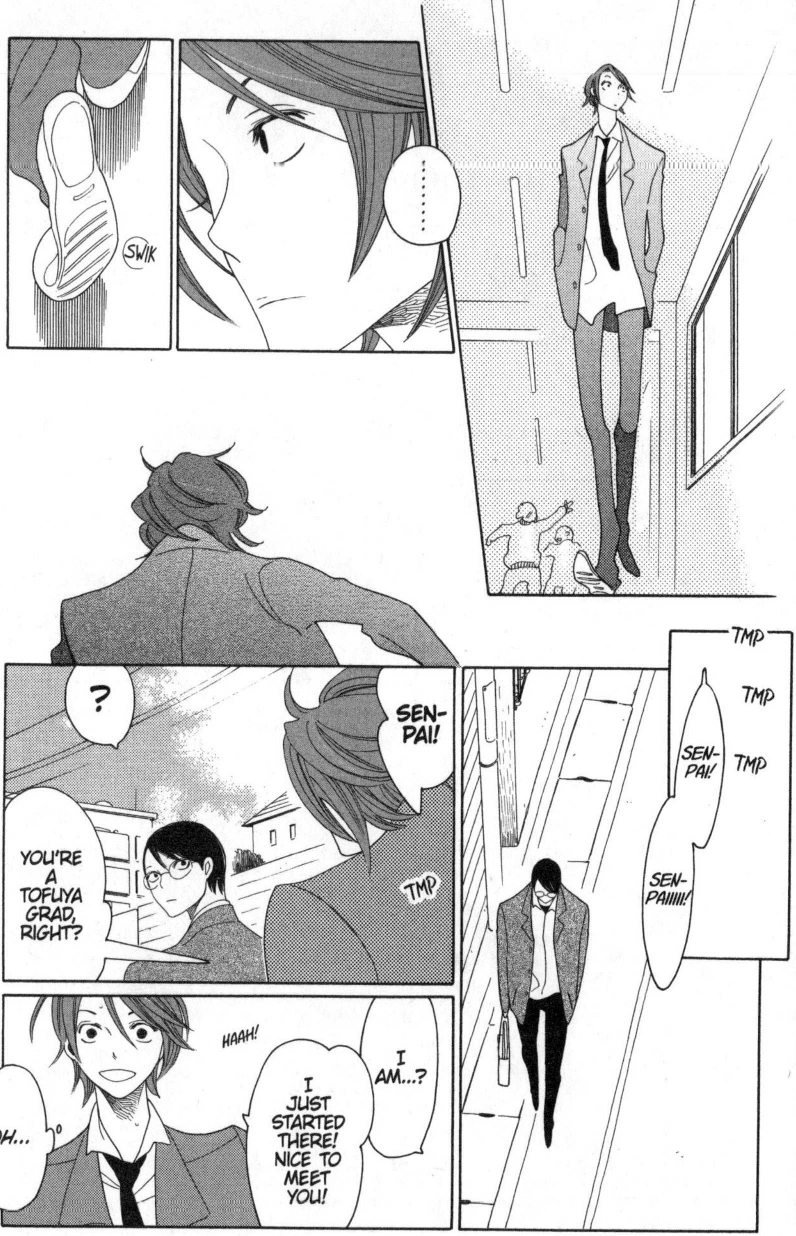
......
SWIK
TMP
TMP
TMP
SEN-PAI!
SEN-PAIIIII!
SEN-PAI!
?
TMP
YOU'RE A TOFUYA GRAD, RIGHT?
I AM...?
HAAH!
I JUST STARTED THERE! NICE TO MEET YOU!
OH...

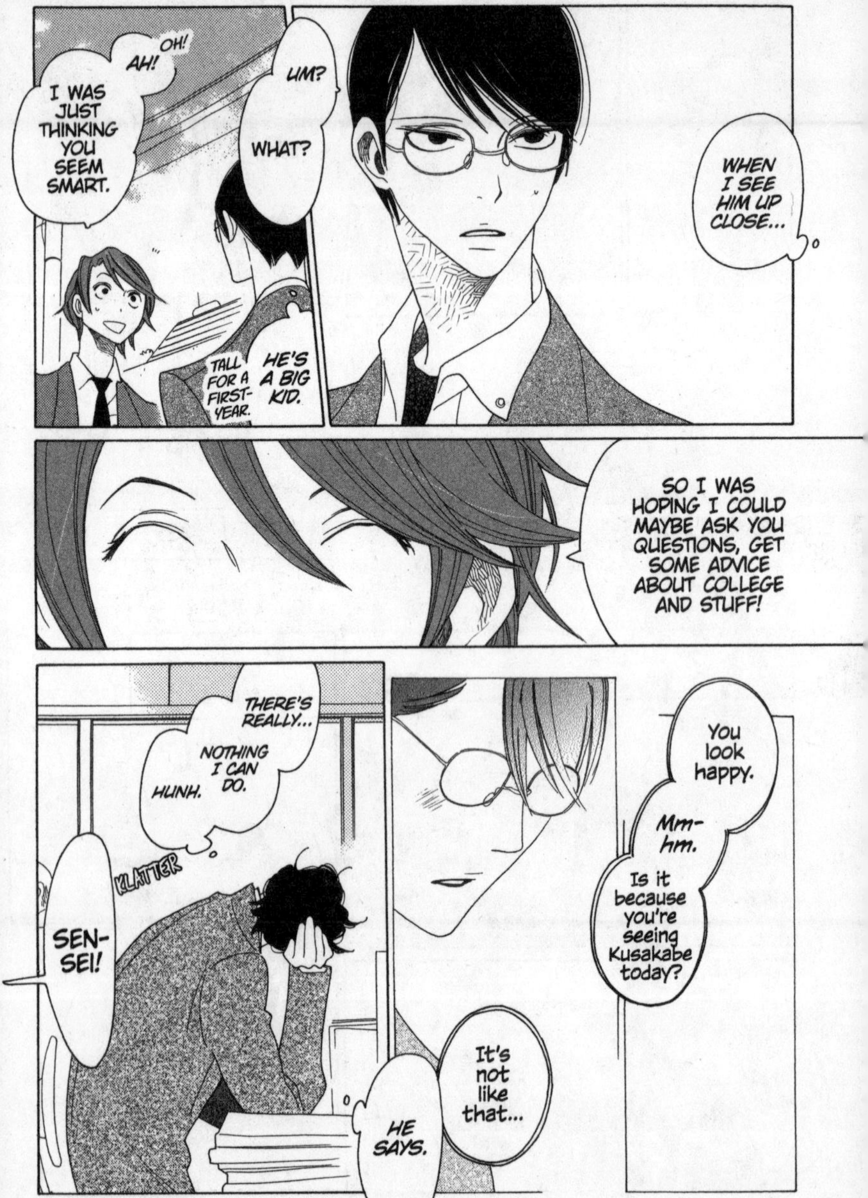
WHEN I SEE HIM UP CLOSE...
UM?
WHAT?
OH!
AH!
I WAS JUST THINKING YOU SEEM SMART.
HE'S A BIG KID.
TALL FOR A FIRST-YEAR.
SO I WAS HOPING I COULD MAYBE ASK YOU QUESTIONS, GET SOME ADVICE ABOUT COLLEGE AND STUFF!
You look happy.
Mm-hm.
Is it because you're seeing Kusakabe today?
It's not like that...
HE SAYS.
THERE'S REALLY...
NOTHING I CAN DO.
HUNH.
KLATTER
SEN-SEI!

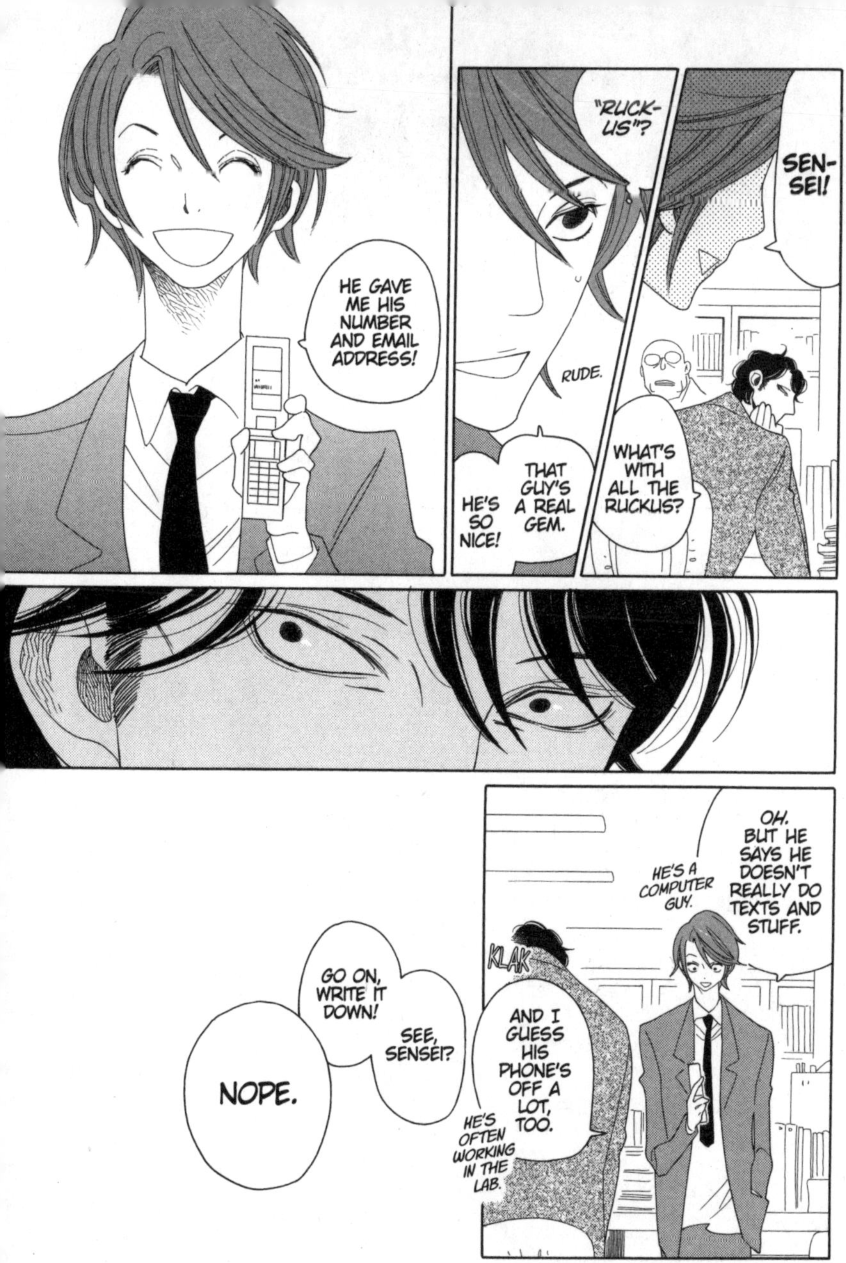
SEN-SEI!
WHAT'S WITH ALL THE RUCKUS?
"RUCK-US"?
RUDE.
THAT GUY'S A REAL GEM.
HE'S SO NICE!
HE GAVE ME HIS NUMBER AND EMAIL ADDRESS!
OH. BUT HE SAYS HE DOESN'T REALLY DO TEXTS AND STUFF.
HE'S A COMPUTER GUY.
KLAK
AND I GUESS HIS PHONE'S OFF A LOT, TOO.
HE'S OFTEN WORKING IN THE LAB.
SEE, SENSEI?
GO ON, WRITE IT DOWN!
NOPE.

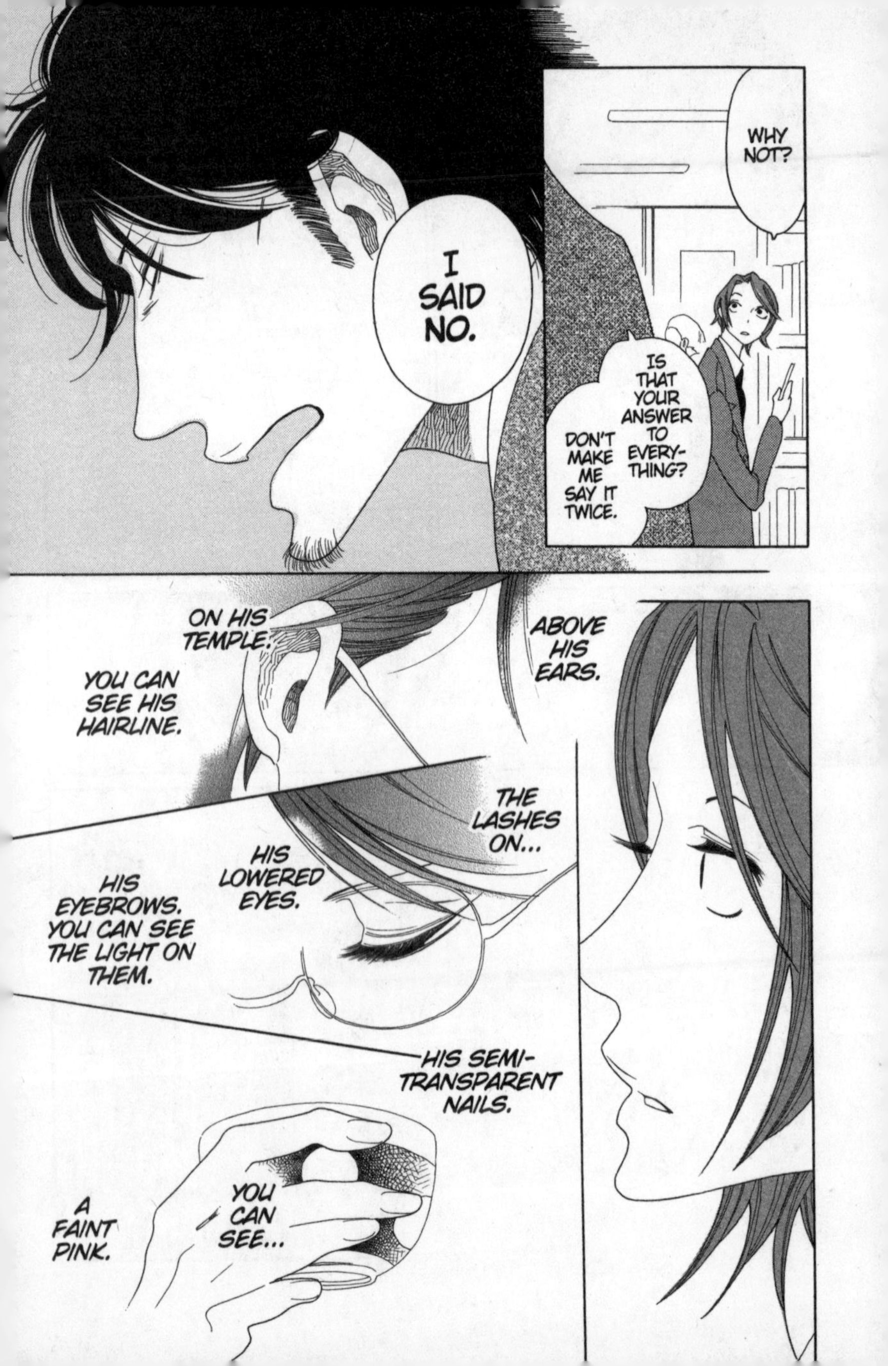
WHY NOT?
IS THAT YOUR ANSWER TO EVERYTHING?
DON'T MAKE ME SAY IT TWICE.
I SAID NO.
ABOVE HIS EARS.
ON HIS TEMPLE.
YOU CAN SEE HIS HAIRLINE.
THE LASHES ON...
HIS LOWERED EYES.
HIS EYEBROWS. YOU CAN SEE THE LIGHT ON THEM.
HIS SEMI-TRANSPARENT NAILS.
YOU CAN SEE...
A FAINT PINK.

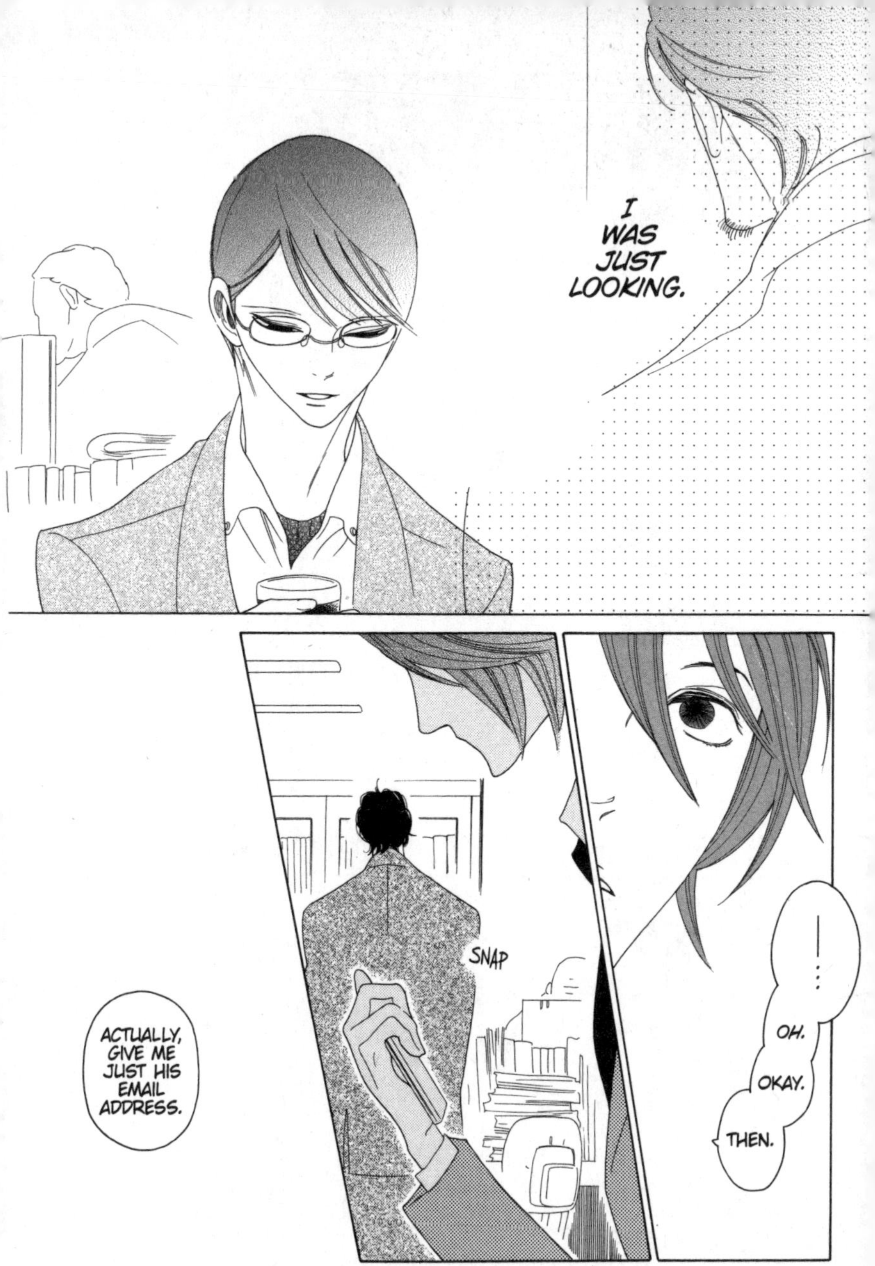
I WAS JUST LOOKING.
......
OH. OKAY. THEN.
SNAP
ACTUALLY, GIVE ME JUST HIS EMAIL ADDRESS.

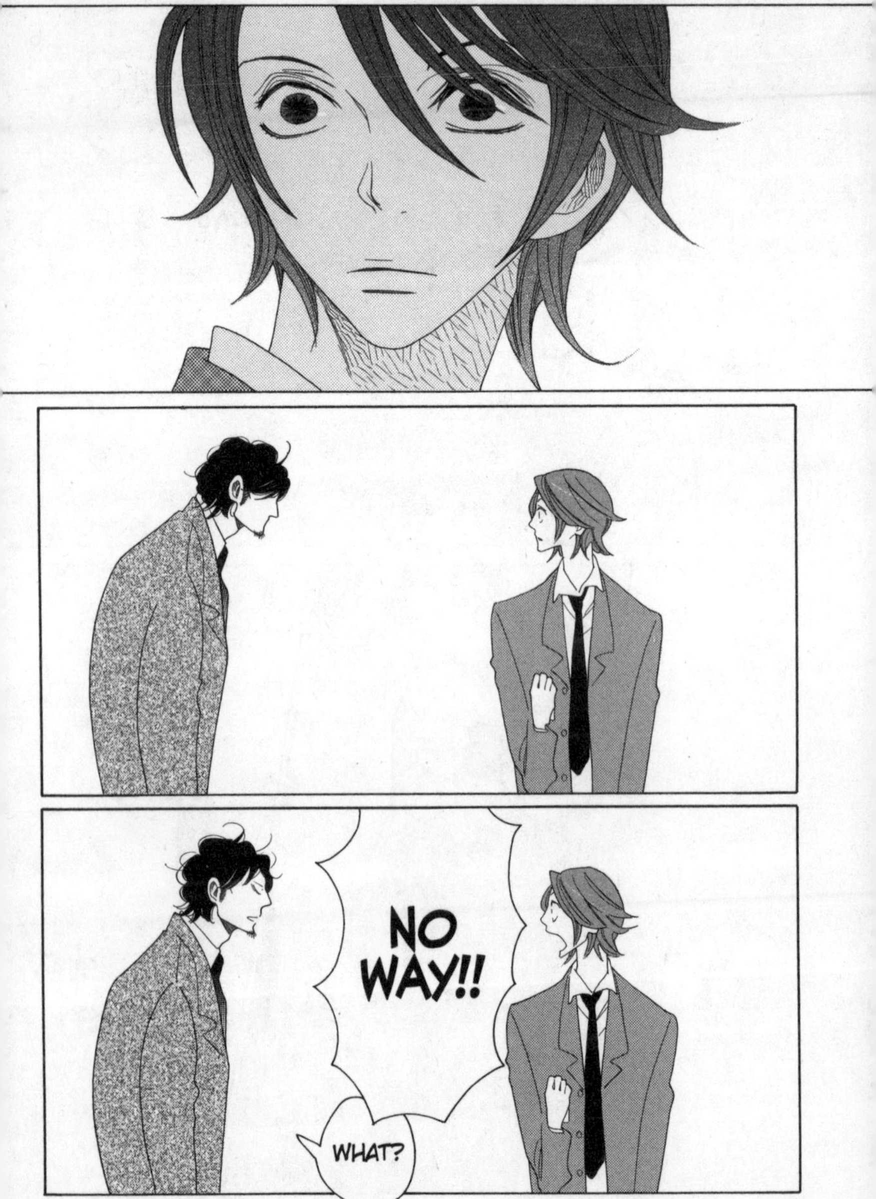
NO WAY!!
WHAT?

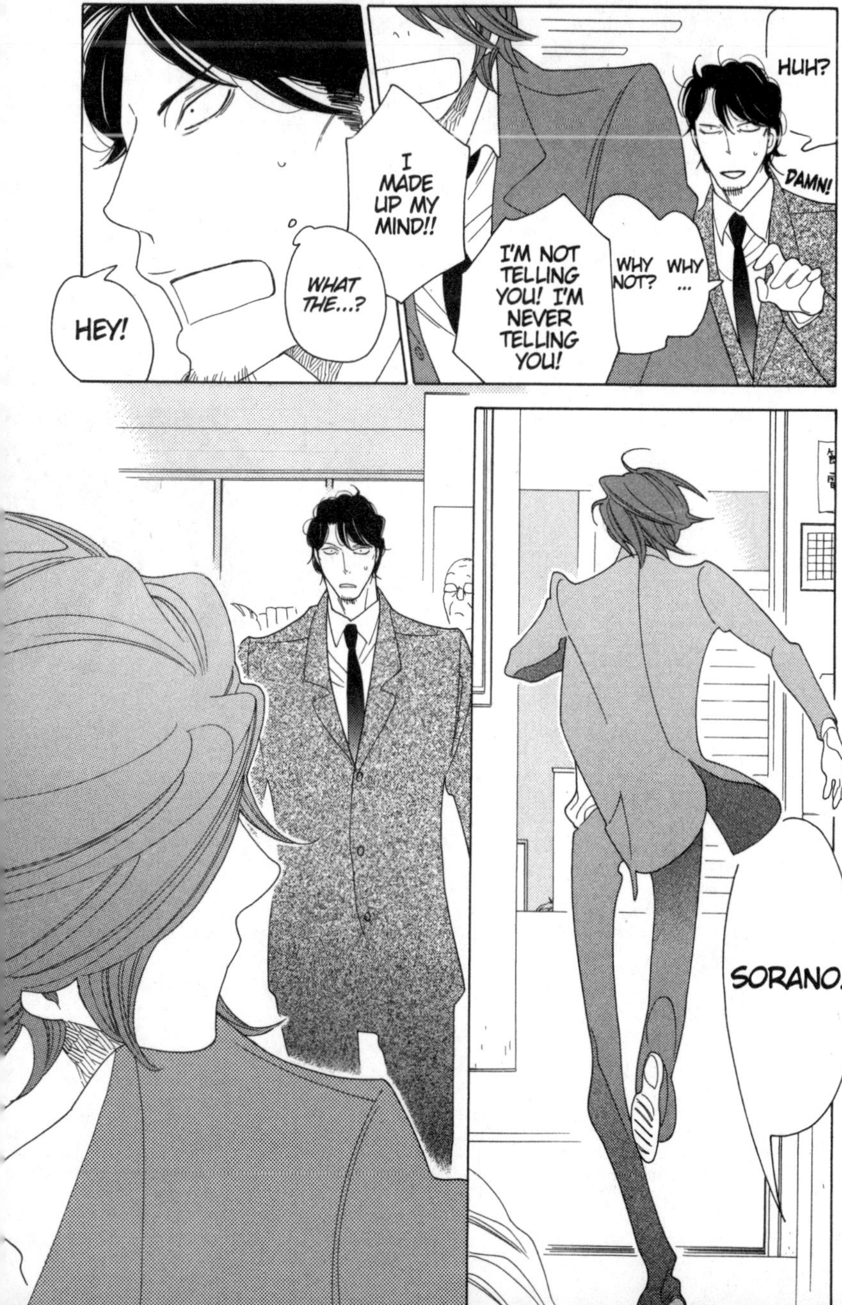
HUH?
DAMN!
WHY ...
WHY NOT?
I'M NOT TELLING YOU! I'M NEVER TELLING YOU!
I MADE UP MY MIND!!
WHAT THE...?
HEY!
SORANO!

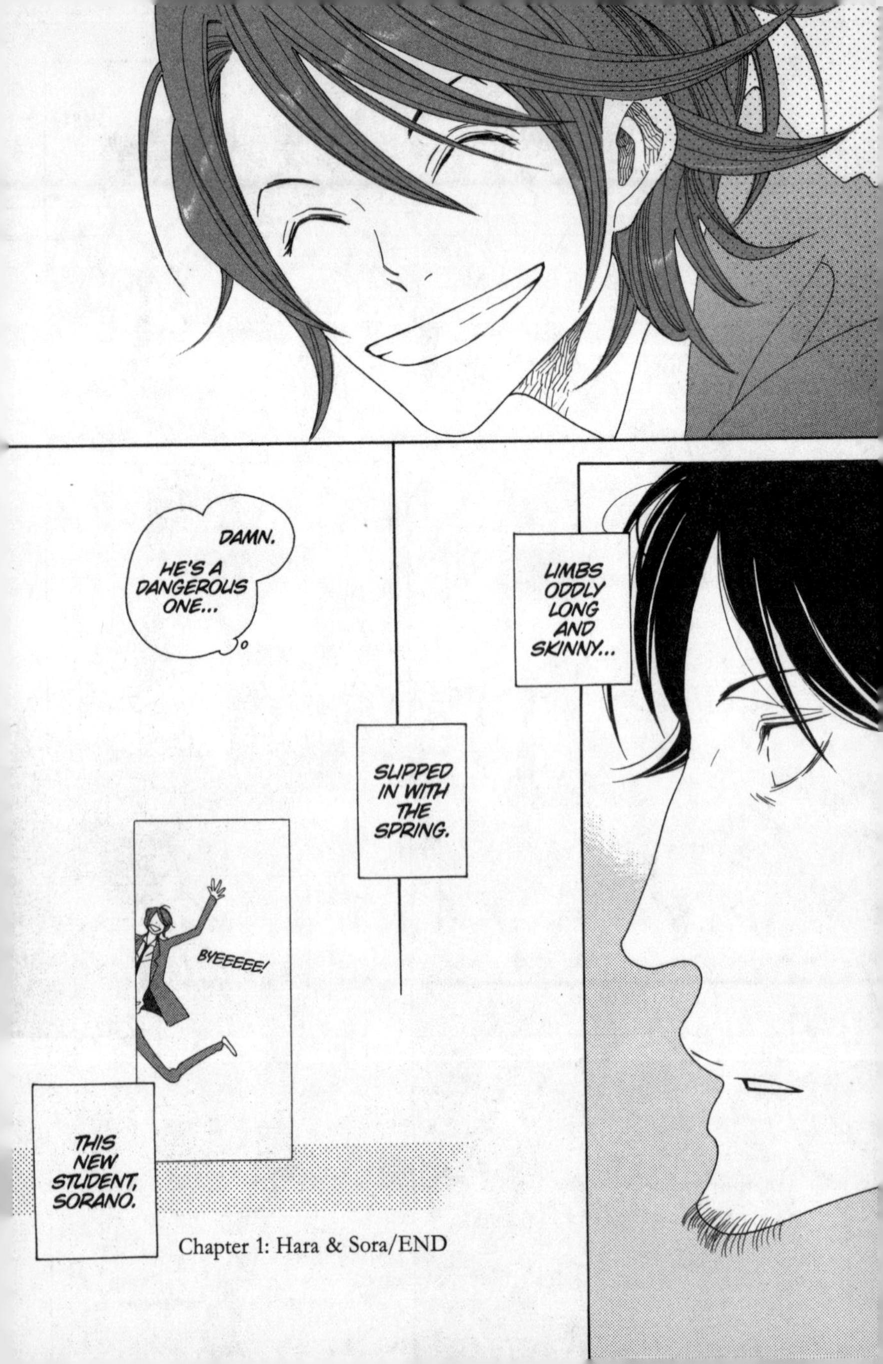
LIMBS ODDLY LONG AND SKINNY...
SLIPPED IN WITH THE SPRING.
DAMN. HE'S A DANGEROUS ONE...
BYEEEEE!
THIS NEW STUDENT, SORANO.

Chapter 1: Hara & Sora/END

[Chapter 2: Adult and Child]

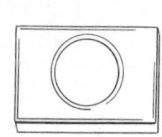

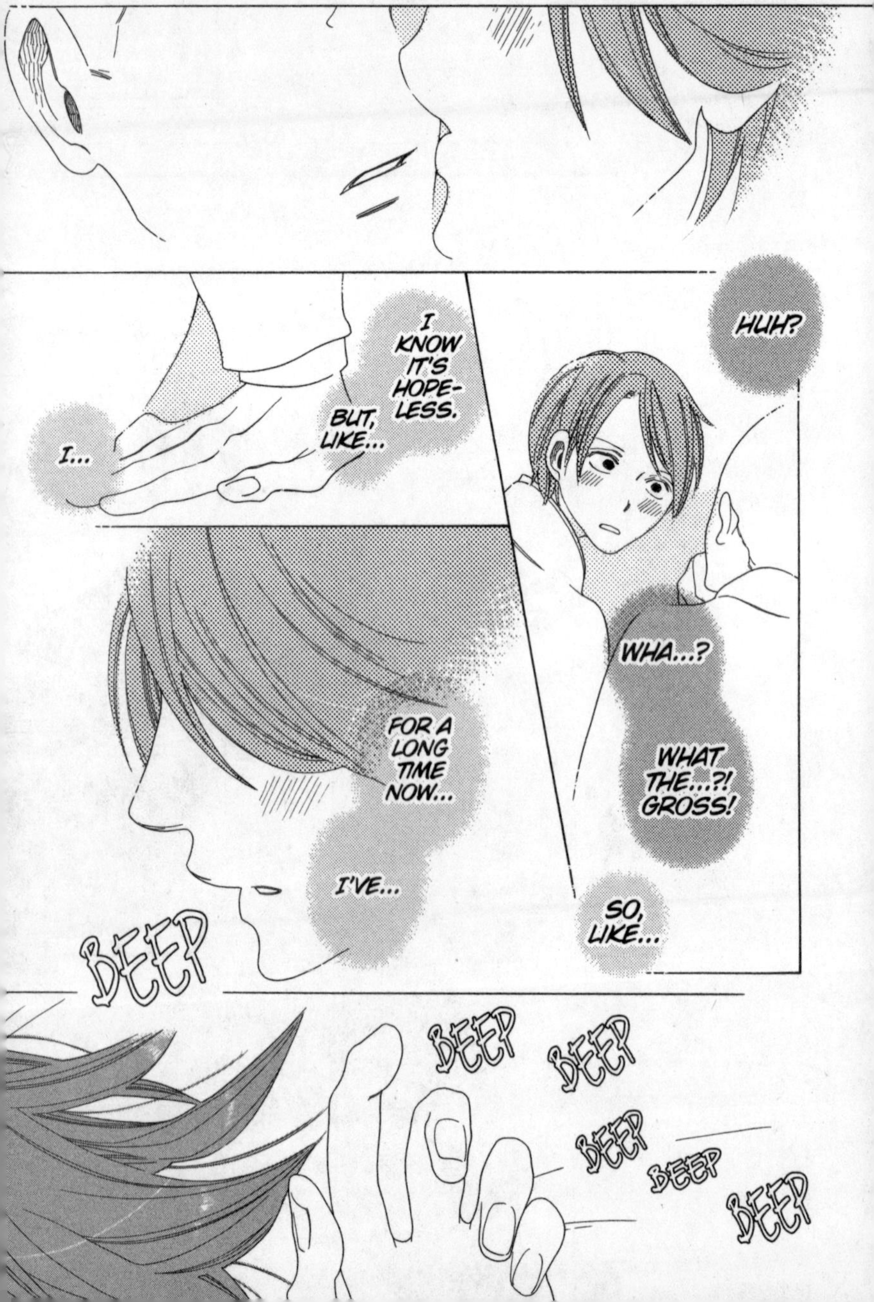
HUH?
WHA...?
WHAT THE...?! GROSS!
SO, LIKE...
I KNOW IT'S HOPE-LESS.
BUT, LIKE...
I...
FOR A LONG TIME NOW...
I'VE...
BEEP
BEEP
BEEP
BEEP
BEEP
BEEP

BEEP
BEEP
PSSSH
PSSSH
SPLSH
SPLSH
SORA-NO!
TIME TO GET UP!
BEEP
BEEP
BEEP
BEEP
SQUEAK

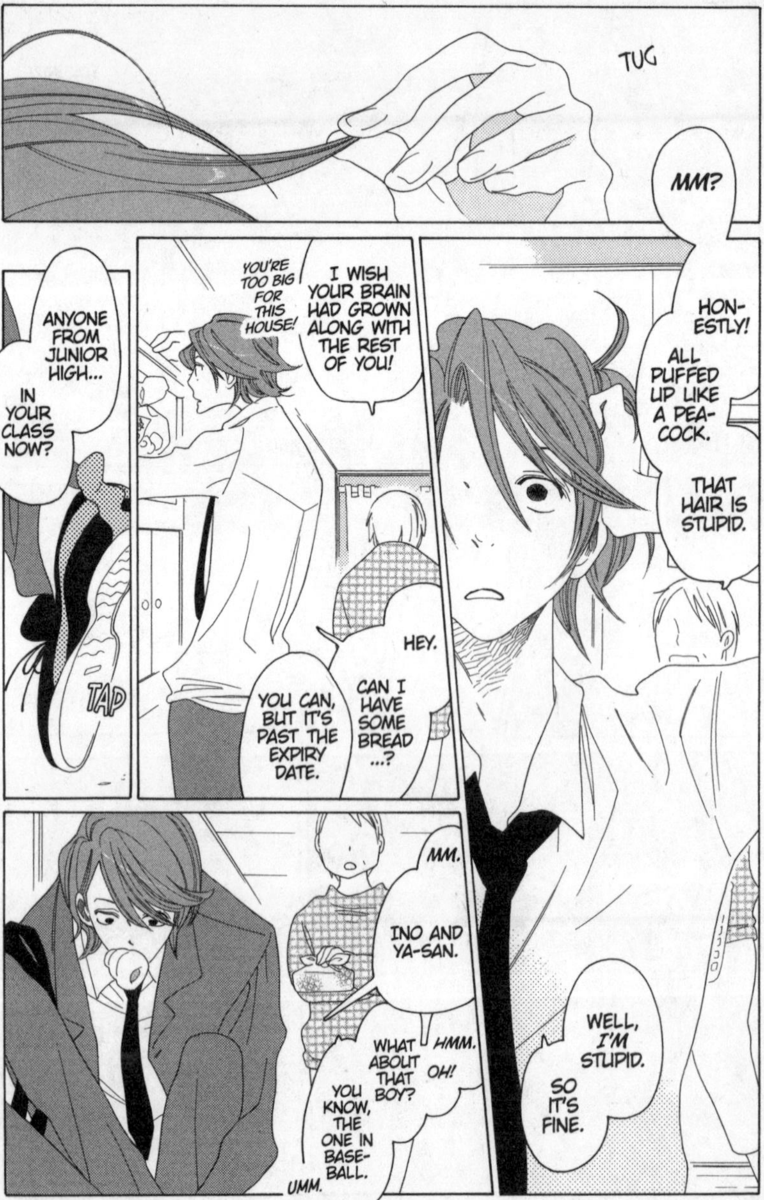
TUG
MM?
HON-ESTLY!
ALL PUFFED UP LIKE A PEA-COCK.
THAT HAIR IS STUPID.
WELL, I'M STUPID.
SO IT'S FINE.
I WISH YOUR BRAIN HAD GROWN ALONG WITH THE REST OF YOU!
YOU'RE TOO BIG FOR THIS HOUSE!
HEY.
CAN I HAVE SOME BREAD ...?
YOU CAN, BUT IT'S PAST THE EXPIRY DATE.
ANYONE FROM JUNIOR HIGH...
IN YOUR CLASS NOW?
TAP
MM.
INO AND YA-SAN.
HMM.
OH!
WHAT ABOUT THAT BOY?
YOU KNOW, THE ONE IN BASE-BALL.
UMM.

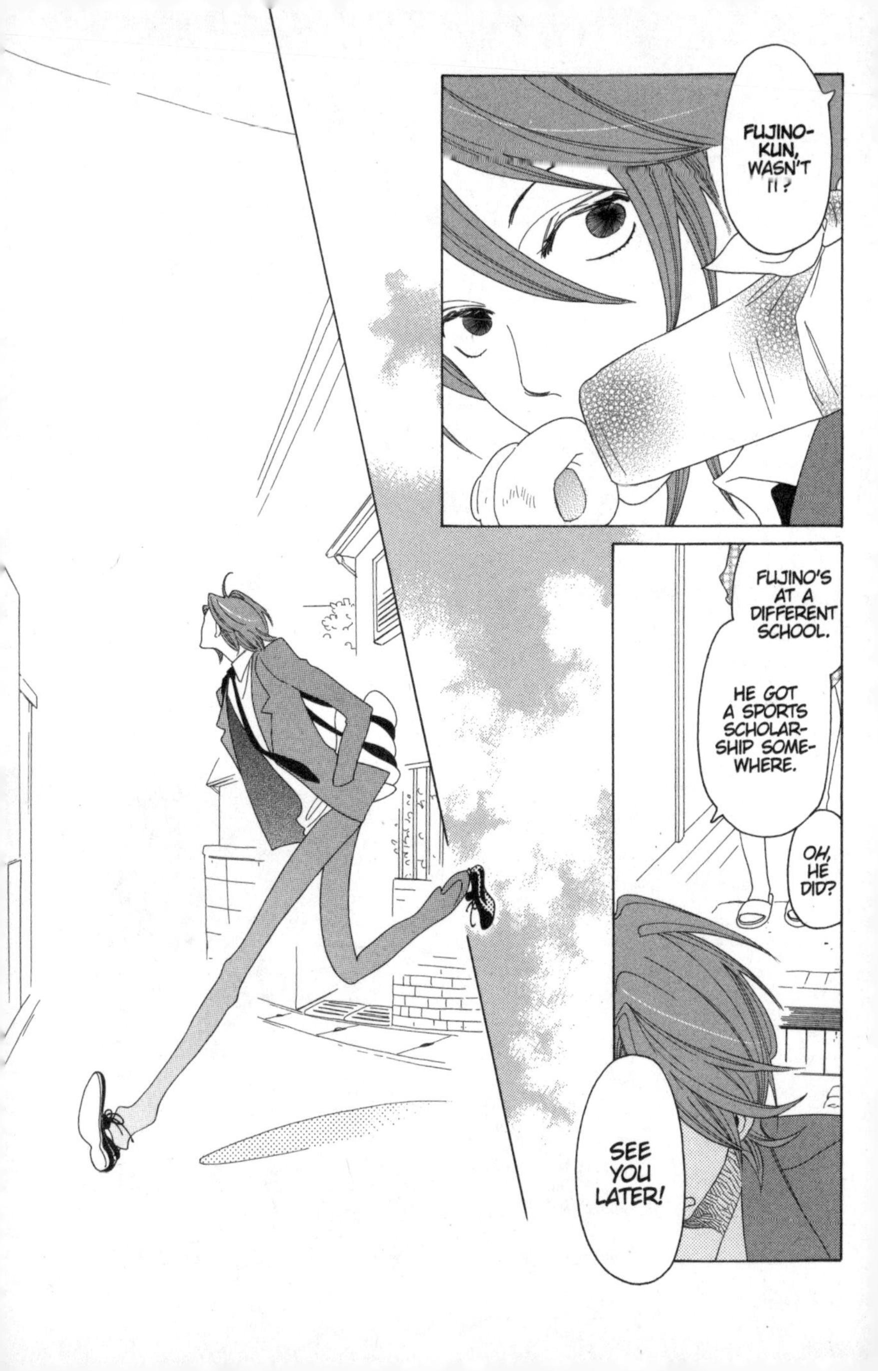
FUJINO-KUN, WASN'T IT?
FUJINO'S AT A DIFFERENT SCHOOL.
HE GOT A SPORTS SCHOLAR-SHIP SOME-WHERE.
OH, HE DID?
SEE YOU LATER!

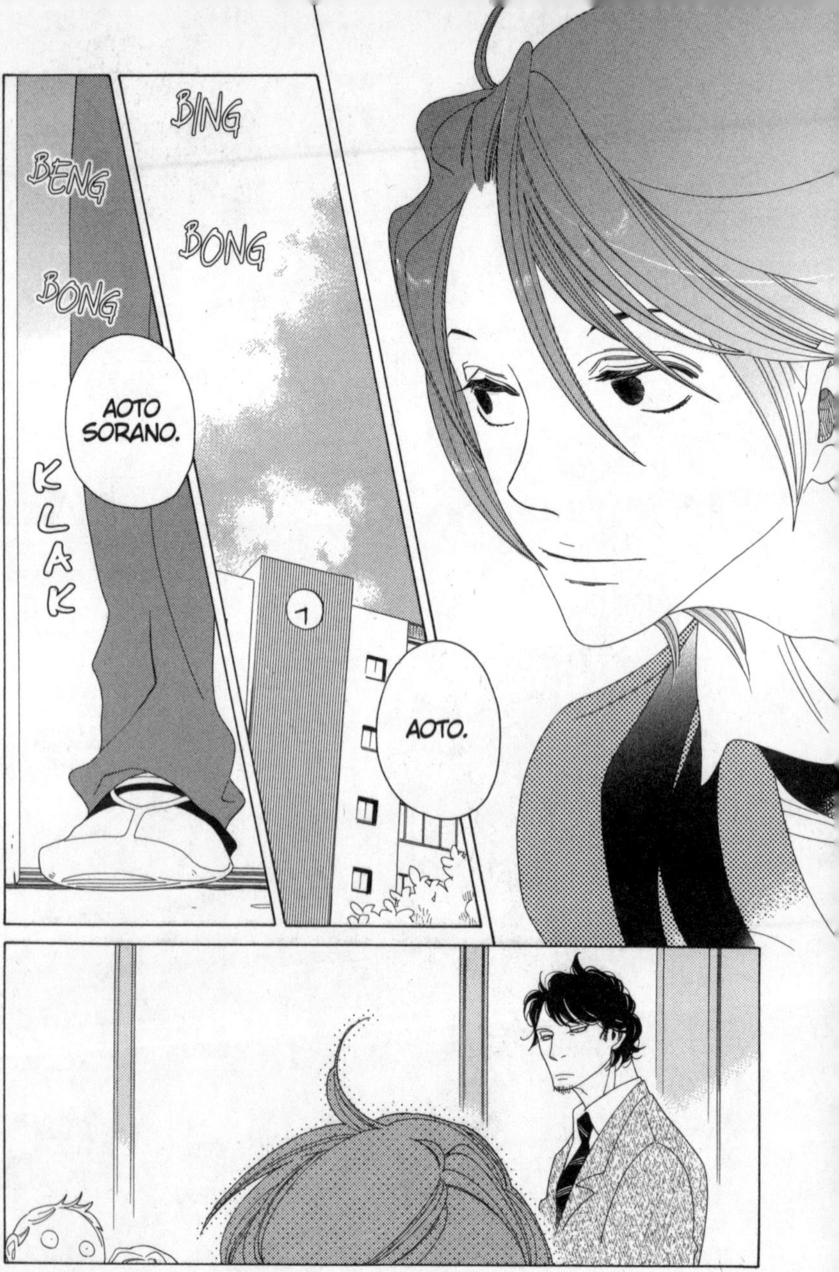
AOTO.
BING
BONG
BENG
BONG
AOTO SORANO.
KLAK

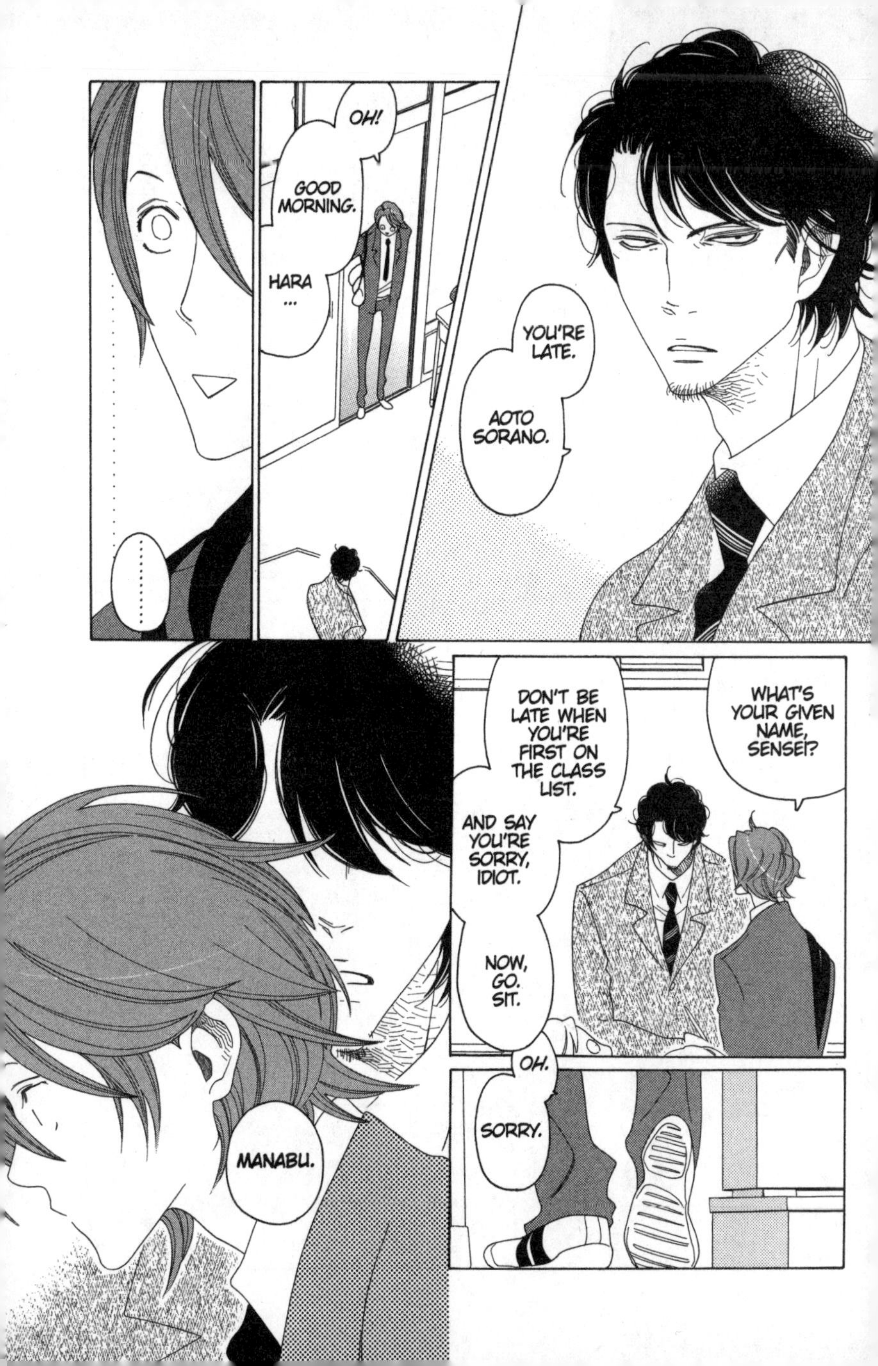
YOU'RE LATE.
AOTO SORANO.
OH!
GOOD MORNING.
HARA...
......
WHAT'S YOUR GIVEN NAME, SENSEI?
DON'T BE LATE WHEN YOU'RE FIRST ON THE CLASS LIST.
AND SAY YOU'RE SORRY, IDIOT.
NOW, GO. SIT.
OH.
SORRY.
MANABU.

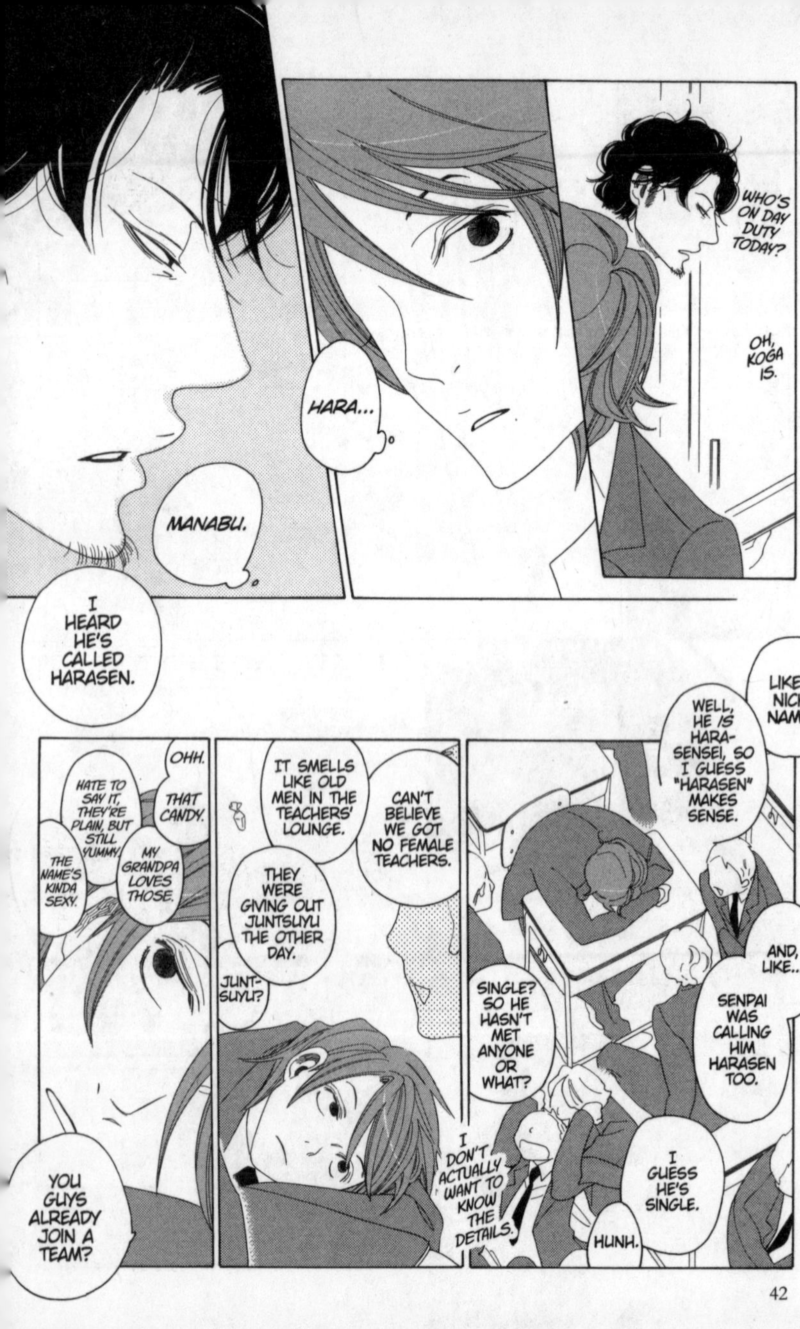
WHO'S ON DAY DUTY TODAY?
OH, KOGA IS.
HARA...
MANABU.
I HEARD HE'S CALLED HARASEN.
LIKE A NICK-NAME?
WELL, HE *IS* HARA-SENSEI, SO I GUESS "HARASEN" MAKES SENSE.
AND, LIKE...
SENPAI WAS CALLING HIM HARASEN TOO.
SINGLE? SO HE HASN'T MET ANYONE OR WHAT?
I GUESS HE'S SINGLE.
HUNH.
I DON'T ACTUALLY WANT TO KNOW THE DETAILS.
CAN'T BELIEVE WE GOT NO FEMALE TEACHERS.
IT SMELLS LIKE OLD MEN IN THE TEACHERS' LOUNGE.
THEY WERE GIVING OUT JUNTSUYU THE OTHER DAY.
JUNT-SUYU?
OHH.
THAT CANDY.
HATE TO SAY IT, THEY'RE PLAIN, BUT STILL YUMMY.
MY GRANDPA LOVES THOSE.
THE NAME'S KINDA SEXY.
YOU GUYS ALREADY JOIN A TEAM?

HUH?
YOU SAID "SENPAI" BEFORE.
OHH. RIGHT, YEAH.
WELL...
MY SENPAI FROM JUNIOR HIGH'S ON THE TEAM, SO...
IT'S ALREADY A DONE DEAL.
OR WHATEVER.
I'LL KEEP GOING WITH...
BASEBALL, THEN.
YEAH, DO IT.
I HEARD YOU'RE SINGLE, HARASEN.
IT TRUE?
WHUT?

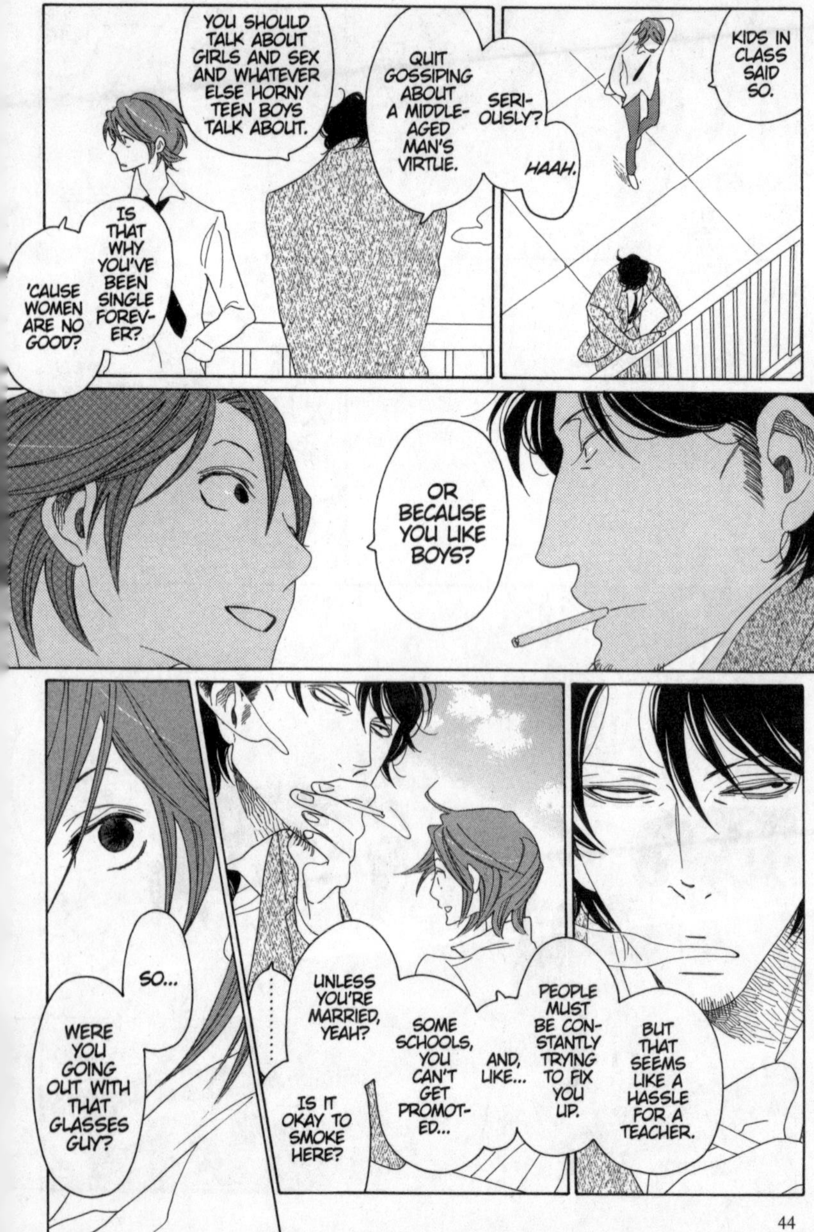
KIDS IN CLASS SAID SO.
SERI-OUSLY?
HAAH.
QUIT GOSSIPING ABOUT A MIDDLE-AGED MAN'S VIRTUE.
YOU SHOULD TALK ABOUT GIRLS AND SEX AND WHATEVER ELSE HORNY TEEN BOYS TALK ABOUT.
IS THAT WHY YOU'VE BEEN SINGLE FOREVER?
'CAUSE WOMEN ARE NO GOOD?
OR BECAUSE YOU LIKE BOYS?
BUT THAT SEEMS LIKE A HASSLE FOR A TEACHER.
PEOPLE MUST BE CONSTANTLY TRYING TO FIX YOU UP.
AND, LIKE...
SOME SCHOOLS, YOU CAN'T GET PROMOTED...
UNLESS YOU'RE MARRIED, YEAH?
IS IT OKAY TO SMOKE HERE?
......
SO...
WERE YOU GOING OUT WITH THAT GLASSES GUY?

SAJO-SAN?
NO.
NOPE.
NUH-UH.
LISTEN.
I EXPLICITLY TOLD YOU, I DON'T LAY A FINGER ON MY STUDENTS.
NO WAY.
AND...
HE'S GOT A STRONG PART-NER.
M'KAY?

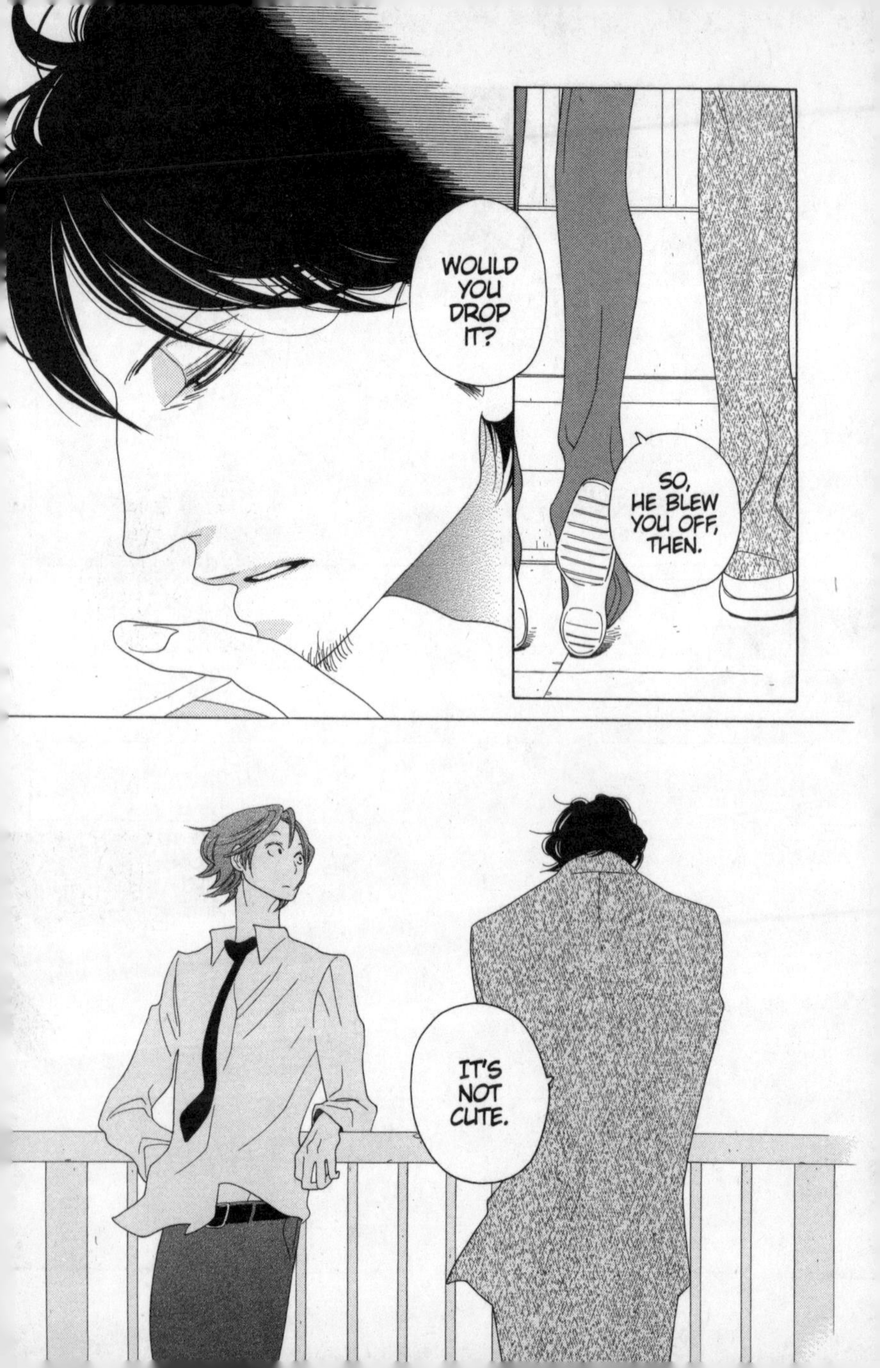
SO, HE BLEW YOU OFF, THEN.
WOULD YOU DROP IT?
IT'S NOT CUTE.

SORRY.
I'M SORRY.
IT'S FINE.
IT'S SERIOUSLY FINE.
MOMENTARY LAPSE.
SORRY.
SENSEI!
I REALLY AM...
SORRY.

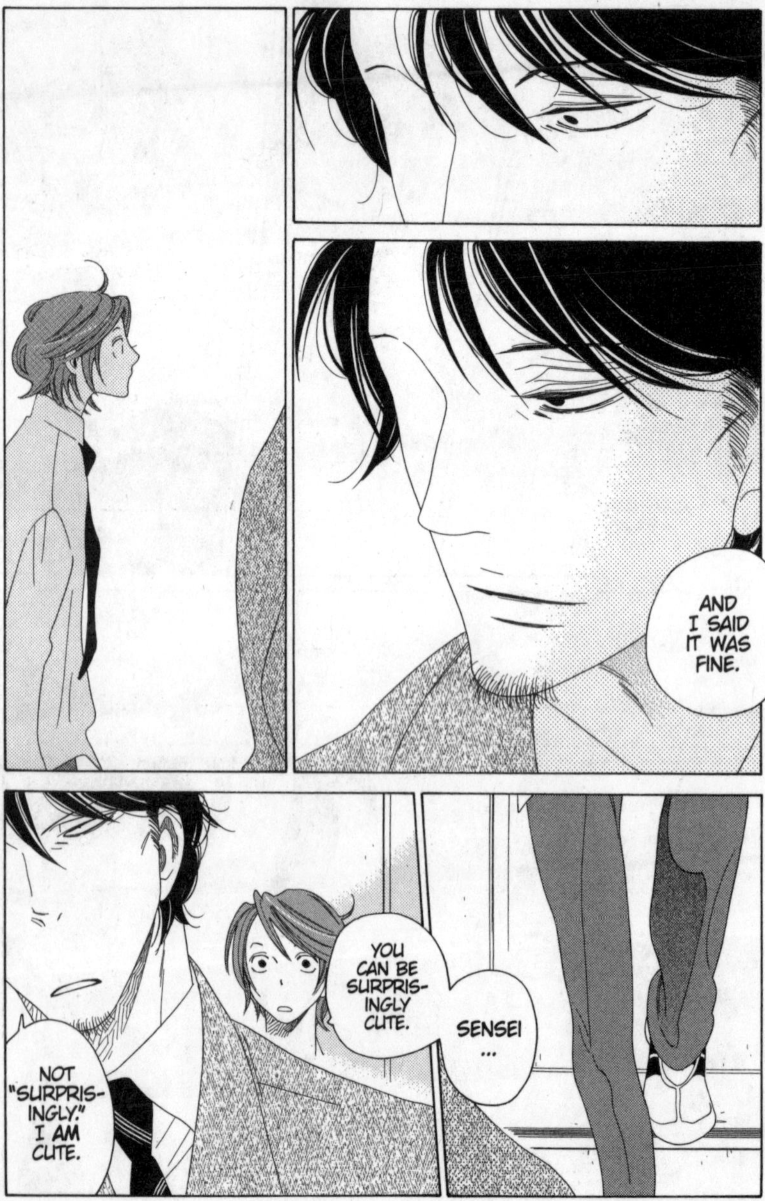
AND I SAID IT WAS FINE.
SENSEI ...
YOU CAN BE SURPRIS-INGLY CUTE.
NOT "SURPRIS-INGLY." I AM CUTE.

AND I'LL TELL YOU NOW ...
THE ROOF'S OFF-LIMITS.
YOU WERE UP THERE FIRST, THOUGH.
I'M ALLOWED.
I'M A GROWN-UP.
IS IT NICE BEING A GROWN-UP?
IT IS.
MUST BE NICE, BEING GROWN UP.
IT IS.
ALL GROWN UP.
MAYBE.
TMP
I GOT BLOWN OFF, YOU KNOW.

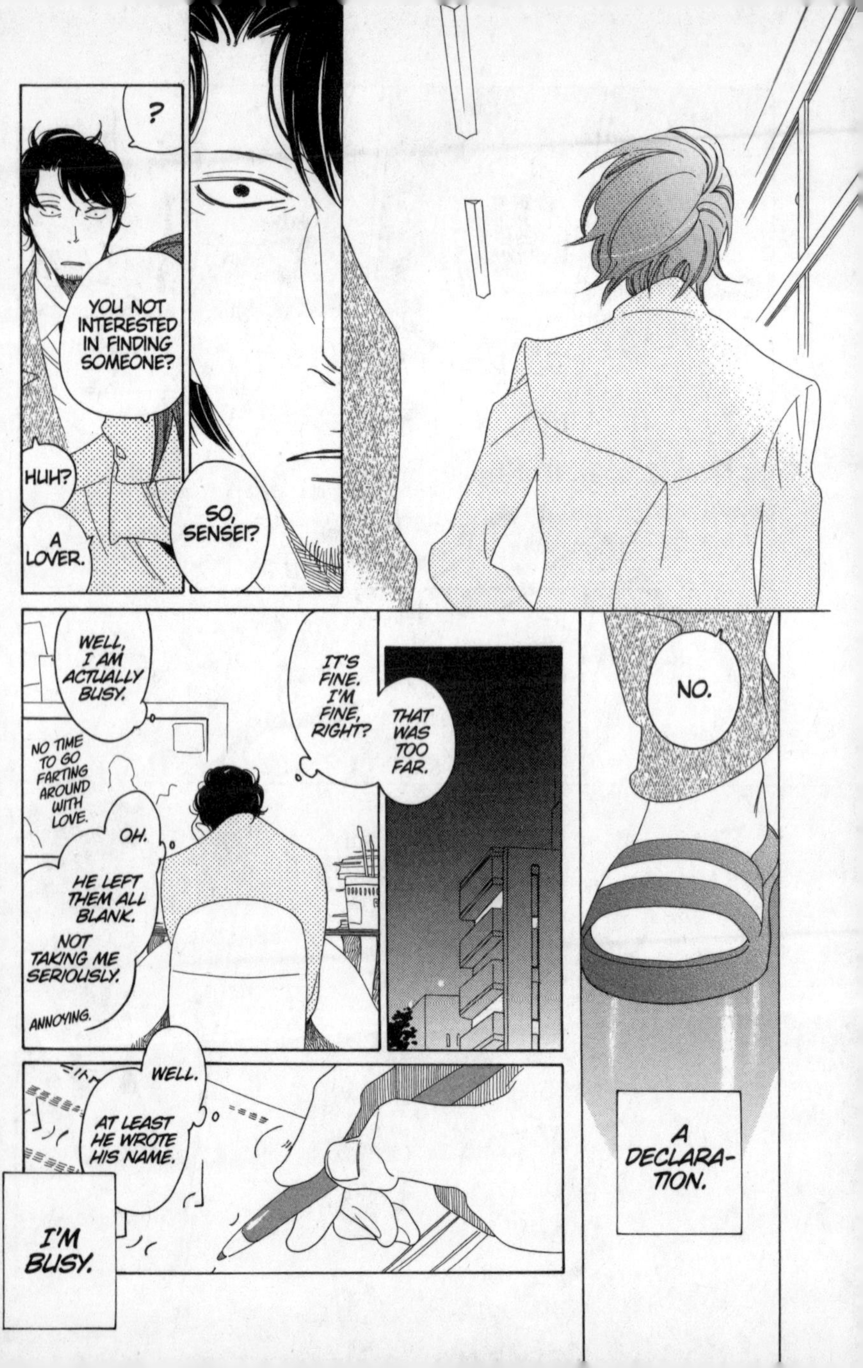
SO, SENSEI?
?
YOU NOT INTERESTED IN FINDING SOMEONE?
HUH?
A LOVER.
NO.
A DECLARATION.
THAT WAS TOO FAR.
IT'S FINE. I'M FINE, RIGHT?
WELL, I AM ACTUALLY BUSY.
NO TIME TO GO FARTING AROUND WITH LOVE.
OH.
HE LEFT THEM ALL BLANK.
NOT TAKING ME SERIOUSLY.
ANNOYING.
WELL.
AT LEAST HE WROTE HIS NAME.
I'M BUSY.

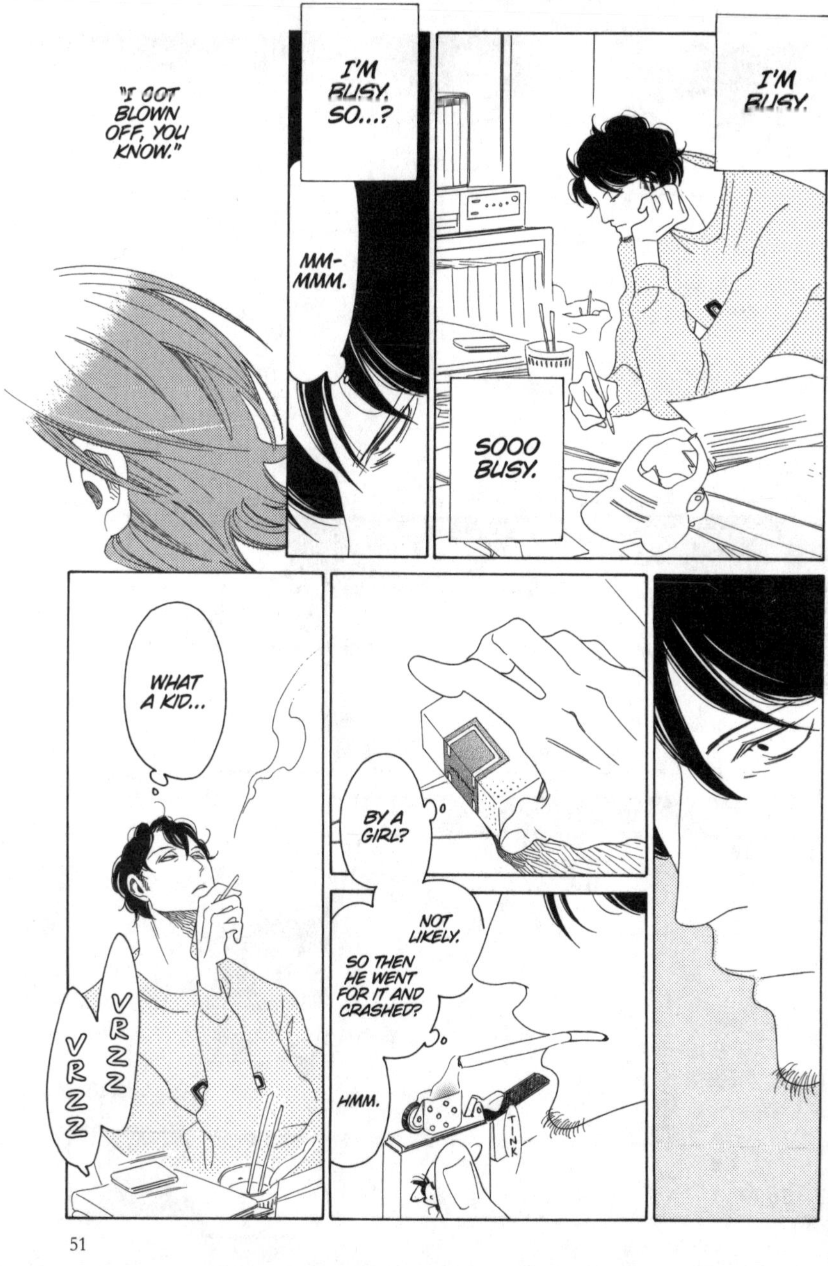
I'M BUSY.
SOOO BUSY.
I'M BUSY. SO...?
MM-MMM.
"I GOT BLOWN OFF, YOU KNOW."
BY A GIRL?
NOT LIKELY.
SO THEN HE WENT FOR IT AND CRASHED?
HMM.
TINK
WHAT A KID...
VRZZ VRZZ

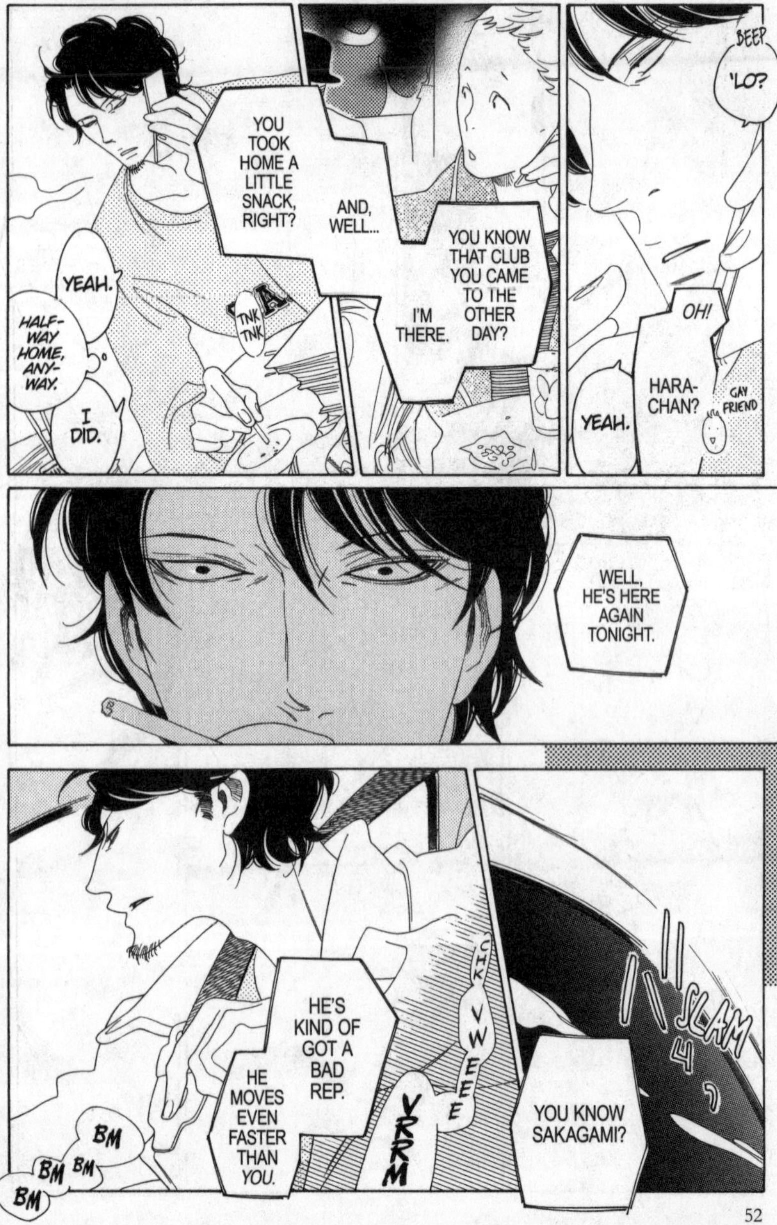
BEEP
'LO?
OH!
HARA-CHAN?
GAY FRIEND
YEAH.
YOU KNOW THAT CLUB YOU CAME TO THE OTHER DAY?
I'M THERE.
AND, WELL...
YOU TOOK HOME A LITTLE SNACK, RIGHT?
YEAH.
HALF-WAY HOME, ANY-WAY.
I DID.
TNK TNK
WELL, HE'S HERE AGAIN TONIGHT.
SLAM
YOU KNOW SAKAGAMI?
CHK
VWEEEE
HE'S KIND OF GOT A BAD REP.
HE MOVES EVEN FASTER THAN *YOU.*
VRRM
BM BM BM BM

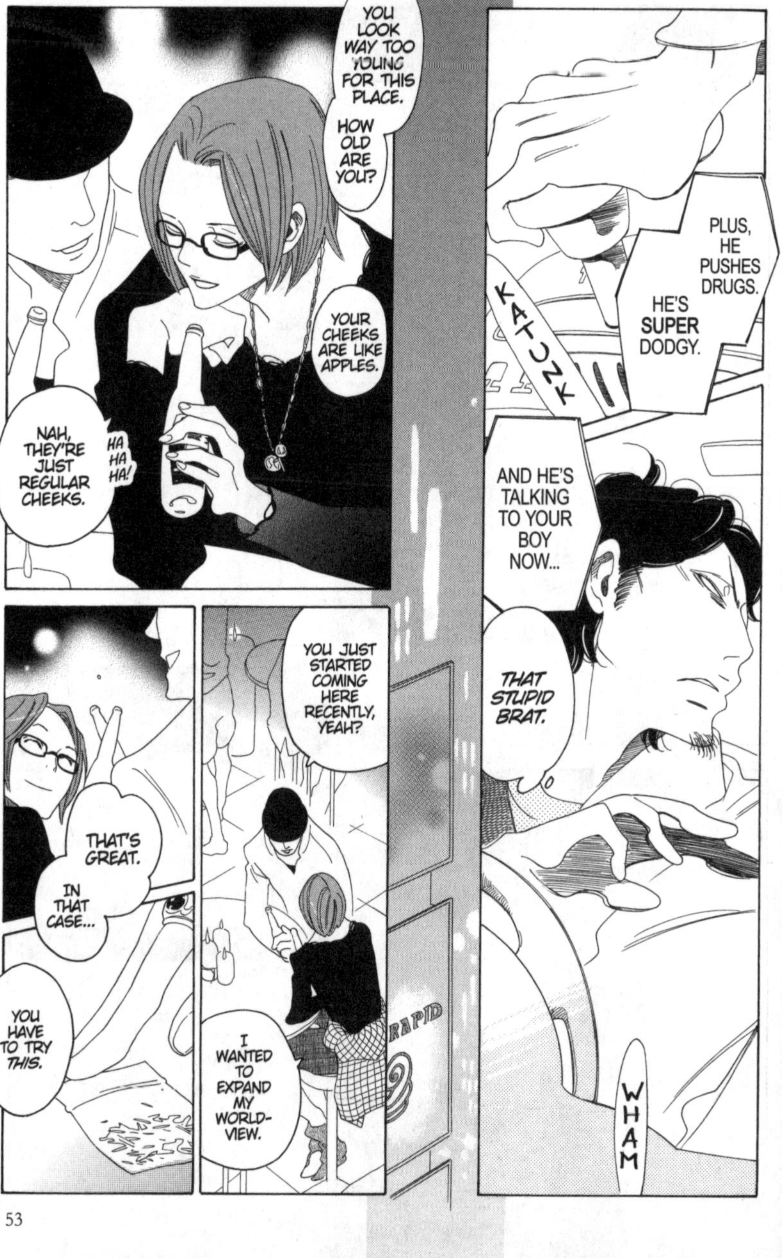
PLUS, HE PUSHES DRUGS.
HE'S **SUPER** DODGY.
KATUNK
AND HE'S TALKING TO YOUR BOY NOW...
THAT STUPID BRAT.
WHAM
YOU LOOK WAY TOO YOUNG FOR THIS PLACE.
HOW OLD ARE YOU?
YOUR CHEEKS ARE LIKE APPLES.
NAH, THEY'RE JUST REGULAR CHEEKS.
HA HA HA!
YOU JUST STARTED COMING HERE RECENTLY, YEAH?
I WANTED TO EXPAND MY WORLD-VIEW.
RAPID
THAT'S GREAT.
IN THAT CASE...
YOU HAVE TO TRY *THIS.*

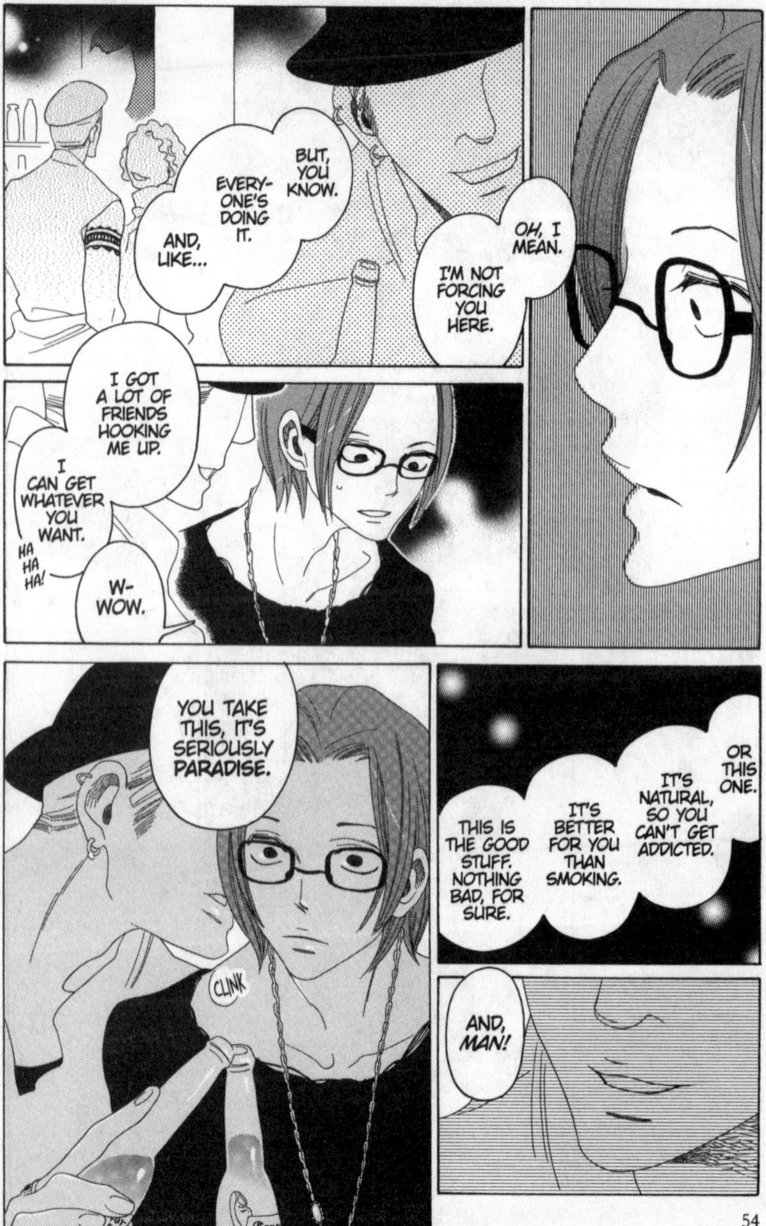
OH, I MEAN.
I'M NOT FORCING YOU HERE.
BUT, YOU KNOW.
EVERY-ONE'S DOING IT.
AND, LIKE...
I GOT A LOT OF FRIENDS HOOKING ME UP.
I CAN GET WHATEVER YOU WANT.
HA HA HA!
W-WOW.
OR THIS ONE.
IT'S NATURAL, SO YOU CAN'T GET ADDICTED.
IT'S BETTER FOR YOU THAN SMOKING.
THIS IS THE GOOD STUFF. NOTHING BAD, FOR SURE.
AND, MAN!
YOU TAKE THIS, IT'S SERIOUSLY PARADISE.
CLINK

RIGHT.
NO WORD OF A LIE!
YOU JUST MELT AWAY.
IT, LIKE, COMES TO YOU FROM YOUR CORE.
SO...
THIS YOUR FIRST TIME?
KLANK
IN THAT CASE, IT'S EXTRA GOOD.
RELAXES THE HELL OUT OF YOU.
SERIOUSLY.
EVEN THE SIDE EFFECTS ARE AWESOME.
IT'LL HAVE YOU CUM--
EXCUSE ME.

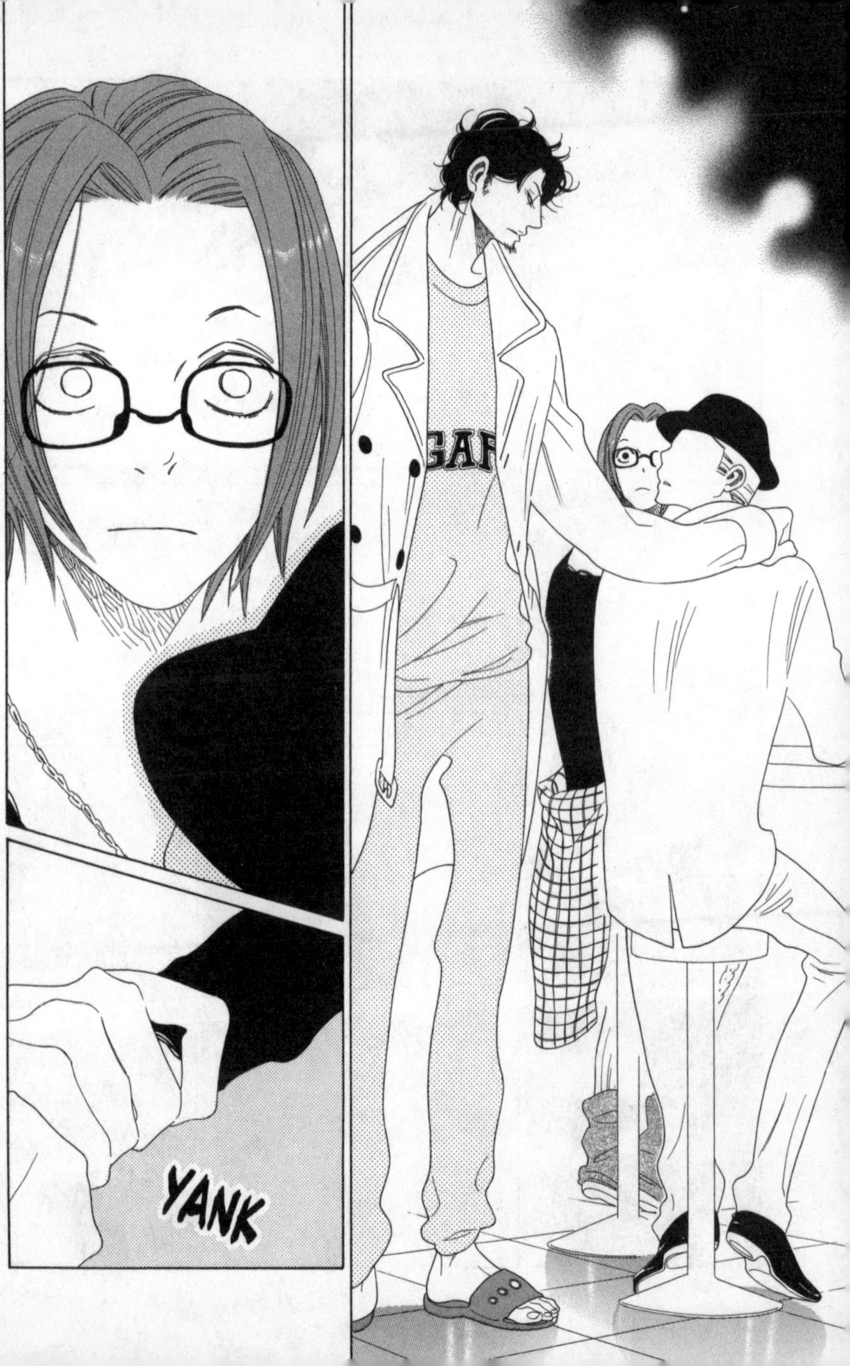
YANK

LET'S GO.
AH!
UH!
HOLD UP!
HEY!
HEY!
WHAT THE HELL, MAN?!
YOU DON'T GET TO BUTT IN--
GRAB
WHAM
GAH!
CRASH
I'M HIS...
HIS...
KLUNK
KANK
KANK

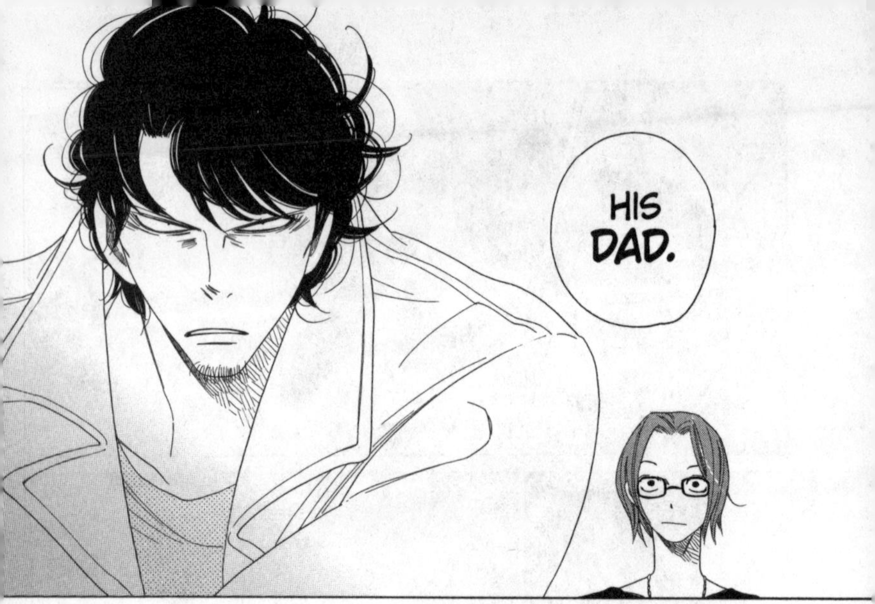
HIS DAD.

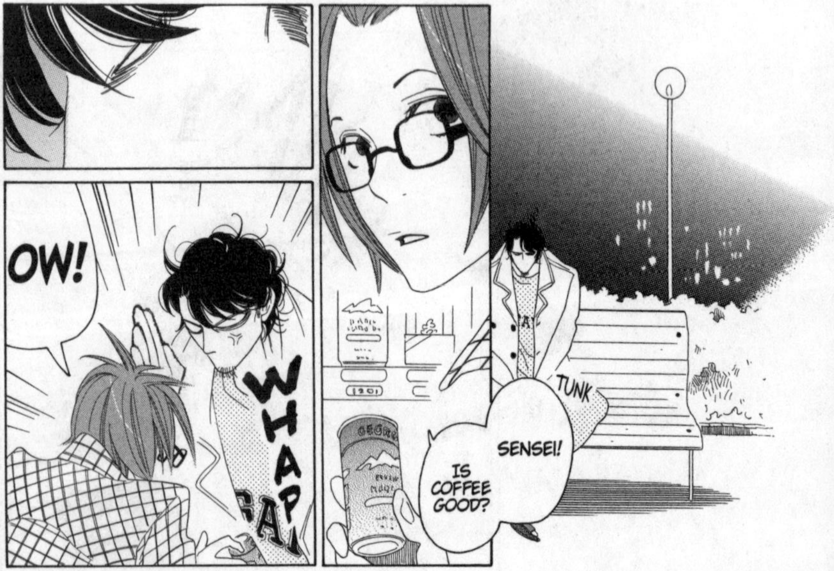
TUNK
SENSEI!
IS COFFEE GOOD?
OW!
WHAP

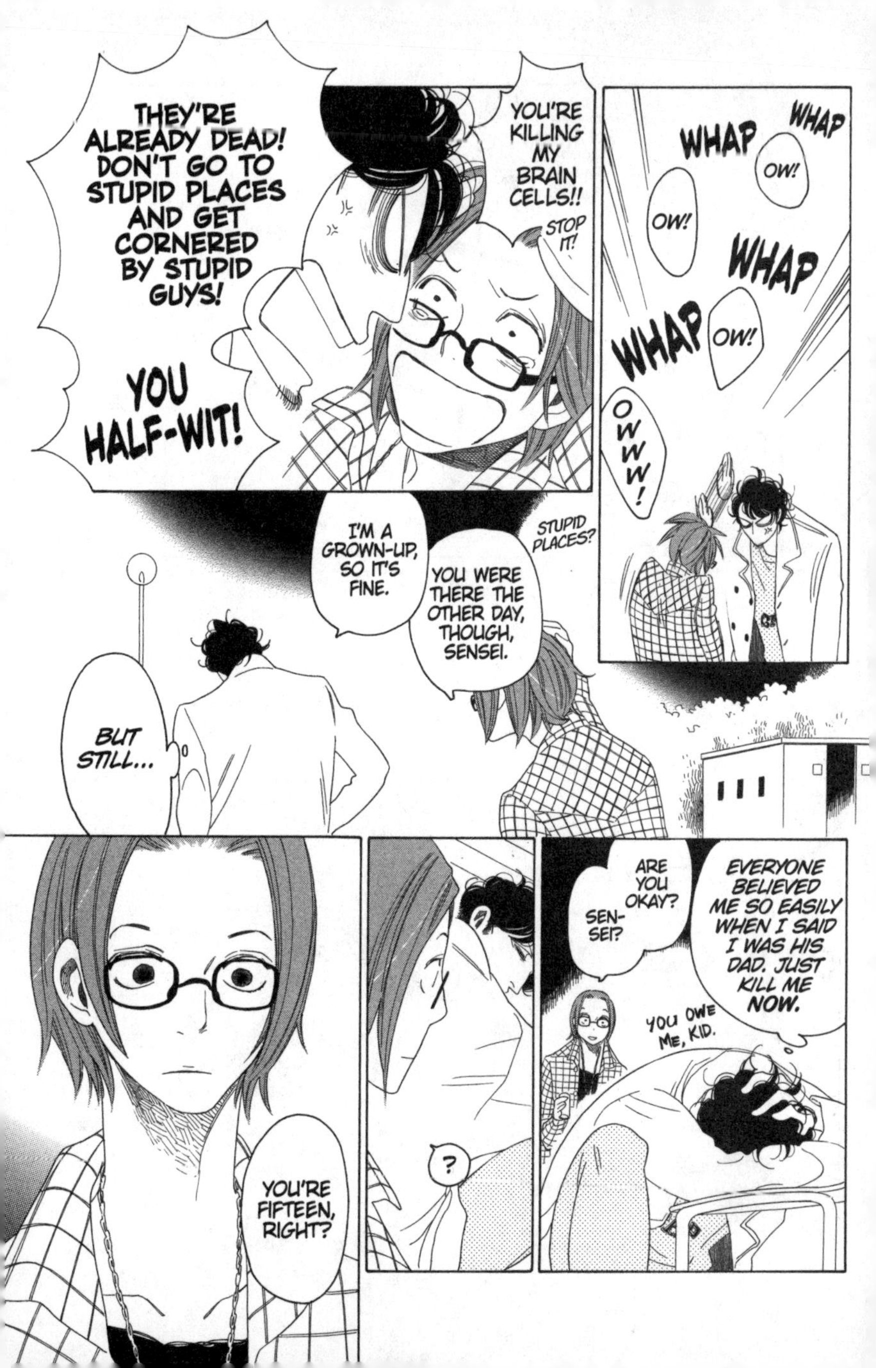
WHAP
WHAP
OW!
OW!
WHAP
OW!
WHAP
OWWW!
YOU'RE KILLING MY BRAIN CELLS!!
STOP IT!
THEY'RE ALREADY DEAD! DON'T GO TO STUPID PLACES AND GET CORNERED BY STUPID GUYS!
YOU HALF-WIT!
STUPID PLACES?
YOU WERE THERE THE OTHER DAY, THOUGH, SENSEI.
I'M A GROWN-UP, SO IT'S FINE.
BUT STILL...
EVERYONE BELIEVED ME SO EASILY WHEN I SAID I WAS HIS DAD. JUST KILL ME NOW.
ARE YOU OKAY?
SEN-SEI?
YOU OWE ME, KID.
?
YOU'RE FIFTEEN, RIGHT?

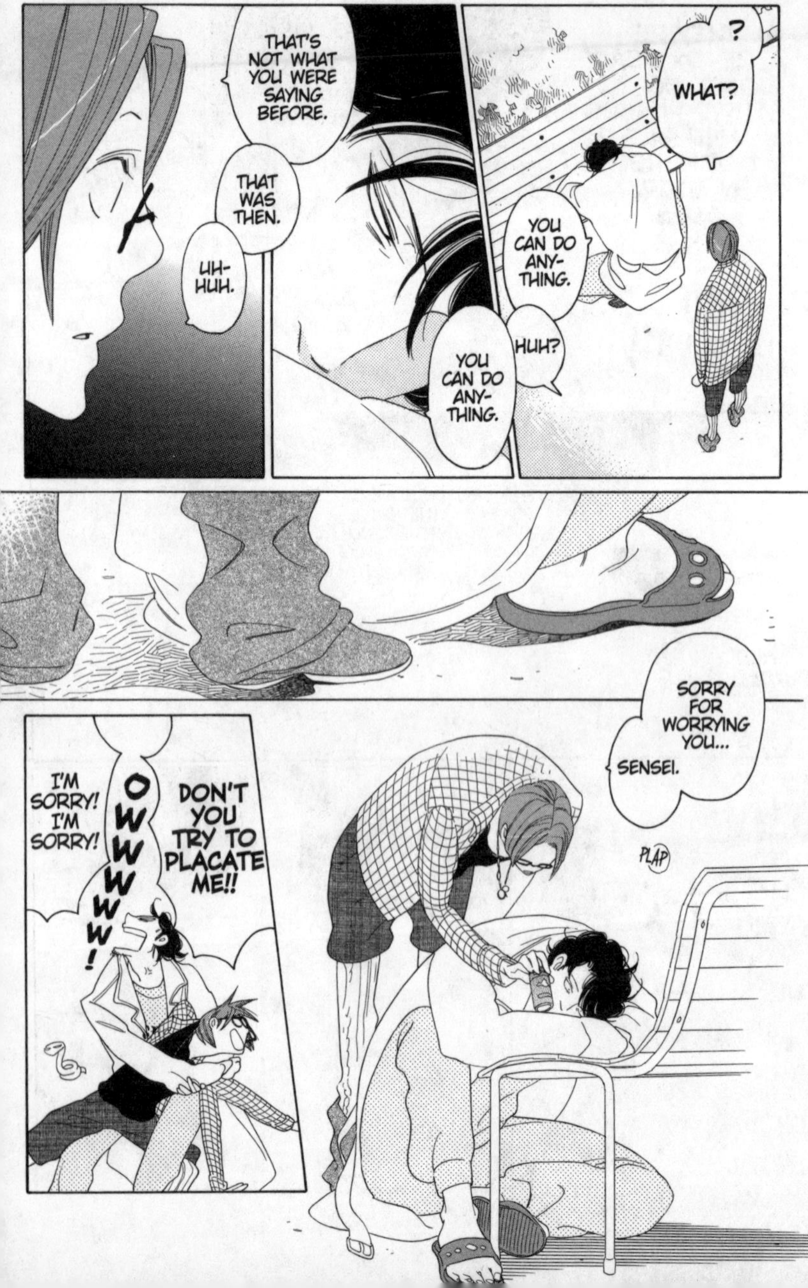

?
WHAT?
YOU CAN DO ANY-THING.
HUH?
YOU CAN DO ANY-THING.
THAT'S NOT WHAT YOU WERE SAYING BEFORE.
THAT WAS THEN.
UH-HUH.
SORRY FOR WORRYING YOU...
SENSEI.
PLAP
DON'T YOU TRY TO PLACATE ME!!
OWWWWW!
I'M SORRY! I'M SORRY!

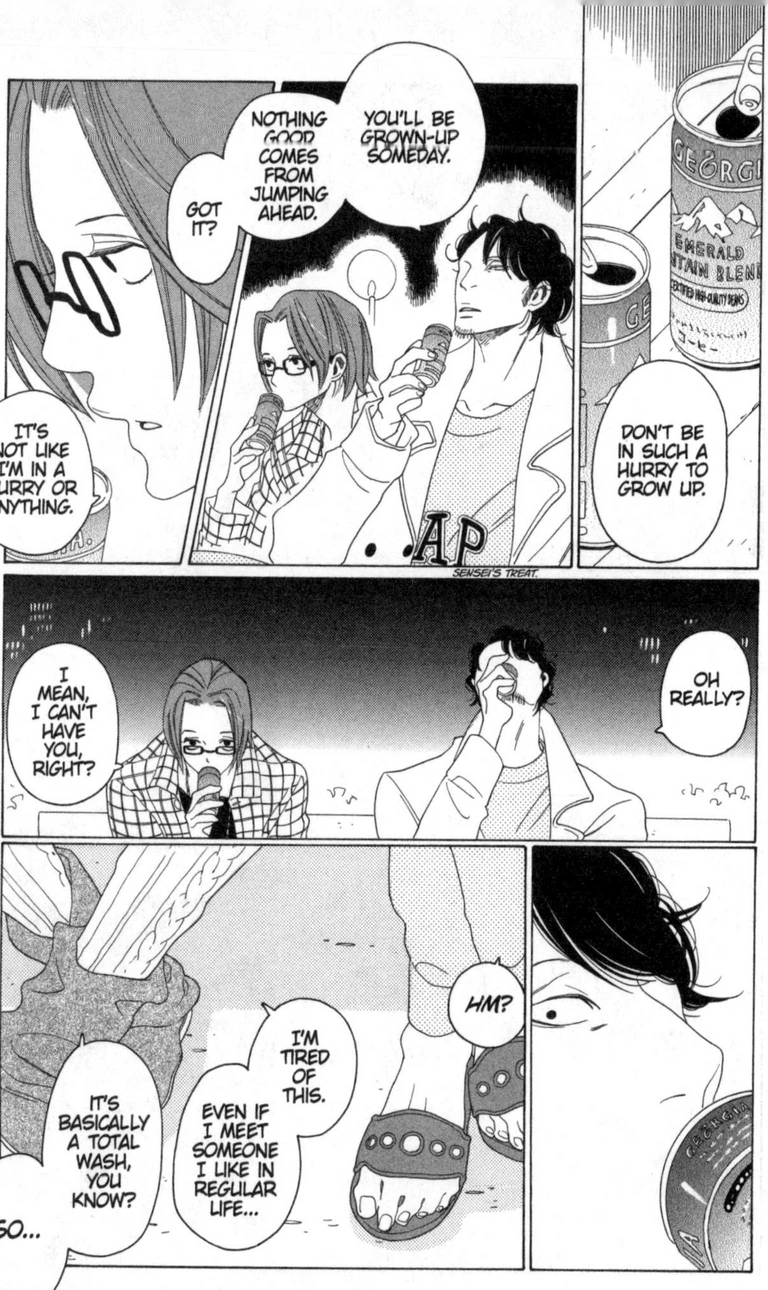
DON'T BE IN SUCH A HURRY TO GROW UP.
YOU'LL BE GROWN-UP SOMEDAY.
NOTHING GOOD COMES FROM JUMPING AHEAD.
GOT IT?
SENSEI'S TREAT.
IT'S NOT LIKE I'M IN A HURRY OR ANYTHING.
OH REALLY?
I MEAN, I CAN'T HAVE YOU, RIGHT?
HM?
I'M TIRED OF THIS.
EVEN IF I MEET SOMEONE I LIKE IN REGULAR LIFE...
IT'S BASICALLY A TOTAL WASH, YOU KNOW?
SO...

I DON'T WANT TO GET DRAWN INTO SOME EXHAUSTING ROMANCE.
SO...
IT'S LIKE HAVING A GOOD BATTING AVERAGE.
OR AT LEAST SEXUAL... PREFERENCE? AT LEAST WE SHARE THAT.
LOOK, YOU...
NON-EXHAUSTING ROMANCE DOESN'T EXIST, OKAY?

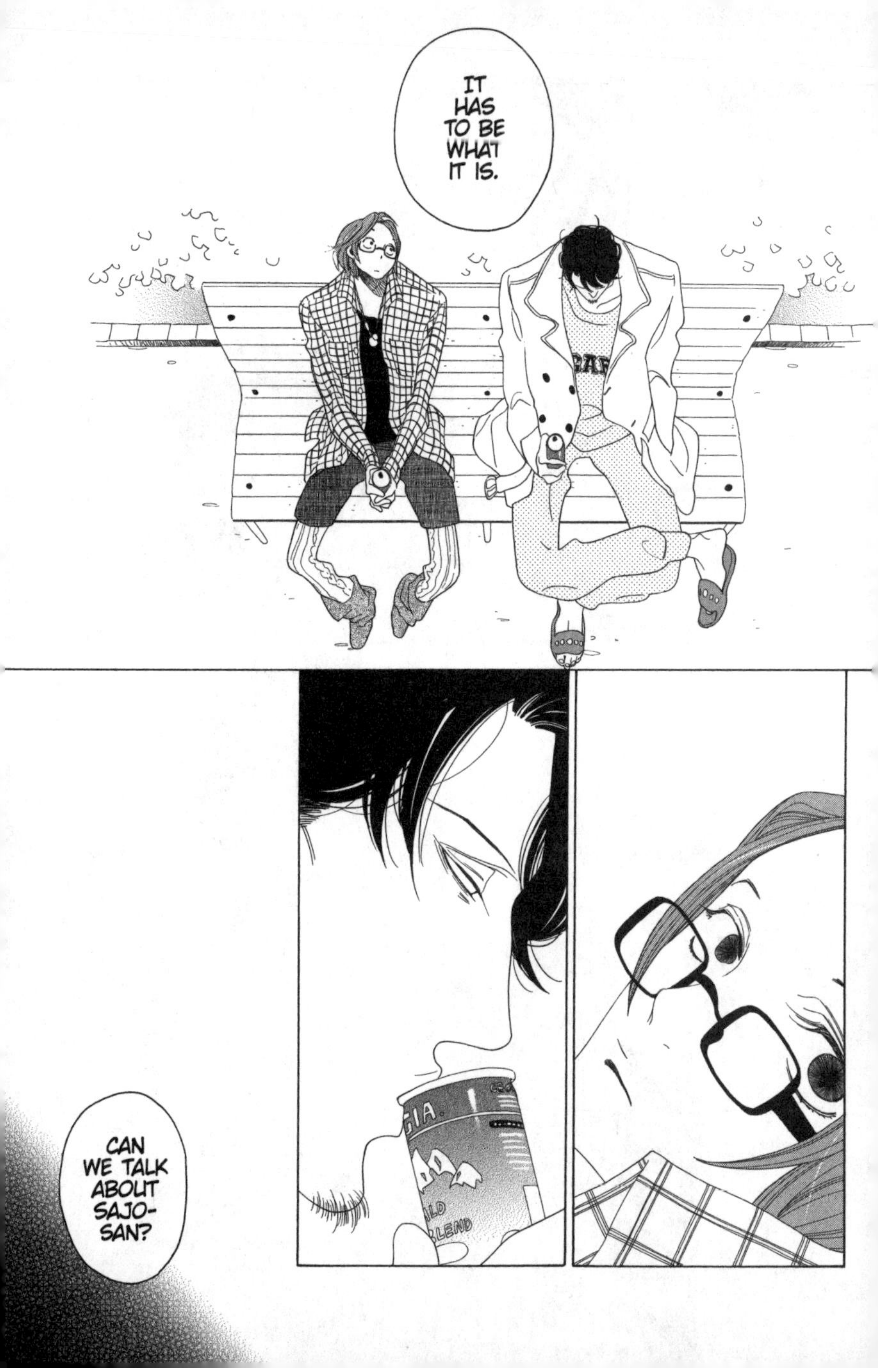
IT HAS TO BE WHAT IT IS.
CAN WE TALK ABOUT SAJO-SAN?

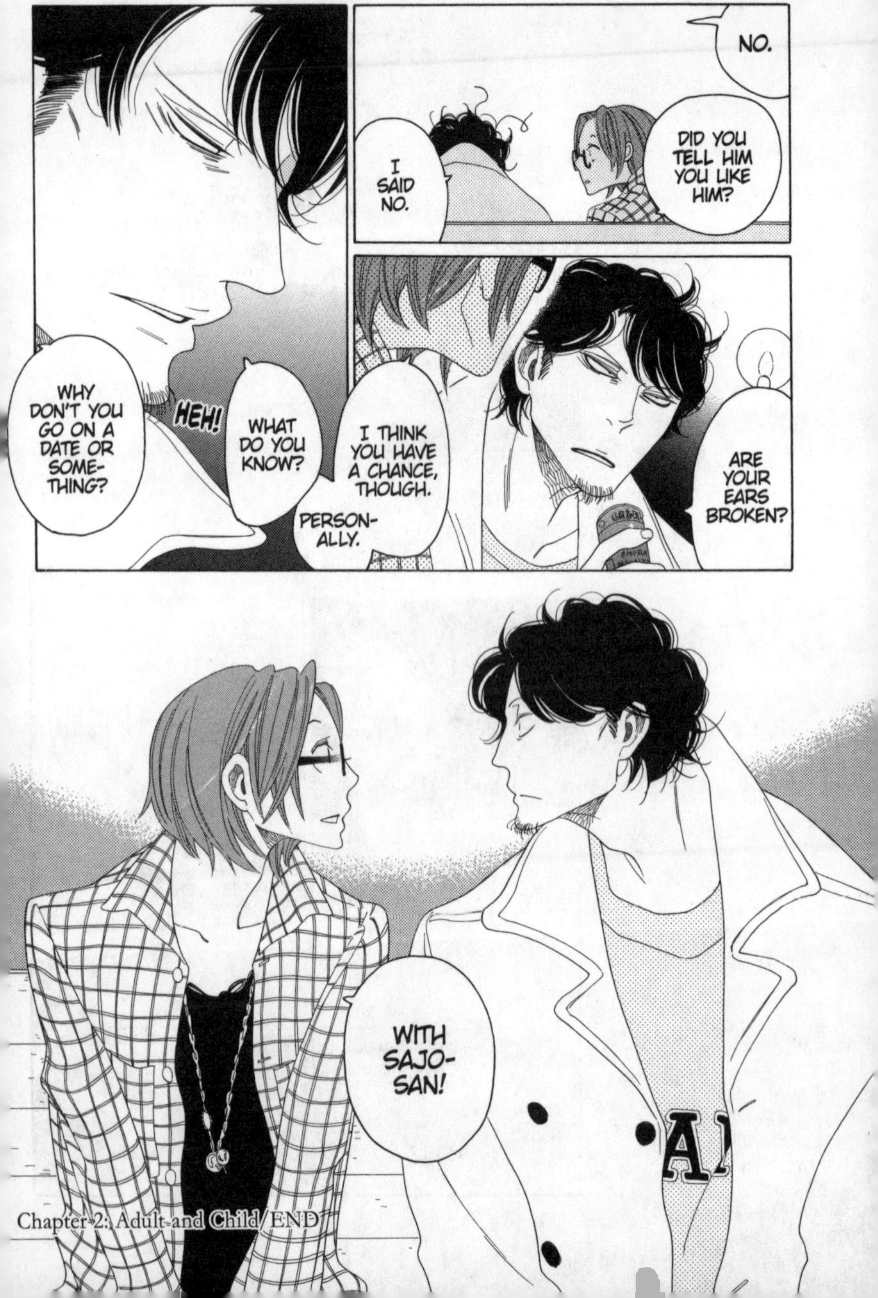
NO.
DID YOU TELL HIM YOU LIKE HIM?
I SAID NO.
ARE YOUR EARS BROKEN?
I THINK YOU HAVE A CHANCE, THOUGH.
PERSONALLY.
WHAT DO YOU KNOW?
HEH!
WHY DON'T YOU GO ON A DATE OR SOME-THING?
WITH SAJO-SAN!

Chapter 2: Adult and Child / END

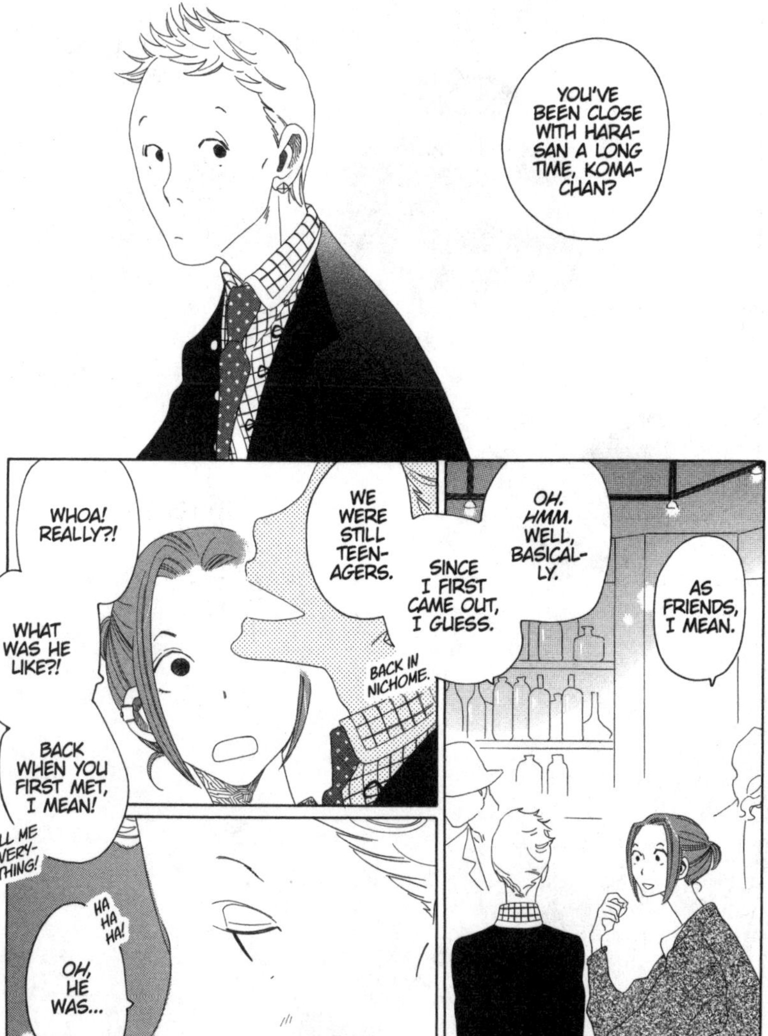
YOU'VE BEEN CLOSE WITH HARA-SAN A LONG TIME, KOMA-CHAN?
OH. HMM. WELL, BASICAL-LY.
SINCE I FIRST CAME OUT, I GUESS.
AS FRIENDS, I MEAN.
WE WERE STILL TEEN-AGERS.
BACK IN NICHOME.
WHOA! REALLY?!
WHAT WAS HE LIKE?!
BACK WHEN YOU FIRST MET, I MEAN!
TELL ME EVERY-THING!
HA HA HA!
OH, HE WAS...

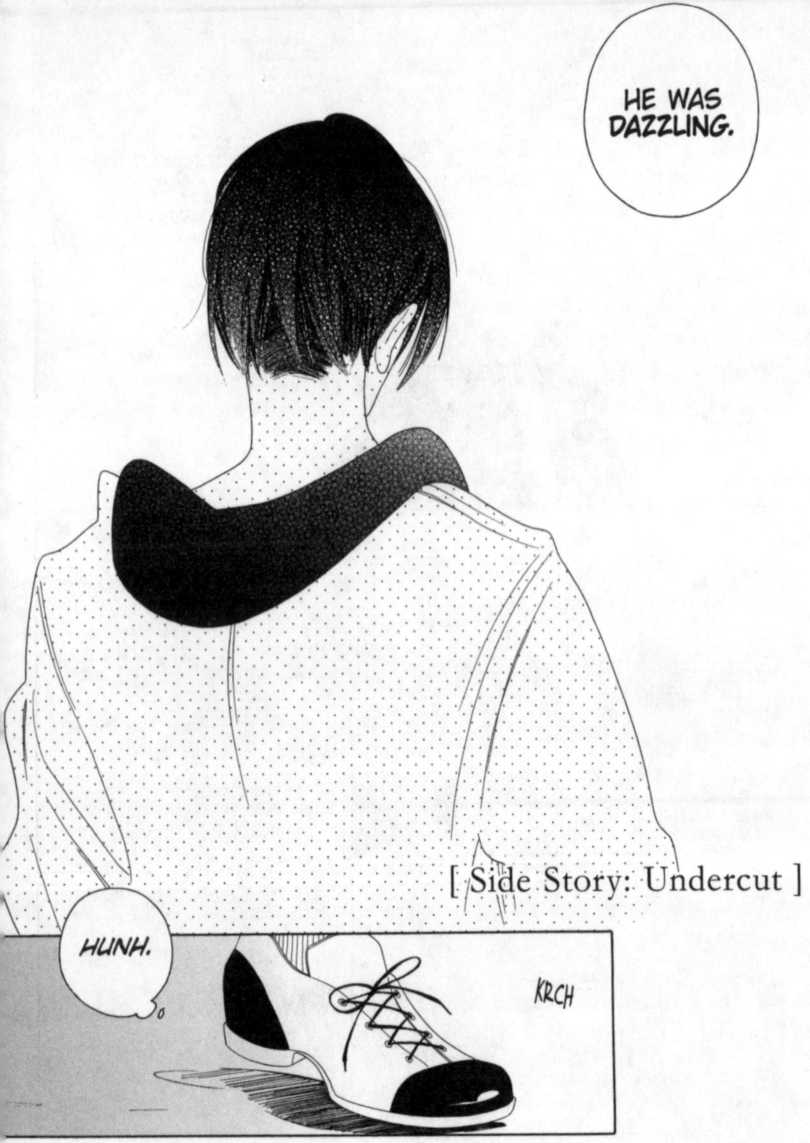
HE WAS DAZZLING.
[Side Story: Undercut]
KRCH
HUNH.

WALKING AROUND HERE, EVERYONE LOOKS KINDA SKETCHY.
I GUESS...
THIS IS THE SKETCHY PART OF TOWN.
OH!
WHOA!
AUUGH! NO WAAAAY! FOR REAAAAL?! WHOAAAAA!
THIS REALLY IS MECCA!
WHOAAAA! I MEAN, IT'S COOL, BUT I'M FREAKED OUT... AAAAH, ACTUALLY...
MAYBE COMING HERE ALONE WASN'T A GREAT IDEA.
BUT...
WHAT IF SOMEONE SCARY STARTS TALKING TO ME?
I DON'T HAVE ANY FRIENDS I COULD BRING HERE...
TAK

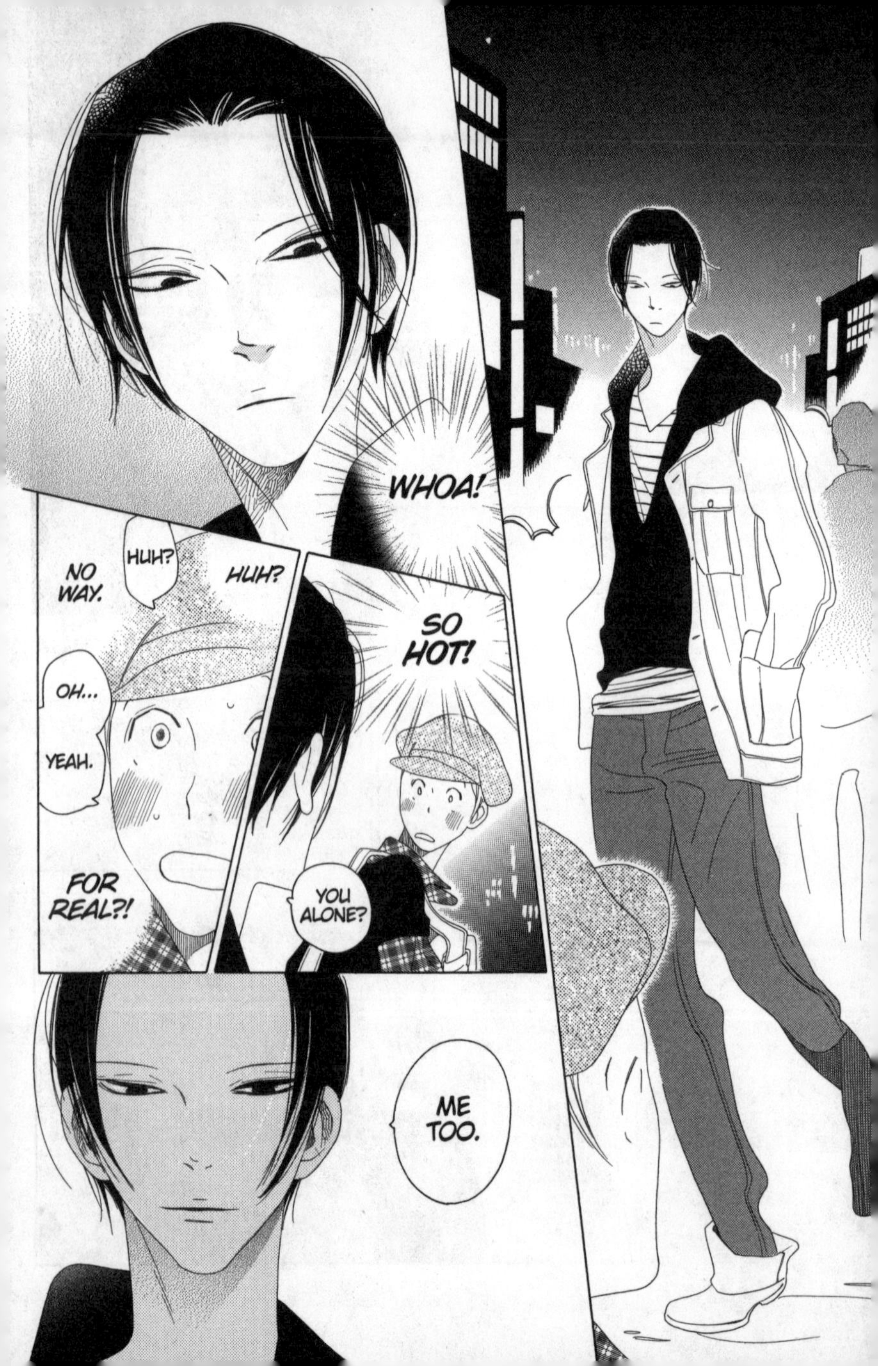
WHOA!
SO HOT!
YOU ALONE?
HUH?
HUH?
NO WAY.
OH...
YEAH.
FOR REAL?!
ME TOO.

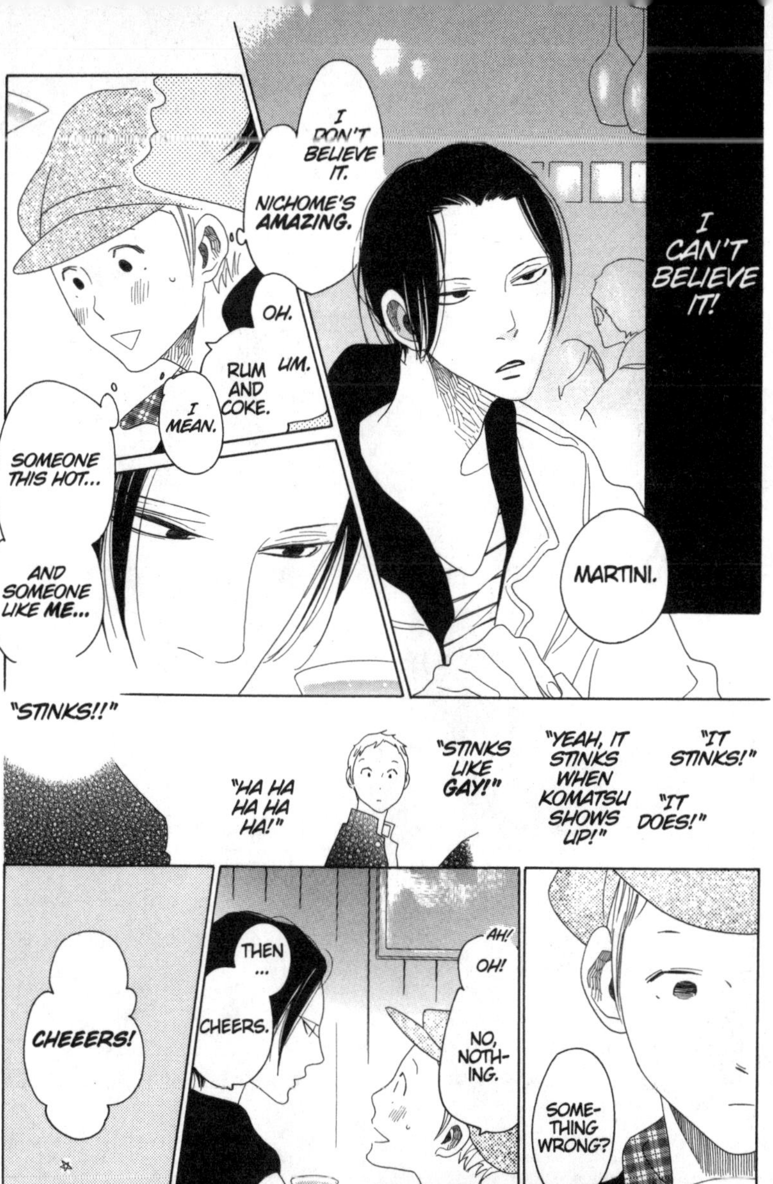

I CAN'T BELIEVE IT!
I DON'T BELIEVE IT.
NICHOME'S AMAZING.
OH.
UM.
RUM AND COKE.
I MEAN.
MARTINI.
SOMEONE THIS HOT...
AND SOMEONE LIKE ME...
"STINKS!!"
"IT STINKS!"
"IT DOES!"
"YEAH, IT STINKS WHEN KOMATSU SHOWS UP!"
"STINKS LIKE GAY!"
"HA HA HA HA HA!"
SOME-THING WRONG?
AH!
OH!
NO, NOTH-ING.
THEN ...
CHEERS.
CHEEERS!

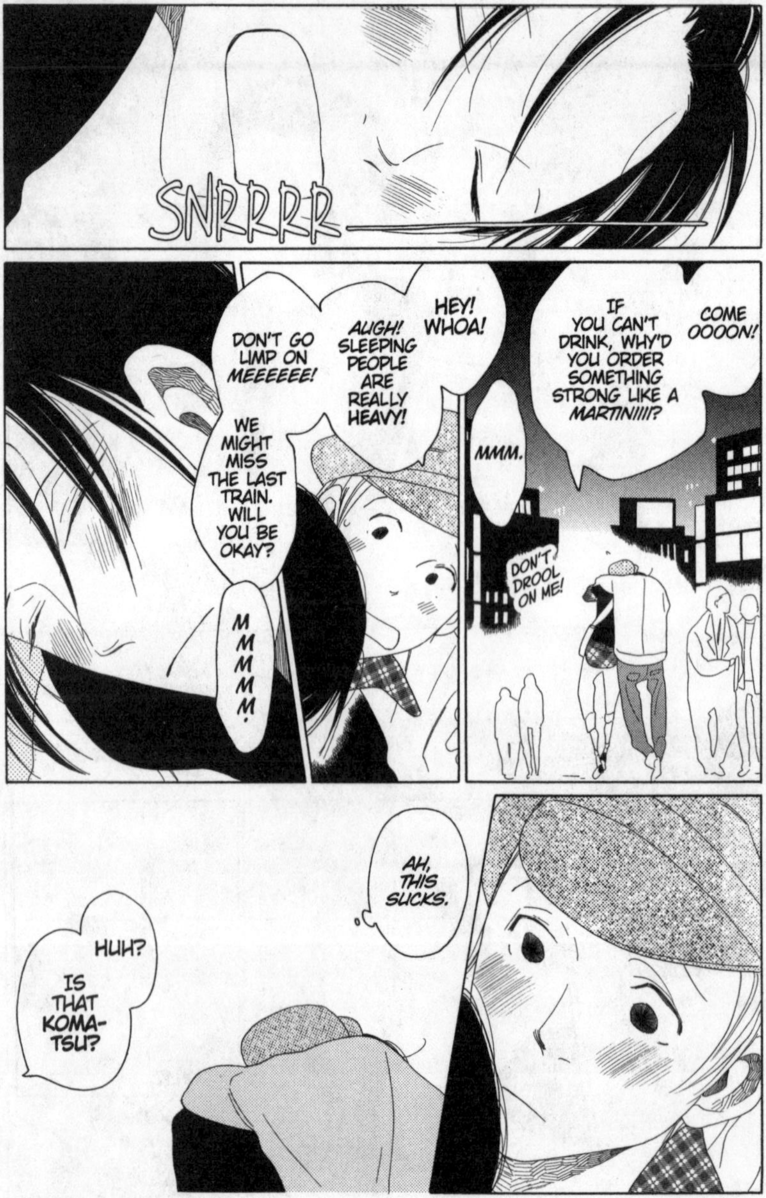
SNRRRR
COME OOOON!
IF YOU CAN'T DRINK, WHY'D YOU ORDER SOMETHING STRONG LIKE A MARTINI!!!?
MMM.
DON'T DROOL ON ME!
HEY! WHOA!
AUGH! SLEEPING PEOPLE ARE REALLY HEAVY!
DON'T GO LIMP ON MEEEEEE!
WE MIGHT MISS THE LAST TRAIN. WILL YOU BE OKAY?
MMMMMM!
AH, THIS SUCKS.
HUH? IS THAT KOMA-TSU?

WHOA! FOR REAL? KOMA-TSU?!
WOW! WITH A BIG GUY!
SO YOU REALLY COME TO NICHOME!
LOOK AT THE LITTLE SICKO!
SNAP
AND YOU'RE ALL DRESSED UP.
GIMME A BREAK!
YOU TRYING TO PICK UP A GUY?
YOU "CRUISING"?
MAN, HOW PATHETIC!
UHHH?
STAGGER
WHAT?
YOU NEED SOME-THING?
EH, MR. BOY-FRIEND?
HYUK HYUK HYUK!
URP.

HRRRRRK!
AUGH!
GROSS!
SPLSH
SPLSH
SPLSH
ZSSHA
PSSH
SWSH
SWSH
SWSH
PEH
SPLASH
SPLASH
OH.
THANKS.
HAAH...
SORRY.

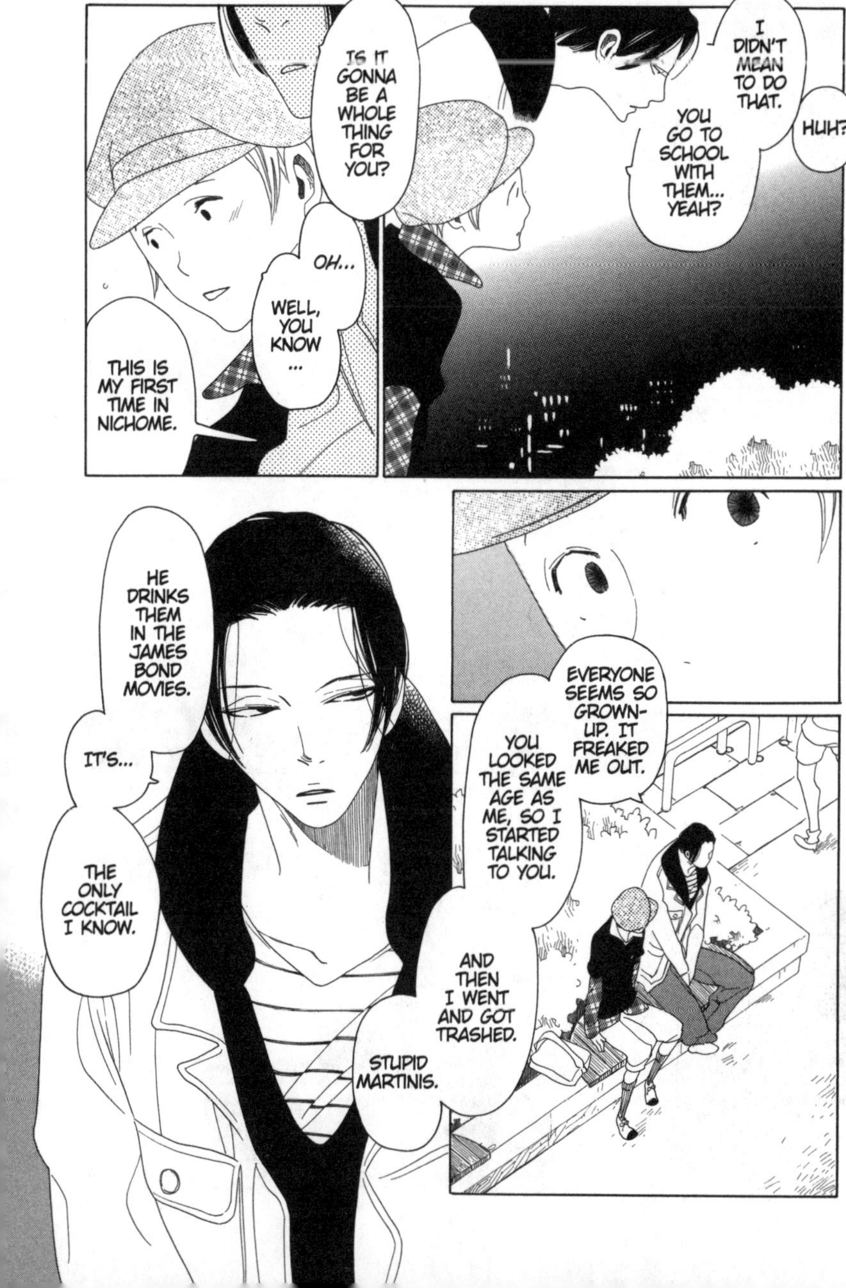
I DIDN'T MEAN TO DO THAT.
HUH?
YOU GO TO SCHOOL WITH THEM... YEAH?
IS IT GONNA BE A WHOLE THING FOR YOU?
OH...
WELL, YOU KNOW ...
THIS IS MY FIRST TIME IN NICHOME.
EVERYONE SEEMS SO GROWN-UP. IT FREAKED ME OUT.
YOU LOOKED THE SAME AGE AS ME, SO I STARTED TALKING TO YOU.
AND THEN I WENT AND GOT TRASHED.
STUPID MARTINIS.
HE DRINKS THEM IN THE JAMES BOND MOVIES.
IT'S...
THE ONLY COCKTAIL I KNOW.

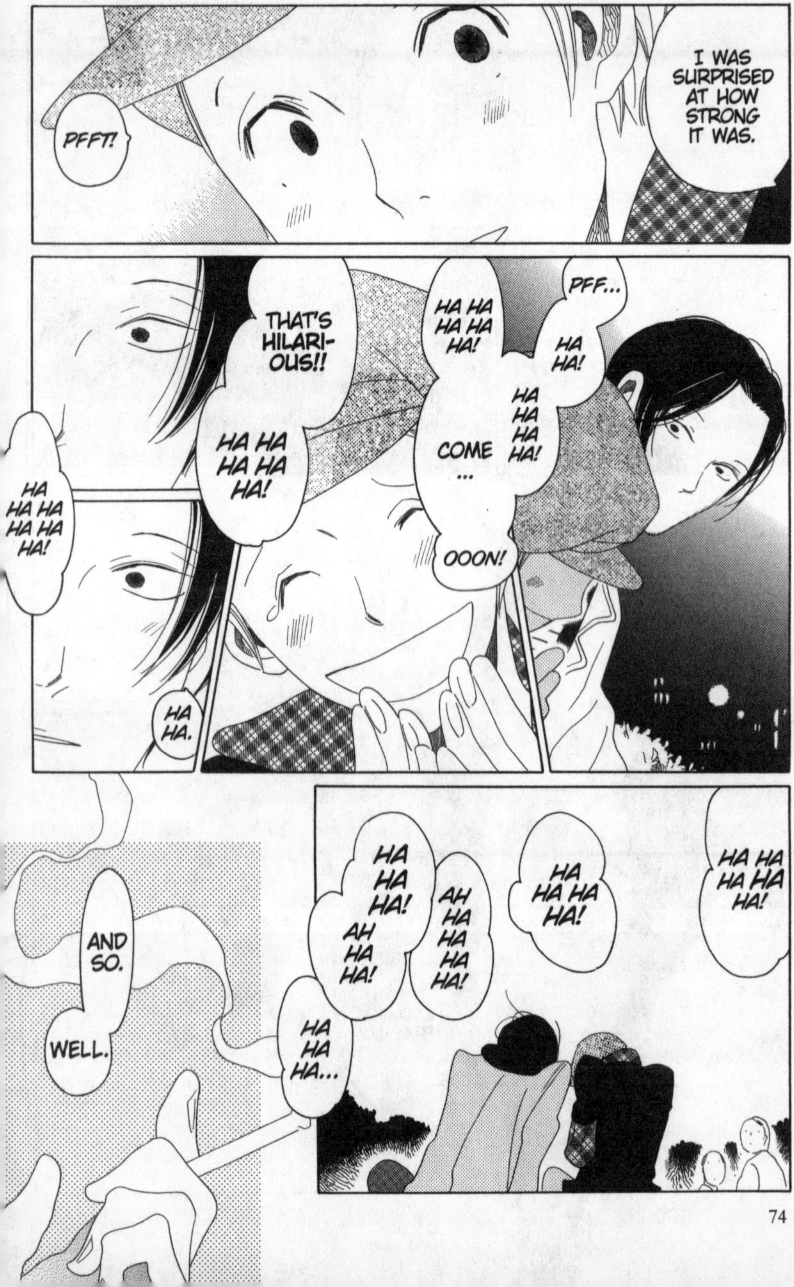
I WAS SURPRISED AT HOW STRONG IT WAS.
PFFT!
PFF... HA HA!
HA HA HA HA!
HA HA HA HA HA!
COME... OOON!
THAT'S HILARIOUS!!
HA HA HA HA HA!
HA HA HA HA HA HA!
HA HA.
HA HA HA HA HA!
HA HA HA HA!
AH HA HA HA HA!
HA HA HA! AH HA HA!
HA HA HA...
AND SO.
WELL.

IT WAS LIKE THAT, BASICALLY.
WOW! WHAT A CRAZY FIRST MEETING!
I GUESS?
HEH HEH.
I LEFT HIGH SCHOOL AFTER THAT.
STARTED FASHION SCHOOL.
OOOOH, YOU DID?
OH! RIGHT!
CAN I GET A DISCOUNT ON YOUR CLOTHES, KOMA-CHAN?
HA HA HA!
SURE.
OH, BUT THERE'S NOT A LOT OF STOCK. COME IN AND ORDER SOMETHING!
HOORAY! I'LL BE THERE WITH BELLS ON!
HUH? SO LIKE...
YOU TWO NEVER GOT TOGETHER?
NOPE, NUH-UH. NEVER.
HUNH. WHY NOT?
WHY NOT?
HMM. WHY NOT? WELL...
HEY!

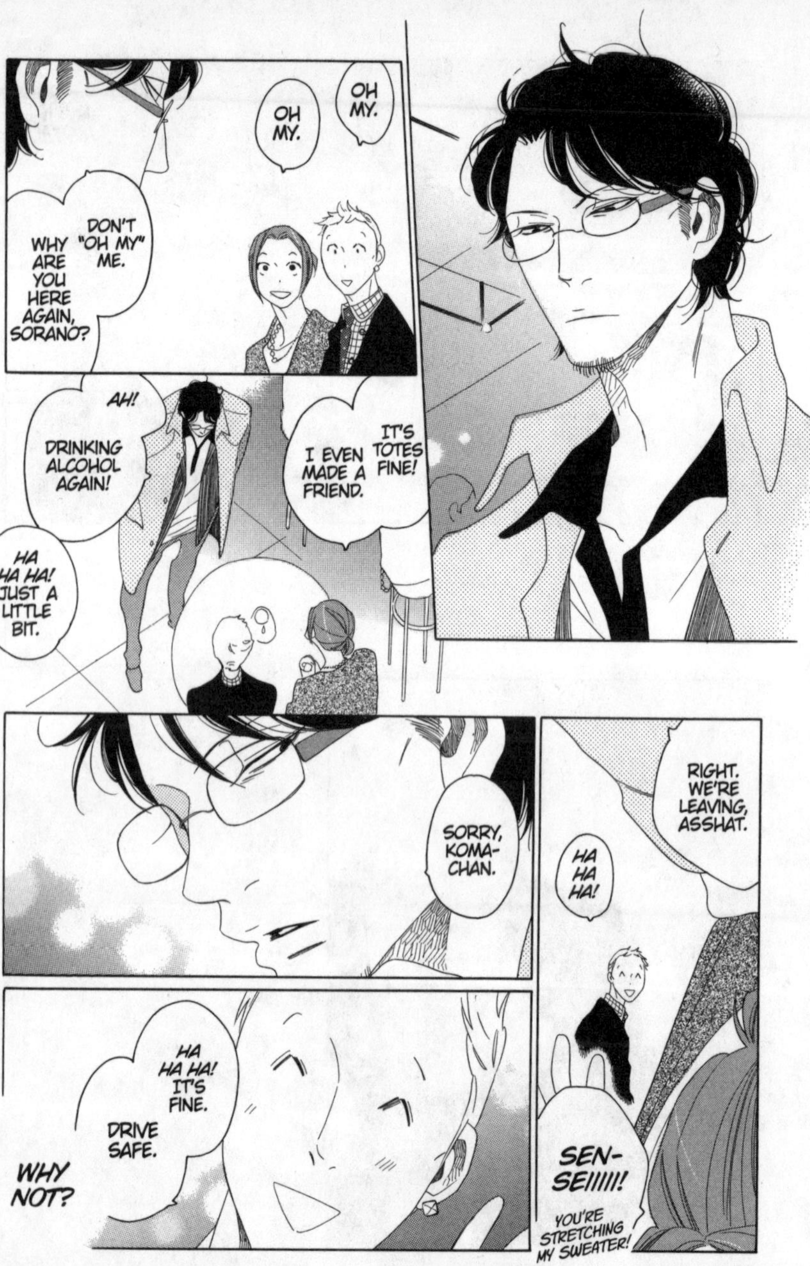
OH MY.
OH MY.
DON'T "OH MY" ME.
WHY ARE YOU HERE AGAIN, SORANO?
IT'S TOTES FINE!
I EVEN MADE A FRIEND.
AH!
DRINKING ALCOHOL AGAIN!
HA HA HA! JUST A LITTLE BIT.
RIGHT. WE'RE LEAVING, ASSHAT.
HA HA HA!
SEN-SEIIIIII!
YOU'RE STRETCHING MY SWEATER!
SORRY, KOMA-CHAN.
HA HA HA! IT'S FINE.
DRIVE SAFE.
WHY NOT?

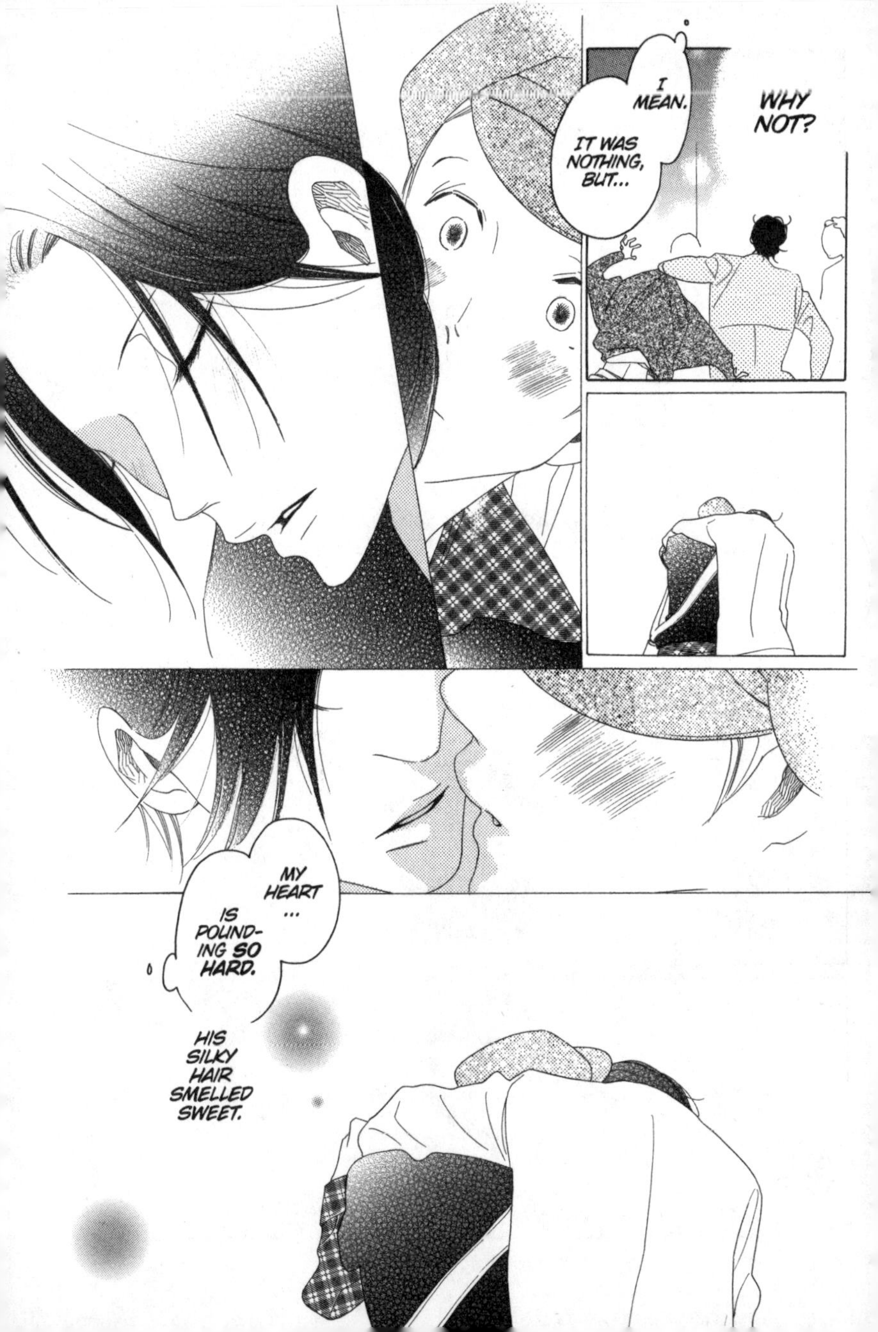
WHY NOT?
I MEAN. IT WAS NOTHING, BUT...
MY HEART ... IS POUNDING SO HARD.
HIS SILKY HAIR SMELLED SWEET.

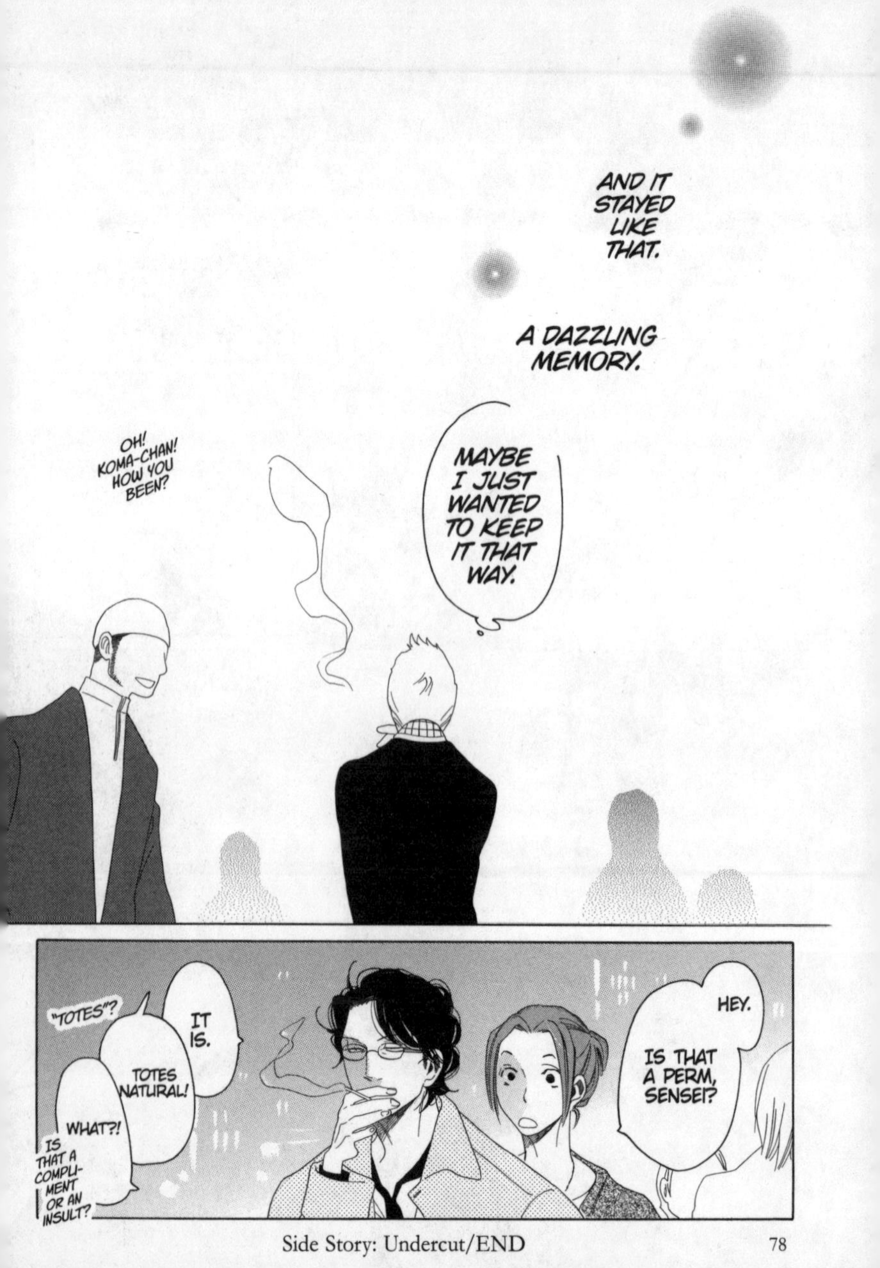
AND IT STAYED LIKE THAT.
A DAZZLING MEMORY.
MAYBE I JUST WANTED TO KEEP IT THAT WAY.
OH! KOMA-CHAN! HOW YOU BEEN?
HEY.
IS THAT A PERM, SENSEI?
IT IS.
TOTES NATURAL!
"TOTES"?
WHAT?!
IS THAT A COMPLI-MENT OR AN INSULT?

Side Story: Undercut/END

[Chapter 3: Hara & Sajo]

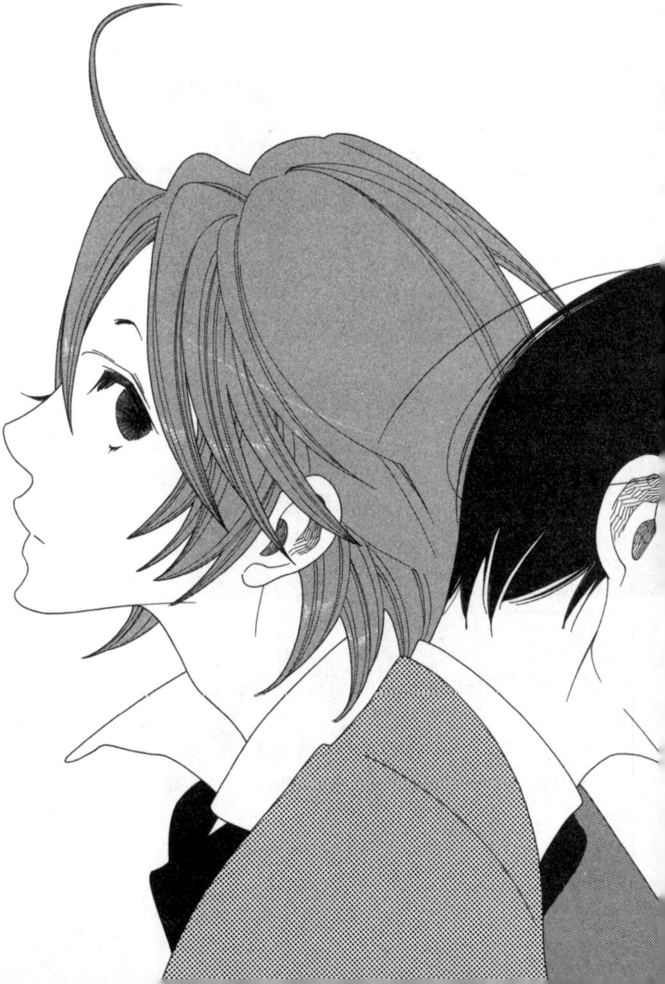

"WHY DON'T YOU...
HARA-SENSEI, DROOL.
"GO ON A DATE OR SOME-THING?
AH?!
YOU'RE DROOLING.
HA HA!
YOU'RE TOO YOUNG TO HAVE WEAK JAW MUSCLES.
JAW MUSCLES
HA HA HA.
NO, NO.
"WITH SAJO-SAN!"
HARA-SENSEI.
IT'S...
REALLY.
REALLY...
A DATE.

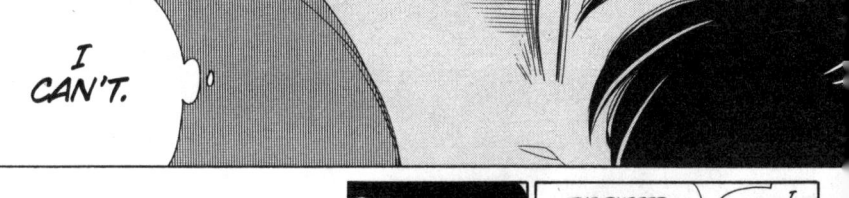

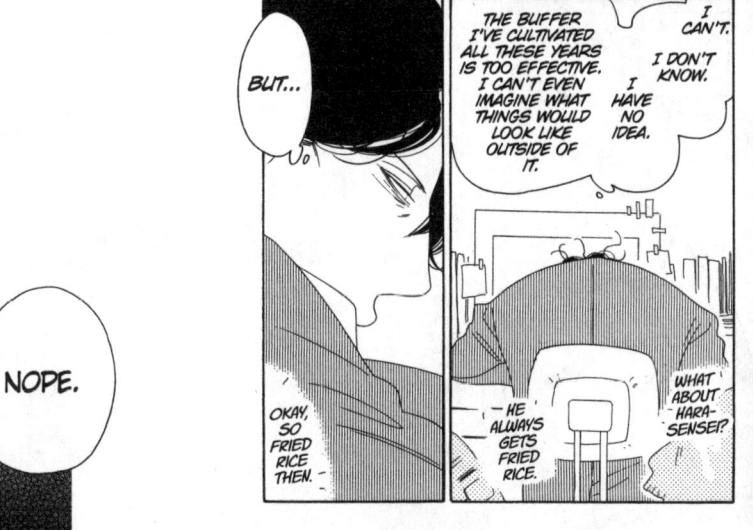

A DATE WITH SAJO.

WHAT SHOULD WE DO FOR LUNCH?

KUNK

SHOULD WE GET TAKE-OUT?

RAMEN FOR ME.

OH, I'LL SIT THIS ONE OUT.

I CAN'T.

I CAN'T. I DON'T KNOW. I HAVE NO IDEA.

THE BUFFER I'VE CULTIVATED ALL THESE YEARS IS TOO EFFECTIVE. I CAN'T EVEN IMAGINE WHAT THINGS WOULD LOOK LIKE OUTSIDE OF IT.

BUT...

WHAT ABOUT HARA-SENSEI!?

HE ALWAYS GETS FRIED RICE.

OKAY, SO FRIED RICE THEN.

NOPE.

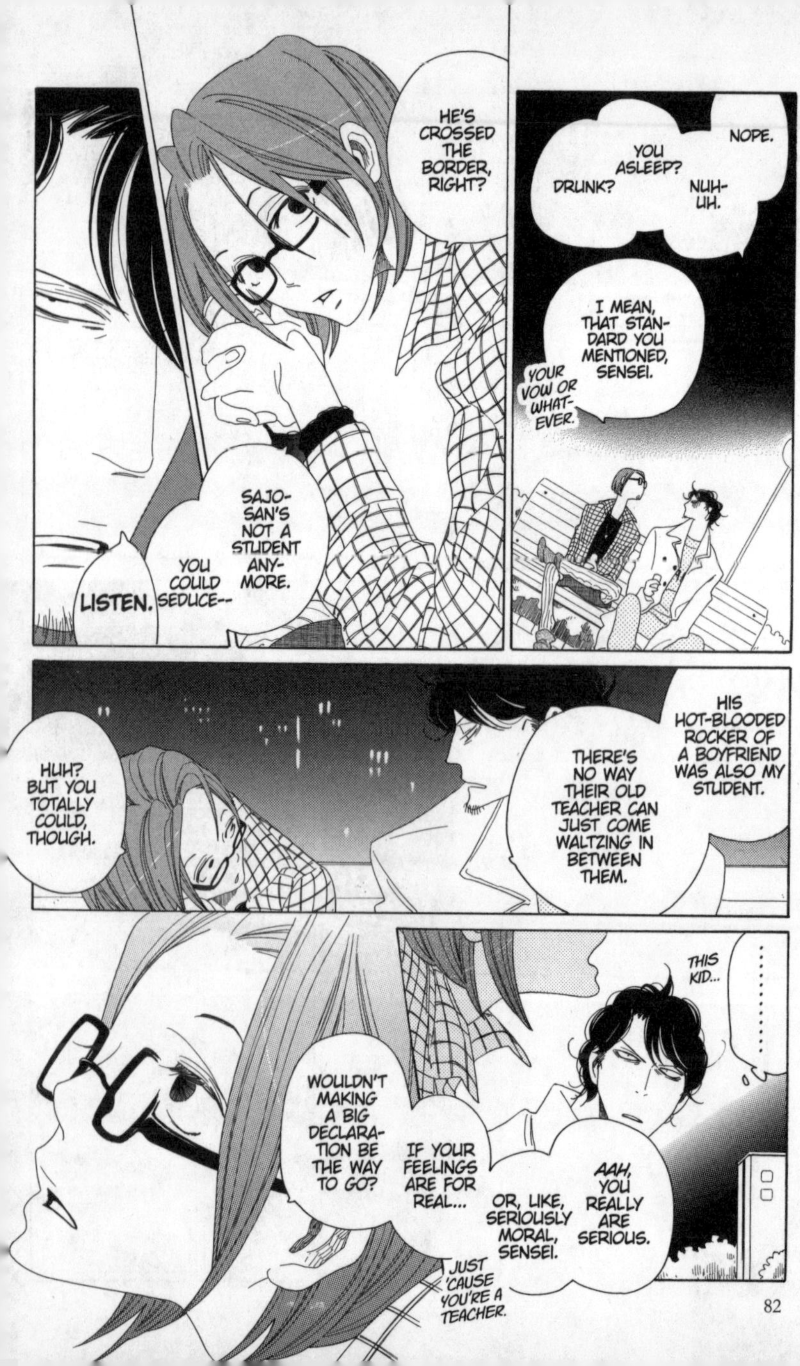
YOU ASLEEP?
NOPE.
DRUNK?
NUH-UH.
I MEAN, THAT STANDARD YOU MENTIONED, SENSEI.
YOUR VOW OR WHATEVER.
HE'S CROSSED THE BORDER, RIGHT?
SAJO-SAN'S NOT A STUDENT ANYMORE.
YOU COULD SEDUCE--
LISTEN.
HIS HOT-BLOODED ROCKER OF A BOYFRIEND WAS ALSO MY STUDENT.
THERE'S NO WAY THEIR OLD TEACHER CAN JUST COME WALTZING IN BETWEEN THEM.
HUH? BUT YOU TOTALLY COULD, THOUGH.
......
THIS KID...
AAH, YOU REALLY ARE SERIOUS.
OR, LIKE, SERIOUSLY MORAL, SENSEI.
JUST 'CAUSE YOU'RE A TEACHER.
IF YOUR FEELINGS ARE FOR REAL...
WOULDN'T MAKING A BIG DECLARATION BE THE WAY TO GO?

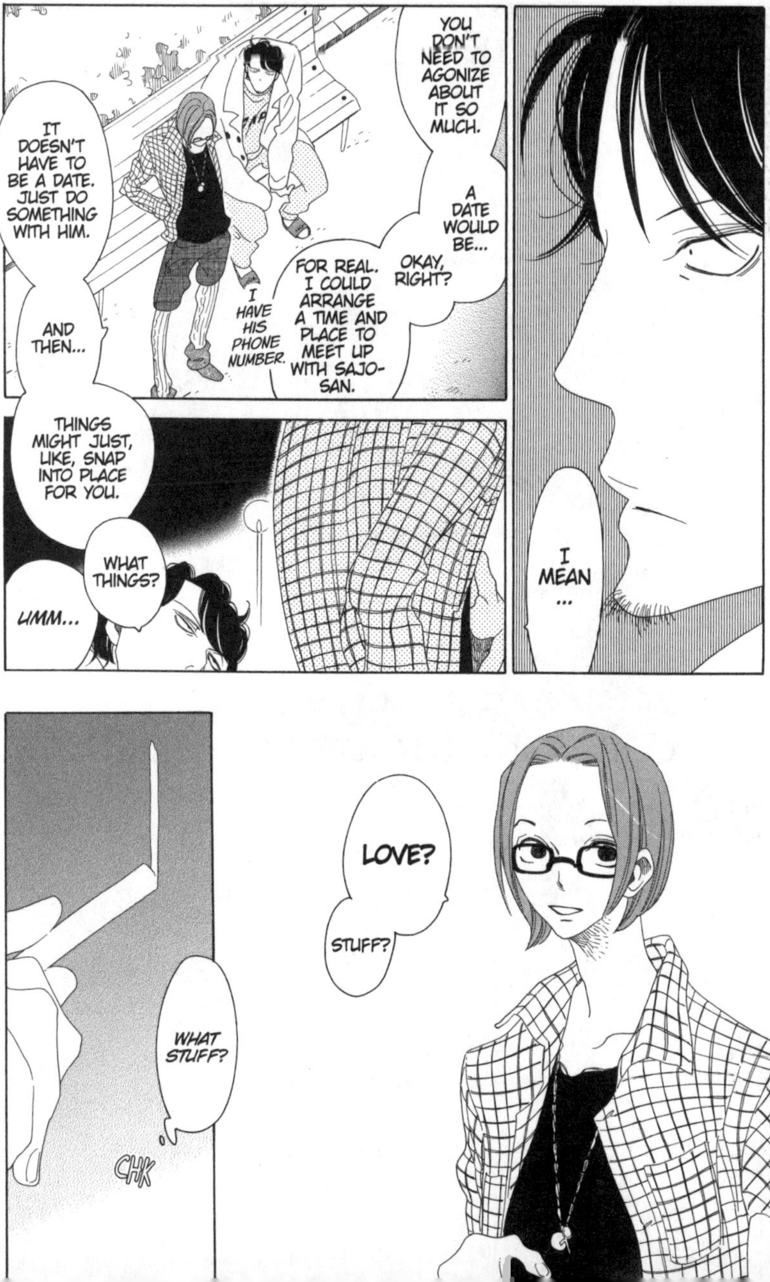
I MEAN...
YOU DON'T NEED TO AGONIZE ABOUT IT SO MUCH.
A DATE WOULD BE...
OKAY, RIGHT?
FOR REAL. I COULD ARRANGE A TIME AND PLACE TO MEET UP WITH SAJO-SAN.
I HAVE HIS PHONE NUMBER.
IT DOESN'T HAVE TO BE A DATE. JUST DO SOMETHING WITH HIM.
AND THEN...
THINGS MIGHT JUST, LIKE, SNAP INTO PLACE FOR YOU.
WHAT THINGS?
UMM...
LOVE?
STUFF?
WHAT STUFF?
CHK

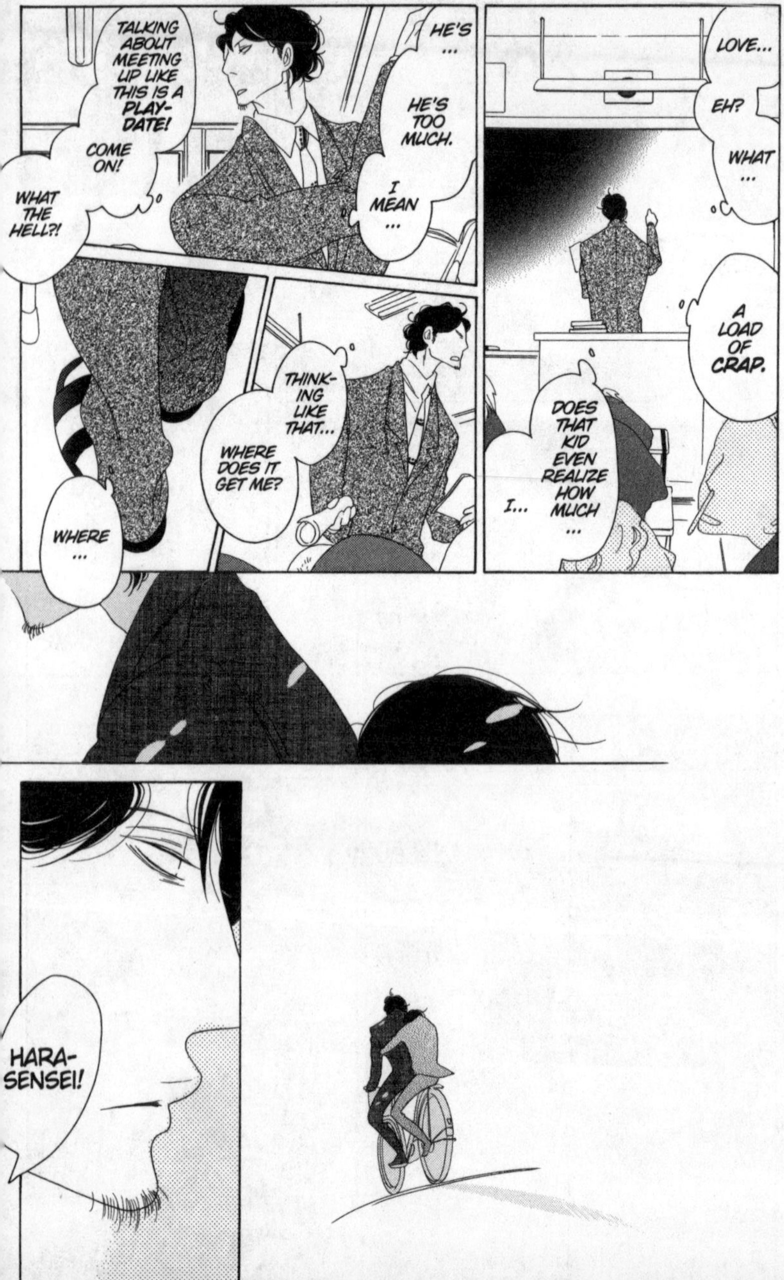
LOVE... EH? WHAT...
A LOAD OF CRAP.
DOES THAT KID EVEN REALIZE HOW MUCH...
I...
HE'S...
HE'S TOO MUCH.
I MEAN...
TALKING ABOUT MEETING UP LIKE THIS IS A PLAY-DATE!
COME ON!
WHAT THE HELL?!
THINKING LIKE THAT...
WHERE DOES IT GET ME?
WHERE...
HARA-SENSEI!

HM?
KLATTER
CAN WE GO NOW?
KLATTER
YEAH.
BING
BONG
THE ONLY THING YOU LOT ARE GOOD AT IS GOING HOME.
SEE YA LATER!
I GOT PRACTICE!
BENG
BONG
BING
BONG
OH.
HENHEI HOOAAI!
DON'T TALK WITH YOUR MOUTH FULL.
HA HA HA!
BENG
BONG
YOU WANT ONE?
NO THANKS.
WHAT CLUB ARE YOU IN?
THE "GO HOME CLUB"?
......
THAT I AM!

MUNCH MUNCH .... MUNCH MUNCH HMM.

SO...

HOW DID IT GO WITH *THAT*?

OH! THE DATE!

HE FORGOT?!

IT'S JUST... YOU GAVE ME SUCH A FIRM NO. A VERY BIG RED LIGHT. IT WAS CLEAR YOU WEREN'T INTO THE IDEA AT ALL, Y'KNOW? MM...

? THAT?

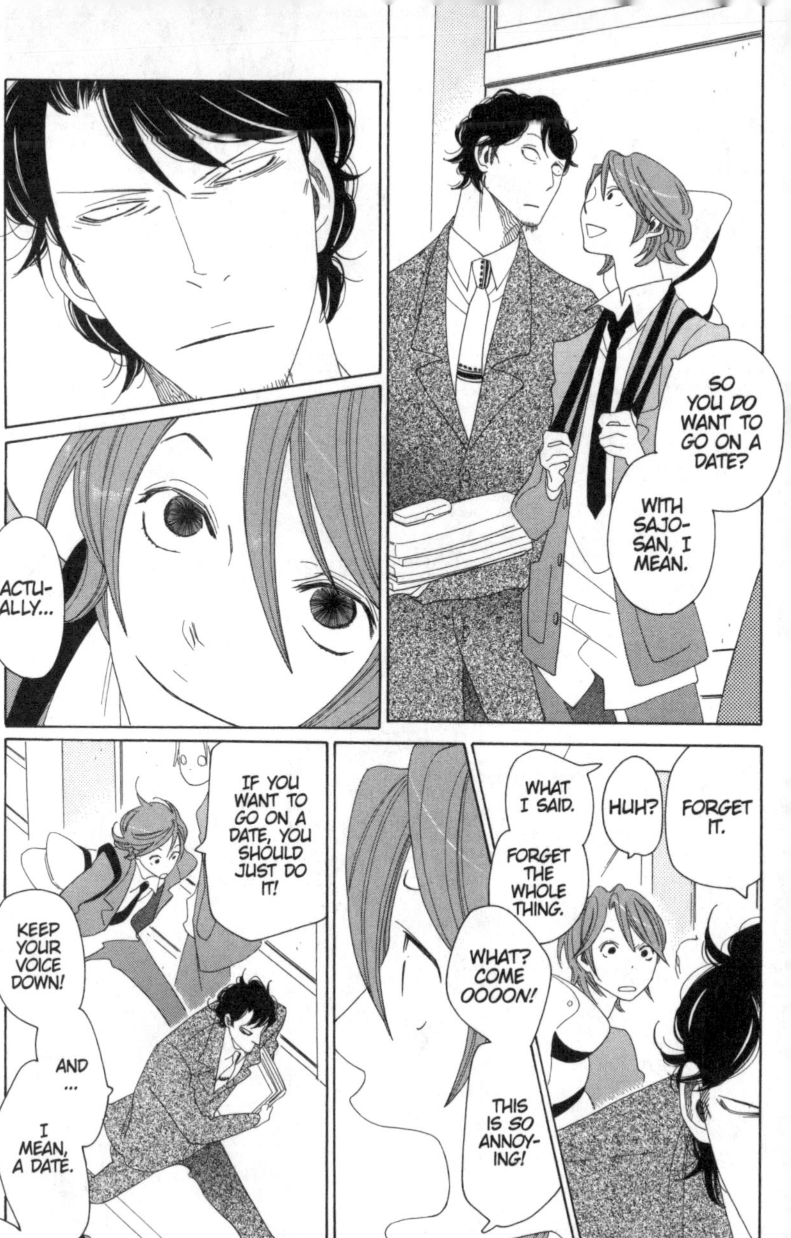
SO YOU *DO* WANT TO GO ON A DATE?
WITH SAJO-SAN, I MEAN.
ACTUALLY...
FORGET IT.
HUH?
WHAT I SAID.
FORGET THE WHOLE THING.
WHAT? COME OOOON!
THIS IS SO ANNOYING!
IF YOU WANT TO GO ON A DATE, YOU SHOULD JUST DO IT!
KEEP YOUR VOICE DOWN!
AND ...
I MEAN, A DATE.
WH...

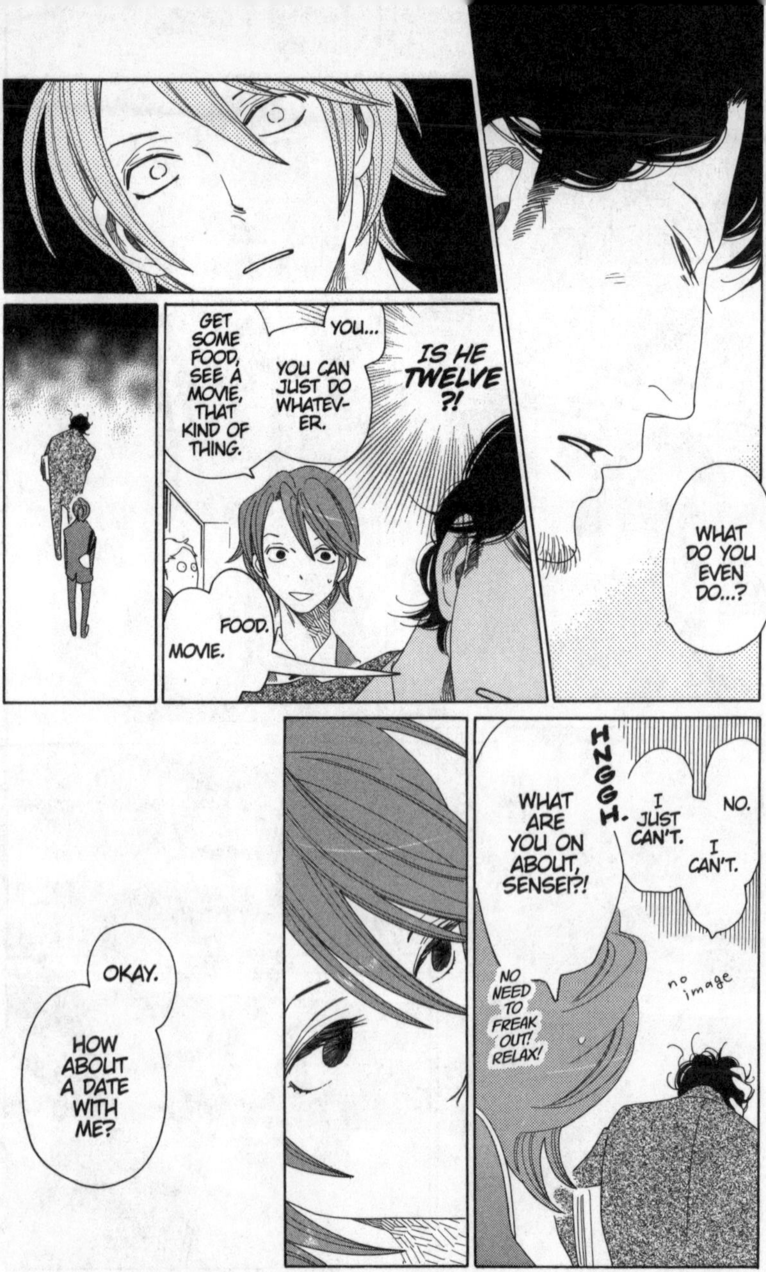
WHAT DO YOU EVEN DO...?
YOU...
YOU CAN JUST DO WHATEVER.
GET SOME FOOD, SEE A MOVIE, THAT KIND OF THING.
IS HE TWELVE ?!
FOOD. MOVIE.
NO. I CAN'T.
I JUST CAN'T.
HNGGH.
WHAT ARE YOU ON ABOUT, SENSEI!?!
NO NEED TO FREAK OUT! RELAX!
no image
OKAY.
HOW ABOUT A DATE WITH ME?

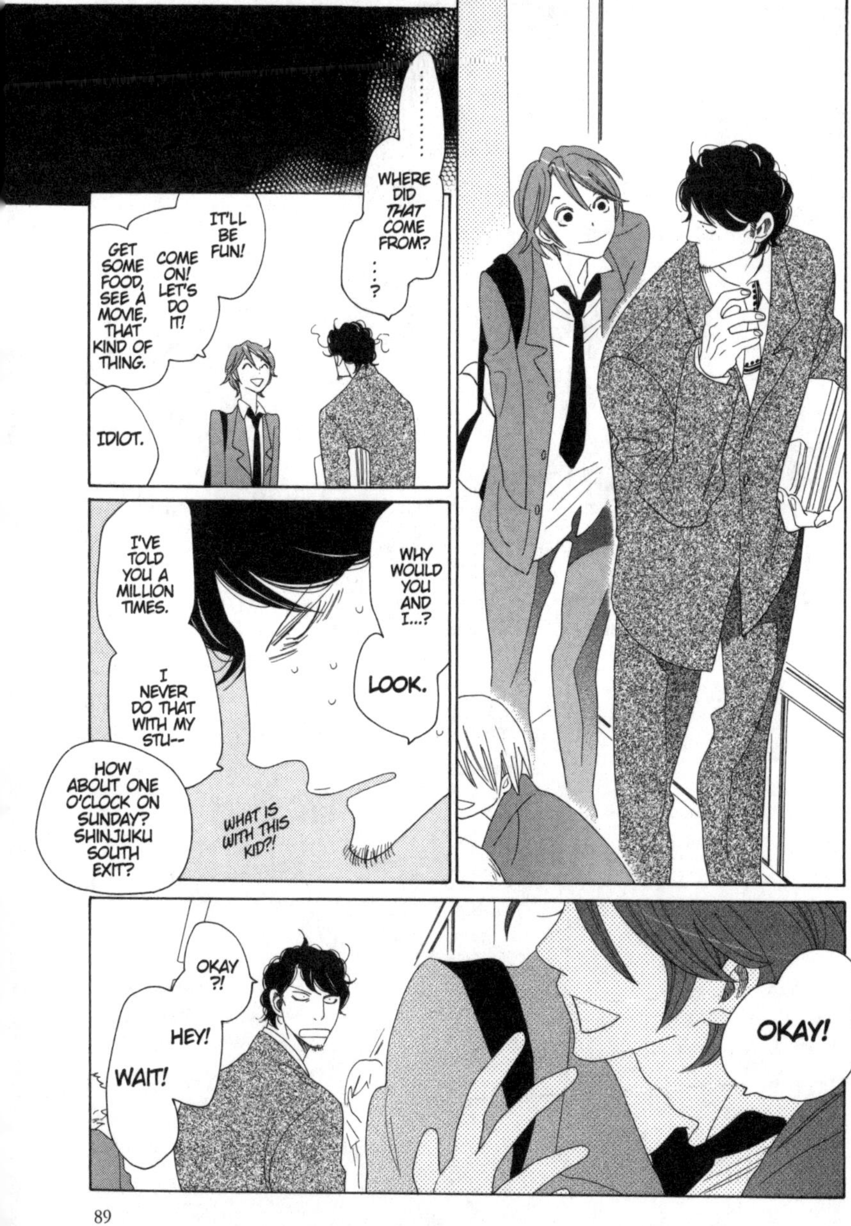
....
WHERE DID THAT COME FROM?
...?
IT'LL BE FUN!
COME ON! LET'S DO IT!
GET SOME FOOD, SEE A MOVIE, THAT KIND OF THING.
IDIOT.
WHY WOULD YOU AND I...?
LOOK.
I'VE TOLD YOU A MILLION TIMES.
I NEVER DO THAT WITH MY STU--
HOW ABOUT ONE O'CLOCK ON SUNDAY? SHINJUKU SOUTH EXIT?
WHAT IS WITH THIS KID?!
OKAY!
OKAY?!
HEY!
WAIT!

MAKE SURE YOU LOOK HOT!

"KISS HIM.

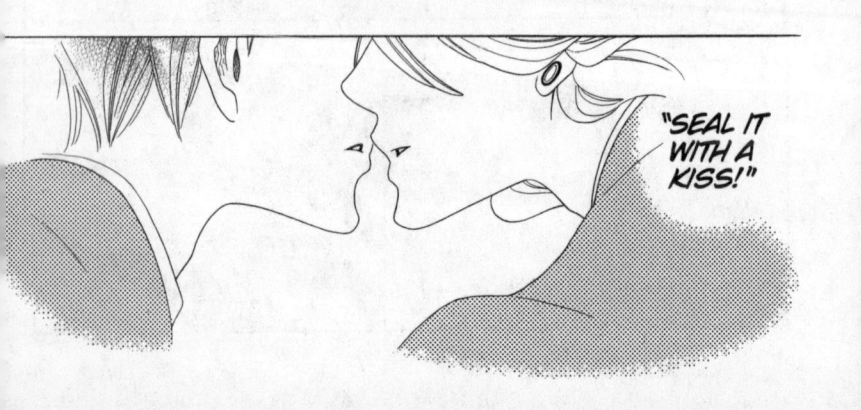

"SEAL IT WITH A KISS!"

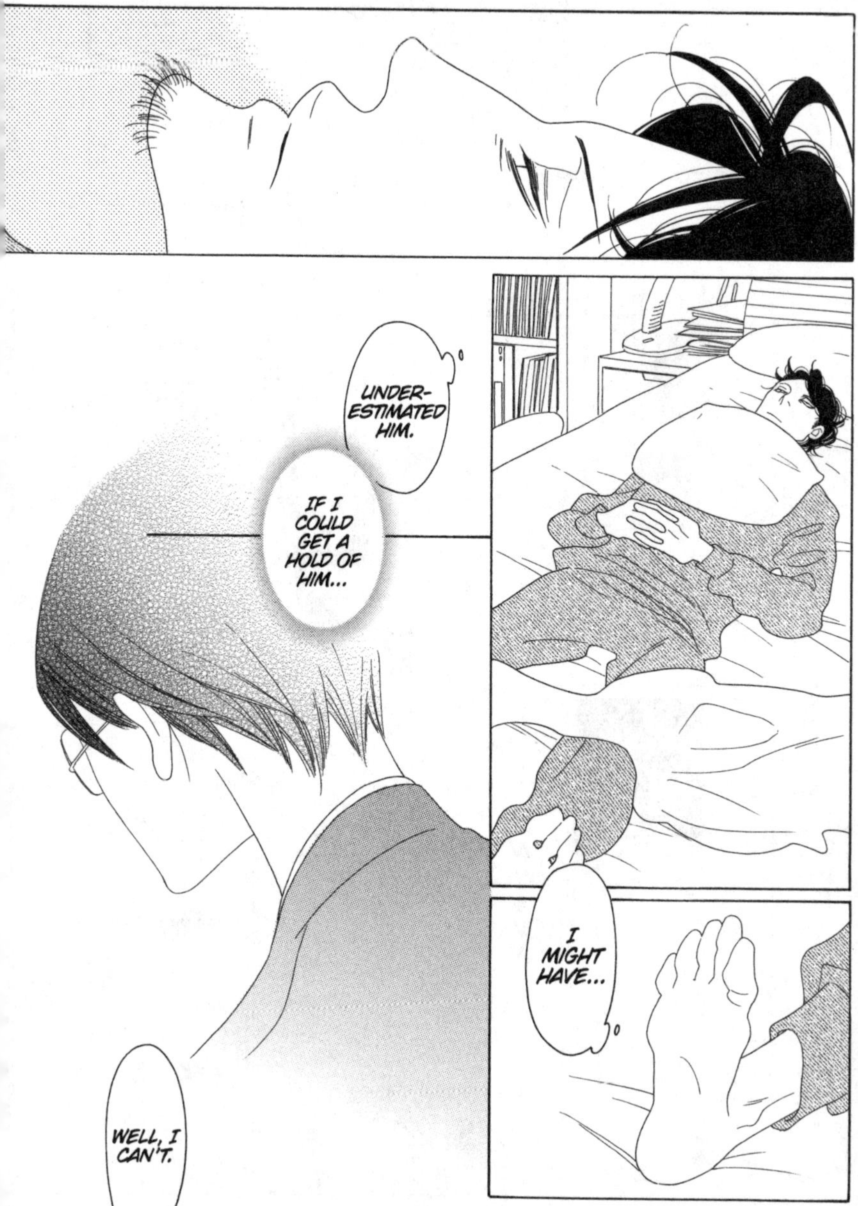
UNDER-ESTIMATED HIM.
IF I COULD GET A HOLD OF HIM...
I MIGHT HAVE...
WELL, I CAN'T.

CON-CEITED.
PRE-SUMPTUOUS.
COWARD.
ARRO-GANT.
FWMP
HAAAH.
NOT COOL.
VRZZ
VRZZ
VRZZ
VRZZ
VRZZ
BEEP
12:00
ALARM 05
LUNCHTIME
12:00
THIS SUNDAY.
ONE O'CLOCK AT SHINJUKU SOUTH EXIT.
UNNNNNNH!
......
SHINJUKU STATION

SHIN-JUKU SOUTH EXIT.
RIGHT.
HE SAID THAT...
BUT THERE'S A BUNCH OF THEM!
SUCH HALF-ASSED DIRECTIONS...
WHERE WOULD HE...
BE...?

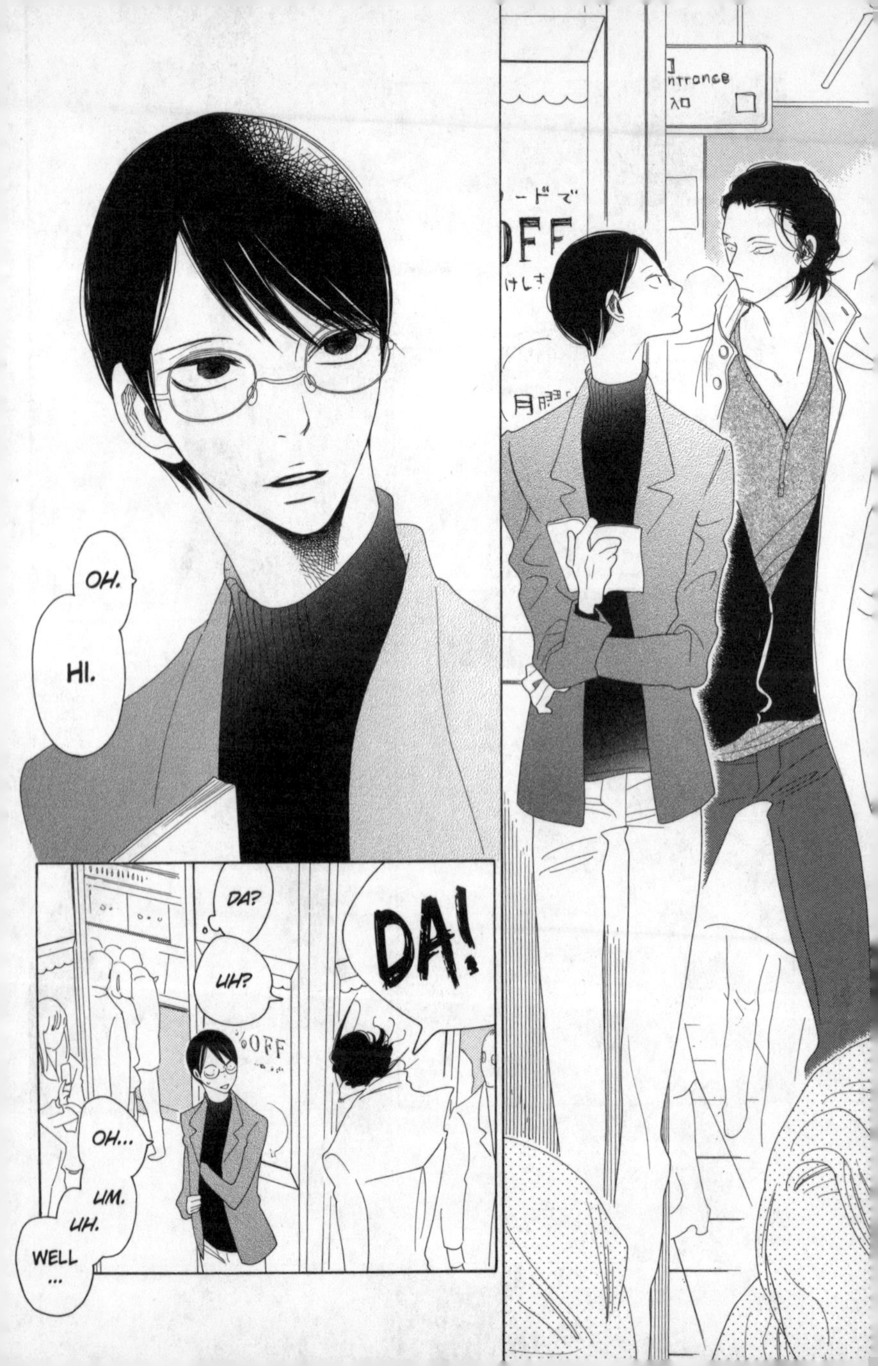
入口
OFF
OH.
HI.
DA!
DA?
UH?
OH...
UM.
UH.
WELL
...

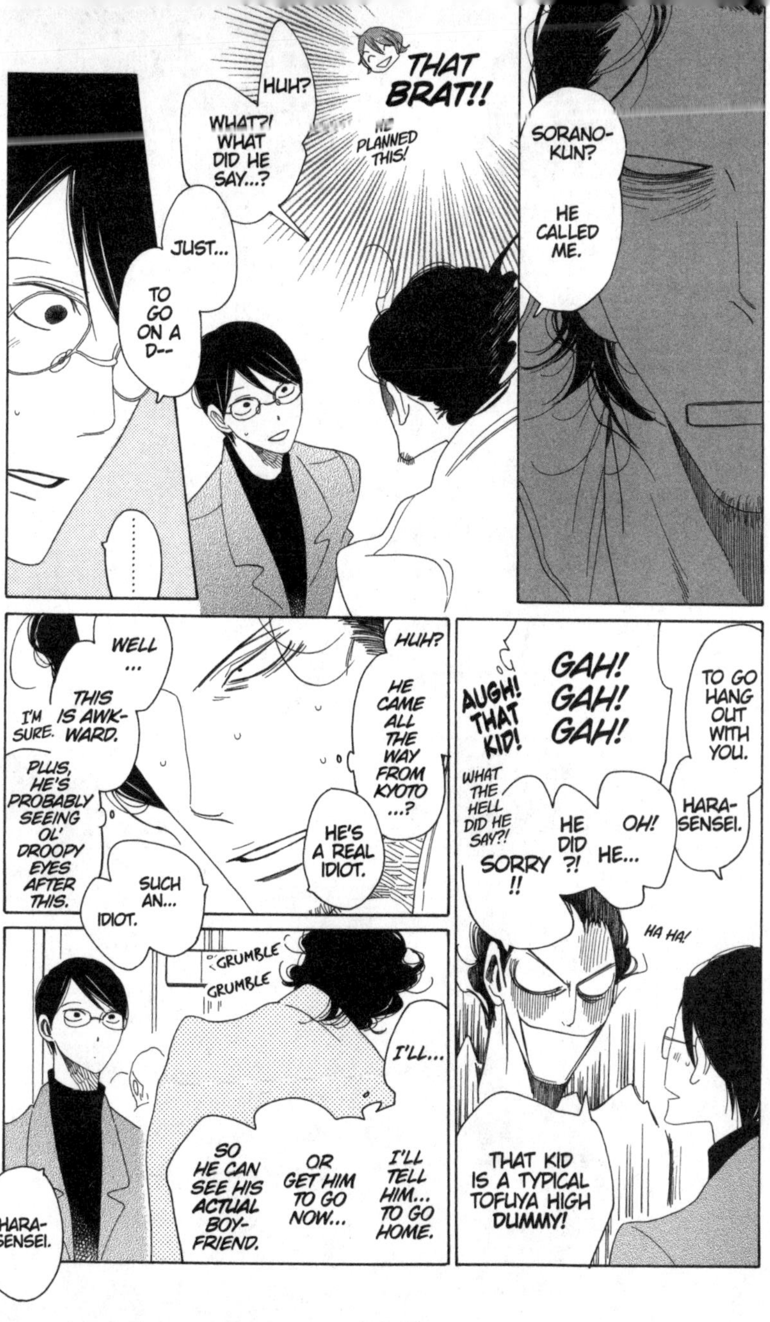
SORANO-KUN?
HE CALLED ME.
THAT BRAT!!
HE PLANNED THIS!
HUH?
WHAT?! WHAT DID HE SAY...?
JUST...
TO GO ON A D--
......
TO GO HANG OUT WITH YOU.
HARA-SENSEI.
OH! HE...
HE DID?!
SORRY!!
GAH! GAH! GAH!
AUGH! THAT KID!
WHAT THE HELL DID HE SAY?!
HUH?
HE CAME ALL THE WAY FROM KYOTO...?
HE'S A REAL IDIOT.
WELL... THIS IS AWKWARD.
I'M SURE.
PLUS, HE'S PROBABLY SEEING OL' DROOPY EYES AFTER THIS.
SUCH AN... IDIOT.
HA HA!
THAT KID IS A TYPICAL TOFUYA HIGH DUMMY!
I'LL...
I'LL TELL HIM... TO GO HOME.
OR GET HIM TO GO NOW...
SO HE CAN SEE HIS ACTUAL BOY-FRIEND.
GRUMBLE
GRUMBLE
HARA-SENSEI.

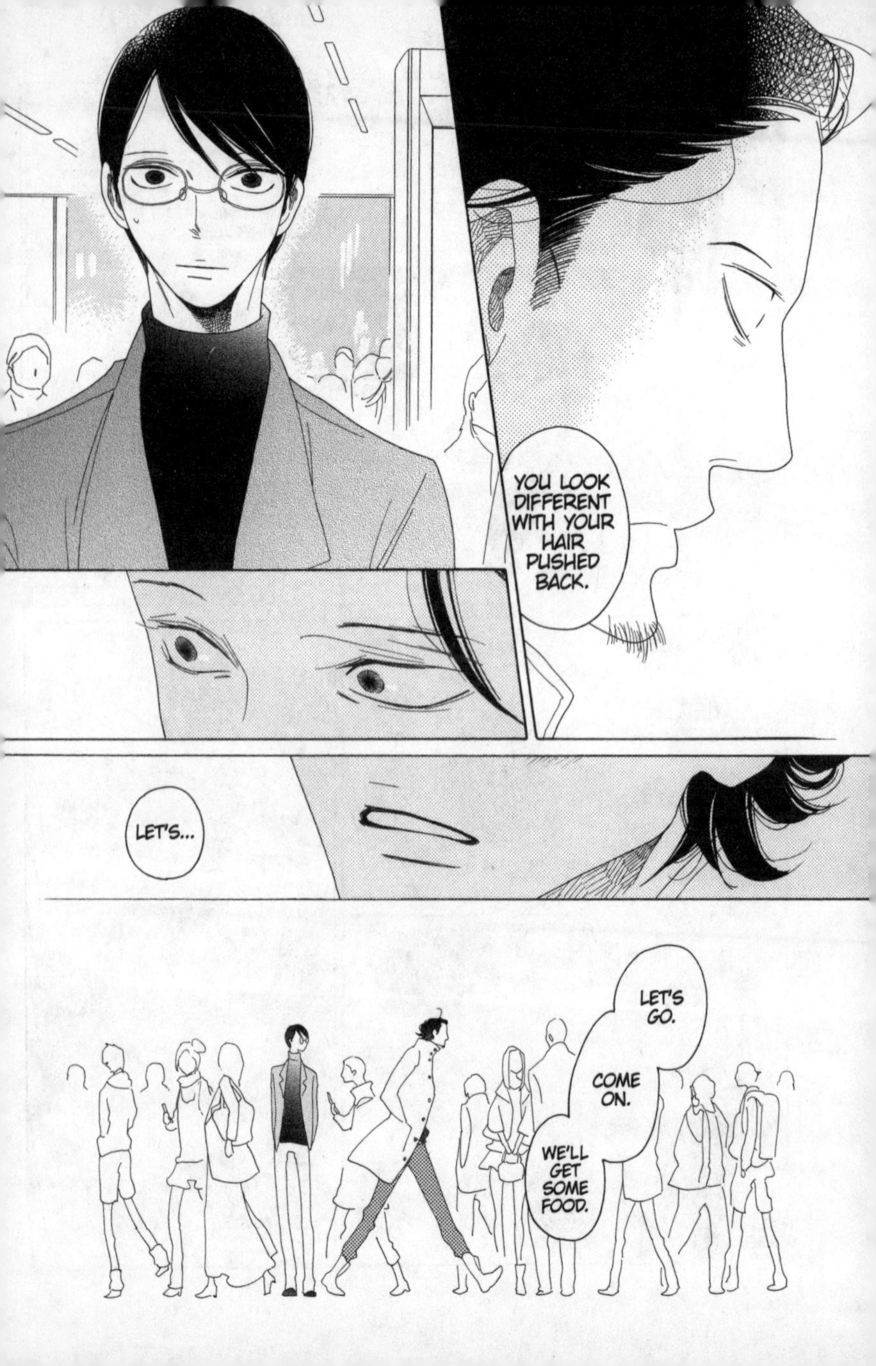
YOU LOOK DIFFERENT WITH YOUR HAIR PUSHED BACK.
LET'S...
LET'S GO.
COME ON.
WE'LL GET SOME FOOD.

GAH, WHAT AM I DOING?!
RATIONAL SELF.
OH!
THEY'RE FINALLY MOVING.
TOOK LONG ENOUGH.
WONDER WHAT THEY SAID.
TAK
WITH YOUR HAMINE CARD
10% OFF
COME ON OUT!
MONDAY
TAK TAK
YOU'RE NOT BUSY?

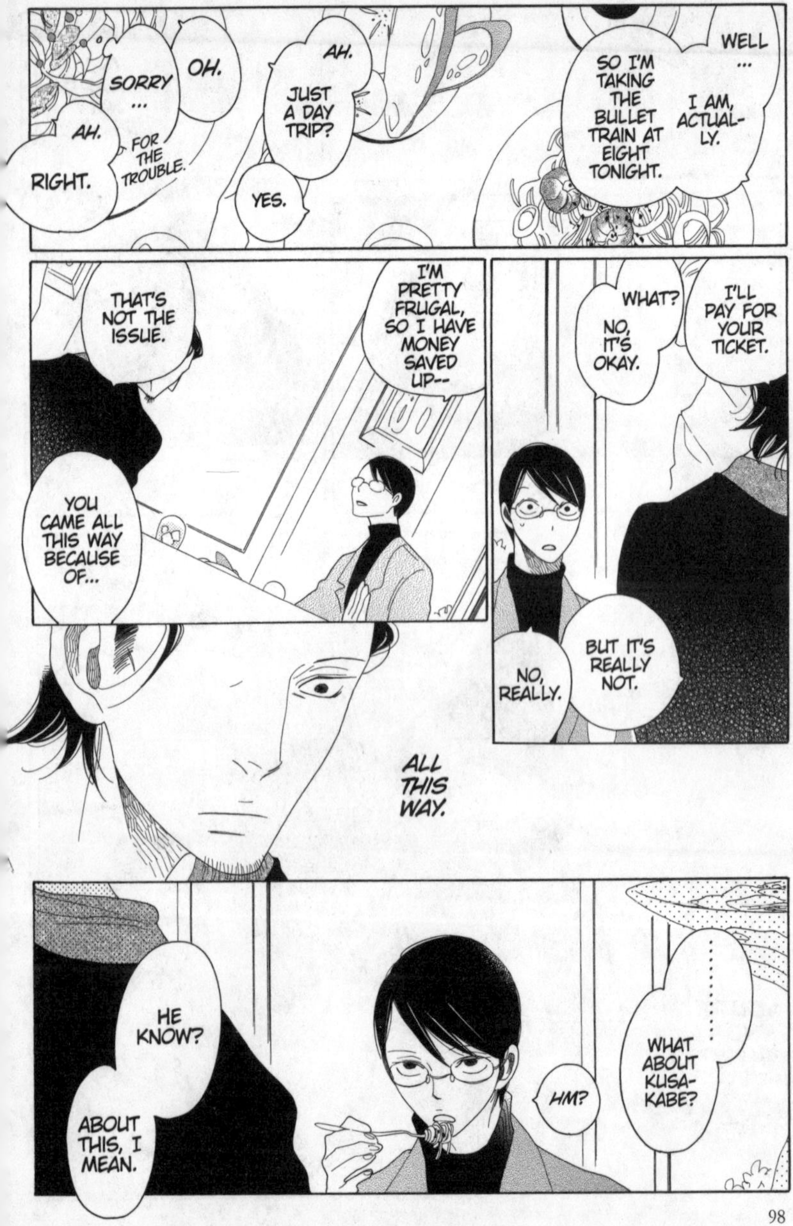
WELL ... I AM, ACTUAL-LY.
SO I'M TAKING THE BULLET TRAIN AT EIGHT TONIGHT.
AH. JUST A DAY TRIP?
YES.
OH.
SORRY ... FOR THE TROUBLE.
AH. RIGHT.
I'LL PAY FOR YOUR TICKET.
WHAT? NO, IT'S OKAY.
BUT IT'S REALLY NOT.
NO, REALLY.
I'M PRETTY FRUGAL, SO I HAVE MONEY SAVED UP--
THAT'S NOT THE ISSUE.
YOU CAME ALL THIS WAY BECAUSE OF...
ALL THIS WAY.
......
WHAT ABOUT KUSA-KABE?
HM?
HE KNOW?
ABOUT THIS, I MEAN.

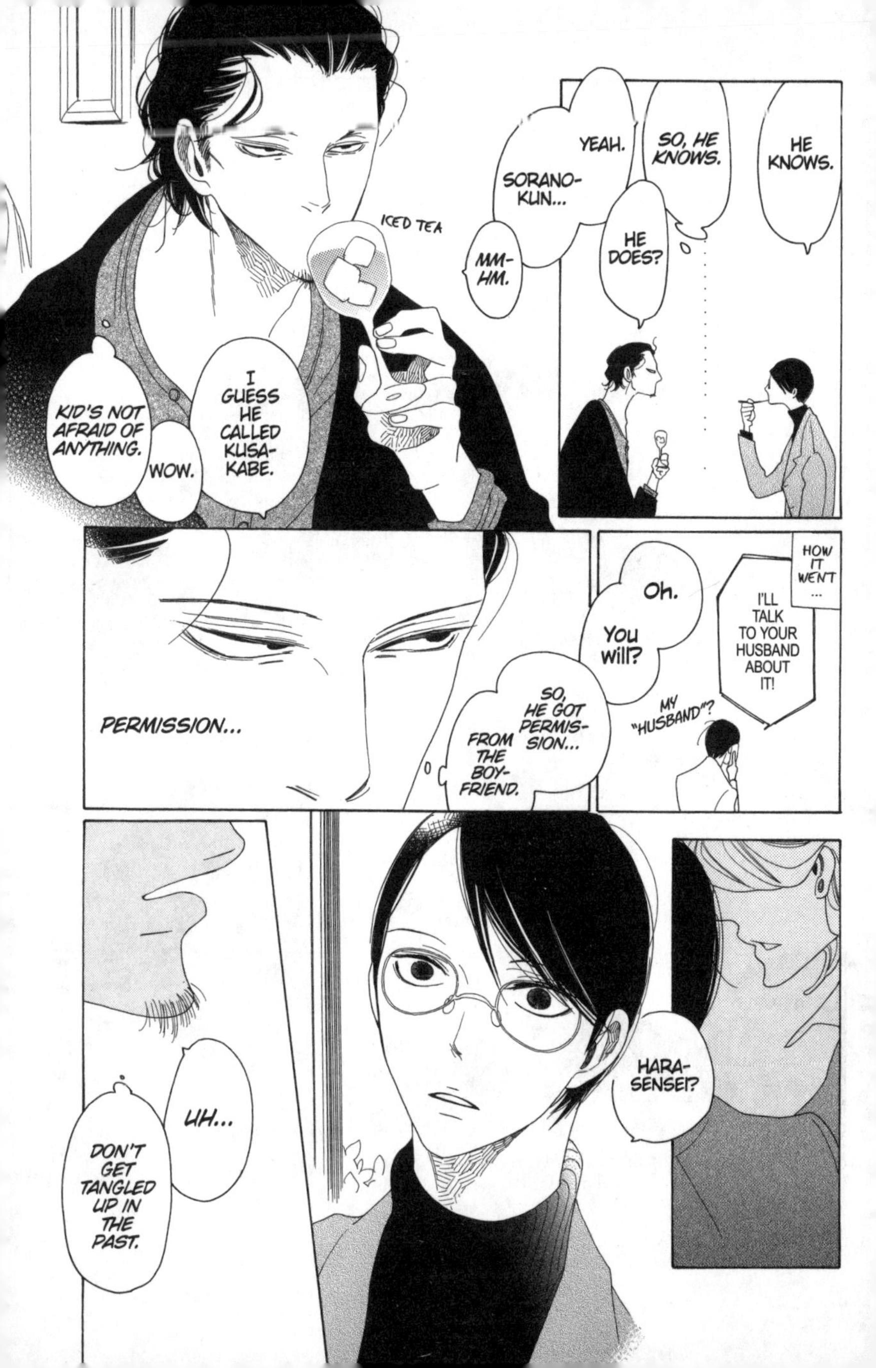
HE KNOWS.
SO, HE KNOWS.
YEAH.
SORANO-KUN...
HE DOES?
MM-HM.
ICED TEA
I GUESS HE CALLED KUSA-KABE.
WOW.
KID'S NOT AFRAID OF ANYTHING.
HOW IT WENT ...
I'LL TALK TO YOUR HUSBAND ABOUT IT!
Oh.
You will?
MY "HUSBAND"?
SO, HE GOT PERMISSION... FROM THE BOY-FRIEND.
PERMISSION...
HARA-SENSEI?
UH...
DON'T GET TANGLED UP IN THE PAST.

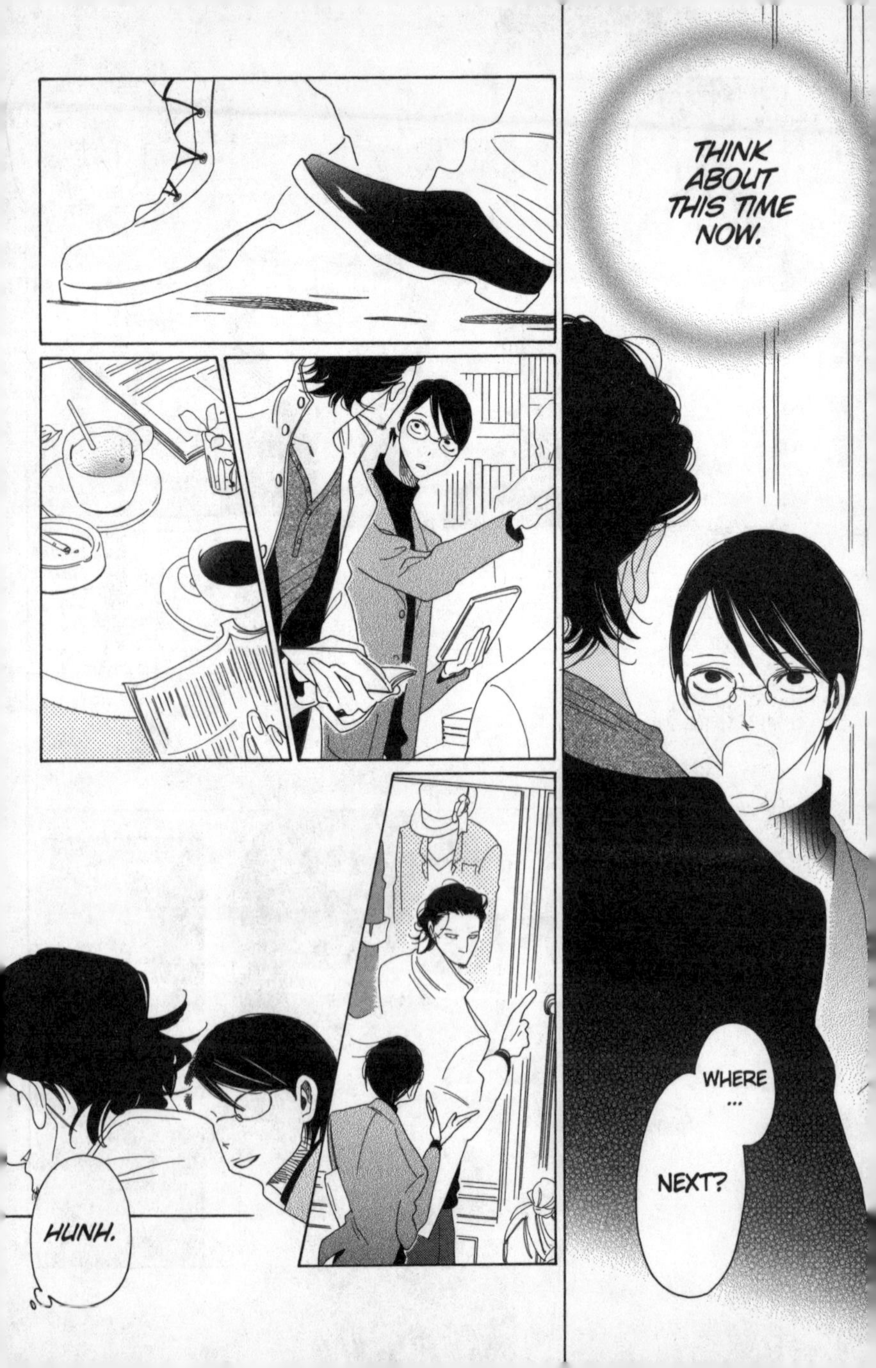
THINK ABOUT THIS TIME NOW.
WHERE ... NEXT?
HUNH.

LOOKS LIKE THEY'RE HAVING A GOOD TIME.
HOW POINT-LESS!
...?
WAIT. WHAT'S POINT-LESS?
GRAB
CRNCH CRNCH CRNCH
...
?
GRAB

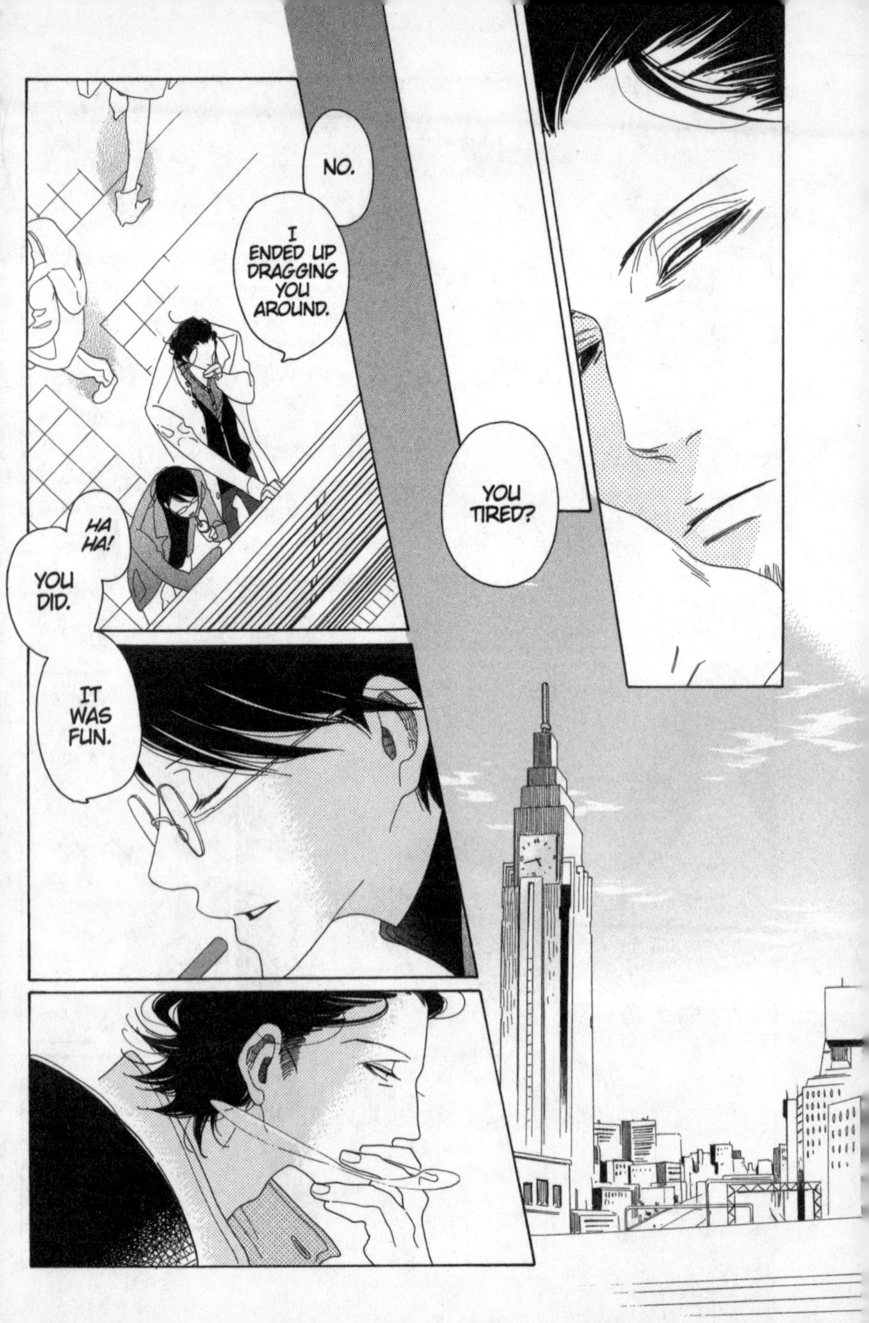
YOU TIRED?
NO.
I ENDED UP DRAGGING YOU AROUND.
HA HA!
YOU DID.
IT WAS FUN.

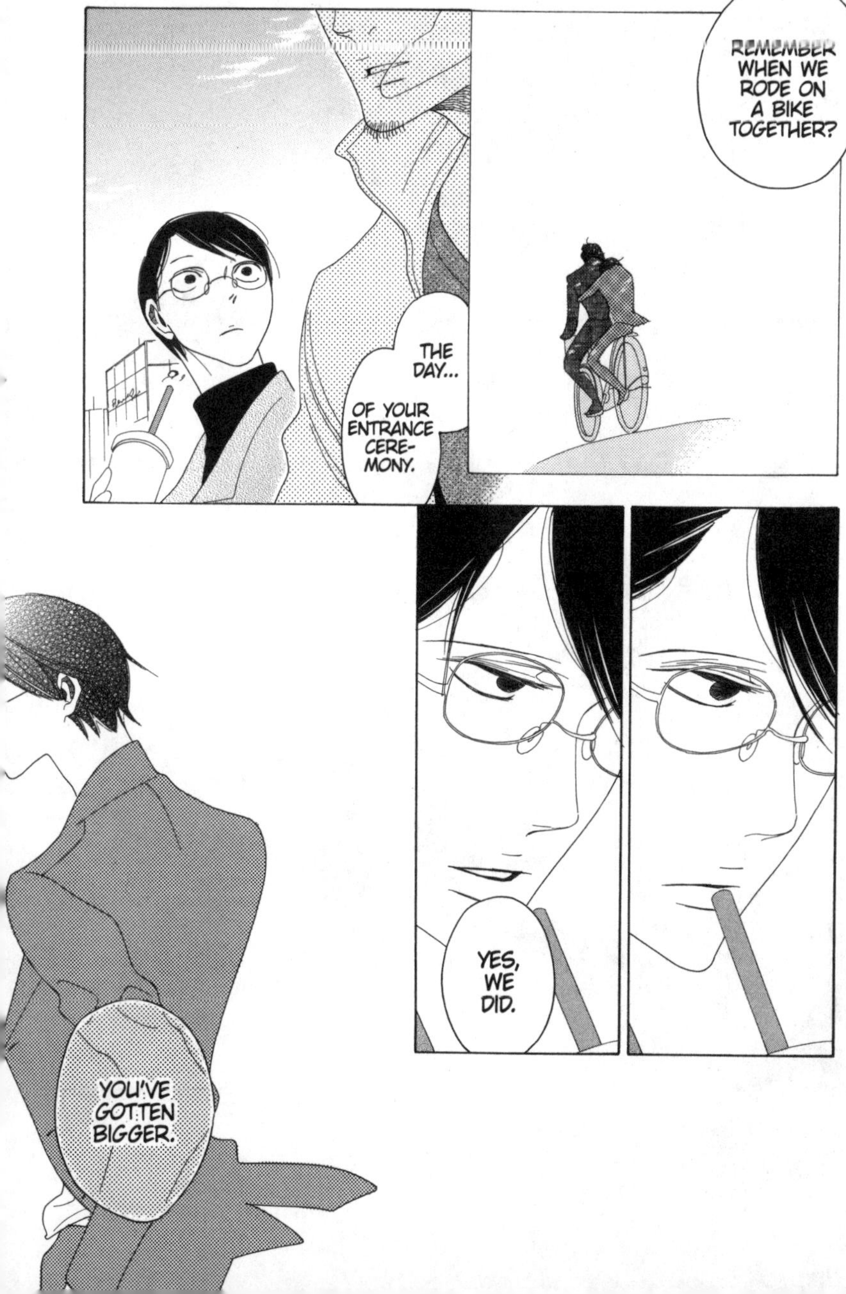
REMEMBER WHEN WE RODE ON A BIKE TOGETHER?
THE DAY...
OF YOUR ENTRANCE CEREMONY.
YES, WE DID.
YOU'VE GOTTEN BIGGER.

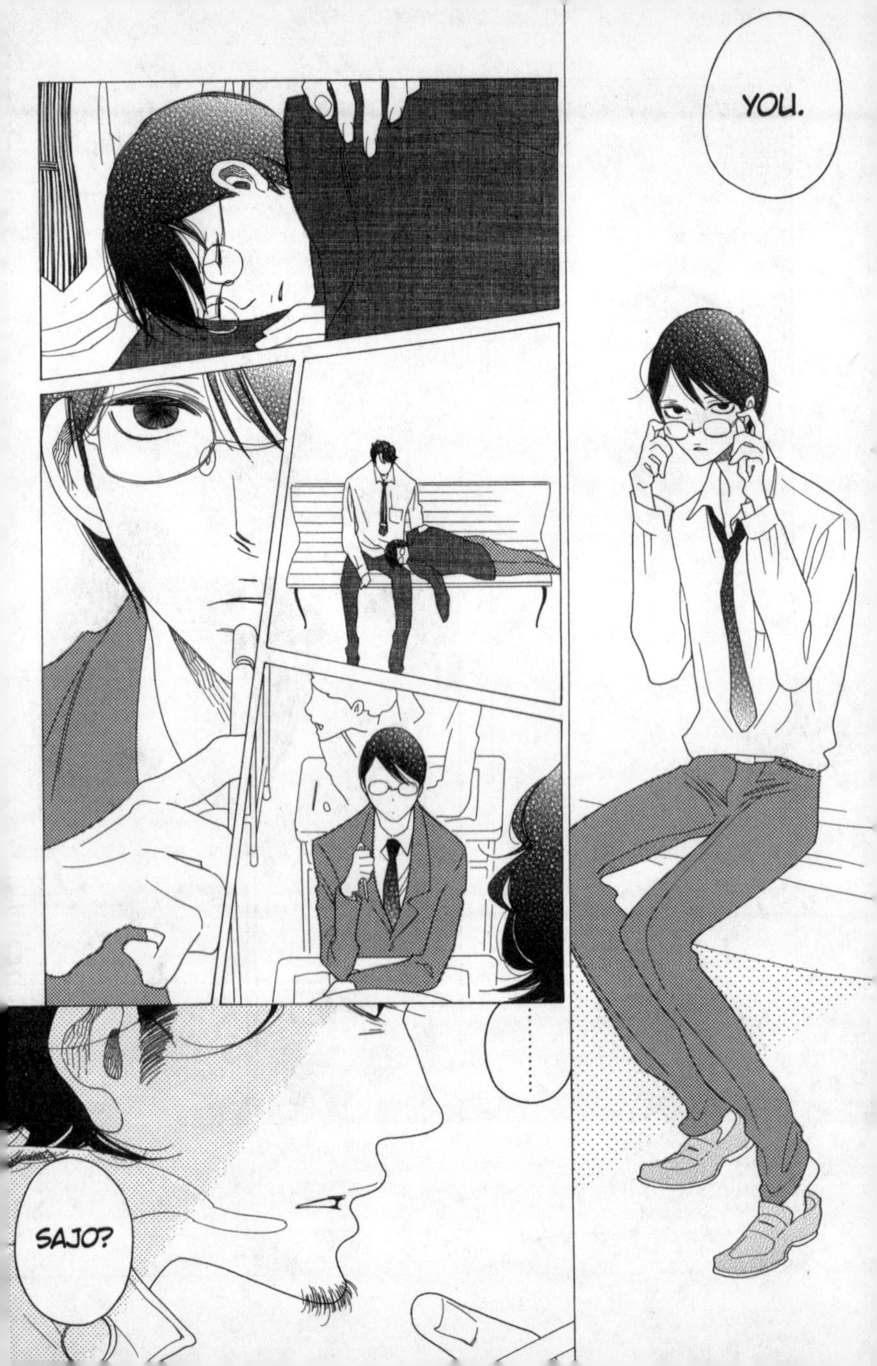
YOU.
……
SAJO?

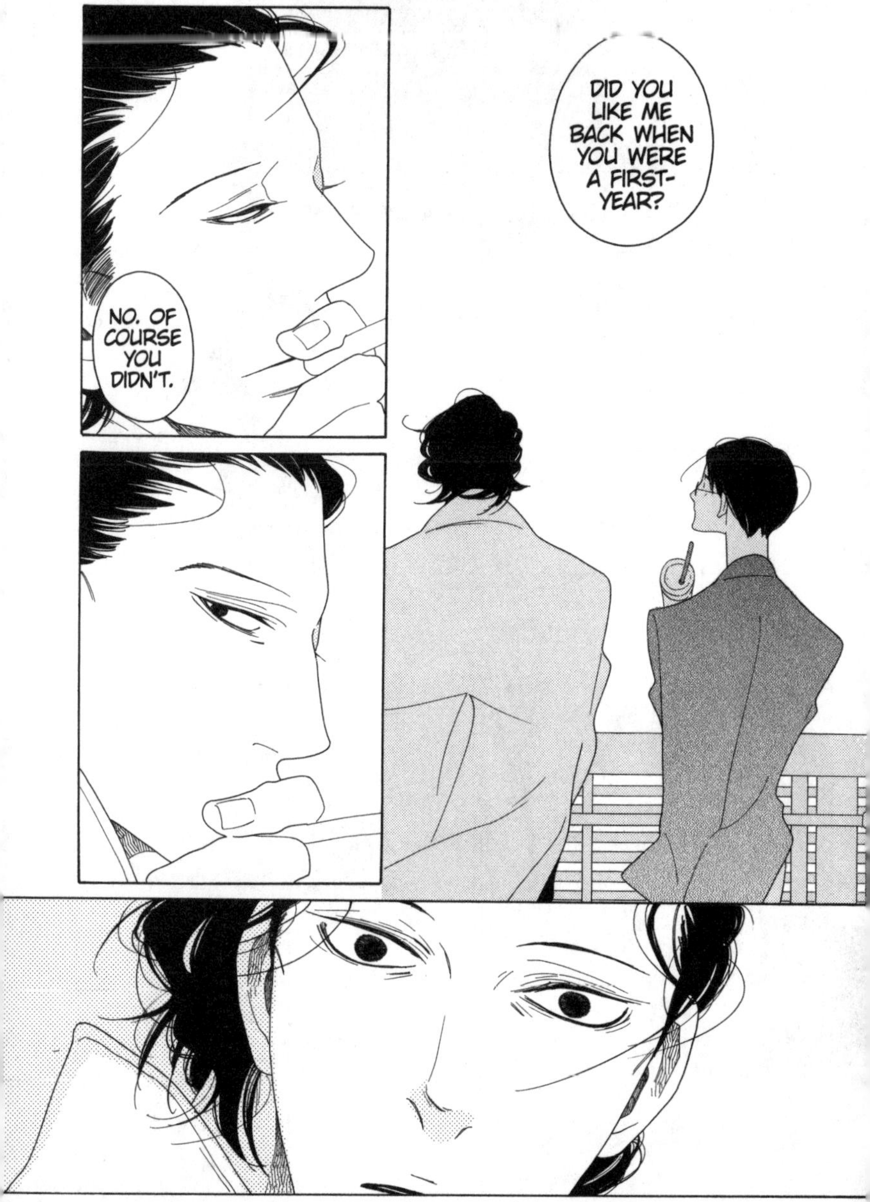
DID YOU LIKE ME BACK WHEN YOU WERE A FIRST-YEAR?
NO. OF COURSE YOU DIDN'T.

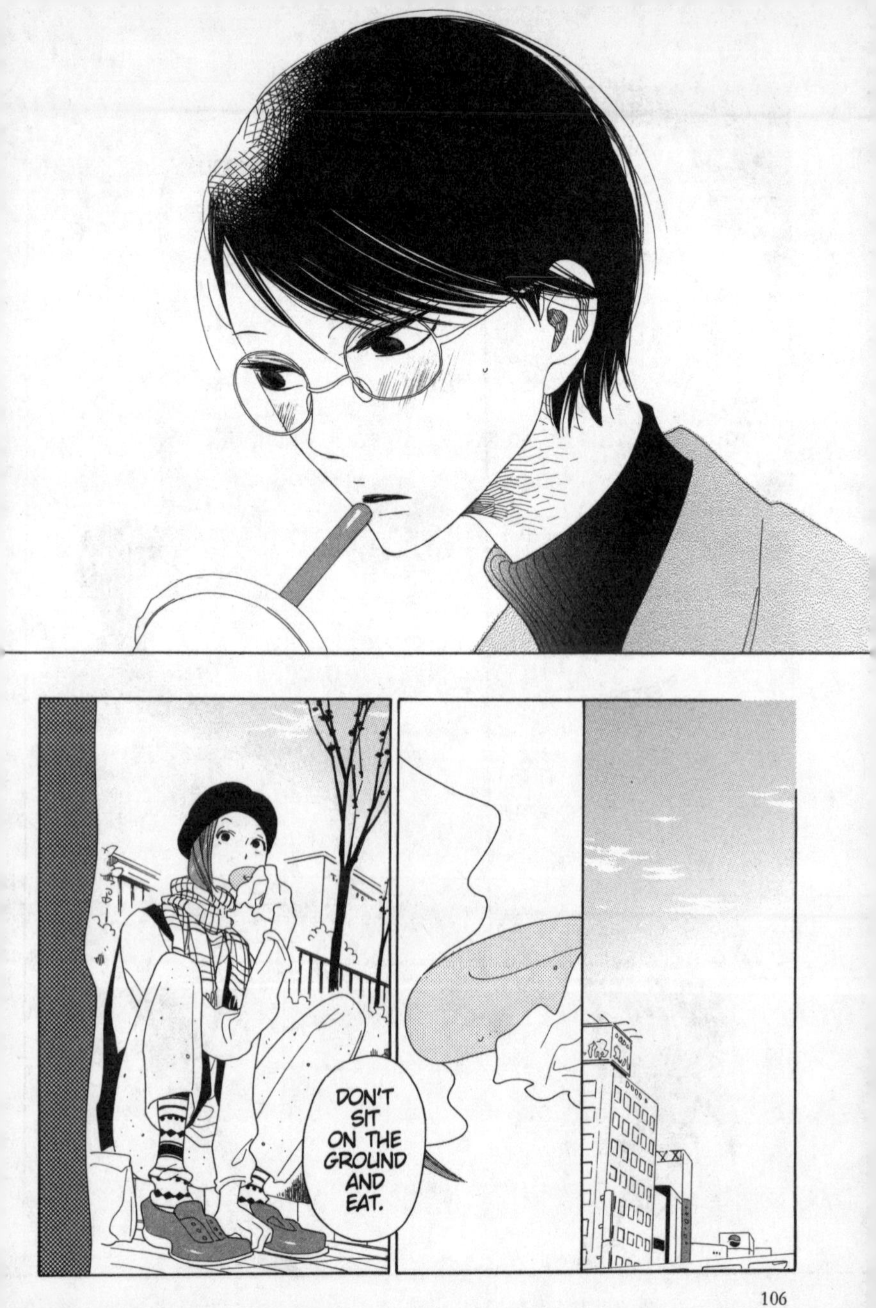
DON'T SIT ON THE GROUND AND EAT.

AH!
SO, YOU ARE HERE, AFTER ALL.
I SENSED YOU.
HUH?
WHERE'S SAJO-SAN?
HE LEFT.
WHAT?! SERIOUS-LY?!
BUT THE NIGHT'S JUST BEGIN-NING!
OH! DID YOU WANT ONE?
WHAT ABOUT DRINKS?!
GETTING TIPSY?!
NO THANKS...
OH!
WHAT ABOUT A KISS?
DON'T BE STUPID. HE'S UNDER-AGE.
YOU AT LEAST KISSED HIM...
RIGHT?!
OF COURSE NOT, IDIOT.
SHUT UP WITH THE "KISS KISS."
OH, COME OOOOON!
I WENT AND SET THIS UP FOR NOTHING.
PAT
PAT
SORANO.
YEAH?

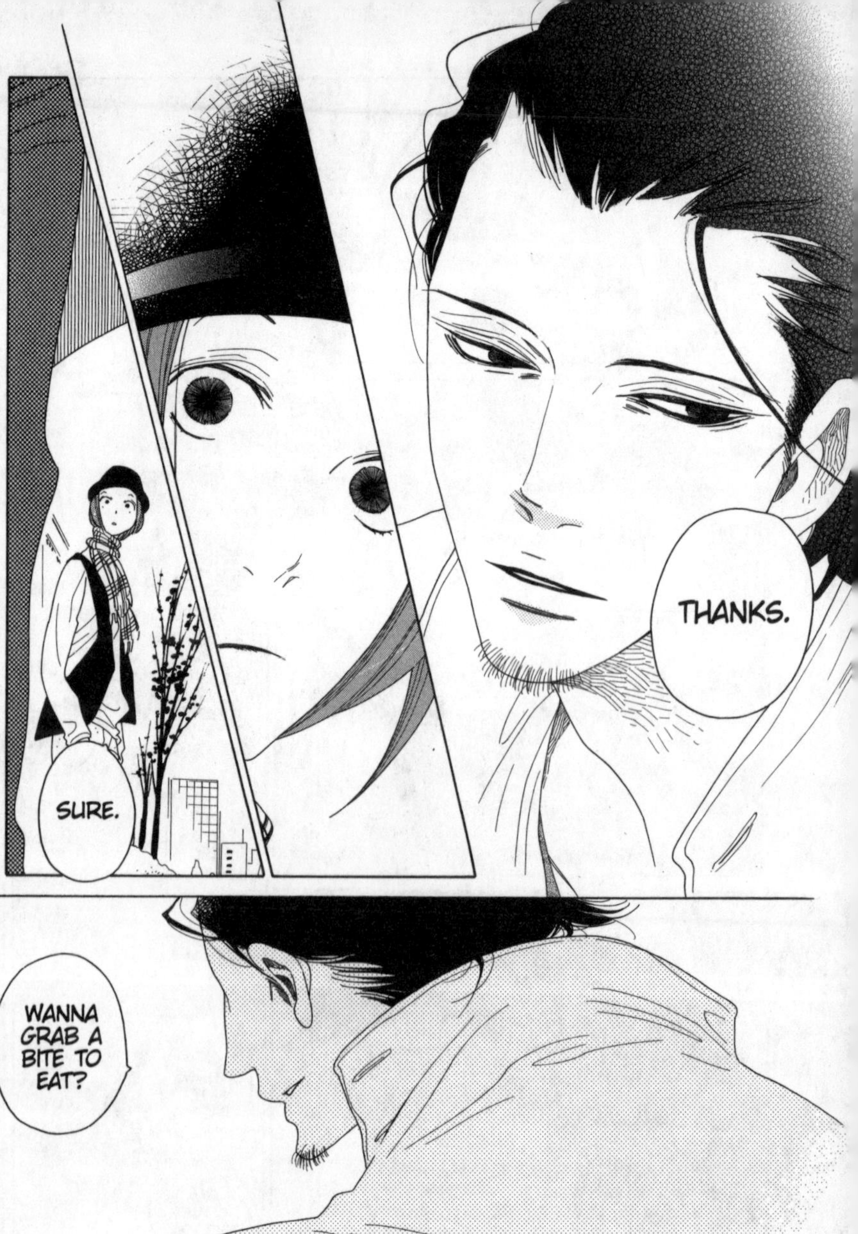
THANKS.
SURE.
WANNA GRAB A BITE TO EAT?

OHH, BUT...
YOU WERE JUST CHOWING DOWN ON THOSE DOUGH-NUTS.
TAK
WHAT DID...
YOU...
TAK
TA-TAK

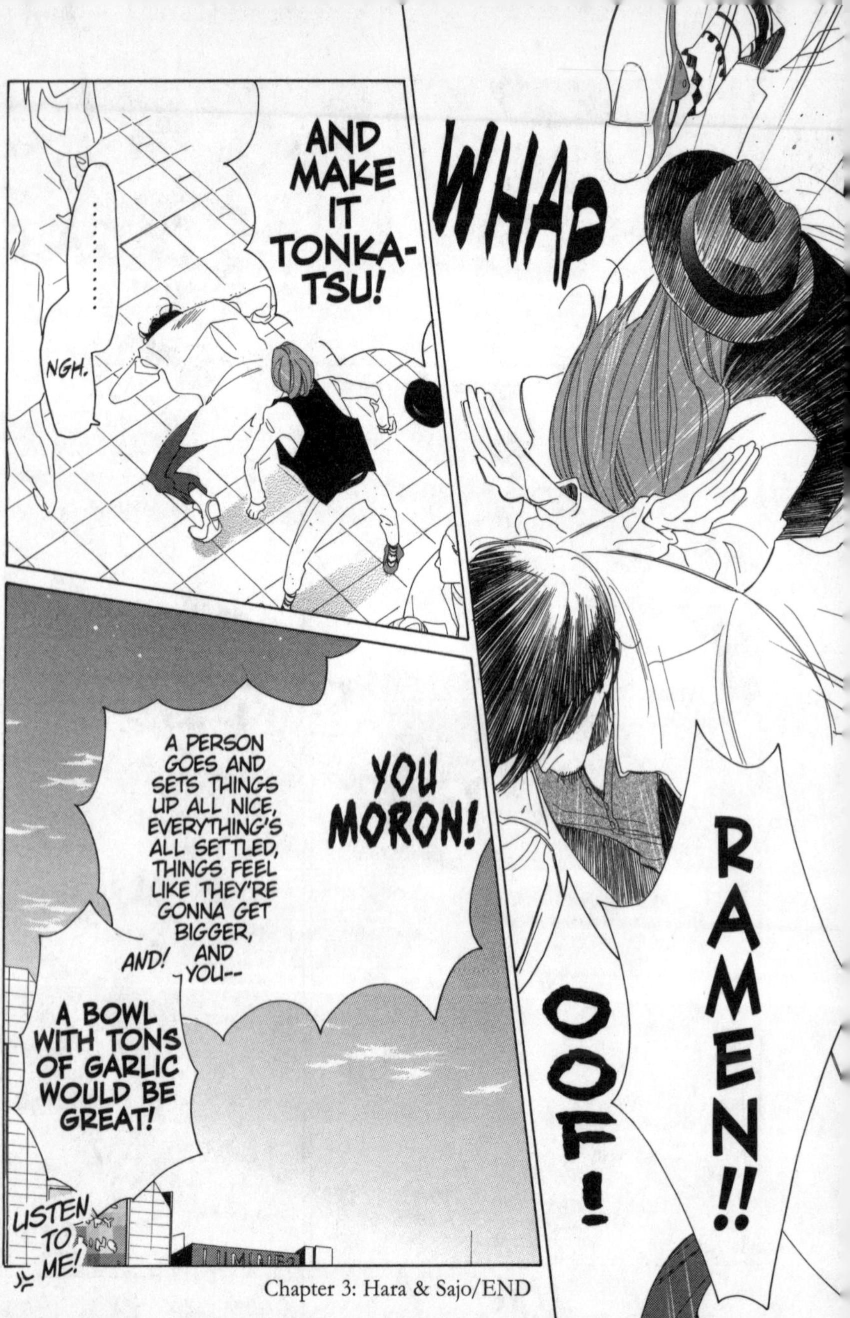
WHAP
RAMEN!!
OOF!
AND MAKE IT TONKA-TSU!
......
NGH.
YOU MORON!
A PERSON GOES AND SETS THINGS UP ALL NICE, EVERYTHING'S ALL SETTLED, THINGS FEEL LIKE THEY'RE GONNA GET BIGGER, AND YOU--
AND!
A BOWL WITH TONS OF GARLIC WOULD BE GREAT!
LISTEN TO ME!

Chapter 3: Hara & Sajo/END

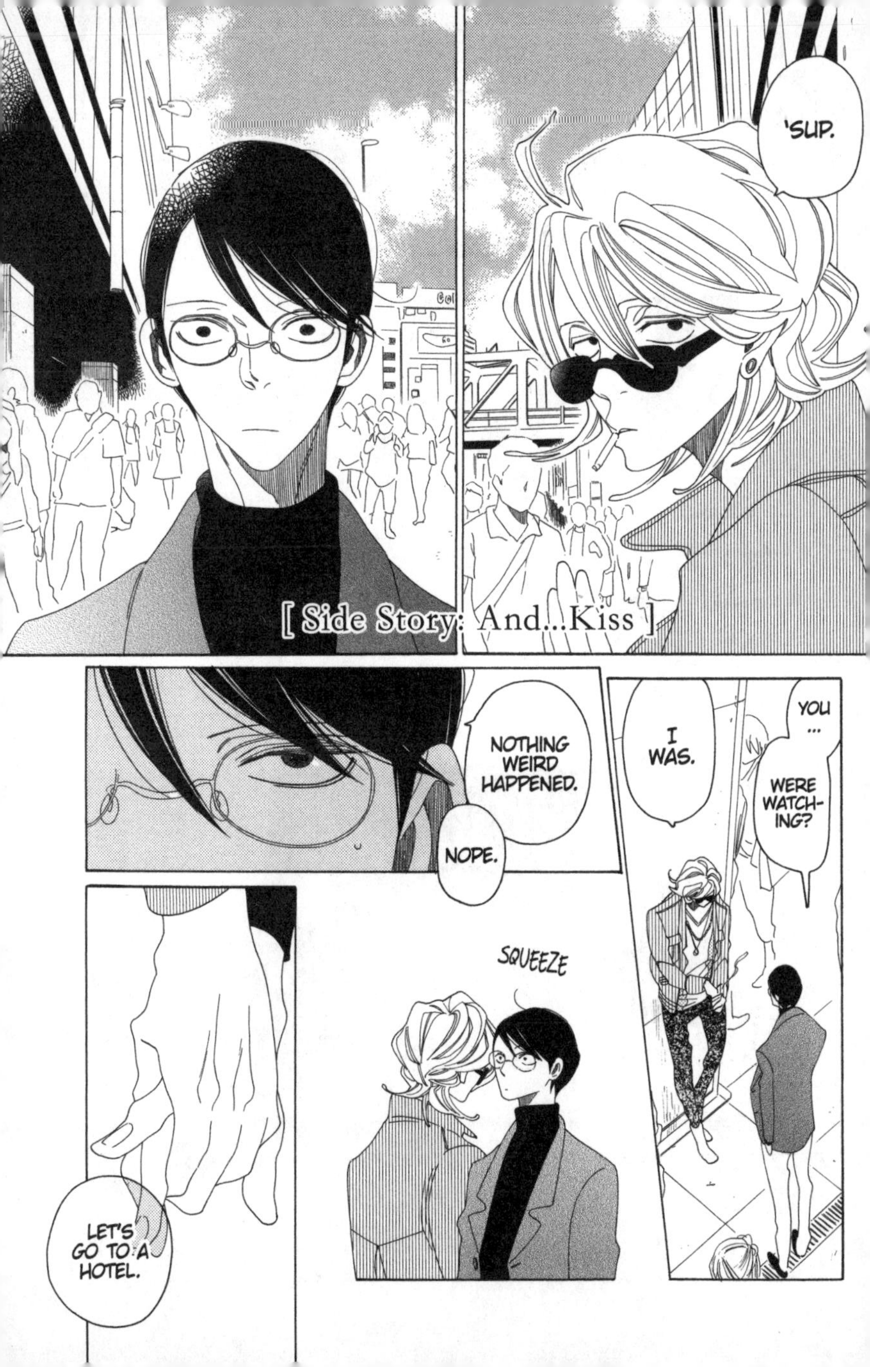
'SUP.
[Side Story: And...Kiss]
YOU ... WERE WATCHING?
I WAS.
NOTHING WEIRD HAPPENED.
NOPE.
SQUEEZE
LET'S GO TO A HOTEL.

SMOKING OR NON?
IT'S A REGULAR HOTEL?
SMOKING.
OH!
REGULAR'S FINE.
IT'S NOT LIKE I WAS THINKING ABOUT ... "THAT."
AND I WASN'T PLANNING TO SPEND THE NIGHT ANYWAY.
SMOKING OKAY?
HUH?
THE ROOM.
YEAH. FINE.
SO... LIKE.
↑ 32
PING
ZSH
ZSH
ZSH
ZSH
IS KUSAKABE... ACTUALLY...
MAD...?
KSHK
KACHAK

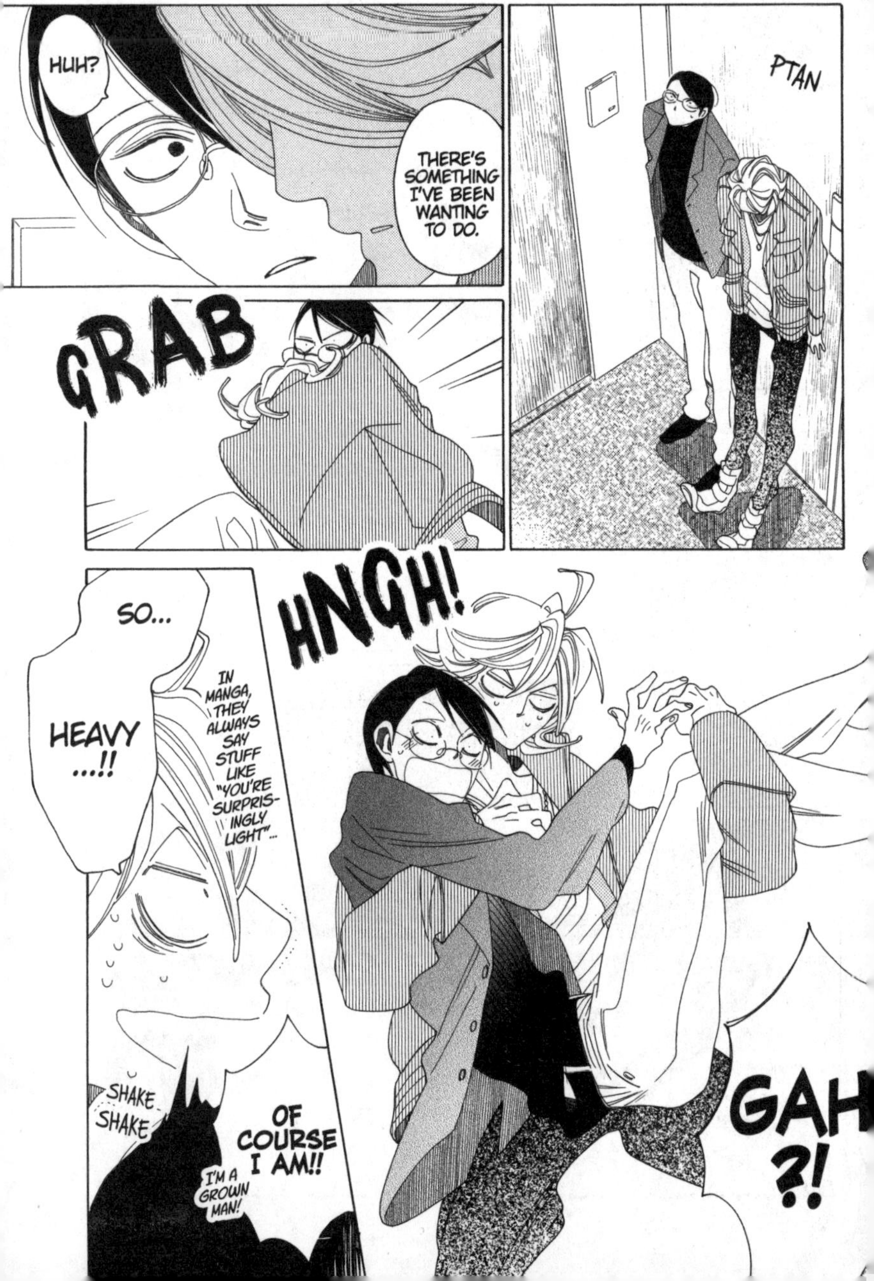
PTAN
HUH?
THERE'S SOMETHING I'VE BEEN WANTING TO DO.
GRAB
HNGH!
GAH ?!
SO... HEAVY ...!!
IN MANGA, THEY ALWAYS SAY STUFF LIKE "YOU'RE SURPRIS-INGLY LIGHT"...
OF COURSE I AM!!
I'M A GROWN MAN!
SHAKE SHAKE

P-PUT ME DOWN!!
RIGHT NOW!!
THIS IS EMBARRASSING!
SWAY
SWAY
HEY!
D-DON'T WIGGLE!
THIS IS HARD AS IT IS!
WHUMP
WHEW!
......
AAAAAAAAAAAAH.
I WAS, LIKE, SUPER FREAKED THERE.
ABOUT WHAT ...?
OH.
......

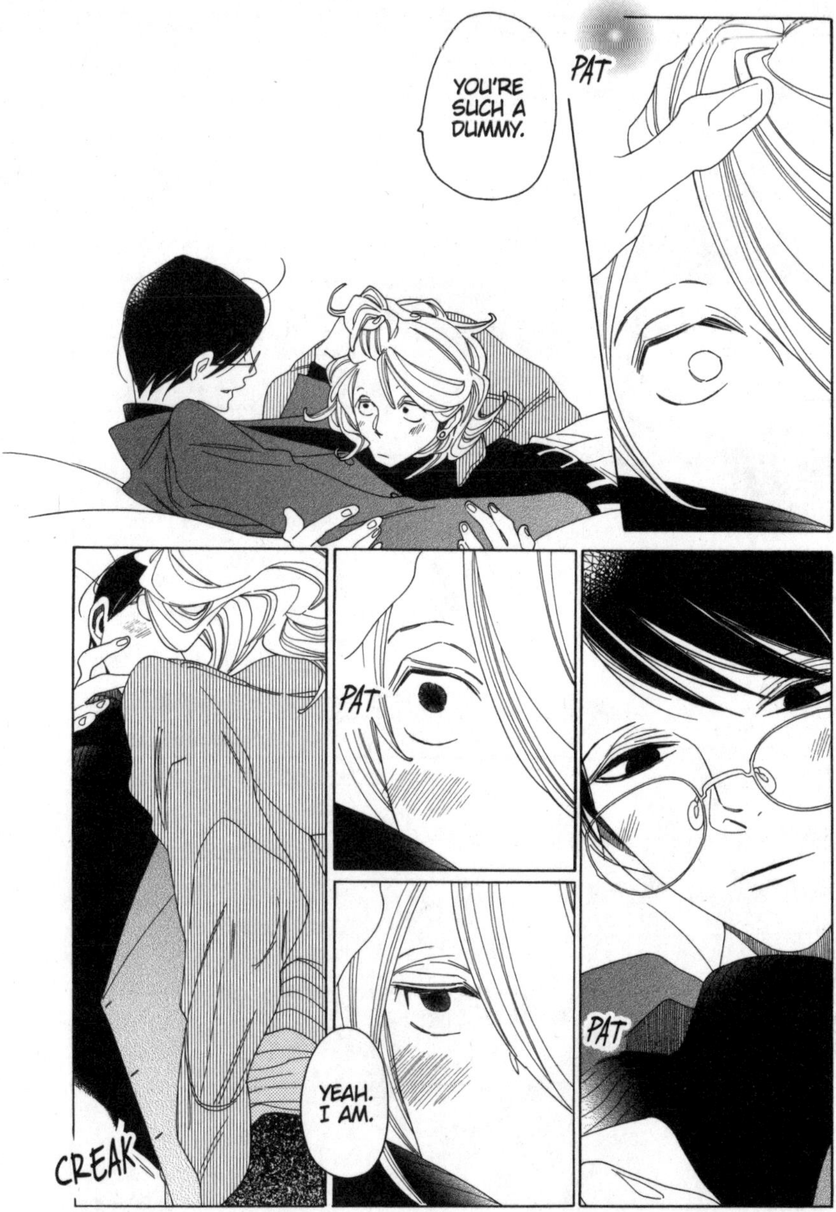
PAT
YOU'RE SUCH A DUMMY.
PAT
PAT
YEAH. I AM.
CREAK

I...
FREEZE
I CAN'T!
SO, LIKE, TODAY ...
HM?
I WON'T BE ABLE TO HOLD BACK.
I KNOW THAT.
YOU'RE GOING HOME, YEAH?
I AM.
WHAT TIME'S YOUR TRAIN?
EIGHT.
HUNH.
EIGHT, EH?
SO, IN TWO HOURS?
AND IT TAKES TIME TO GET TO TOKYO STATION, TOO.
AH.
DAM-MIT.
WHY...?
THE TIME HE WAS WITH THAT GEEZER COULD HAVE BEEN TIME SPENT WITH ME!
......

WHAT ARE YOU THINKING ABOUT?
HUH?
WHAT ARE YOU THINKING ABOUT RIGHT NOW?
OH, UH!
TELL ME.
NAH...
IF I TOLD YOU...
I'D JUST MAKE THINGS WEIRD.
JUST TELL ME.

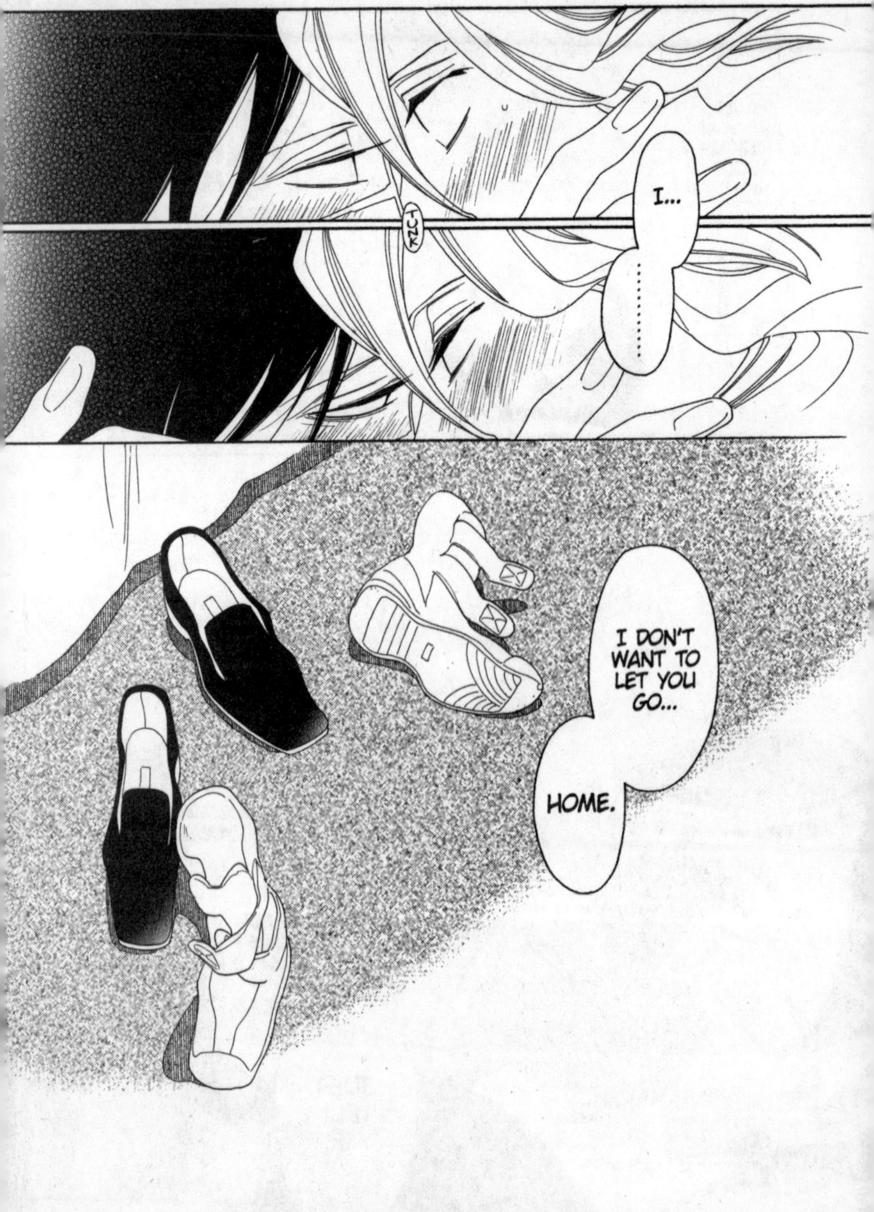

I...
TUNK
......
I DON'T WANT TO LET YOU GO...
HOME.

Side Story: And...Kiss/END

Chapter 4: Sorano & Fujino

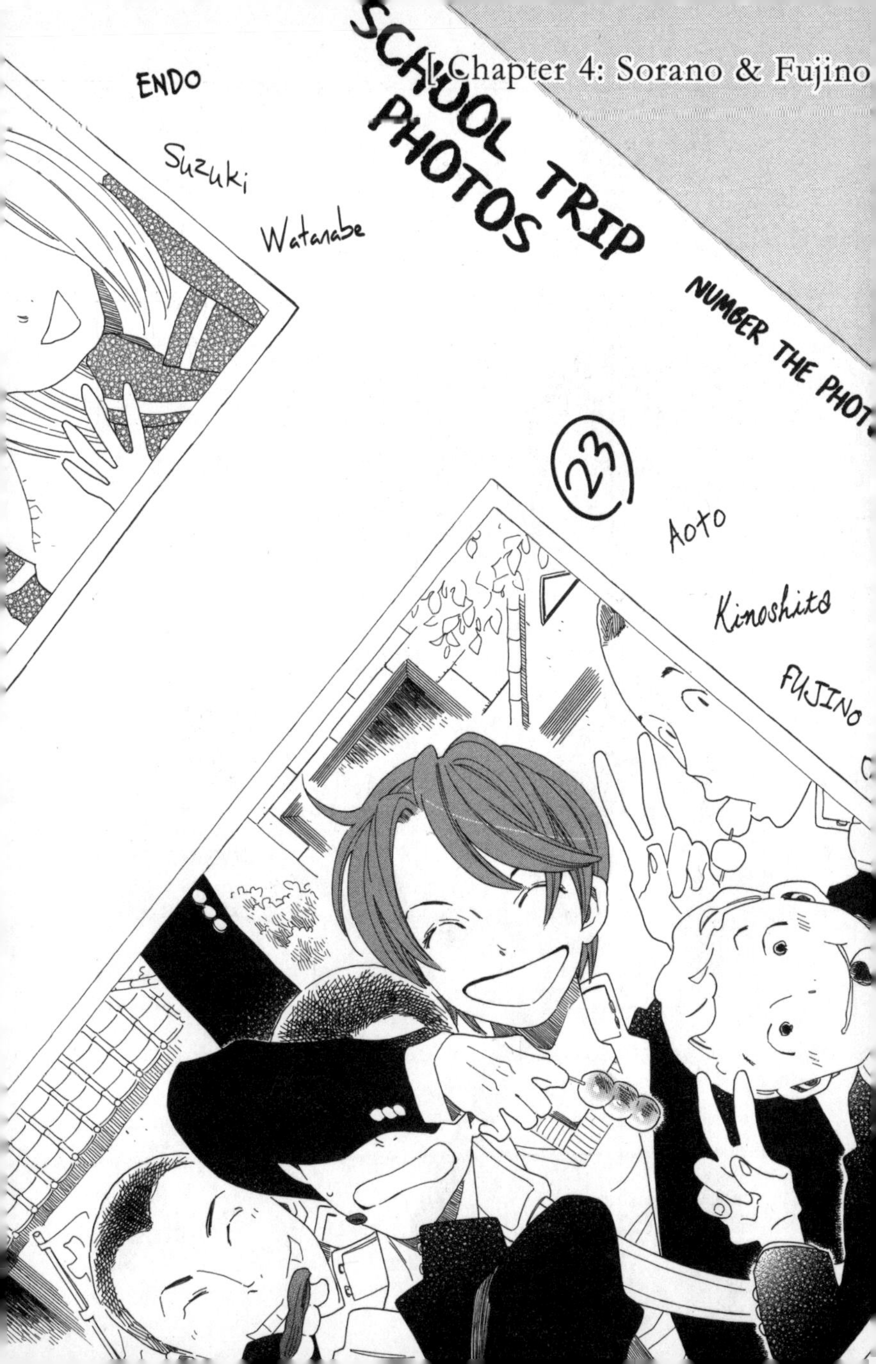
SCHOOL TRIP PHOTOS
ENDO
Suzuki
Watanabe
NUMBER THE PHOT
23
Aoto
Kinoshita
FUJINO

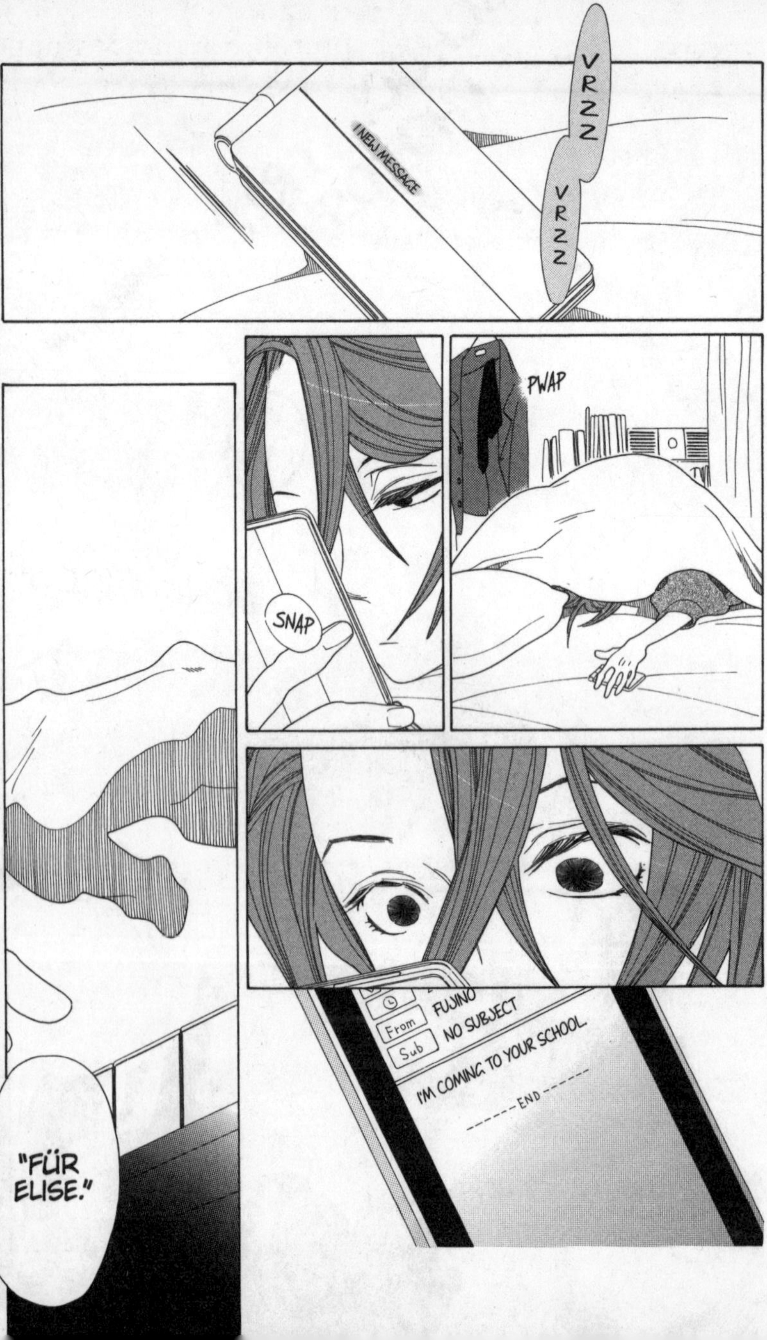
VRZZ
VRZZ
1 NEW MESSAGE
PWAP
SNAP
From FUJINO
Sub NO SUBJECT
I'M COMING TO YOUR SCHOOL.
END
"FÜR ELISE."

WELL
THIS PIANO PIECE IS SO FAMOUS, BASICALLY EVERYONE KNOWS IT.
UNABLE TO BE TOGETHER BECAUSE OF THEIR DIFFERENT SOCIAL STAND-INGS...
BEETHOVEN WROTE HER THIS SONG, TO AT LEAST GIVE HER SOMETHING.
SO...
BUT IN FACT, THE SONG WAS NOT DEDICATED TO ELISE ...
BUT A NOBLE-WOMAN NAMED THERESE.
BUT...
WHY DID "THERESE" BECOME "ELISE"?
IT'S STILL A MYSTERY.
SOME SAY THAT BEETHOVEN'S HANDWRITING WAS SO BAD, IT WAS MISREAD.
OR...
TO AVOID A SCANDAL FOR THE WOMAN HE ONCE LOVED, HE CHANGED THE NAME.
THIS...
IS ONE OF MANY POSSIBLE EXPLANA-TIONS.
DOES HARASEN SEEM HAPPIER LATELY?

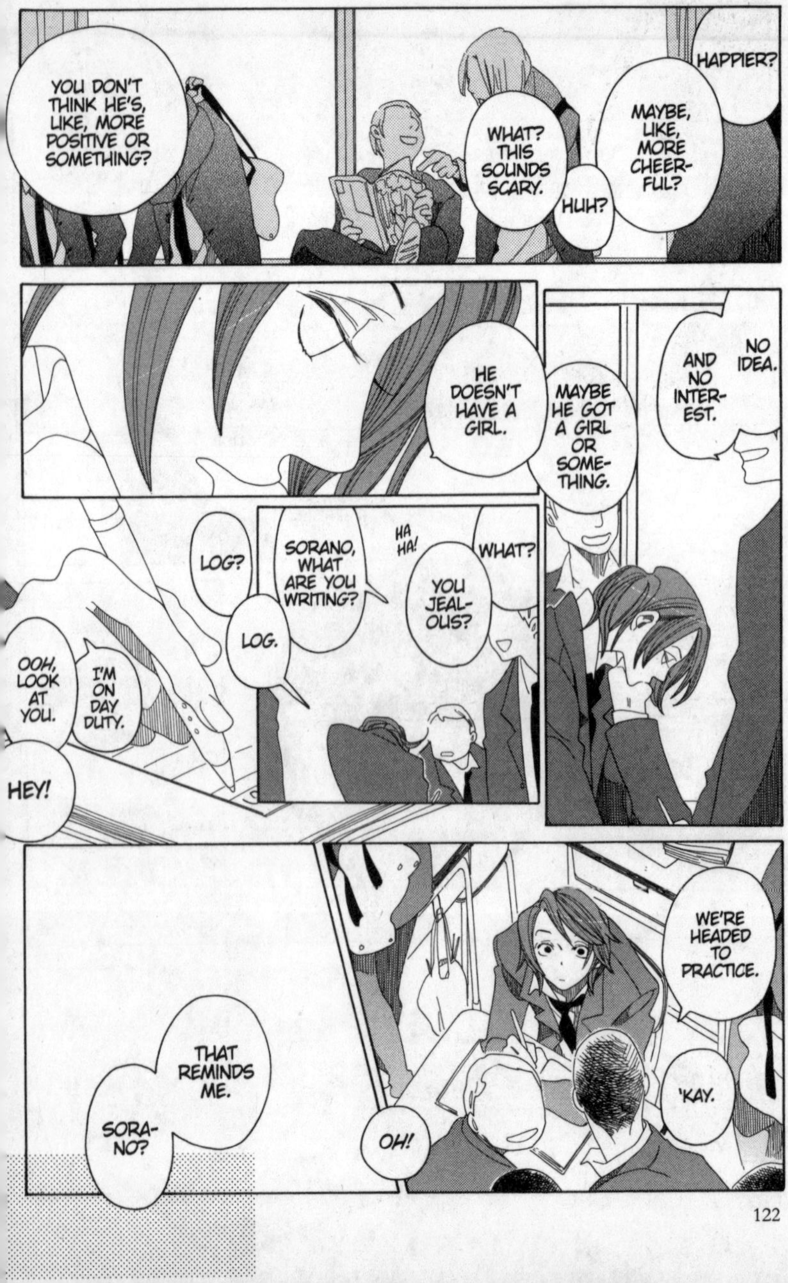
HAPPIER?
MAYBE, LIKE, MORE CHEER-FUL?
HUH?
WHAT? THIS SOUNDS SCARY.
YOU DON'T THINK HE'S, LIKE, MORE POSITIVE OR SOMETHING?
NO IDEA.
AND NO INTER-EST.
MAYBE HE GOT A GIRL OR SOME-THING.
HE DOESN'T HAVE A GIRL.
WHAT?
YOU JEAL-OUS?
HA HA!
SORANO, WHAT ARE YOU WRITING?
LOG?
LOG.
I'M ON DAY DUTY.
OOH, LOOK AT YOU.
HEY!
WE'RE HEADED TO PRACTICE.
'KAY.
OH!
THAT REMINDS ME.
SORA-NO?

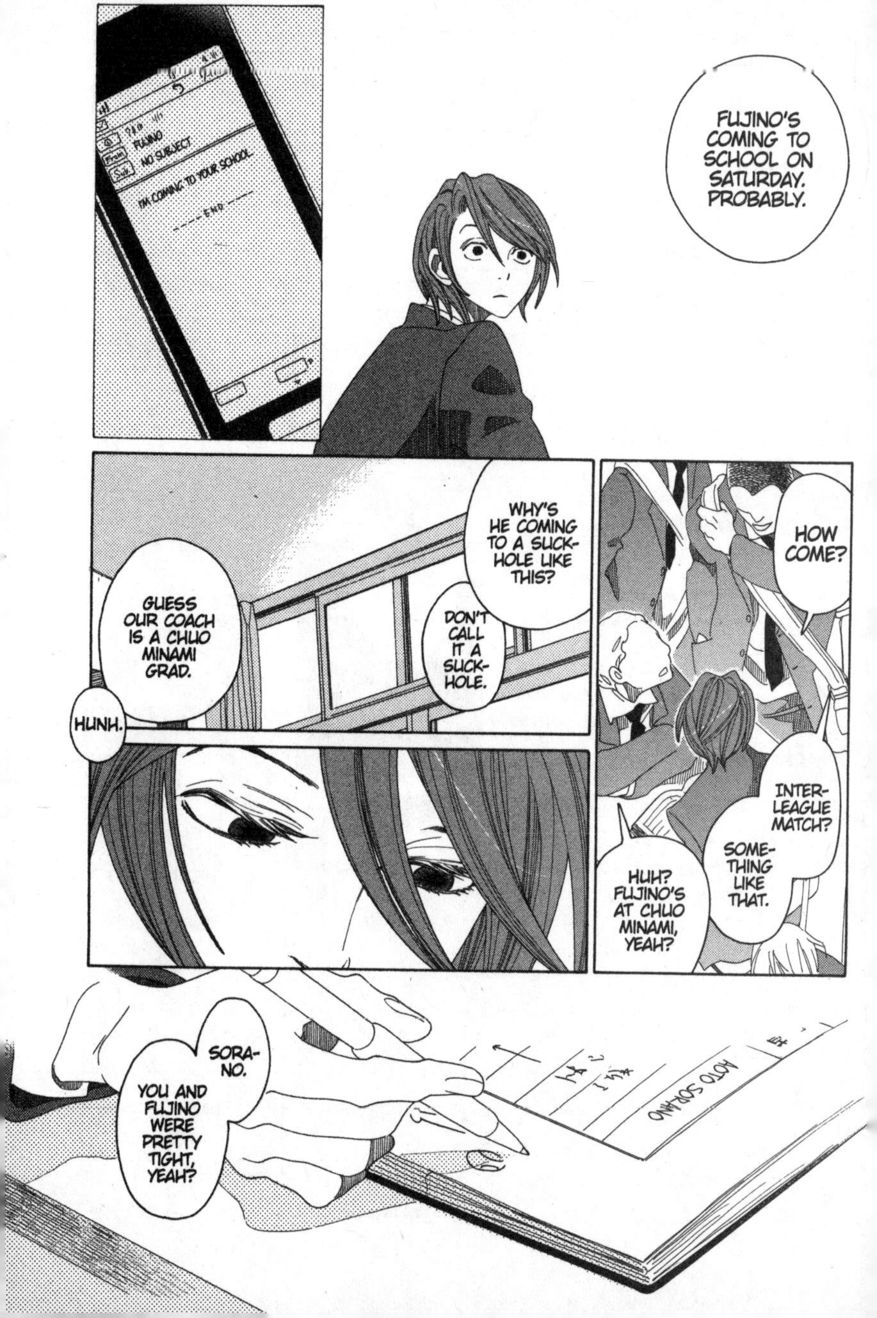
FUJINO'S COMING TO SCHOOL ON SATURDAY. PROBABLY.
From FUJINO
Sub NO SUBJECT
I'M COMING TO YOUR SCHOOL
END
HOW COME?
INTER-LEAGUE MATCH?
SOMETHING LIKE THAT.
HUH? FUJINO'S AT CHUO MINAMI, YEAH?
WHY'S HE COMING TO A SUCK-HOLE LIKE THIS?
DON'T CALL IT A SUCK-HOLE.
GUESS OUR COACH IS A CHUO MINAMI GRAD.
HUNH.
SORA-NO.
YOU AND FUJINO WERE PRETTY TIGHT, YEAH?
HOTO SORANO

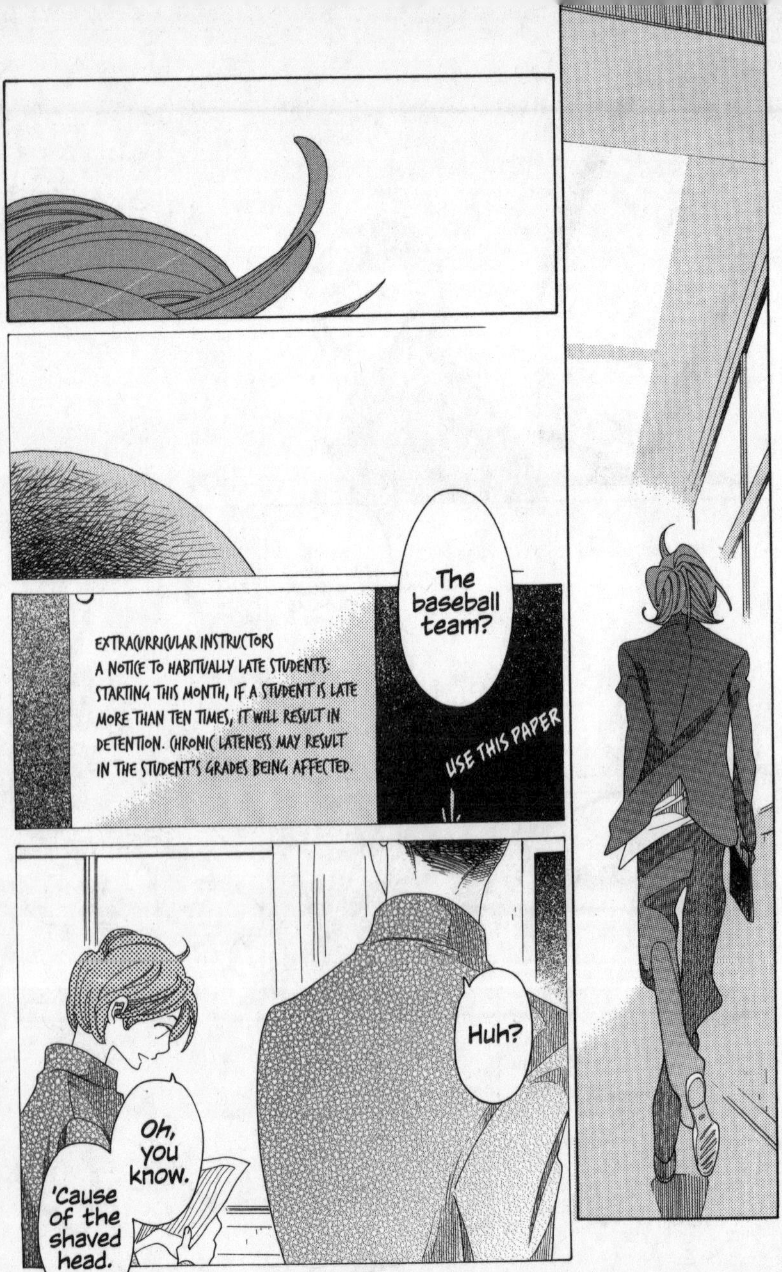
The baseball team?
EXTRACURRICULAR INSTRUCTORS
A NOTICE TO HABITUALLY LATE STUDENTS: STARTING THIS MONTH, IF A STUDENT IS LATE MORE THAN TEN TIMES, IT WILL RESULT IN DETENTION. CHRONIC LATENESS MAY RESULT IN THE STUDENT'S GRADES BEING AFFECTED.
USE THIS PAPER
Huh?
Oh, you know. 'Cause of the shaved head.

Or maybe you're not sporty?
Is it for fashion?
baseball means morning practice, right?
Why were you late?
That's just it. Morning practice went long, so I was late.
Hunh.
They should be letting you off the hook, then!
I mean, if you were at practice--
It wasn't manda-tory practice.
No, it's for base-ball.
Ha ha! I knew it.
Got it in one!
So...
Hunh.
Why were *you* late?
Me? Nothing special.
Just over-slept.
Wow.
Must be nice.

I wanna sleep in late like that someday!
EXCUSE ME!
TEACHERS' ROOM
KLATTER

HAH!
MYAAH!
RAR! RAR!
DON'T BE SO DAMN CREEPY!!
HA HA HA HA HA HA!!
BWA HA HA!!
GOOSEBUMPS
SO?
WHAT DO YOU WANT?
LOG.
OHH.
YOU'RE ON DUTY TODAY?
UH-HUH.
GOOD WORK.
AH.
DON'T STARTLE ME NEXT TIME.
HE'S GOT SLEEP MARKS ON HIS FACE.
OH.
I'M STARVING.
I'D LOVE SOME RAMEN.
OH!
HEY, LET'S GO GET RAMEN AGAIN.
IDIOT.
THAT WAS A ONE-OFF.
MM.

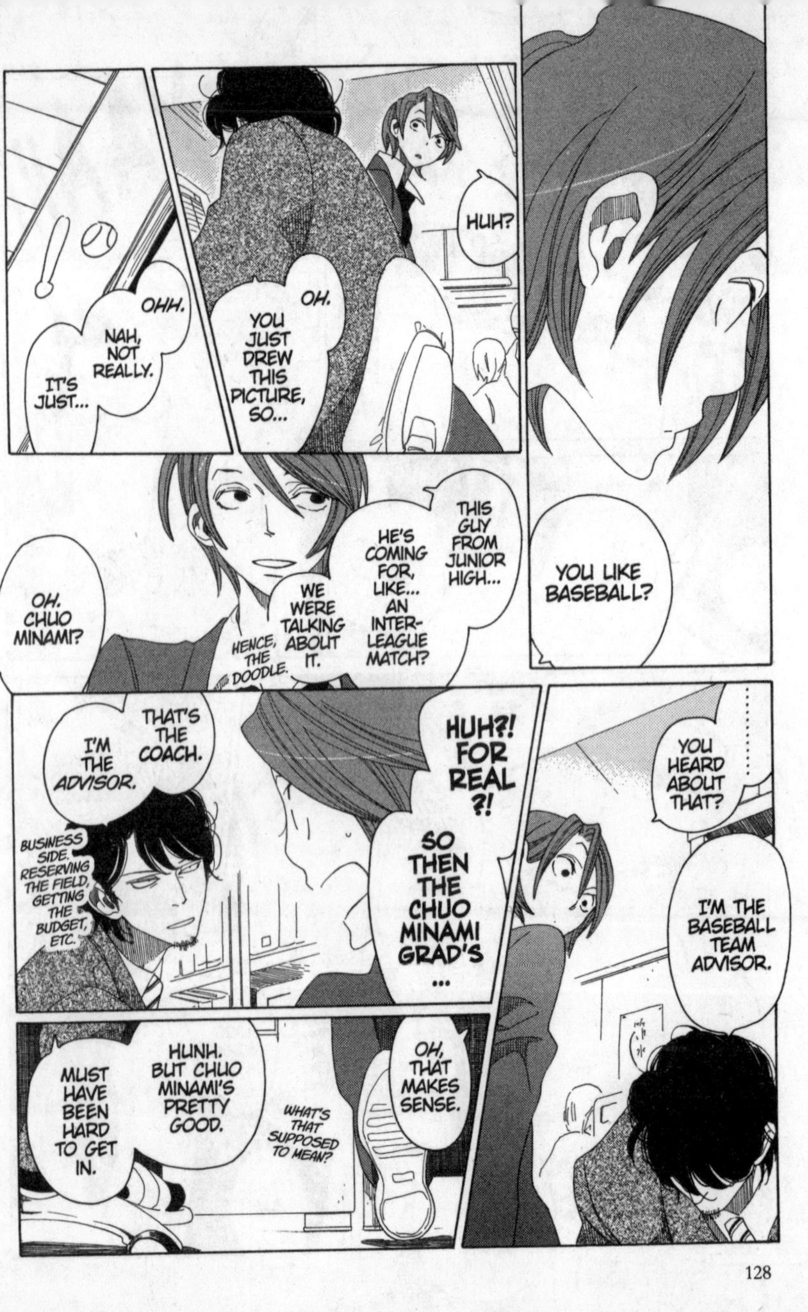

YOU LIKE BASEBALL?
HUH?
OH. YOU JUST DREW THIS PICTURE, SO...
OHH.
NAH, NOT REALLY.
IT'S JUST...
THIS GUY FROM JUNIOR HIGH...
HE'S COMING FOR, LIKE... AN INTER-LEAGUE MATCH?
WE WERE TALKING ABOUT IT.
HENCE, THE DOODLE.
OH. CHUO MINAMI?
......
YOU HEARD ABOUT THAT?
I'M THE BASEBALL TEAM ADVISOR.
HUH?! FOR REAL?!
SO THEN THE CHUO MINAMI GRAD'S...
THAT'S THE COACH.
I'M THE ADVISOR.
BUSINESS SIDE. RESERVING THE FIELD, GETTING THE BUDGET, ETC.
OH, THAT MAKES SENSE.
WHAT'S THAT SUPPOSED TO MEAN?
HUNH. BUT CHUO MINAMI'S PRETTY GOOD.
MUST HAVE BEEN HARD TO GET IN.

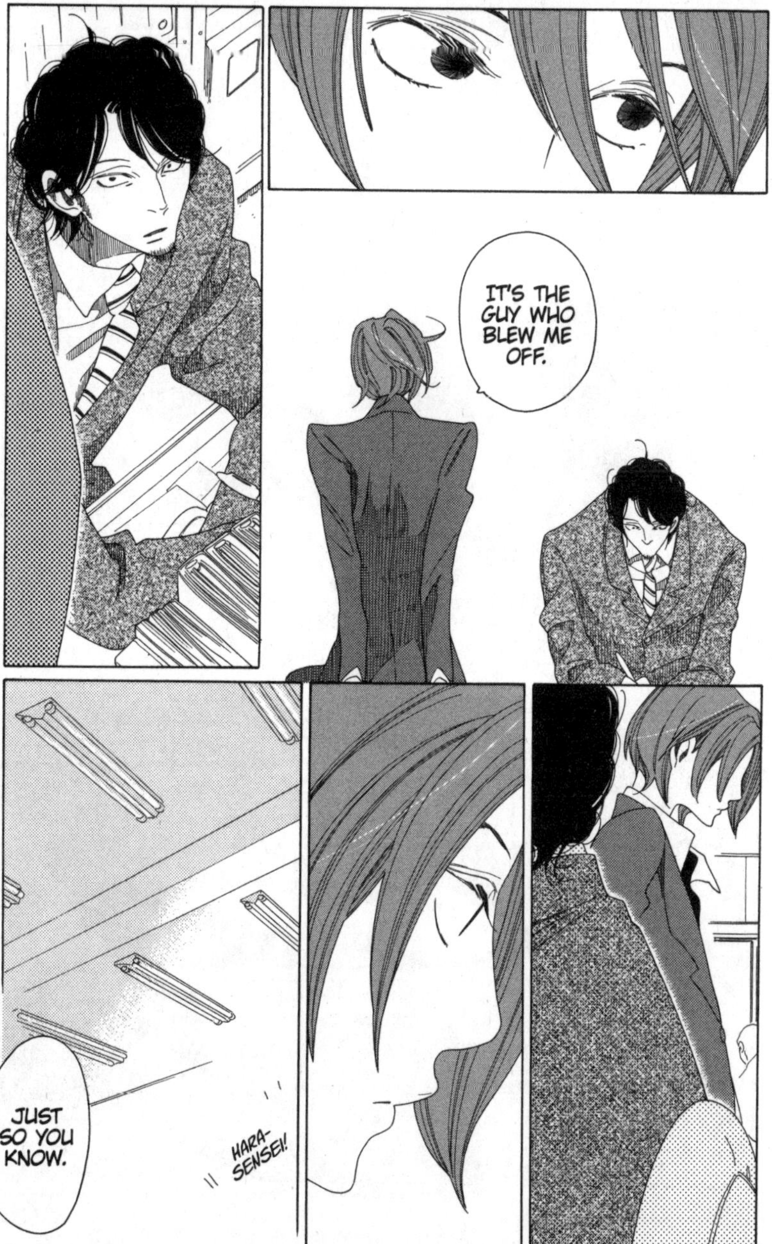
IT'S THE GUY WHO BLEW ME OFF.
JUST SO YOU KNOW.
HARA-SENSEI!

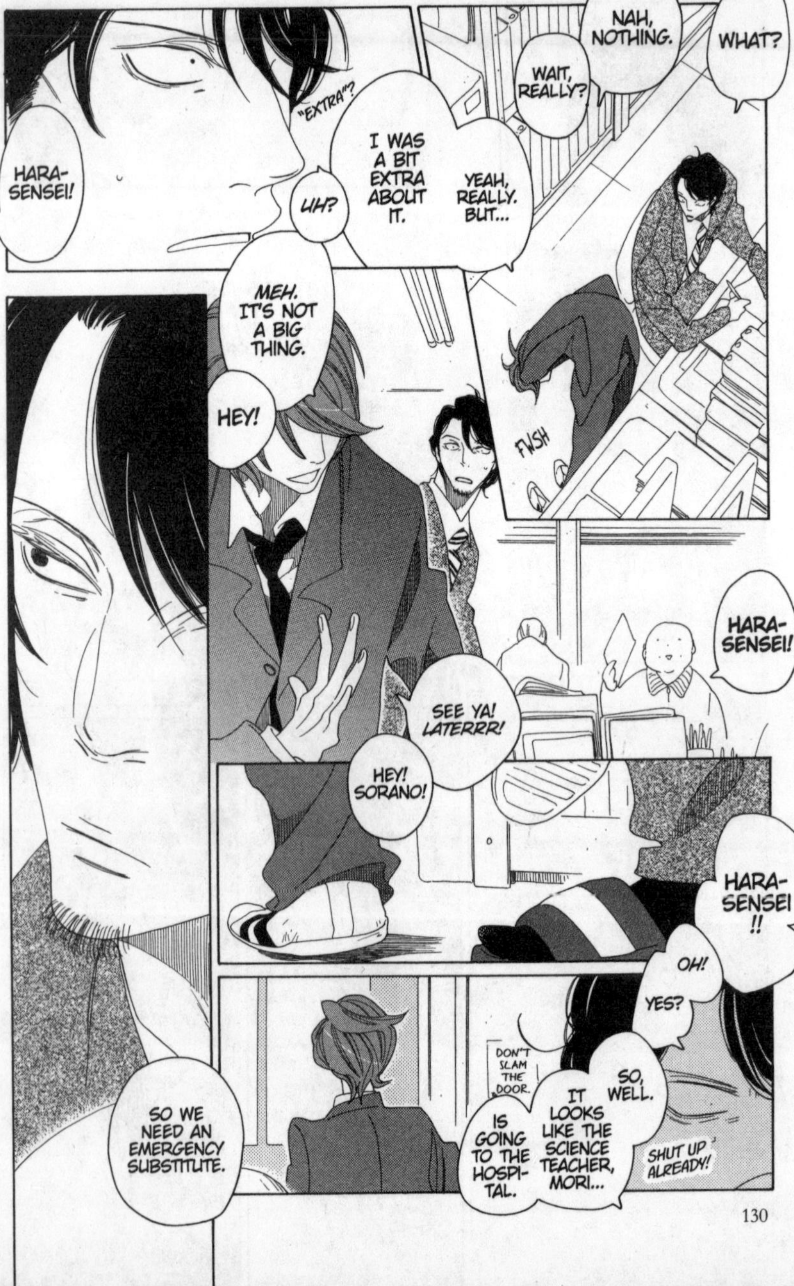
WHAT?
NAH, NOTHING.
WAIT, REALLY?
YEAH, REALLY. BUT...
I WAS A BIT EXTRA ABOUT IT.
"EXTRA"?
UH?
HARA-SENSEI!
MEH. IT'S NOT A BIG THING.
HEY!
FWSH
HARA-SENSEI!
SEE YA! LATERRR!
HEY! SORANO!
HARA-SENSEI !!
OH!
YES?
SO, WELL.
IT LOOKS LIKE THE SCIENCE TEACHER, MORI...
IS GOING TO THE HOSPITAL.
DON'T SLAM THE DOOR.
SHUT UP ALREADY!
SO WE NEED AN EMERGENCY SUBSTITUTE.

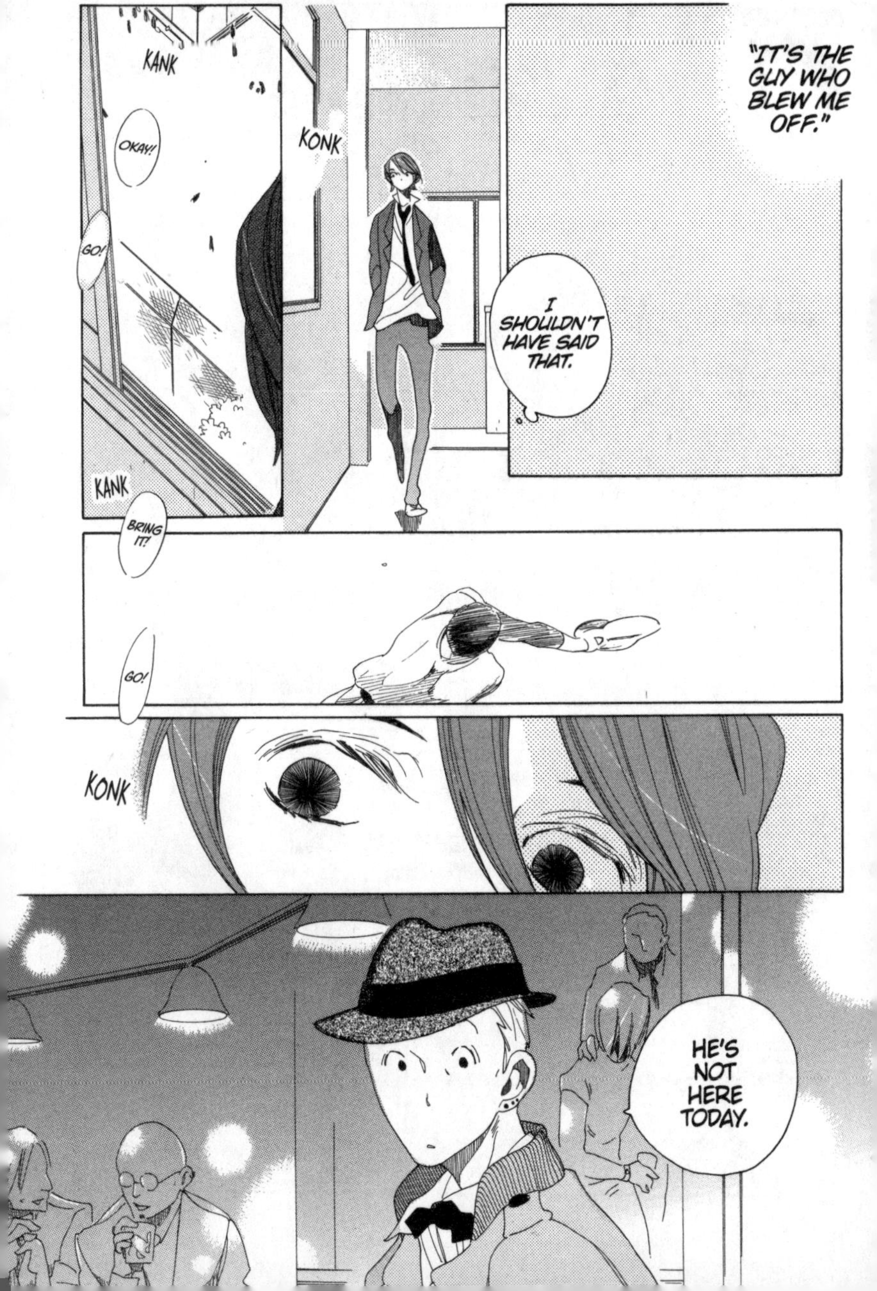
"IT'S THE GUY WHO BLEW ME OFF."
I SHOULDN'T HAVE SAID THAT.
KONK
KANK
OKAY!
GO!
KANK
BRING IT!
GO!
KONK
HE'S NOT HERE TODAY.

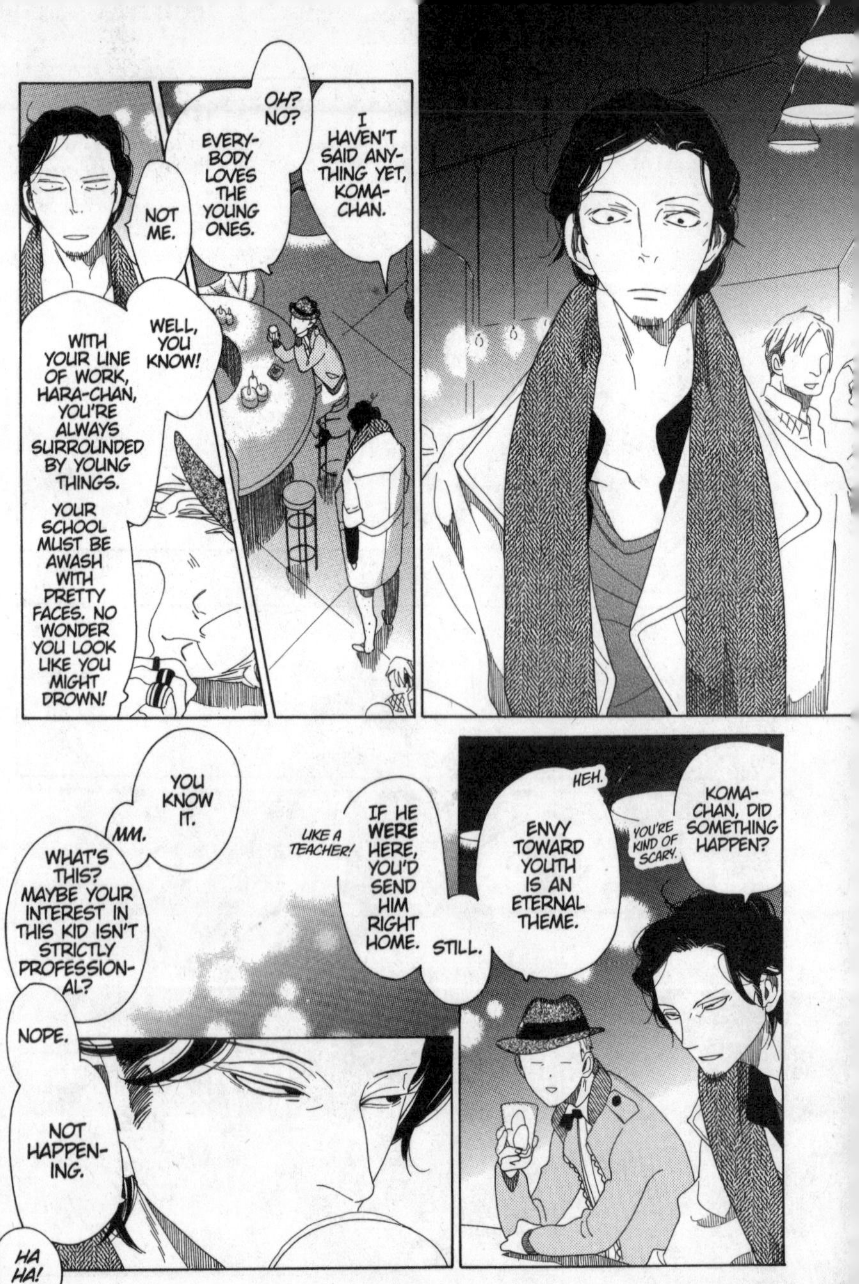
I HAVEN'T SAID ANYTHING YET, KOMA-CHAN.
OH? NO?
EVERYBODY LOVES THE YOUNG ONES.
NOT ME.
WELL, YOU KNOW!
WITH YOUR LINE OF WORK, HARA-CHAN, YOU'RE ALWAYS SURROUNDED BY YOUNG THINGS.
YOUR SCHOOL MUST BE AWASH WITH PRETTY FACES. NO WONDER YOU LOOK LIKE YOU MIGHT DROWN!
KOMA-CHAN, DID SOMETHING HAPPEN?
YOU'RE KIND OF SCARY.
HEH.
ENVY TOWARD YOUTH IS AN ETERNAL THEME.
STILL.
IF HE WERE HERE, YOU'D SEND HIM RIGHT HOME.
LIKE A TEACHER!
YOU KNOW IT.
MM.
WHAT'S THIS? MAYBE YOUR INTEREST IN THIS KID ISN'T STRICTLY PROFESSIONAL?
NOPE.
NOT HAPPENING.
HA HA!

WELL ...
HE'S DIFFERENT FROM YOUR USUAL TYPE, THIS SORA-KUN.
YOU USUALLY GO FOR THE INNOCENTS.
I DO?
SURE. YOU LIKE THEM NAÏVE, SPOTLESS.
OH.
SORA-KUN'S MORE OF...
YOU KNOW.
HE'S LIKE YOU!
EH ?! HOW SO?!
ERR, JUST IN THAT WAY.
YOU KNOW.
ACTING ALL GROWN UP.
......
LIKE HOW HE ACTS ALL COOL?
HE'D COME ASAP.
YOU COULD CALL HIM.
BEEP
NAH.
I'LL PASS.
TOO MUCH HASSLE.
I DON'T HAVE HIS NUMBER ANYWAY.
RRRRRING
RRRRRING
I'M CALLING HIM NOW.
CHK
EH?!
HERE.
BA-DMP
HELLO?

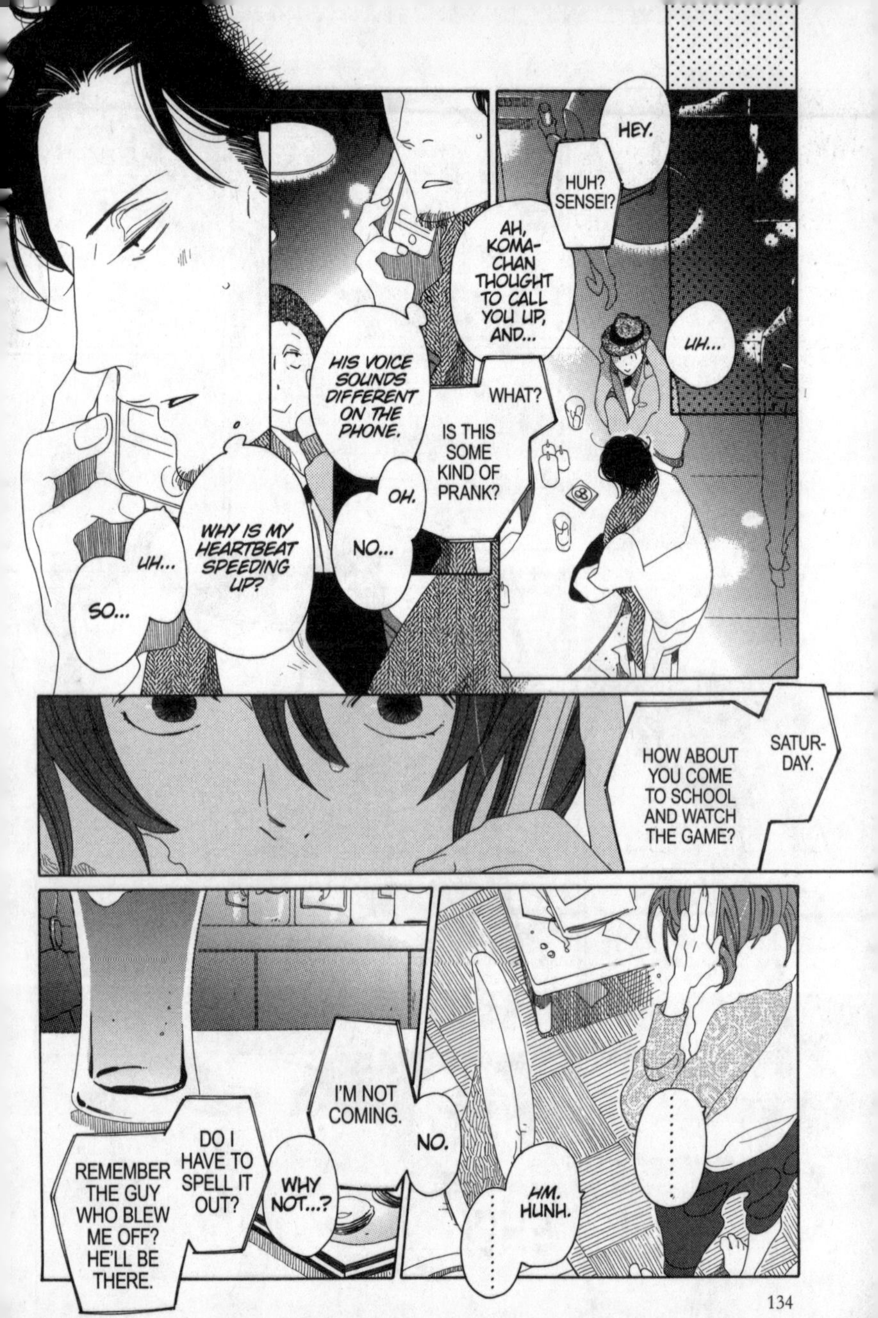
HEY.
HUH? SENSEI?
AH, KOMA-CHAN THOUGHT TO CALL YOU UP, AND...
UH...
WHAT?
IS THIS SOME KIND OF PRANK?
HIS VOICE SOUNDS DIFFERENT ON THE PHONE.
OH.
NO...
WHY IS MY HEARTBEAT SPEEDING UP?
UH...
SO...
SATUR-DAY.
HOW ABOUT YOU COME TO SCHOOL AND WATCH THE GAME?
...
HM. HUNH.
...
NO.
I'M NOT COMING.
WHY NOT...?
DO I HAVE TO SPELL IT OUT?
REMEMBER THE GUY WHO BLEW ME OFF? HE'LL BE THERE.

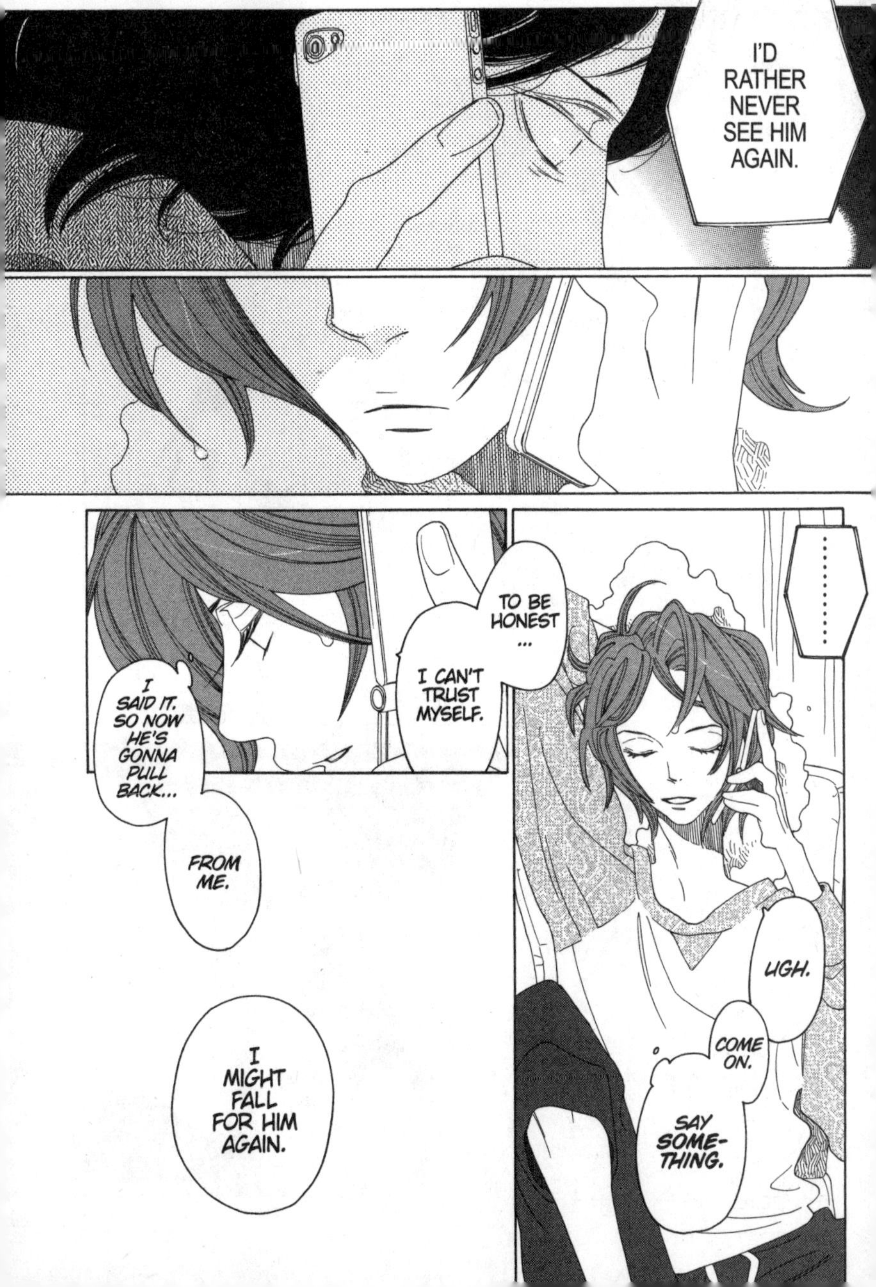
I'D RATHER NEVER SEE HIM AGAIN.
......
UGH.
COME ON.
SAY SOME-THING.
TO BE HONEST...
I CAN'T TRUST MYSELF.
I SAID IT. SO NOW HE'S GONNA PULL BACK...
FROM ME.
I MIGHT FALL FOR HIM AGAIN.

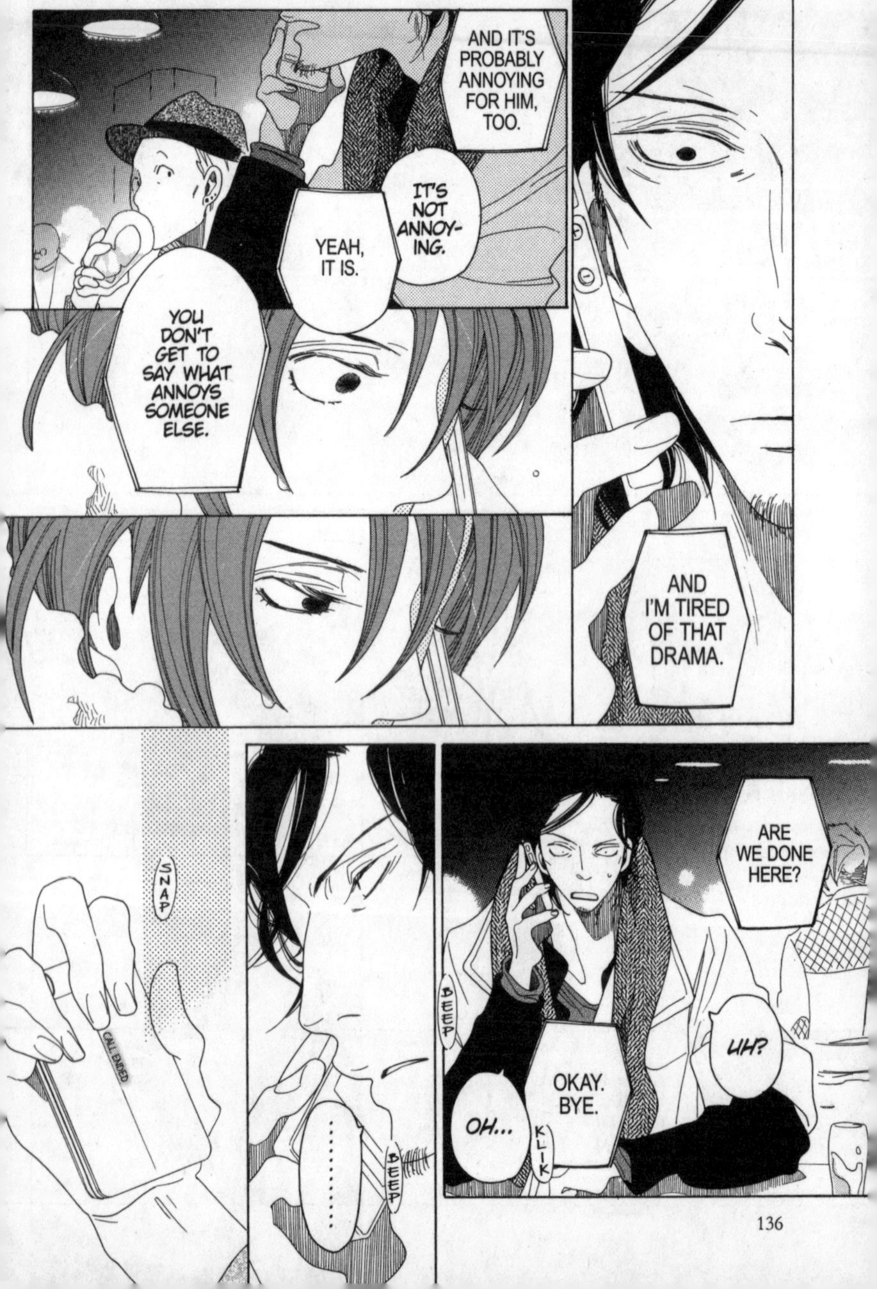
AND I'M TIRED OF THAT DRAMA.
AND IT'S PROBABLY ANNOYING FOR HIM, TOO.
IT'S NOT ANNOYING.
YEAH, IT IS.
YOU DON'T GET TO SAY WHAT ANNOYS SOMEONE ELSE.
ARE WE DONE HERE?
UH?
OKAY. BYE.
BEEP
OH...
KLIK
......
BEEP
SNAP
CALL ENDED

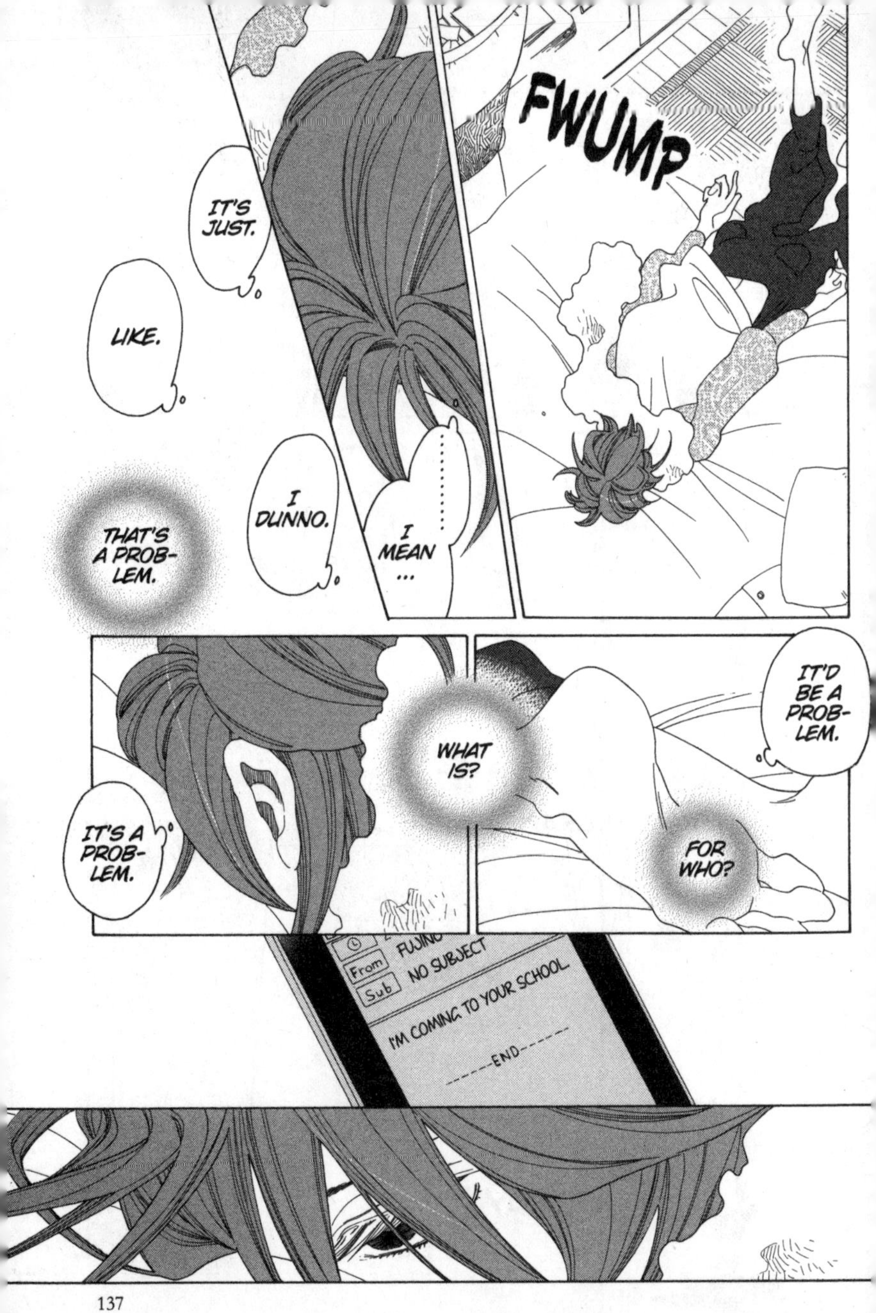
FWUMP
IT'S JUST.
LIKE.
I DUNNO.
I MEAN...
THAT'S A PROBLEM.
IT'D BE A PROBLEM.
WHAT IS?
FOR WHO?
IT'S A PROBLEM.
From FUJINO
Sub NO SUBJECT
I'M COMING TO YOUR SCHOOL
------END------

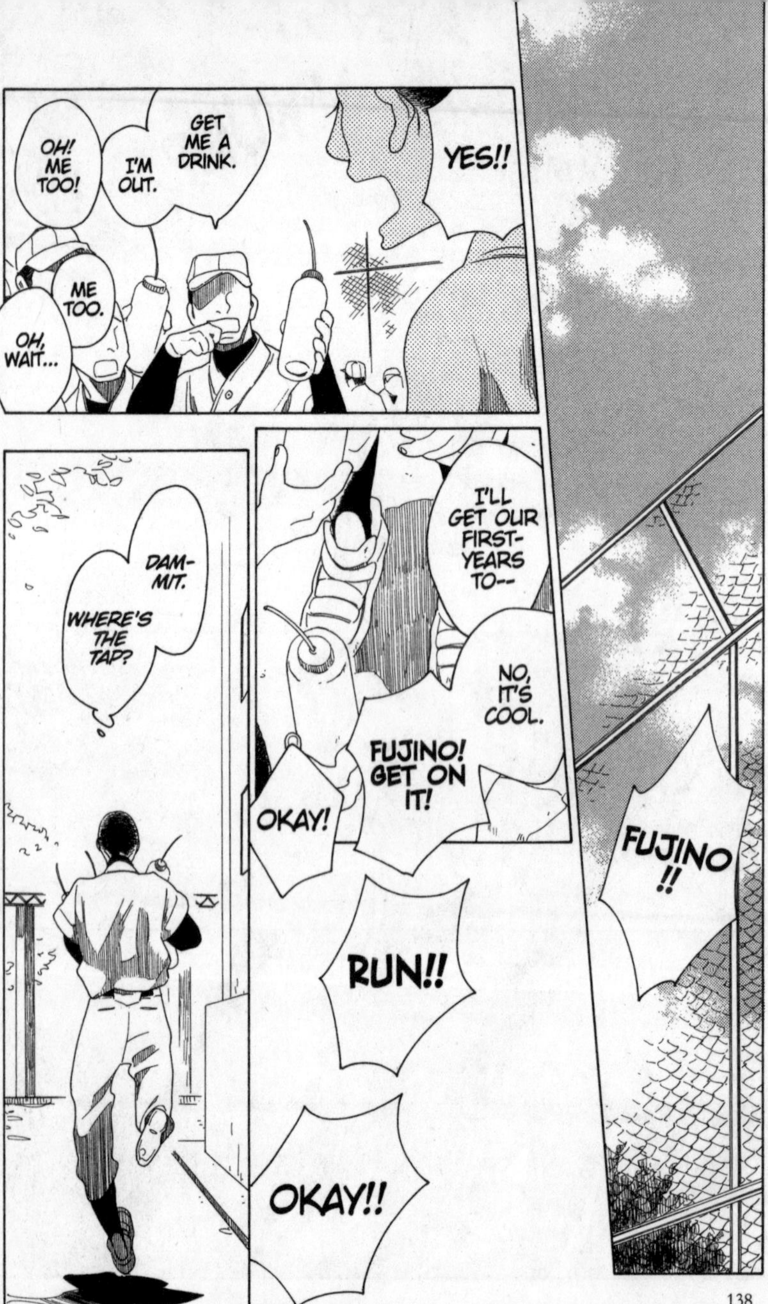
YES!!
GET ME A DRINK.
I'M OUT.
OH! ME TOO!
ME TOO.
OH, WAIT...
I'LL GET OUR FIRST-YEARS TO--
NO, IT'S COOL.
FUJINO! GET ON IT!
OKAY!
FUJINO !!
RUN!!
OKAY!!
DAM-MIT.
WHERE'S THE TAP?

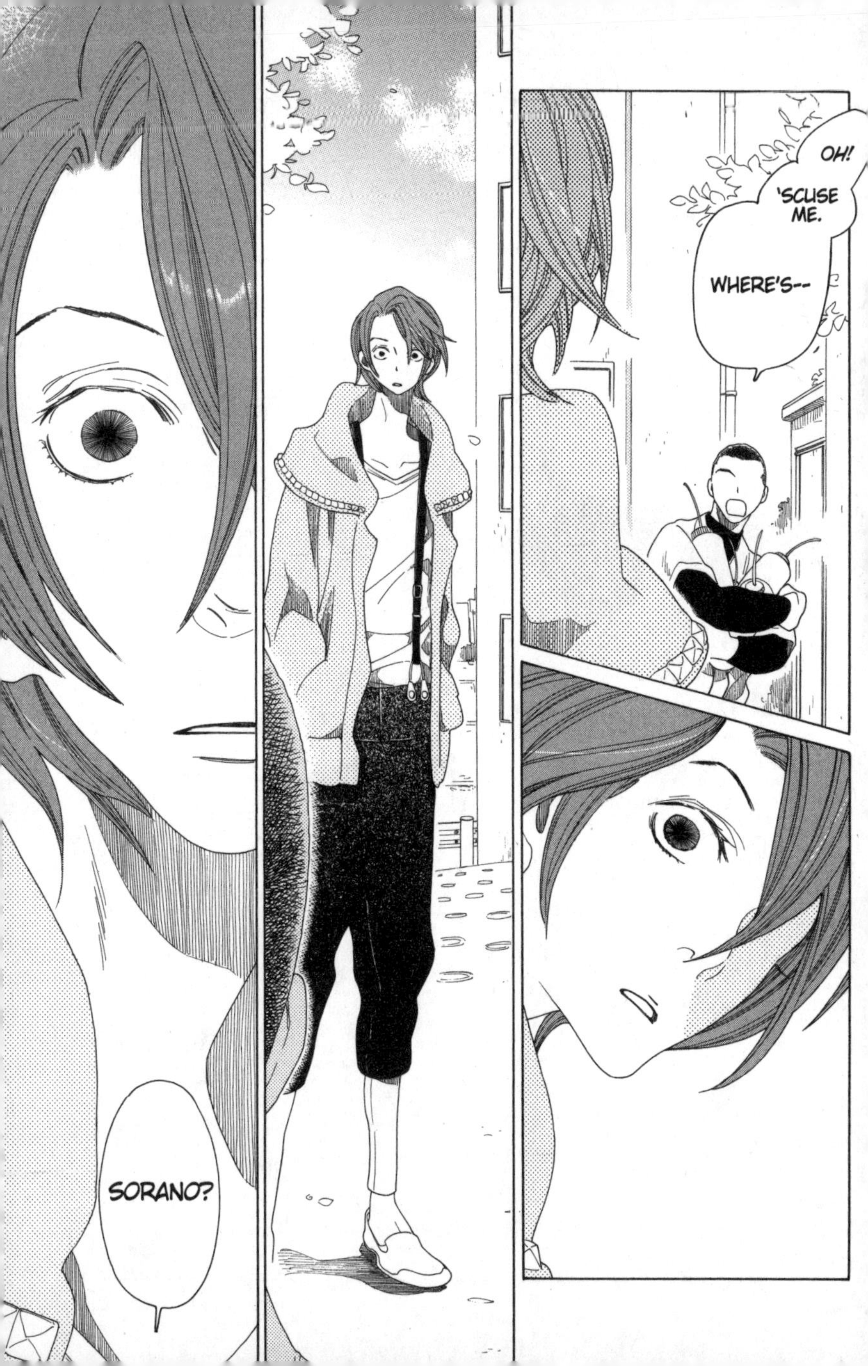
OH!
'SCUSE ME.
WHERE'S--
SORANO?

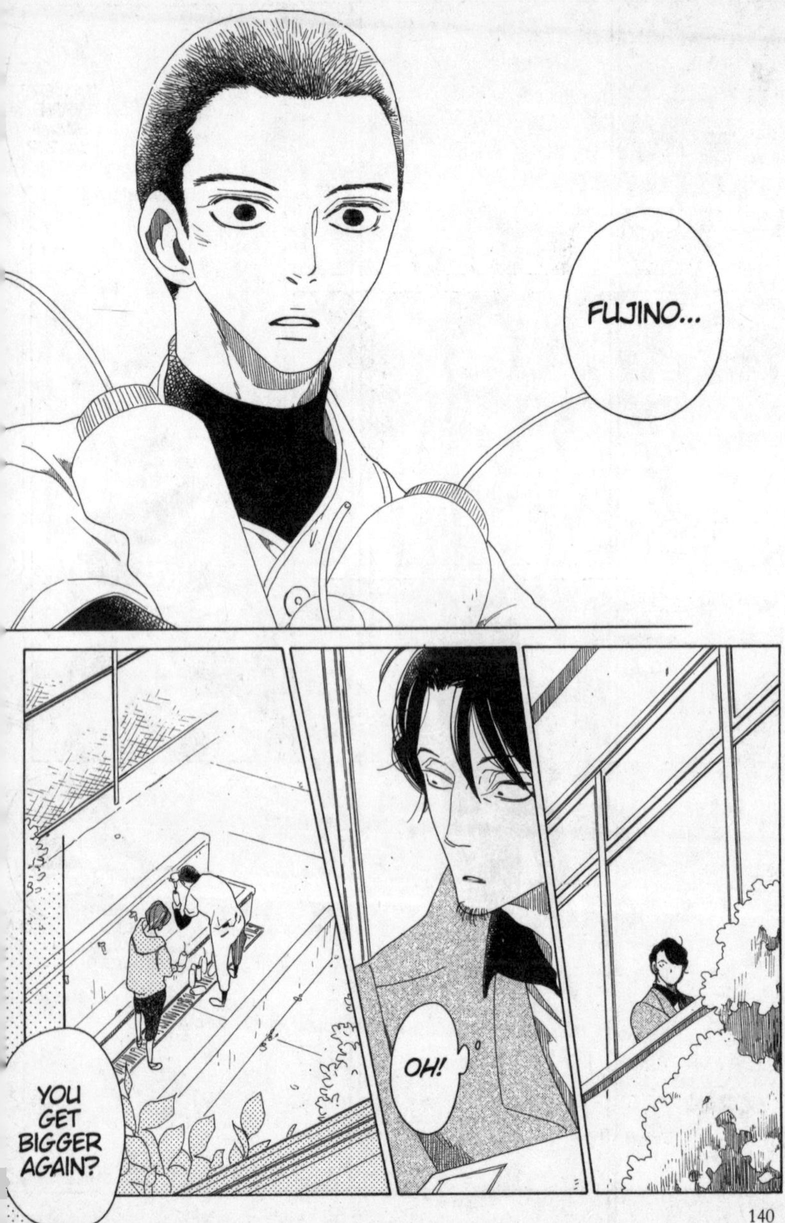
FUJINO...
OH!
YOU GET BIGGER AGAIN?

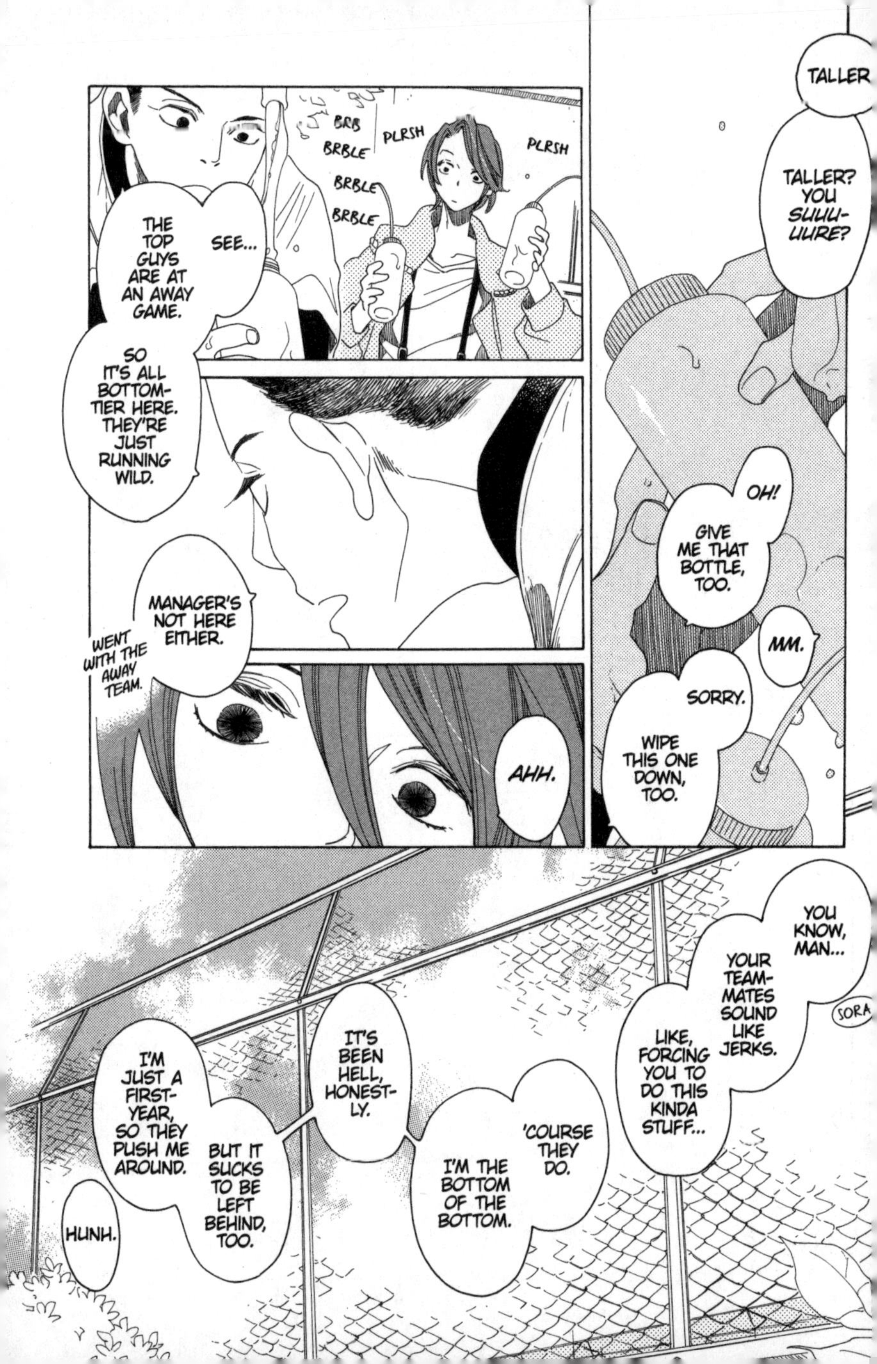
TALLER
TALLER? YOU SUUUURE?
OH!
GIVE ME THAT BOTTLE, TOO.
MM.
SORRY.
WIPE THIS ONE DOWN, TOO.
SEE...
THE TOP GUYS ARE AT AN AWAY GAME.
PLRSH
PLRSH
BRB
BRBLE
BRBLE
BRBLE
SO IT'S ALL BOTTOM-TIER HERE. THEY'RE JUST RUNNING WILD.
AHH.
MANAGER'S NOT HERE EITHER.
WENT WITH THE AWAY TEAM.
SORA
YOU KNOW, MAN...
YOUR TEAM-MATES SOUND LIKE JERKS.
LIKE, FORCING YOU TO DO THIS KINDA STUFF...
'COURSE THEY DO.
I'M THE BOTTOM OF THE BOTTOM.
IT'S BEEN HELL, HONEST-LY.
BUT IT SUCKS TO BE LEFT BEHIND, TOO.
I'M JUST A FIRST-YEAR, SO THEY PUSH ME AROUND.
HUNH.

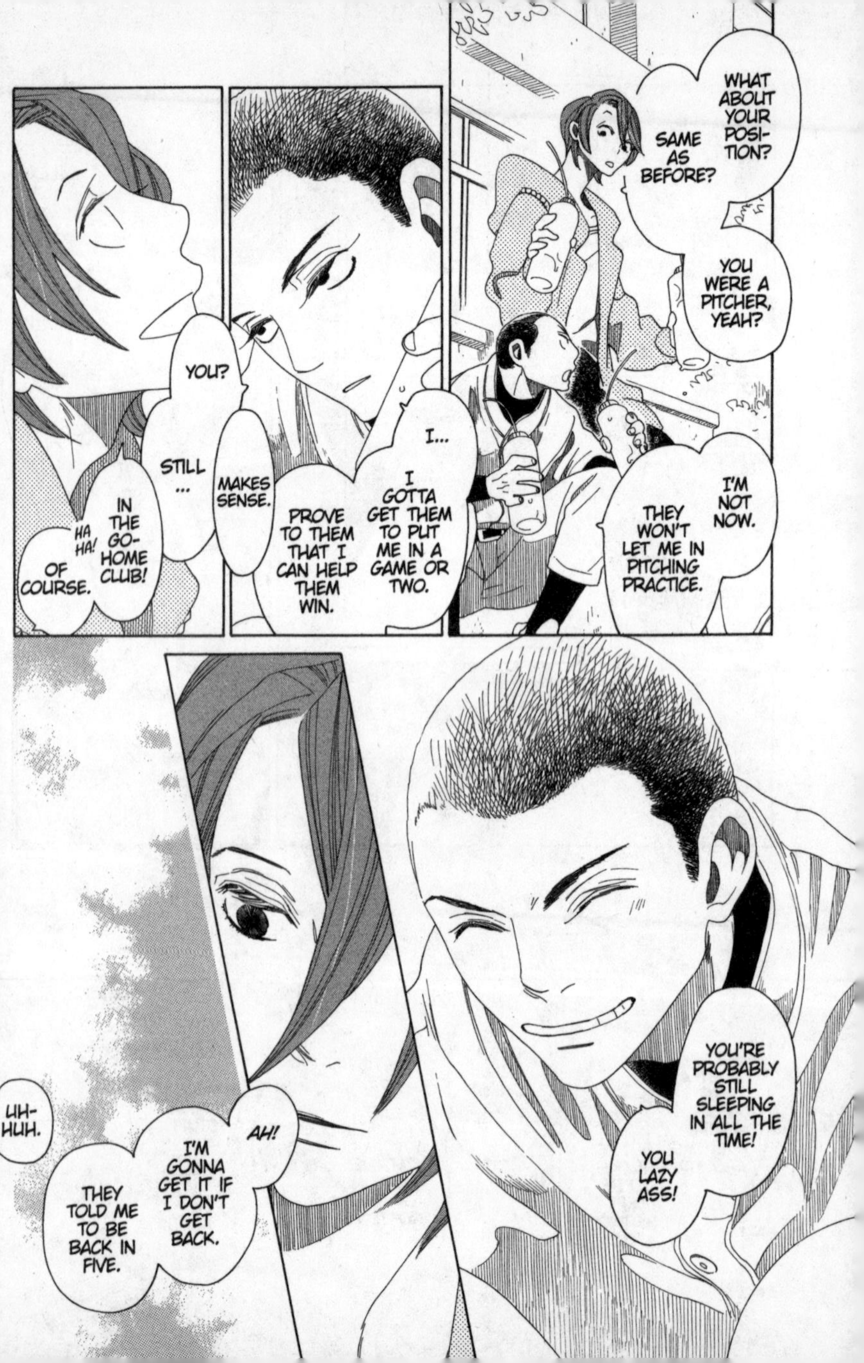
WHAT ABOUT YOUR POSITION?
SAME AS BEFORE?
YOU WERE A PITCHER, YEAH?
I'M NOT NOW.
THEY WON'T LET ME IN PITCHING PRACTICE.
I...
I GOTTA GET THEM TO PUT ME IN A GAME OR TWO.
PROVE TO THEM THAT I CAN HELP THEM WIN.
MAKES SENSE.
YOU?
STILL ...
IN THE GO-HOME CLUB!
HA HA!
OF COURSE.
YOU'RE PROBABLY STILL SLEEPING IN ALL THE TIME!
YOU LAZY ASS!
AH!
I'M GONNA GET IT IF I DON'T GET BACK.
THEY TOLD ME TO BE BACK IN FIVE.
UH-HUH.

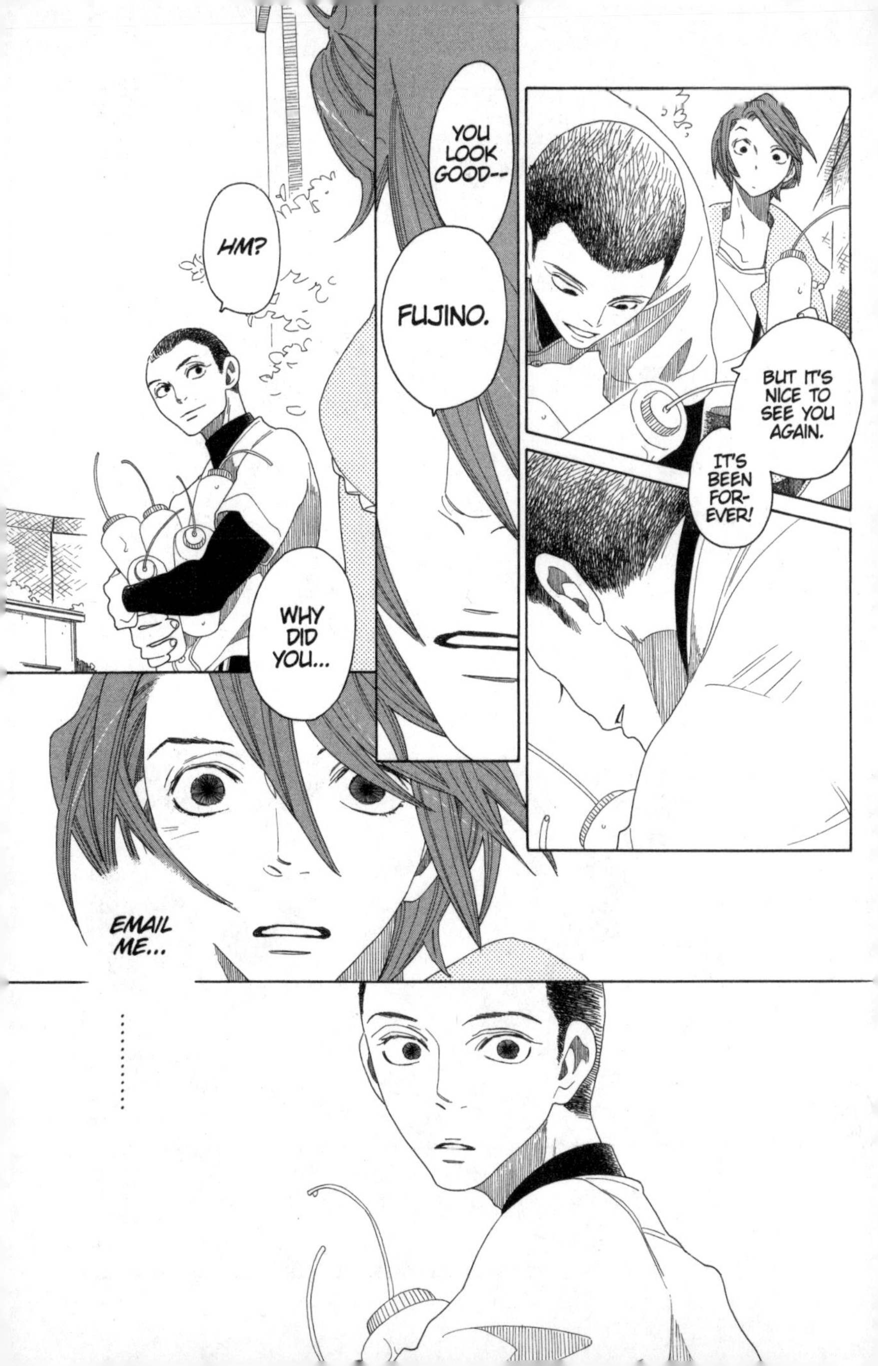
BUT IT'S NICE TO SEE YOU AGAIN.
IT'S BEEN FOR-EVER!
YOU LOOK GOOD--
FUJINO.
HM?
WHY DID YOU...
EMAIL ME...
......

I'VE GOT A GIRLFRIEND.
WHAT?! FOR REAL?!
FOR REAL, YEAH.
FOR REAL REAL ?!
AND YOU'RE AT A BOYS' SCHOOL!
YOU MEET ON A GROUP DATE?!
YUP!
WHOA! FOR REAL?! SHIT!
HA HA HA!
DAMN.
BUT...
THAT'S GREAT.

HEEEY!
FUJINO-OOO!
OH, CRAP!
COMING!!
WHAT THE HELL'S TAKING YA SO LONG?!
COMING!
I'LL BE RIGHT THERE!!
OH, HEY, SORRY.
BOTTLES! BOTTLES!
AND THANKS!
SEE YA!

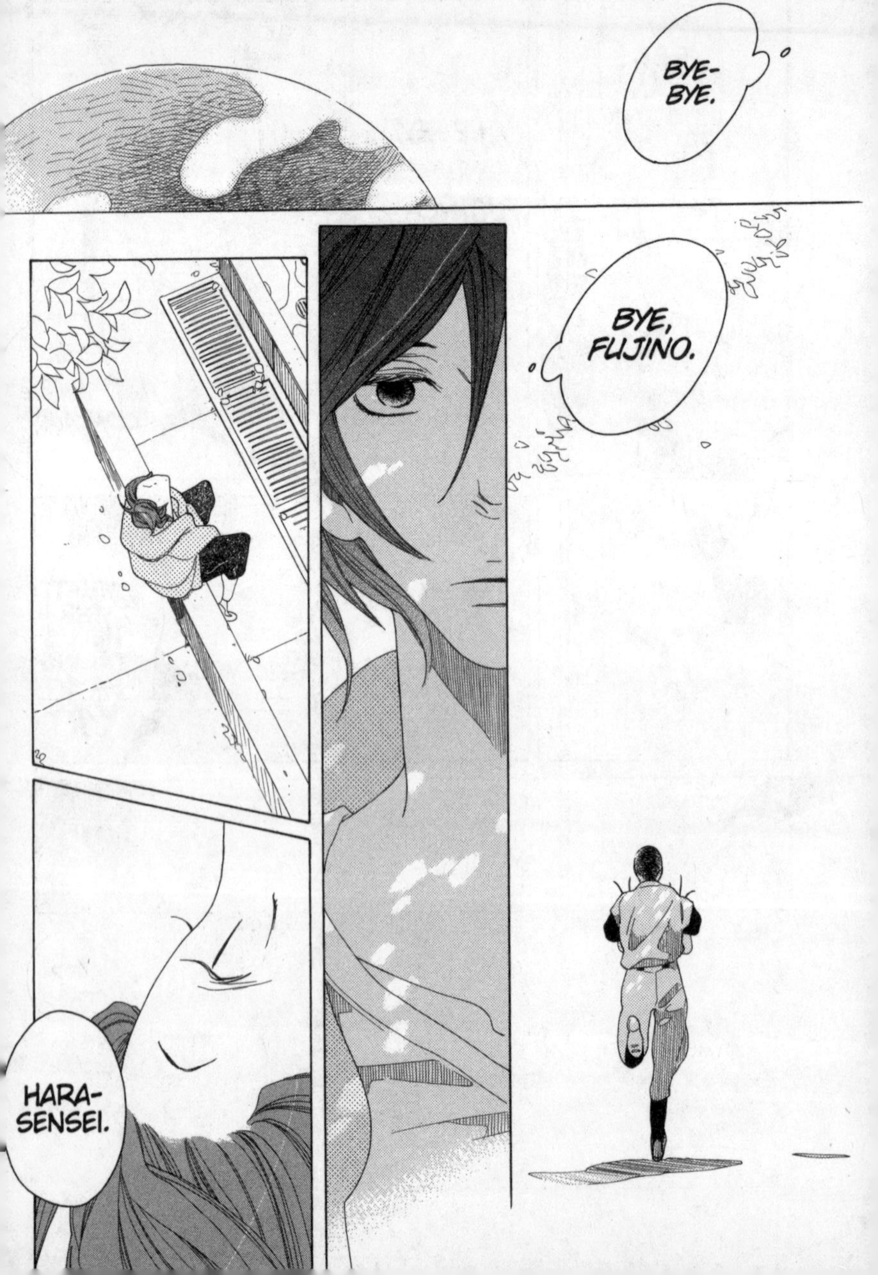
BYE-BYE.
BYE, FUJINO.
HARA-SENSEI.

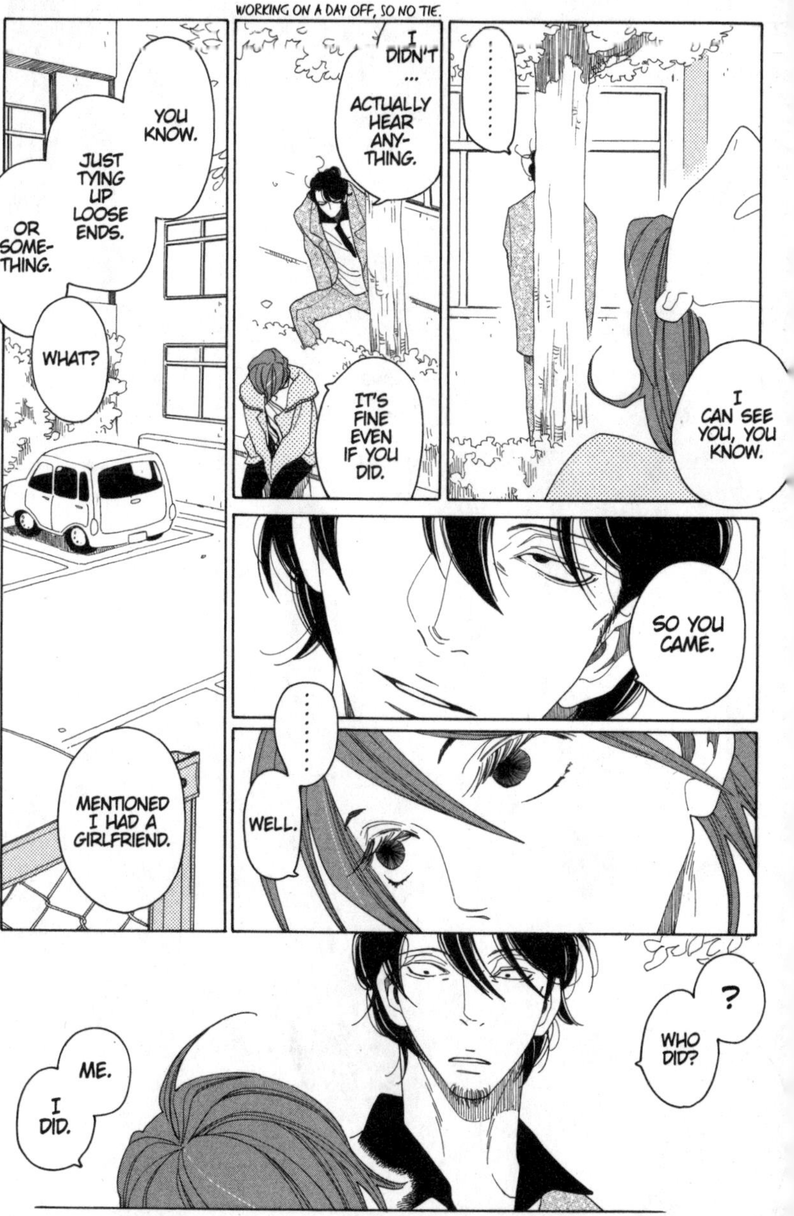
WORKING ON A DAY OFF, SO NO TIE.
......
I CAN SEE YOU, YOU KNOW.
I DIDN'T ... ACTUALLY HEAR ANYTHING.
IT'S FINE EVEN IF YOU DID.
SO YOU CAME.
......
WELL.
YOU KNOW.
JUST TYING UP LOOSE ENDS.
OR SOMETHING.
WHAT?
MENTIONED I HAD A GIRLFRIEND.
?
WHO DID?
ME.
I DID.

IT...
WAS A LIE.
BUT, LIKE...
A WHITE LIE.
HE LOOKED SUPER RELIEVED.
YOU...
THAT KINDA STUFF'S NOT GOOD.
LYING LIKE THAT--
NO.
LET'S STOP TALKING ABOUT THIS.
YOU AND I HAVE DIFFERENT TAKES ON THIS STUFF.
WE *DON'T.*
YOU SAID THE SAME TO ME, DIDN'T YOU?
IT'S BEST TO TELL PEOPLE HOW YOU ACTUALLY FEEL.
GET IT OUT IN THE OPEN.
THAT WAS DIFFERENT.
HOW?

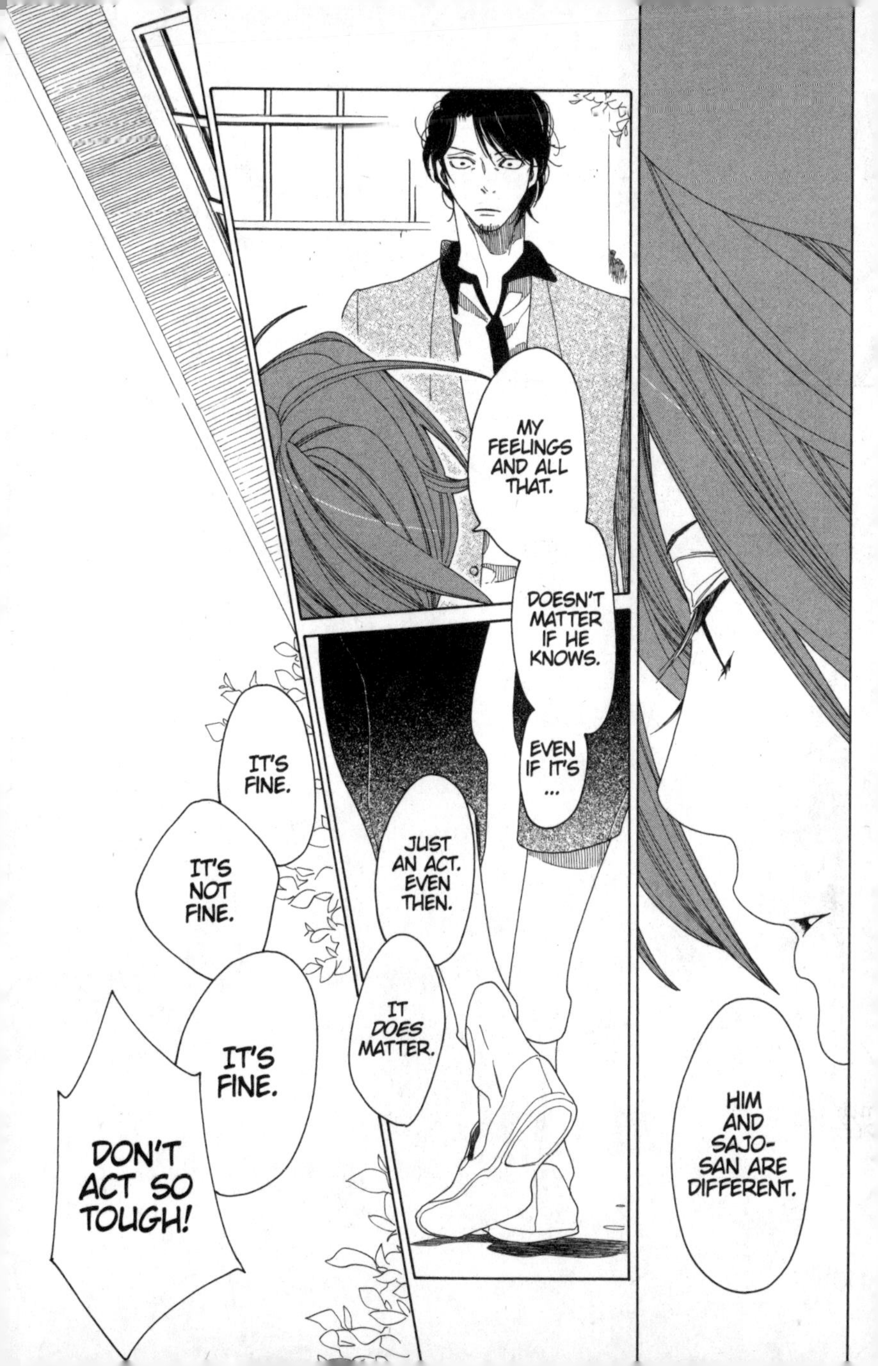
HIM AND SAJO-SAN ARE DIFFERENT.
MY FEELINGS AND ALL THAT.
DOESN'T MATTER IF HE KNOWS.
EVEN IF IT'S ...
JUST AN ACT. EVEN THEN.
IT DOES MATTER.
IT'S FINE.
IT'S NOT FINE.
IT'S FINE.
DON'T ACT SO TOUGH!

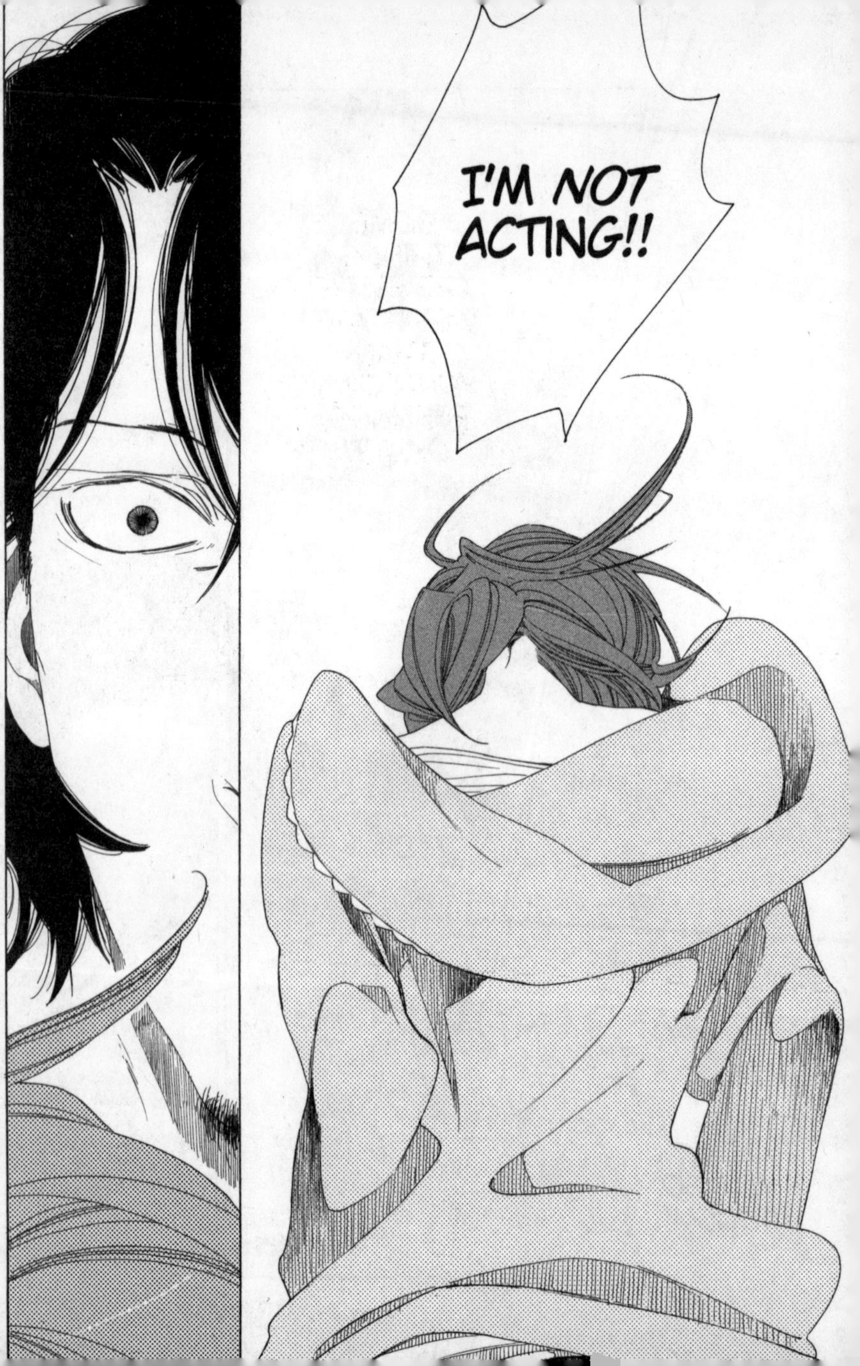
I'M NOT ACTING!!

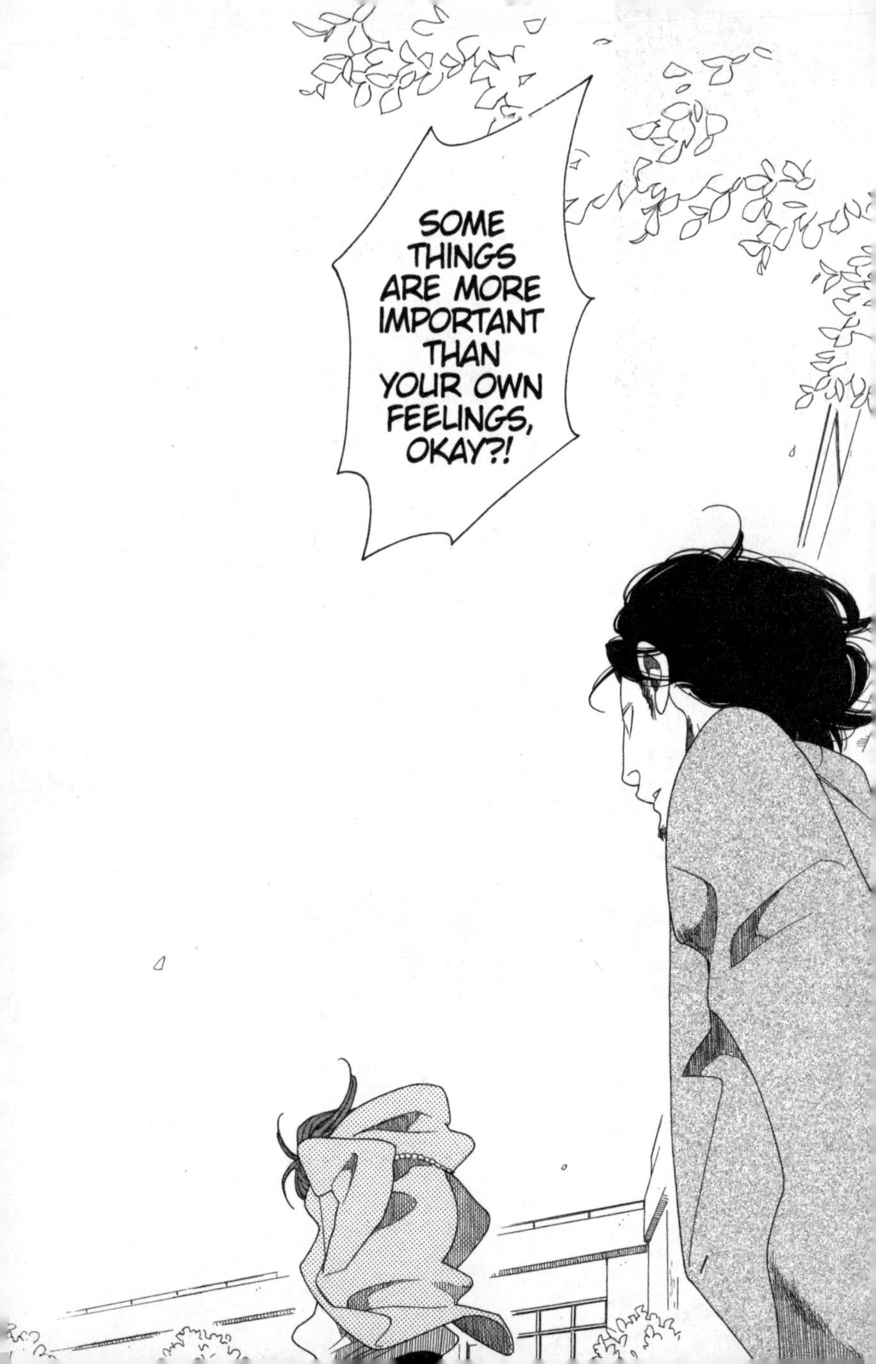
SOME THINGS ARE MORE IMPORTANT THAN YOUR OWN FEELINGS, OKAY?!

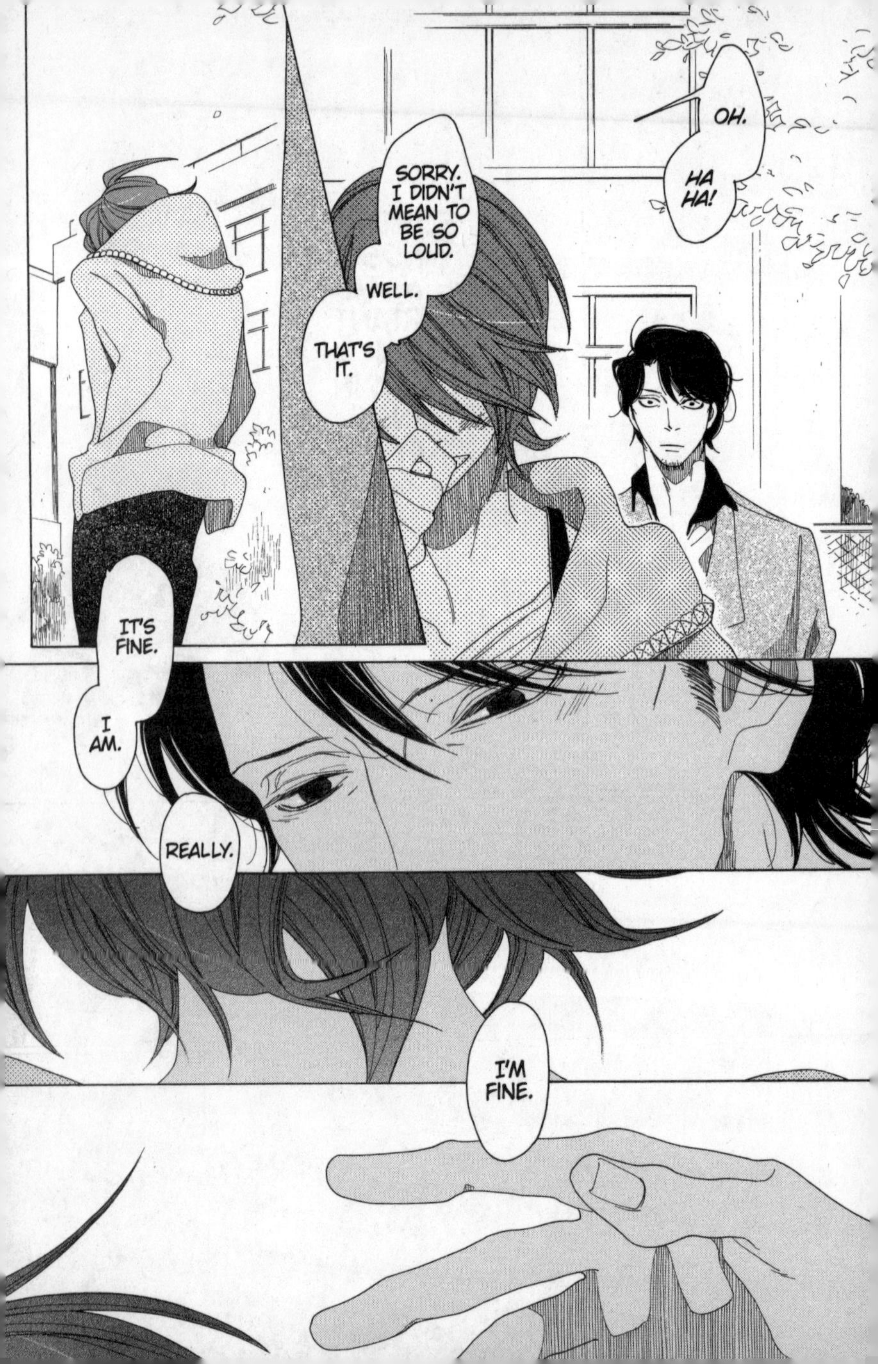
OH.
HA HA!
SORRY. I DIDN'T MEAN TO BE SO LOUD.
WELL.
THAT'S IT.
IT'S FINE.
I AM.
REALLY.
I'M FINE.

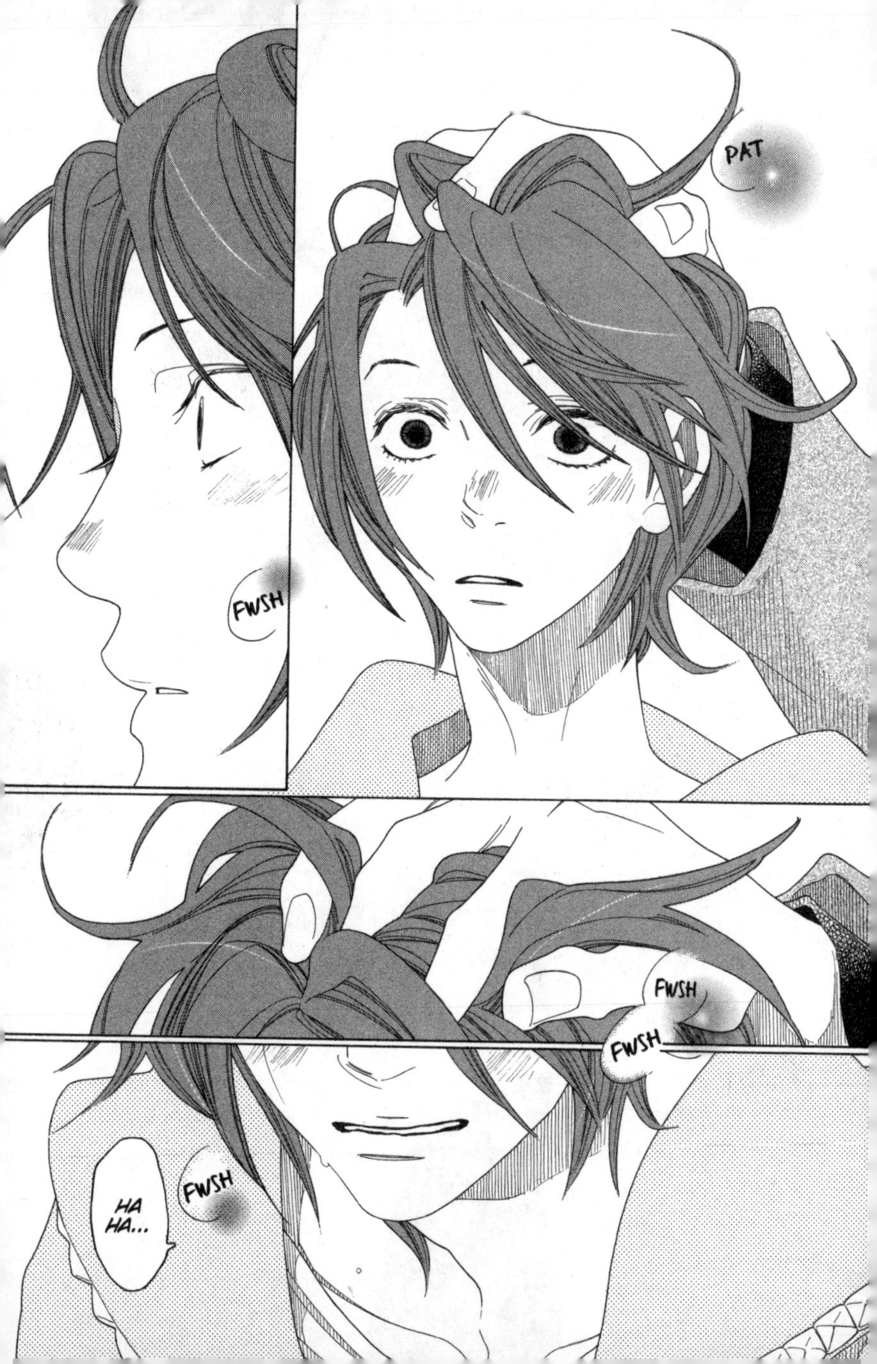
PAT
FWSH
FWSH
FWSH
FWSH
HA HA...

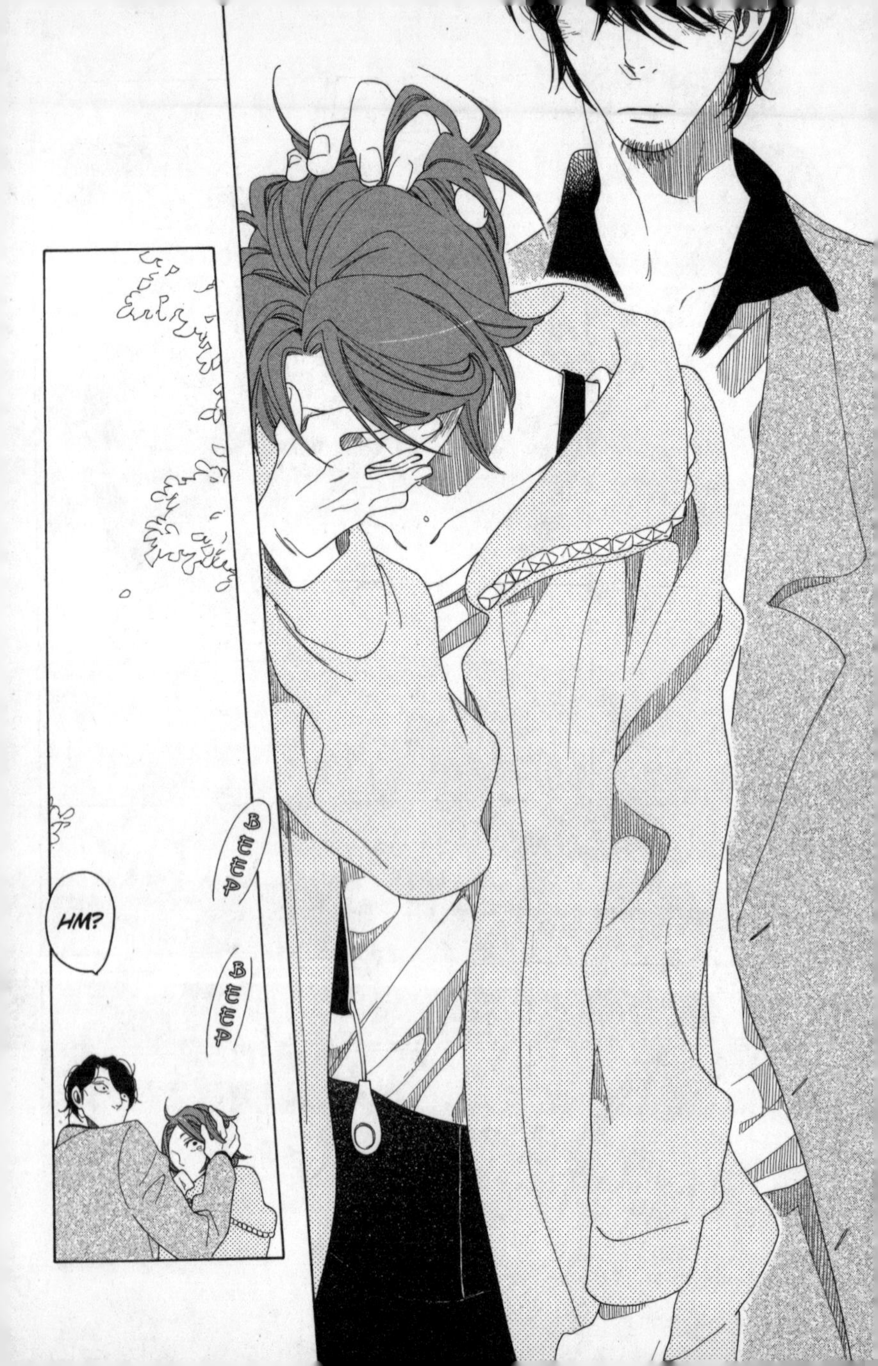
BEEP
BEEP
HM?

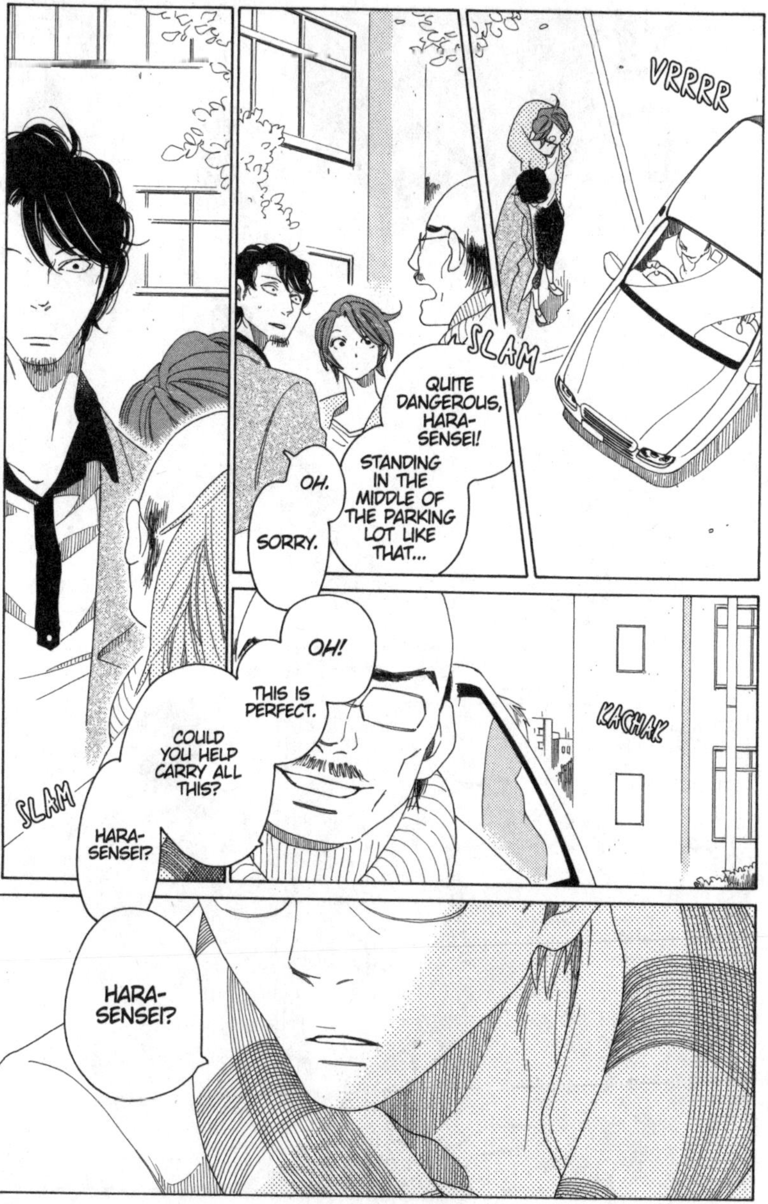
VRRRR
SLAM
QUITE DANGEROUS, HARA-SENSEI!
STANDING IN THE MIDDLE OF THE PARKING LOT LIKE THAT...
OH.
SORRY.
KACHAK
OH!
THIS IS PERFECT.
COULD YOU HELP CARRY ALL THIS?
SLAM
HARA-SENSEI?
HARA-SENSEI?

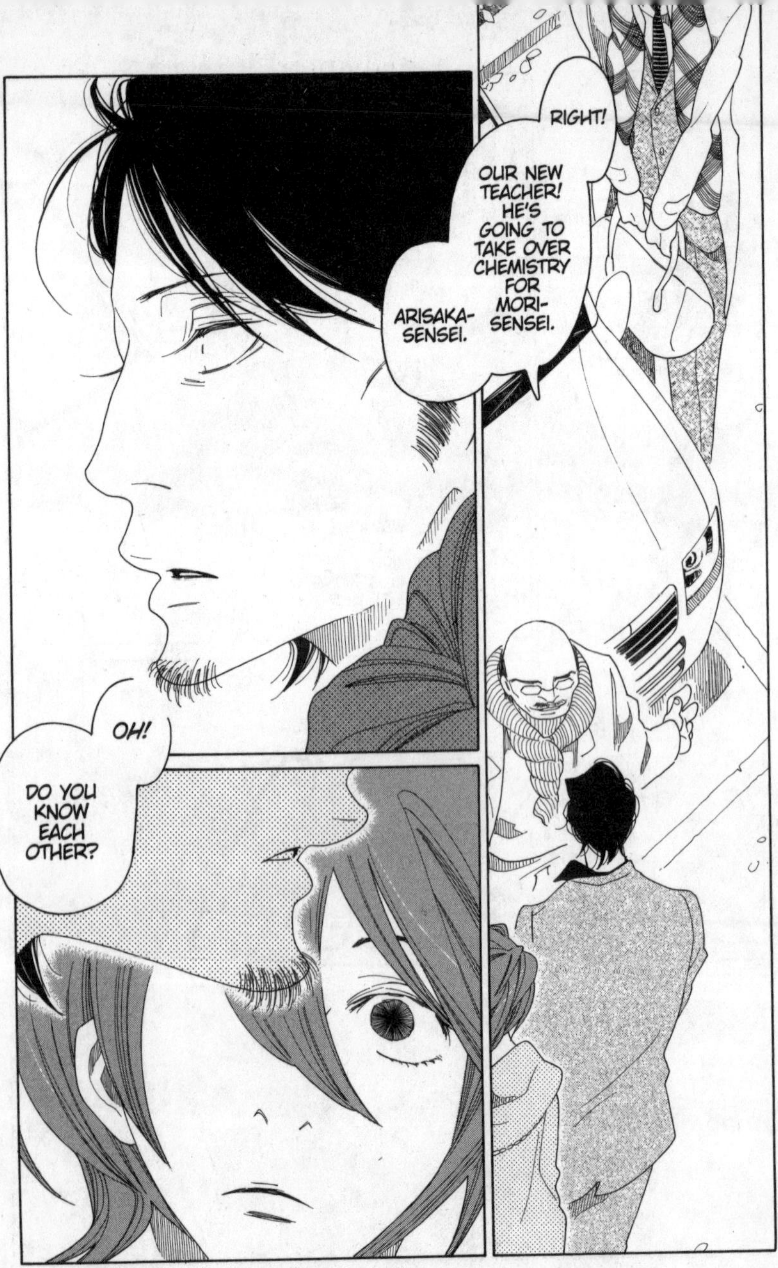
RIGHT!
OUR NEW TEACHER! HE'S GOING TO TAKE OVER CHEMISTRY FOR MORI-SENSEI.
ARISAKA-SENSEI.
OH!
DO YOU KNOW EACH OTHER?

[Chapter 5: Hara & Arisaka

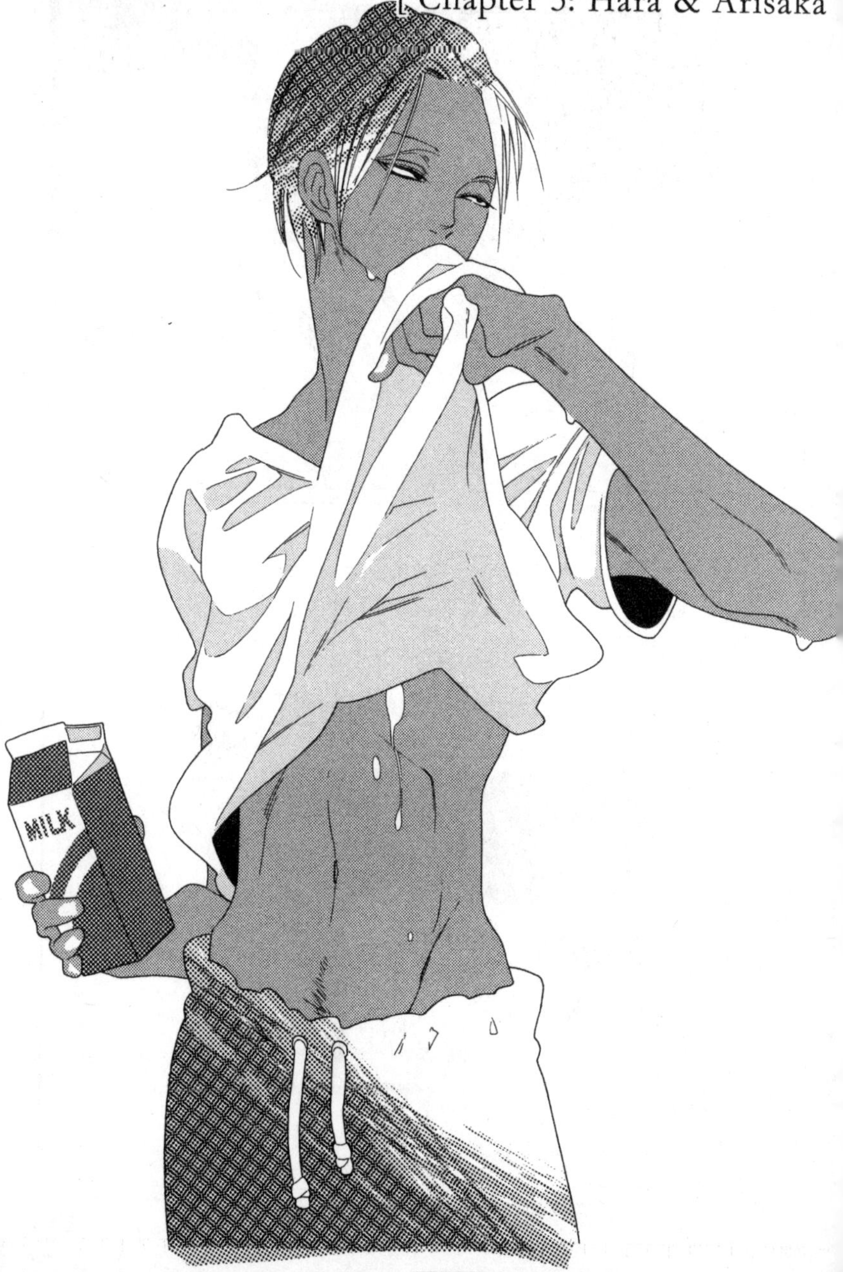
MILK

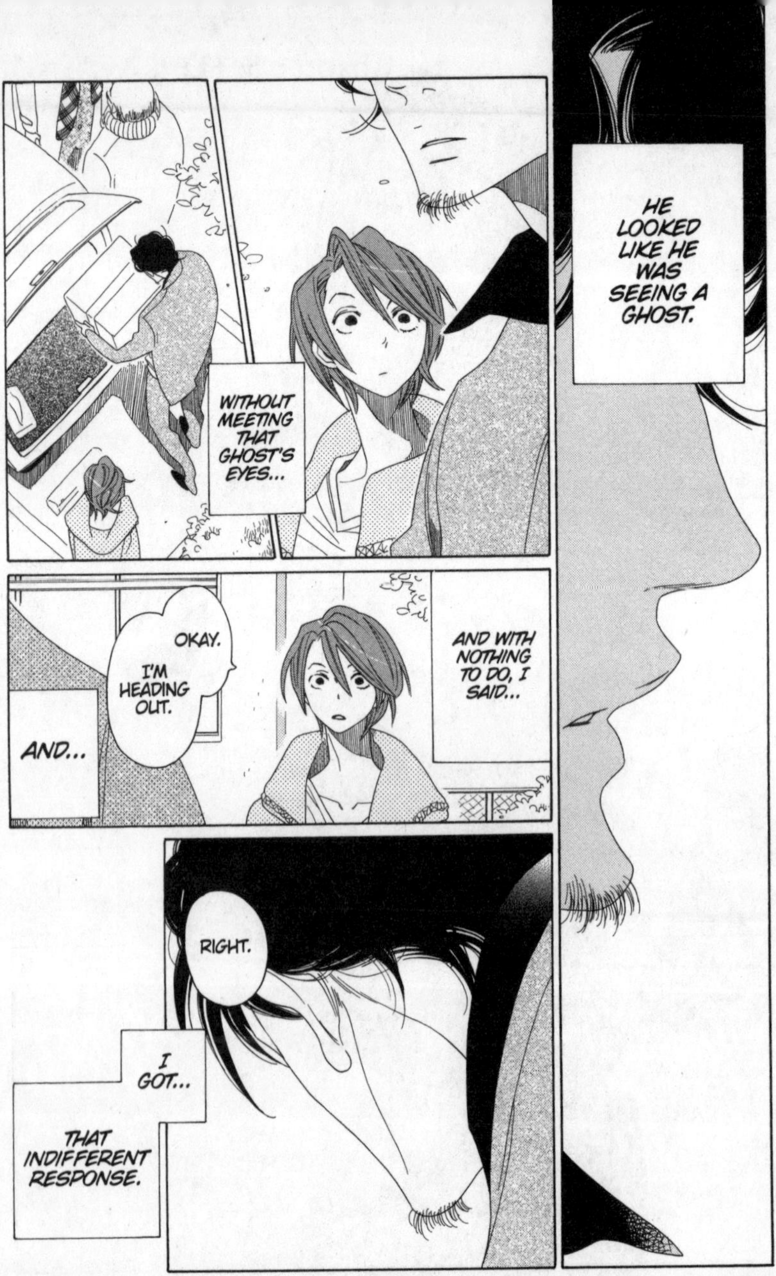
HE LOOKED LIKE HE WAS SEEING A GHOST.
WITHOUT MEETING THAT GHOST'S EYES...
AND WITH NOTHING TO DO, I SAID...
OKAY. I'M HEADING OUT.
AND...
RIGHT.
I GOT...
THAT INDIFFERENT RESPONSE.

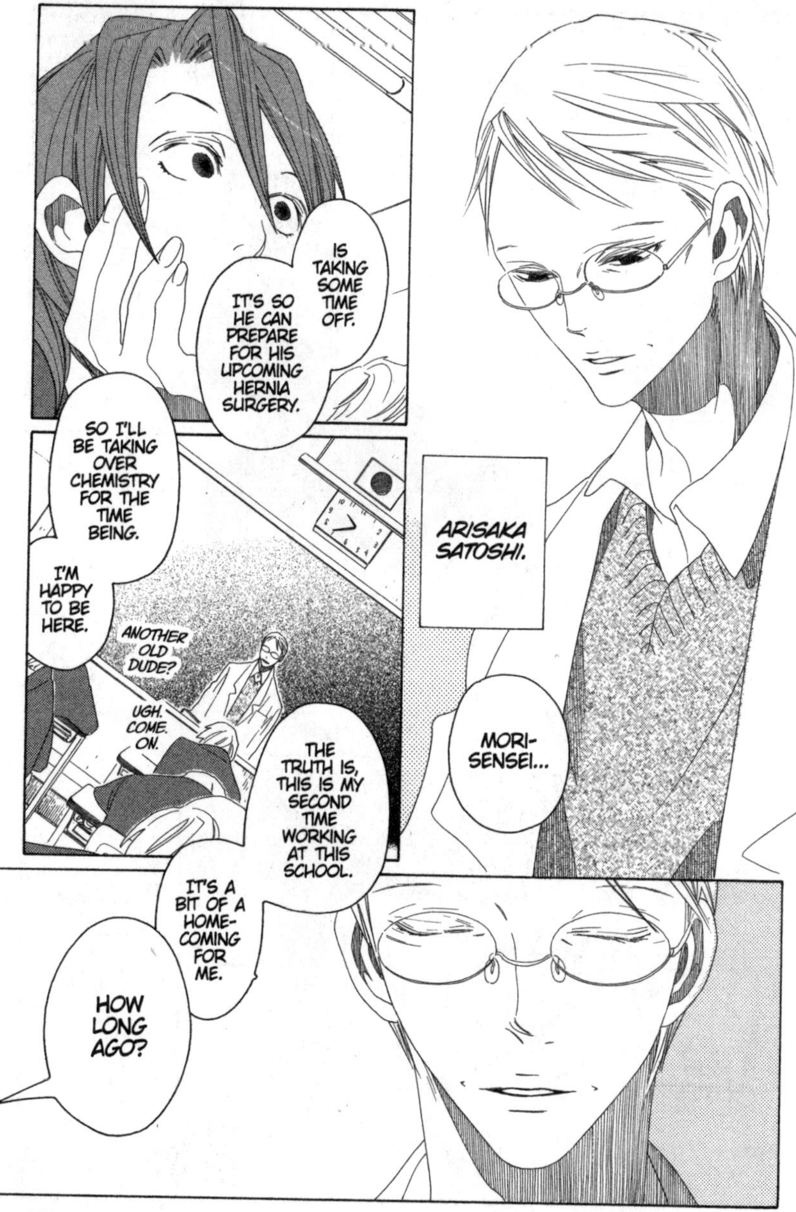
ARISAKA SATOSHI.
MORI-SENSEI...
IS TAKING SOME TIME OFF.
IT'S SO HE CAN PREPARE FOR HIS UPCOMING HERNIA SURGERY.
SO I'LL BE TAKING OVER CHEMISTRY FOR THE TIME BEING.
I'M HAPPY TO BE HERE.
ANOTHER OLD DUDE?
UGH. COME. ON.
THE TRUTH IS, THIS IS MY SECOND TIME WORKING AT THIS SCHOOL.
IT'S A BIT OF A HOMECOMING FOR ME.
HOW LONG AGO?

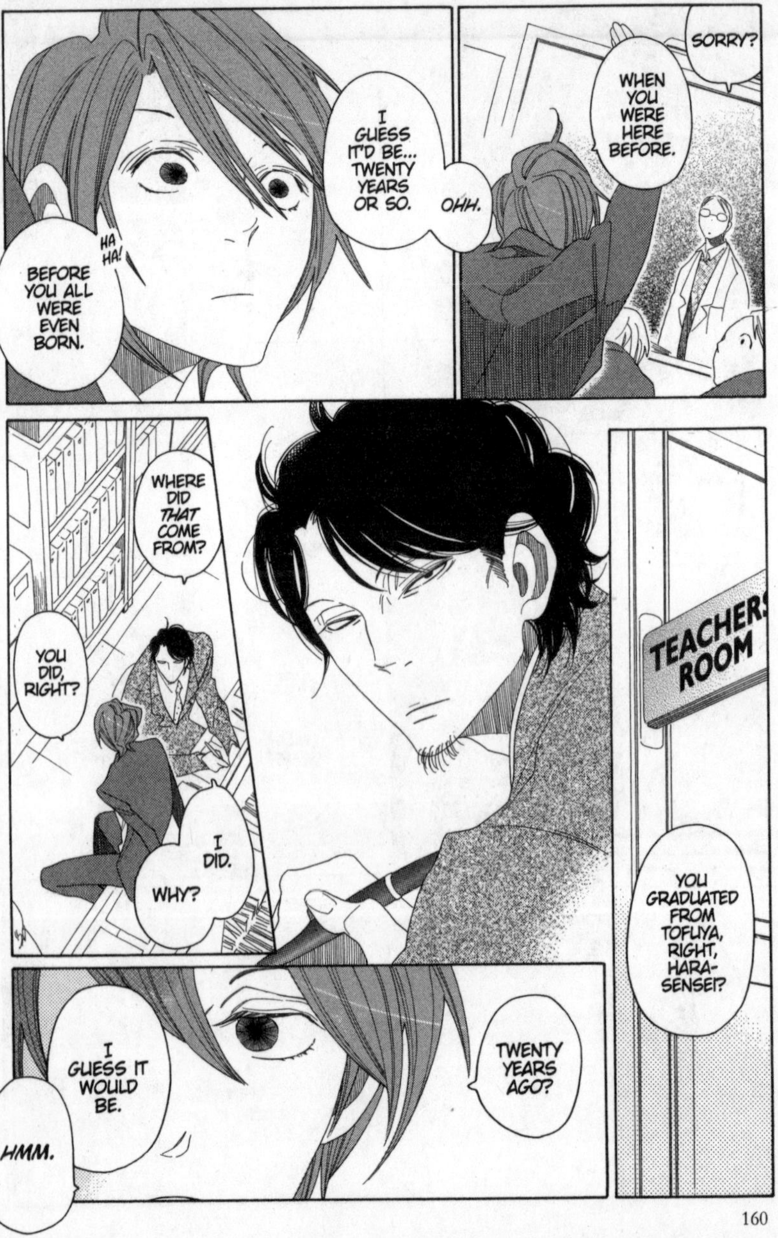
SORRY?
WHEN YOU WERE HERE BEFORE.
I GUESS IT'D BE... TWENTY YEARS OR SO.
OHH.
HA HA!
BEFORE YOU ALL WERE EVEN BORN.
TEACHERS ROOM
YOU GRADUATED FROM TOFUYA, RIGHT, HARA-SENSEI!?
WHERE DID *THAT* COME FROM?
YOU DID, RIGHT?
I DID.
WHY?
TWENTY YEARS AGO?
I GUESS IT WOULD BE.
HMM.

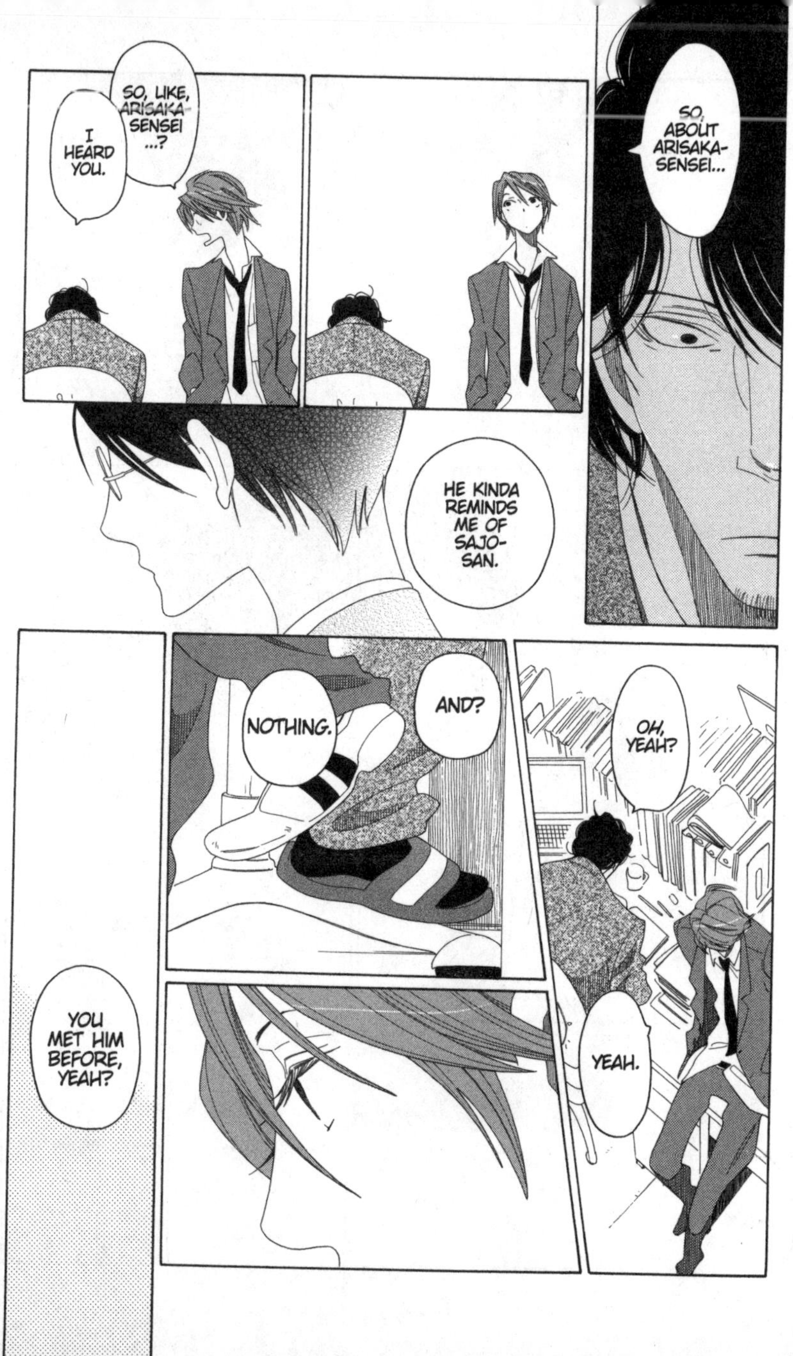
SO, ABOUT ARISAKA-SENSEI...
SO, LIKE, ARISAKA-SENSEI ...?
I HEARD YOU.
HE KINDA REMINDS ME OF SAJO-SAN.
OH, YEAH?
YEAH.
AND?
NOTHING.
YOU MET HIM BEFORE, YEAH?

YOU JUST KEEP TALKING...
HARA-SENSEI.
GAH!
YES?
KLATTER
OH!
ERR.
ABOUT THE KEY TO THE CHEM PREP ROOM...
"NOT AT ALL."
COME ON!
TCH!
SQUEAK
I'M SORRY.
WERE YOU IN THE MIDDLE OF SOME-THING?
NOT AT ALL!
MR. GOATEE ...
VRZZ
VRZZ
GOAT FACE!
BEEP
OH! MAIL.

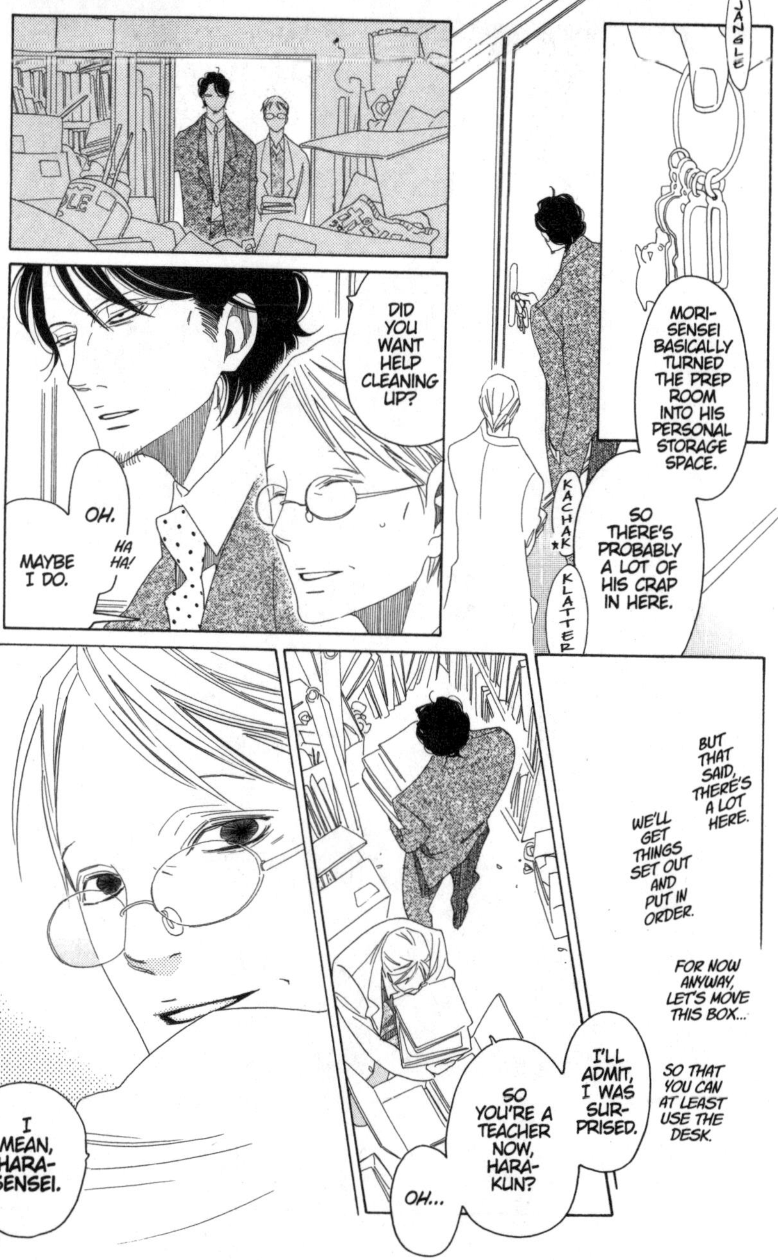
JANGLE
MORI-SENSEI BASICALLY TURNED THE PREP ROOM INTO HIS PERSONAL STORAGE SPACE.
KACHAK★
KLATTER
SO THERE'S PROBABLY A LOT OF HIS CRAP IN HERE.
DID YOU WANT HELP CLEANING UP?
OH.
MAYBE I DO.
HA HA!
BUT THAT SAID, THERE'S A LOT HERE.
WE'LL GET THINGS SET OUT AND PUT IN ORDER.
FOR NOW ANYWAY, LET'S MOVE THIS BOX...
SO THAT YOU CAN AT LEAST USE THE DESK.
I'LL ADMIT, I WAS SURPRISED.
SO YOU'RE A TEACHER NOW, HARA-KUN?
OH...
I MEAN, HARA-SENSEI.

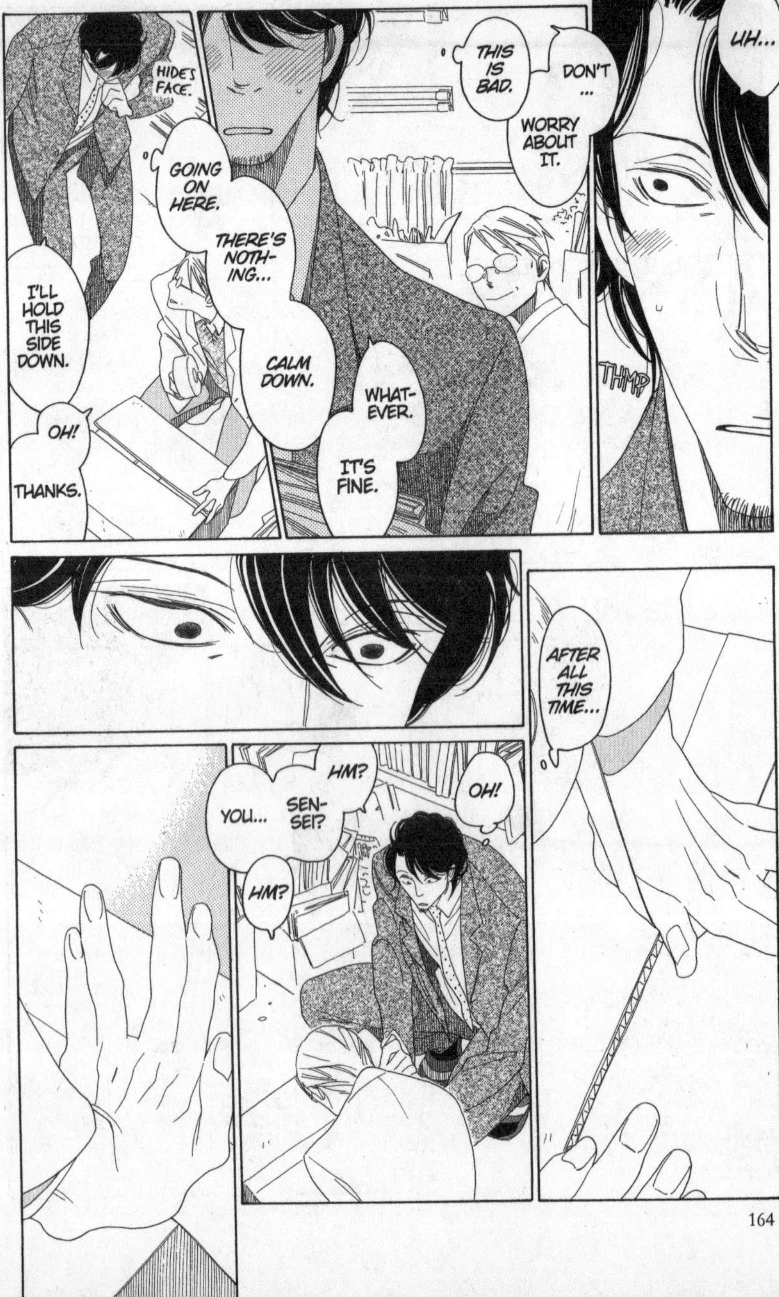
UH...
THMP
DON'T ...
WORRY ABOUT IT.
THIS IS BAD.
THERE'S NOTHING...
GOING ON HERE.
WHAT-EVER.
IT'S FINE.
CALM DOWN.
HIDES FACE.
I'LL HOLD THIS SIDE DOWN.
OH!
THANKS.
AFTER ALL THIS TIME...
OH!
HM?
SEN-SEI?
YOU...
HM?

OH.
NO RING?
IT'S NOTHING.
IF I ASK WHAT HAPPENED...
IT'LL LOOK LIKE I'M INTERESTED.
Desk ③
LIKE ...
"YOU MET HIM BEFORE, YEAH?"
HE KNOWS?
NO.
I MEAN ...
KNOWS WHAT?
THERE'S NOTHING TO KNOW. AND EVEN IF HE DID...
WHIRL
WHIRL
OH!
KLATTER
THERE YOU ARE, ARISAKA-SENSEI!
WE'RE THROWING YOU A WELCOME PARTY ONCE SCHOOL'S OUT TODAY! SO DON'T GO ANYWHERE!

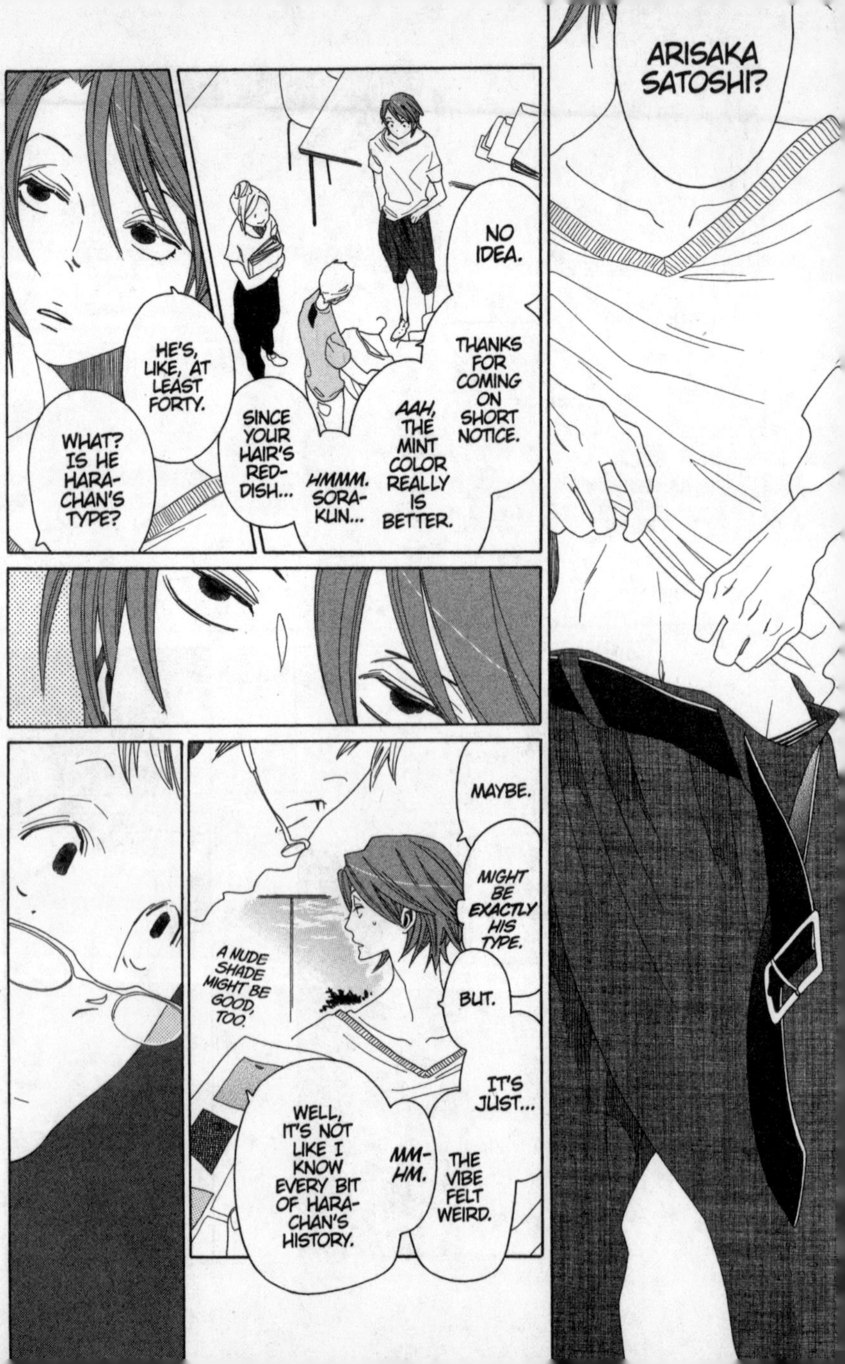
ARISAKA SATOSHI?
NO IDEA.
THANKS FOR COMING ON SHORT NOTICE.
AAH, THE MINT COLOR REALLY IS BETTER.
HMMM. SORA-KUN...
SINCE YOUR HAIR'S RED-DISH...
HE'S, LIKE, AT LEAST FORTY.
WHAT? IS HE HARA-CHAN'S TYPE?
MAYBE.
MIGHT BE EXACTLY HIS TYPE.
BUT.
IT'S JUST...
THE VIBE FELT WEIRD.
A NUDE SHADE MIGHT BE GOOD, TOO.
MM-HM.
WELL, IT'S NOT LIKE I KNOW EVERY BIT OF HARA-CHAN'S HISTORY.

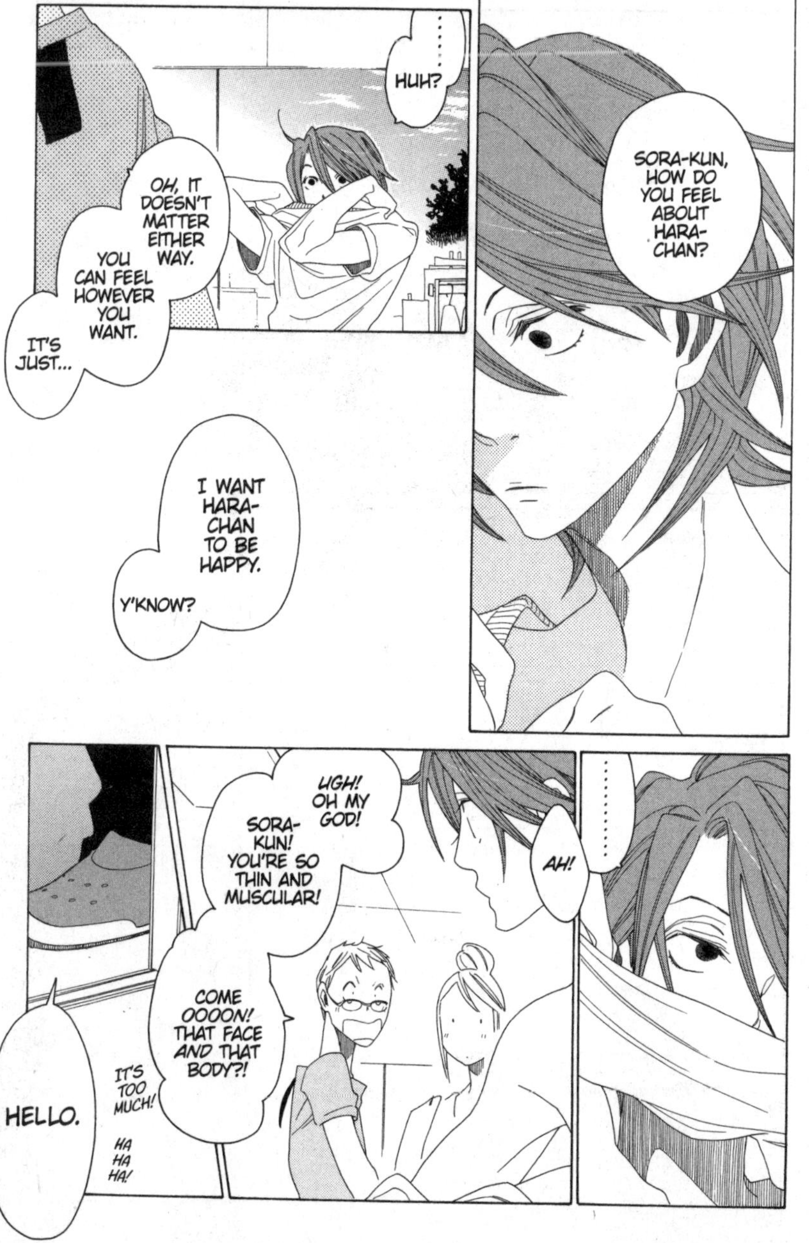
SORA-KUN, HOW DO YOU FEEL ABOUT HARA-CHAN?
...
HUH?
OH, IT DOESN'T MATTER EITHER WAY.
YOU CAN FEEL HOWEVER YOU WANT.
IT'S JUST...
I WANT HARA-CHAN TO BE HAPPY.
Y'KNOW?
...
AH!
UGH! OH MY GOD!
SORA-KUN! YOU'RE SO THIN AND MUSCULAR!
COME OOOON! THAT FACE AND THAT BODY?!
IT'S TOO MUCH!
HA HA HA!
HELLO.

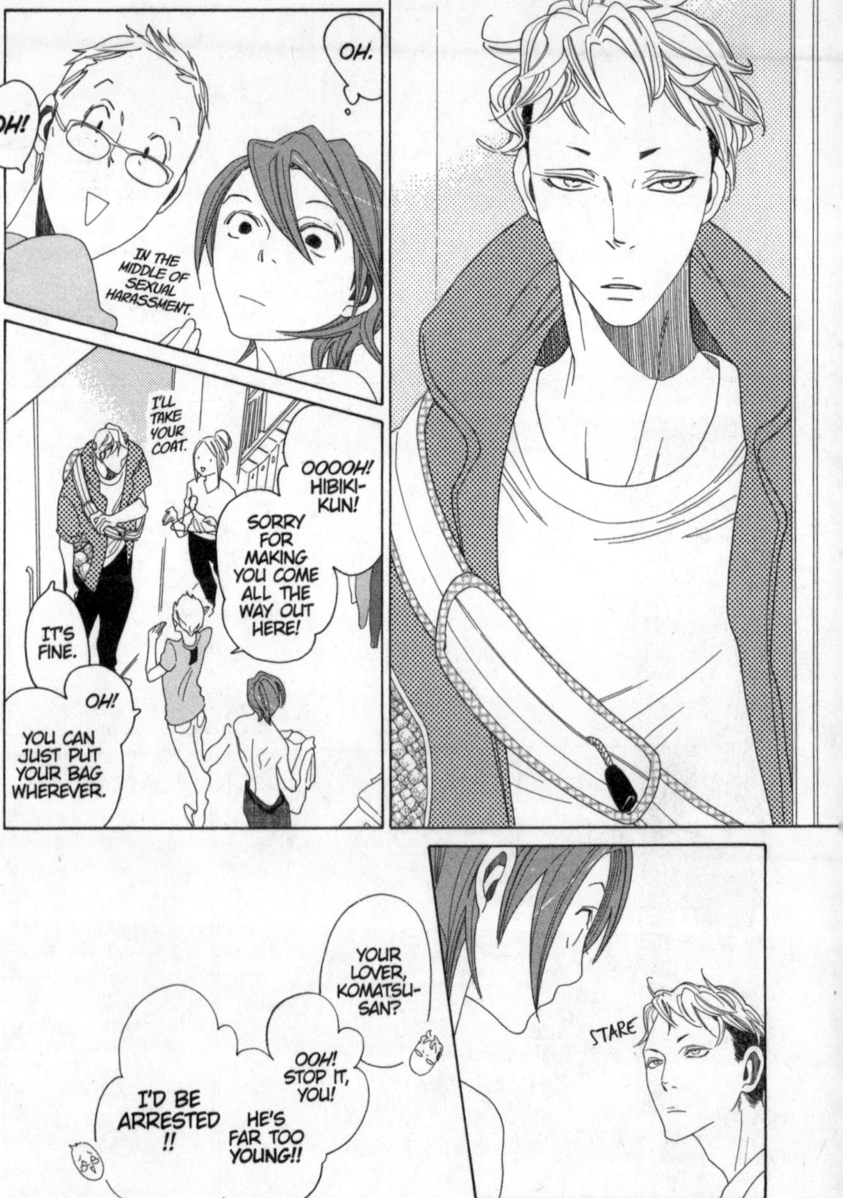
OH.
OH!
IN THE MIDDLE OF SEXUAL HARASSMENT.
OOOOH! HIBIKI-KUN!
SORRY FOR MAKING YOU COME ALL THE WAY OUT HERE!
I'LL TAKE YOUR COAT.
IT'S FINE.
OH!
YOU CAN JUST PUT YOUR BAG WHEREVER.
STARE
YOUR LOVER, KOMATSU-SAN?
OOH! STOP IT, YOU!
HE'S FAR TOO YOUNG!!
I'D BE ARRESTED !!

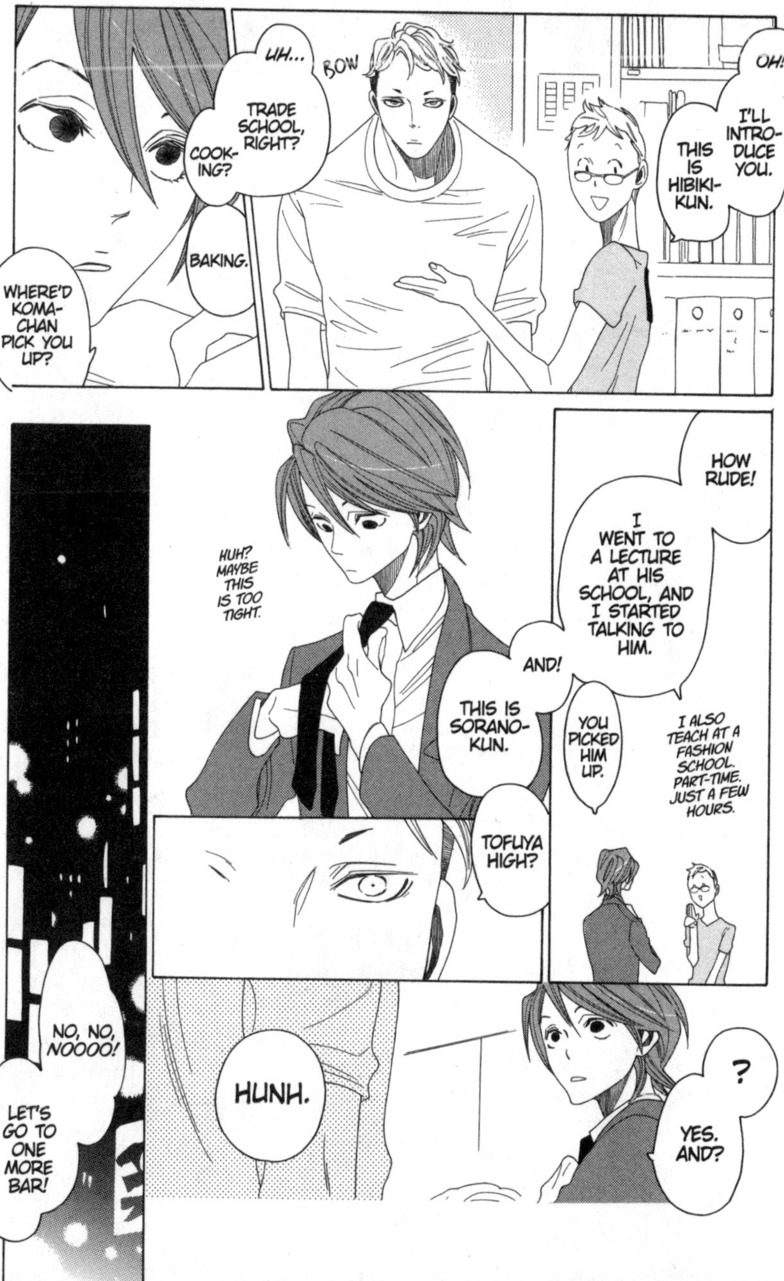
OH!
I'LL INTRODUCE YOU.
THIS IS HIBIKI-KUN.
UH...
BOW
TRADE SCHOOL, RIGHT?
COOKING?
BAKING.
WHERE'D KOMA-CHAN PICK YOU UP?
HOW RUDE!
I WENT TO A LECTURE AT HIS SCHOOL, AND I STARTED TALKING TO HIM.
I ALSO TEACH AT A FASHION SCHOOL. PART-TIME. JUST A FEW HOURS.
YOU PICKED HIM UP.
AND!
THIS IS SORANO-KUN.
HUH? MAYBE THIS IS TOO TIGHT.
TOFUYA HIGH?
?
YES. AND?
HUNH.
NO, NO, *NOOOO!*
LET'S GO TO ONE MORE BAR!

YOU'RE THE GUEST OF HONOR! YOU CAN'T LEAVE!
COME ON!
THE NIGHT'S YOUNG!
LET'S GO DO KARA-OKE!!
SORRY. I'M ALREADY FEELING THOSE DRINKS.
OH.
I'LL SEE YOU OFF.
WHAAAAT? THE TWO YOUNG'UNS ARE LEAVING?
"YOUNG'UNS"?
DO THE YOUNG PEOPLE NOT DRINK THESE DAYS?
SENSEI, YOU HAVE TO SING THAT ONE! "DAITOKAI"!
WHOOPSY! SORRY!
I DON'T KNOOOOW.
SLAM
SEPARATE CABS
HAAH ...
YUP.
VRRRR
SAME AS IT EVER WAS.
THEY'RE SO FULL OF LIFE.
HA HA!
DID YOU USED TO GO WITH THEM?
THAT I DID.
I'D SING "FUNAUTA."
HA HA HA!
KRCH
AAH.
THE BREEZE IS NICE.
THEY WERE WHEN I WORKED HERE BEFORE, TOO.
AT ANY RATE, THEY ALL LOVE KARAOKE.

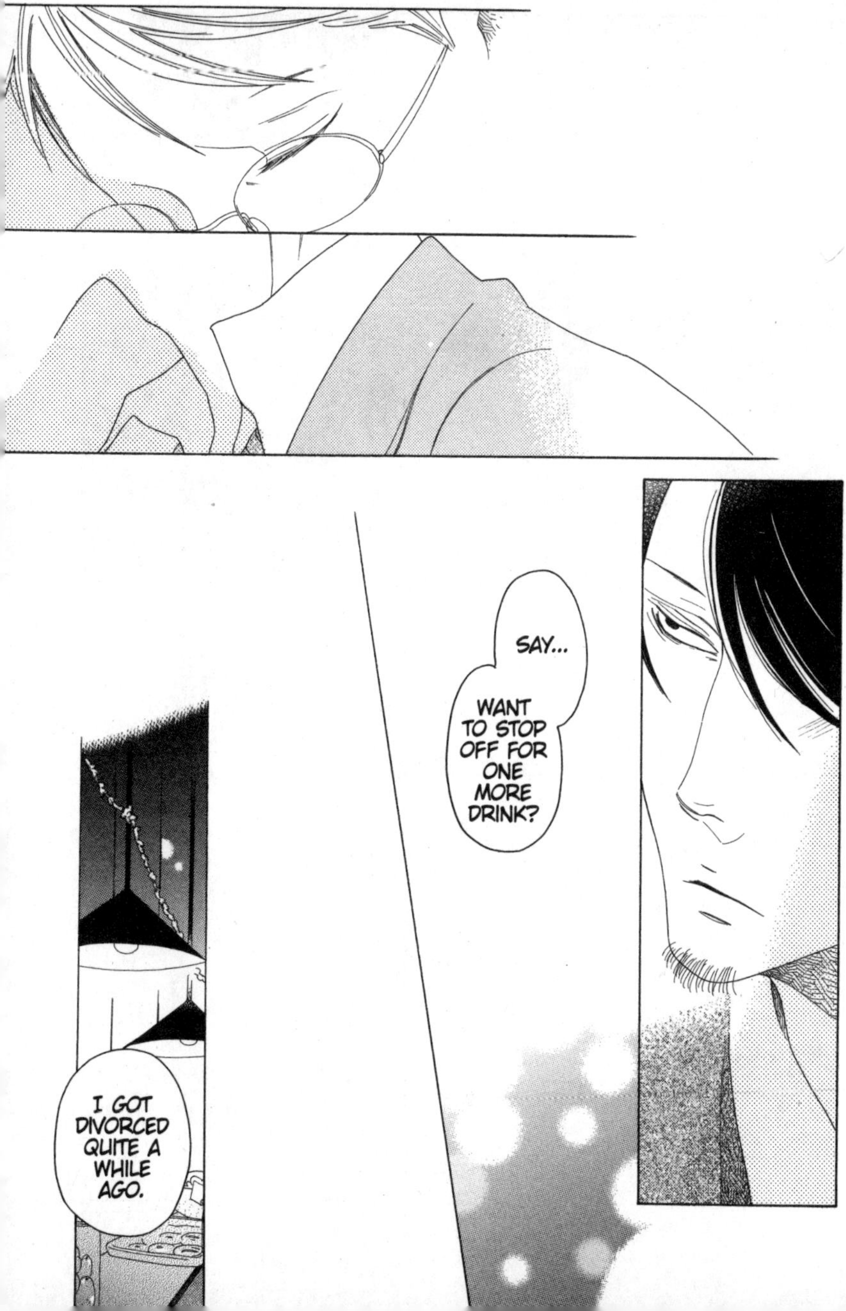
SAY...
WANT TO STOP OFF FOR ONE MORE DRINK?
I GOT DIVORCED QUITE A WHILE AGO.

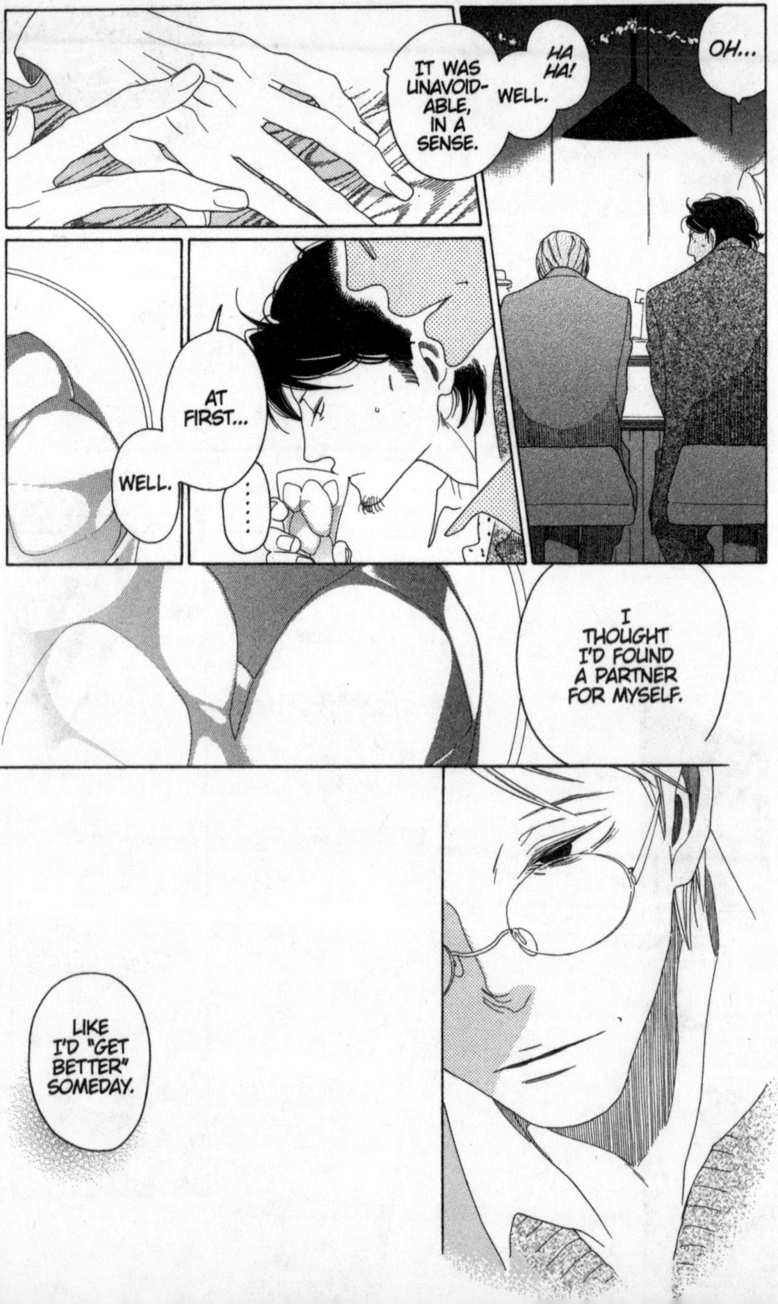
OH...
HA HA!
WELL.
IT WAS UNAVOIDABLE, IN A SENSE.
......
AT FIRST...
WELL.
I THOUGHT I'D FOUND A PARTNER FOR MYSELF.
LIKE I'D "GET BETTER" SOMEDAY.

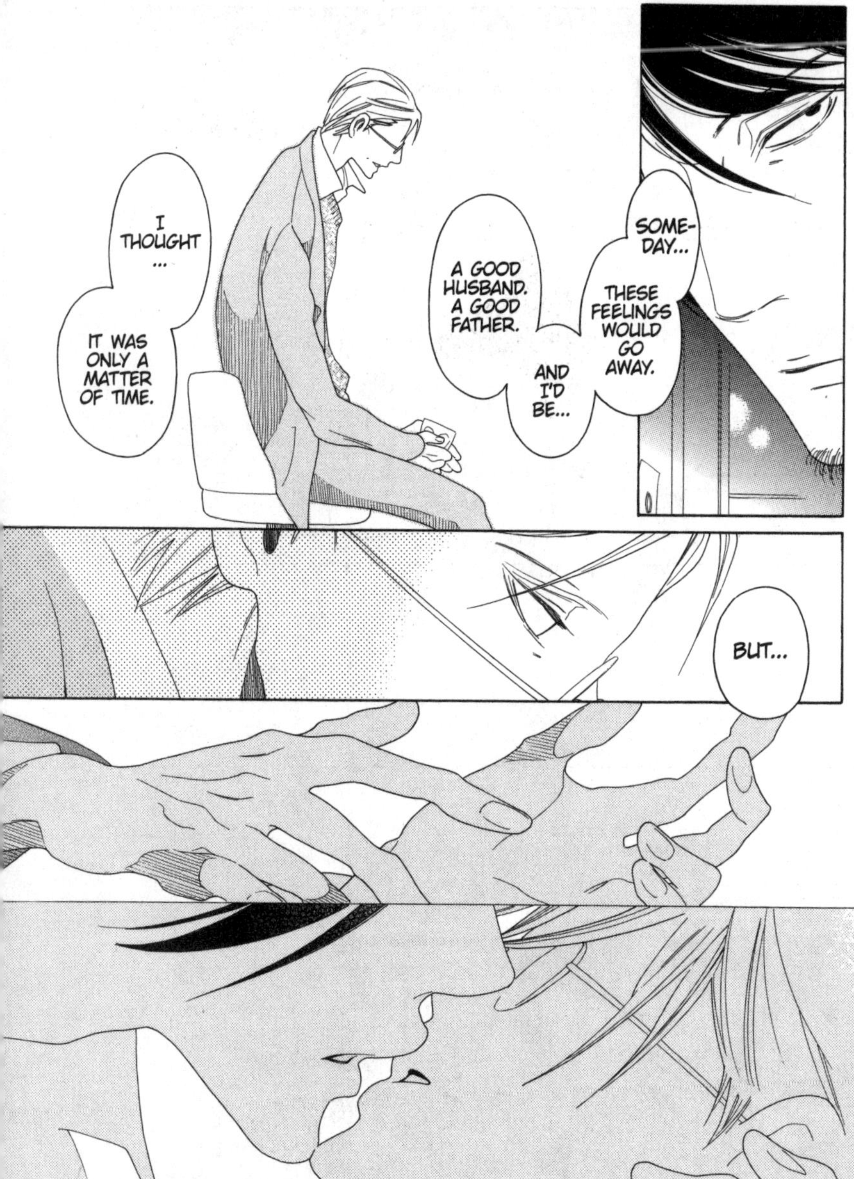
SOME-DAY...
THESE FEELINGS WOULD GO AWAY.
AND I'D BE...
A GOOD HUSBAND. A GOOD FATHER.
I THOUGHT ...
IT WAS ONLY A MATTER OF TIME.
BUT...

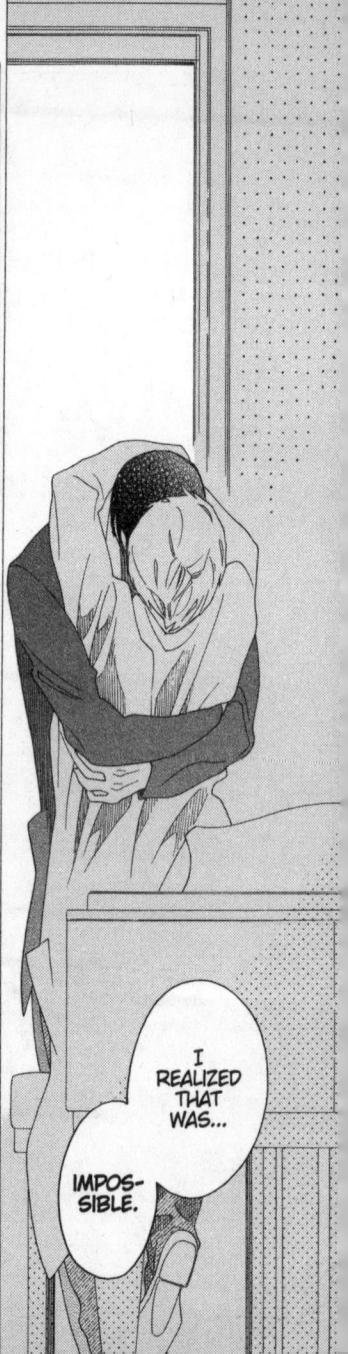

SORRY. I'M JUST JABBERING AWAY.

NO.

AND TO A FORMER STUDENT.

I'M NOT YOUR STUDENT ANYMORE.

SO. WHAT HAPPENED?

YIKES.

UH...

AH!

......

I REALIZED THAT WAS...

IMPOSSIBLE.

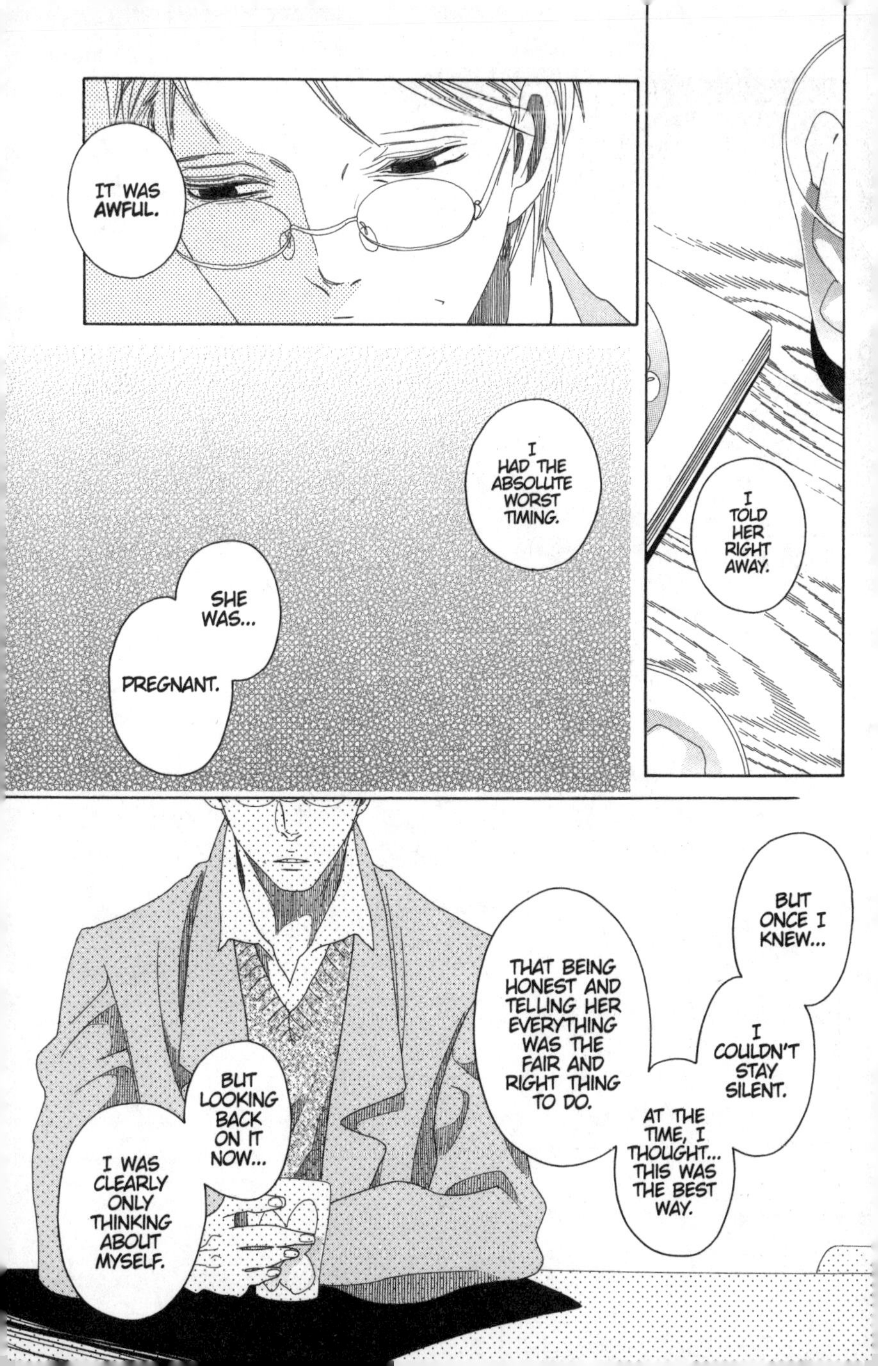
I TOLD HER RIGHT AWAY.
IT WAS AWFUL.
I HAD THE ABSOLUTE WORST TIMING.
SHE WAS... PREGNANT.
BUT ONCE I KNEW...
I COULDN'T STAY SILENT.
THAT BEING HONEST AND TELLING HER EVERYTHING WAS THE FAIR AND RIGHT THING TO DO.
AT THE TIME, I THOUGHT... THIS WAS THE BEST WAY.
BUT LOOKING BACK ON IT NOW...
I WAS CLEARLY ONLY THINKING ABOUT MYSELF.

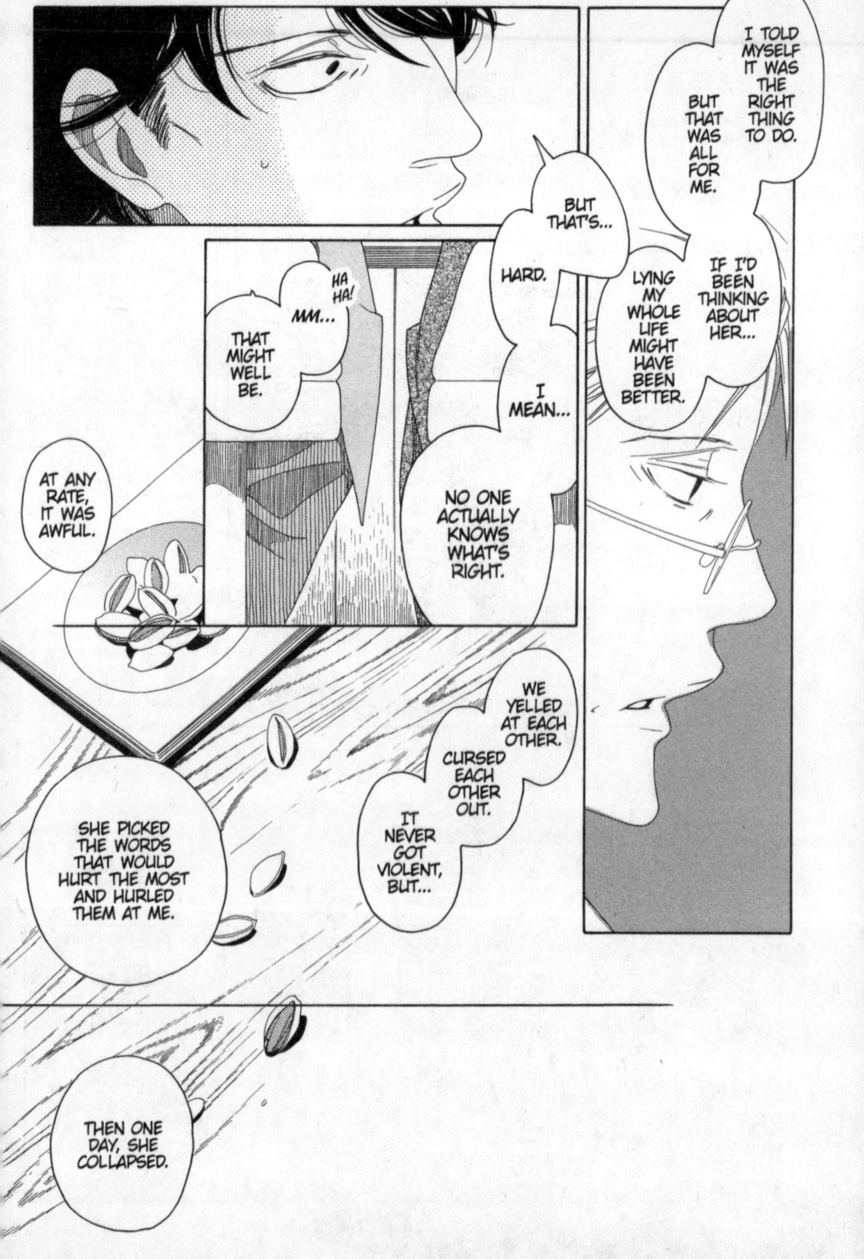
I TOLD MYSELF IT WAS THE RIGHT THING TO DO.
BUT THAT WAS ALL FOR ME.
IF I'D BEEN THINKING ABOUT HER...
LYING MY WHOLE LIFE MIGHT HAVE BEEN BETTER.
BUT THAT'S...
HARD.
I MEAN...
NO ONE ACTUALLY KNOWS WHAT'S RIGHT.
HA HA!
MM...
THAT MIGHT WELL BE.
AT ANY RATE, IT WAS AWFUL.
WE YELLED AT EACH OTHER.
CURSED EACH OTHER OUT.
IT NEVER GOT VIOLENT, BUT...
SHE PICKED THE WORDS THAT WOULD HURT THE MOST AND HURLED THEM AT ME.
THEN ONE DAY, SHE COLLAPSED.

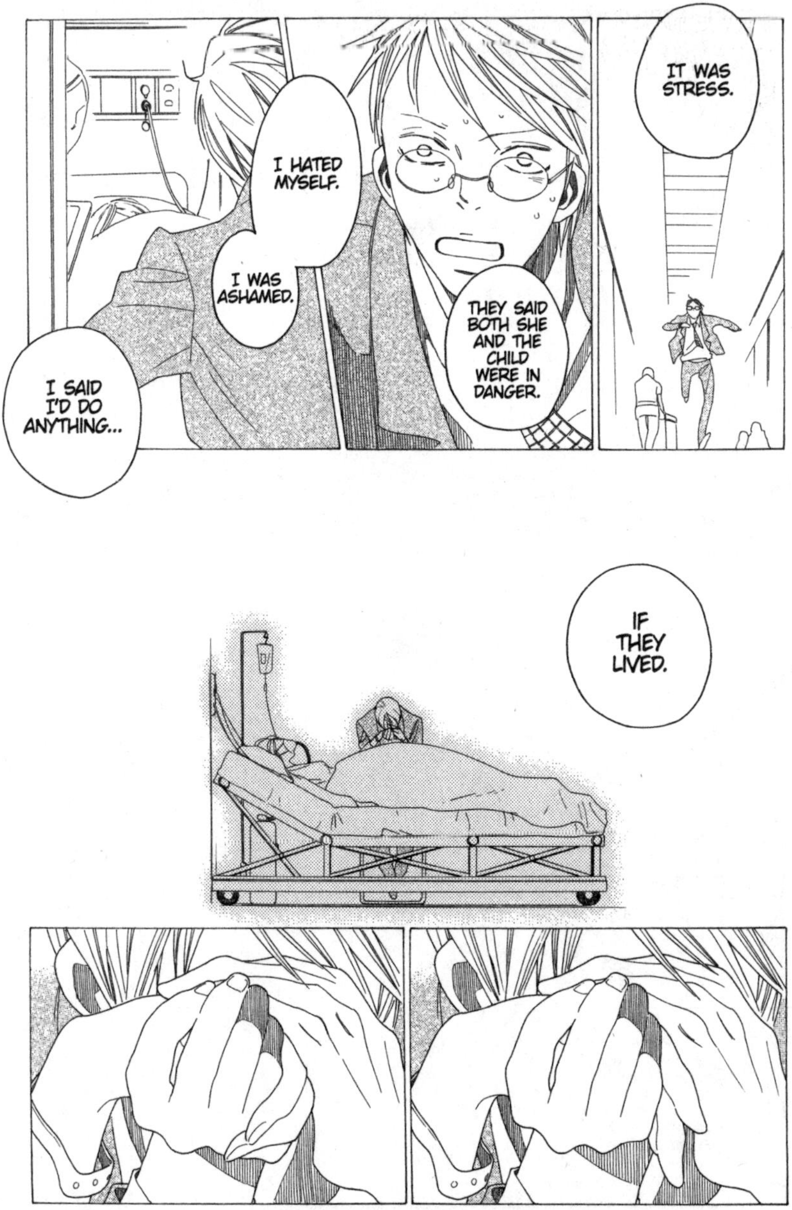
IT WAS STRESS.
THEY SAID BOTH SHE AND THE CHILD WERE IN DANGER.
I HATED MYSELF.
I WAS ASHAMED.
I SAID I'D DO ANYTHING...
IF THEY LIVED.

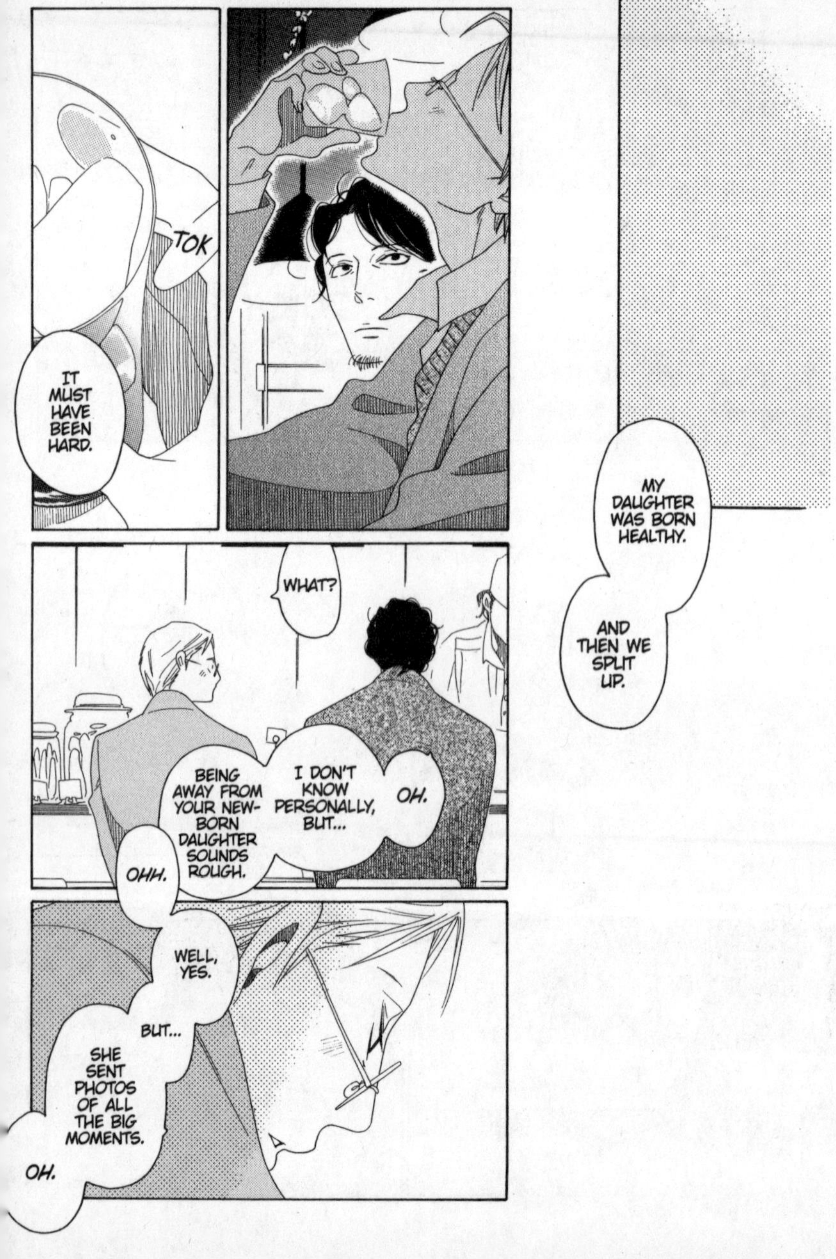
MY DAUGHTER WAS BORN HEALTHY.
AND THEN WE SPLIT UP.
TOK
IT MUST HAVE BEEN HARD.
WHAT?
OH.
I DON'T KNOW PERSONALLY, BUT...
BEING AWAY FROM YOUR NEW-BORN DAUGHTER SOUNDS ROUGH.
OHH.
WELL, YES.
BUT...
SHE SENT PHOTOS OF ALL THE BIG MOMENTS.
OH.

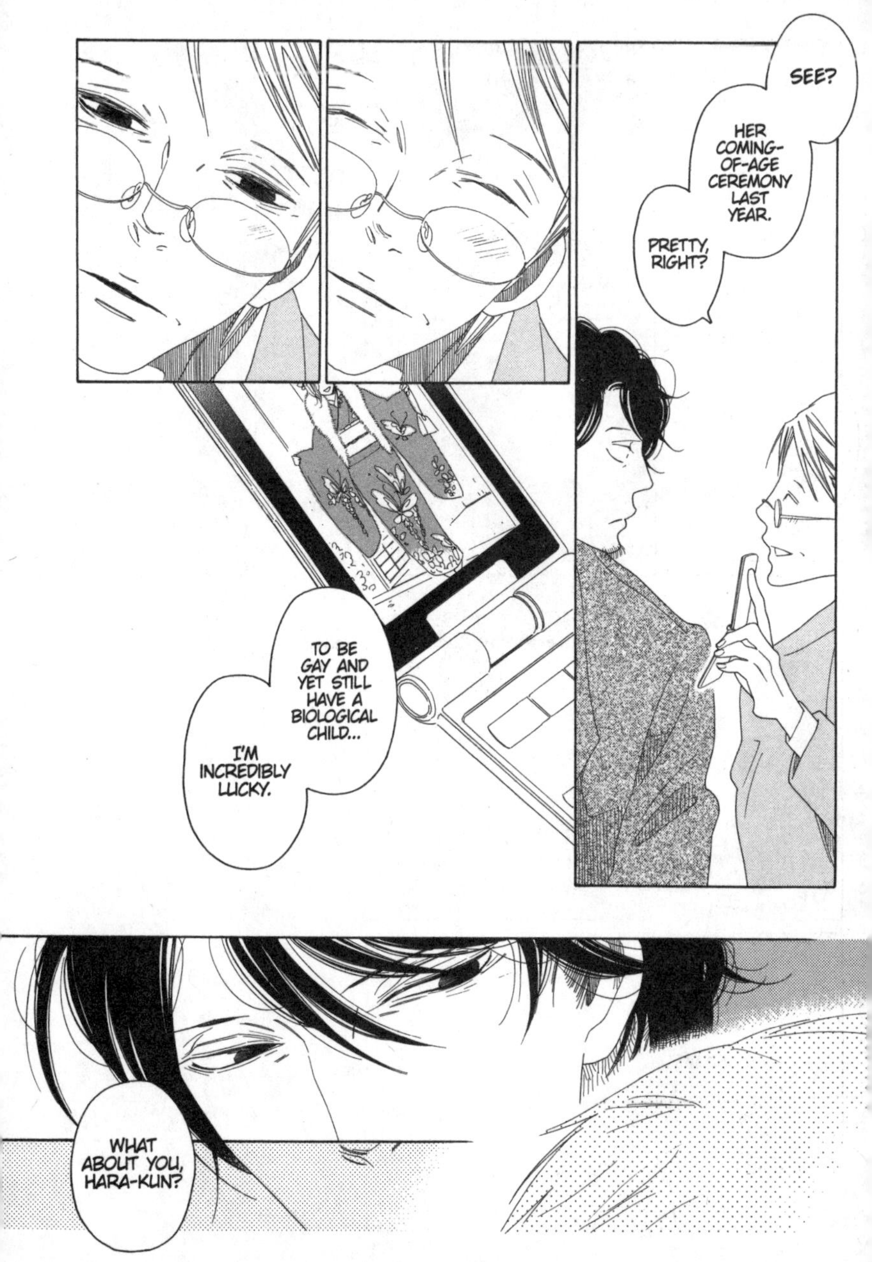
SEE?
HER COMING-OF-AGE CEREMONY LAST YEAR.
PRETTY, RIGHT?
TO BE GAY AND YET STILL HAVE A BIOLOGICAL CHILD...
I'M INCREDIBLY LUCKY.
WHAT ABOUT YOU, HARA-KUN?

UH?!
MAR-RIED?
UH?!
NO! NOT YET!
NO? OH, WELL.
WAIT. DOES HE...
SO...A PARTNER?
UH!
NO. THAT'S, WELL...
NOPE, NOTHING.
MAYBE HE DOESN'T KNOW I'M GAY.
WHAT?
BUT YOU SEEM LIKE YOU'D BE LUCKY IN LOVE.
SO CASUAL!
OR...
HA HA! LISTEN TO ME!
I SOUND LIKE AN OLD MAN!
SORRY.
ALTHOUGH I AM AN OLD MAN!
TO START WITH, YOU...

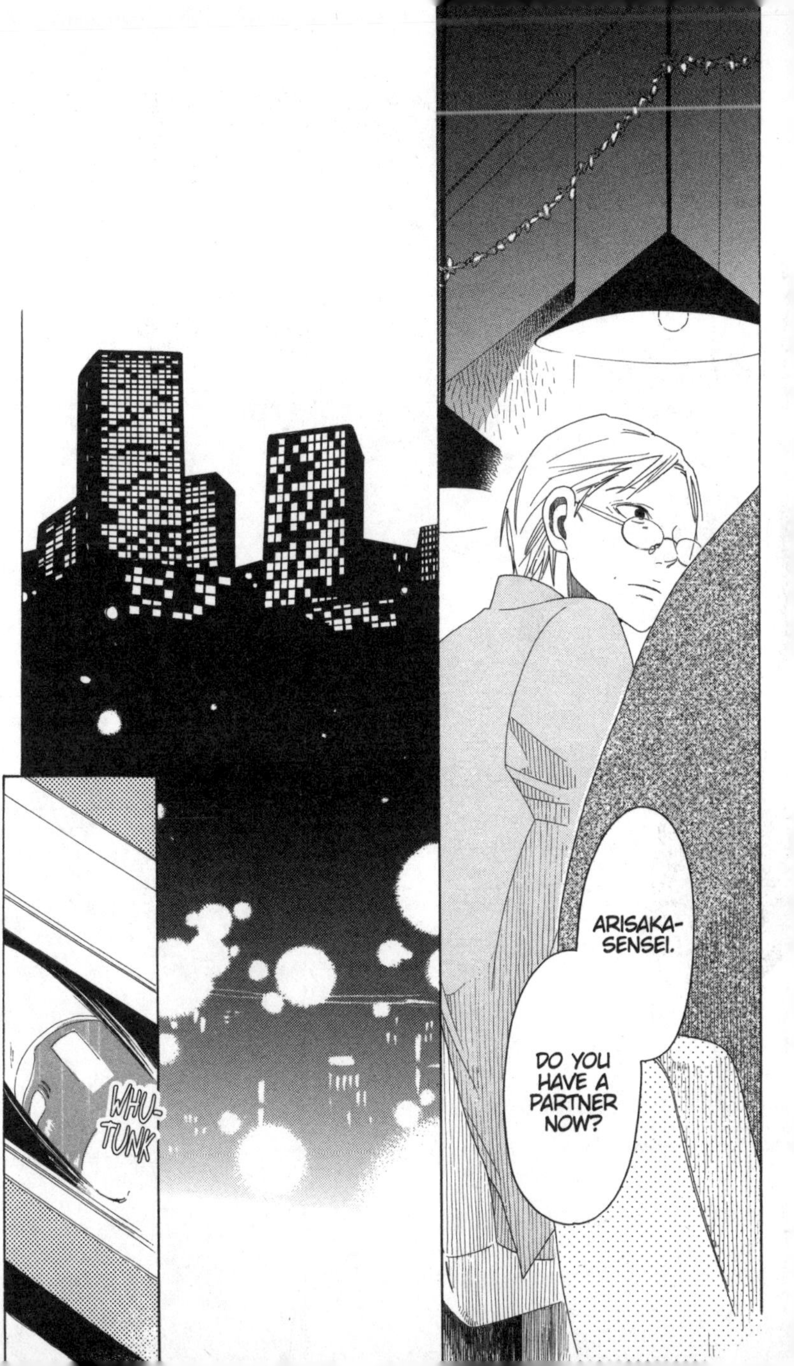
ARISAKA-SENSEI.
DO YOU HAVE A PARTNER NOW?
WHU-TUNK

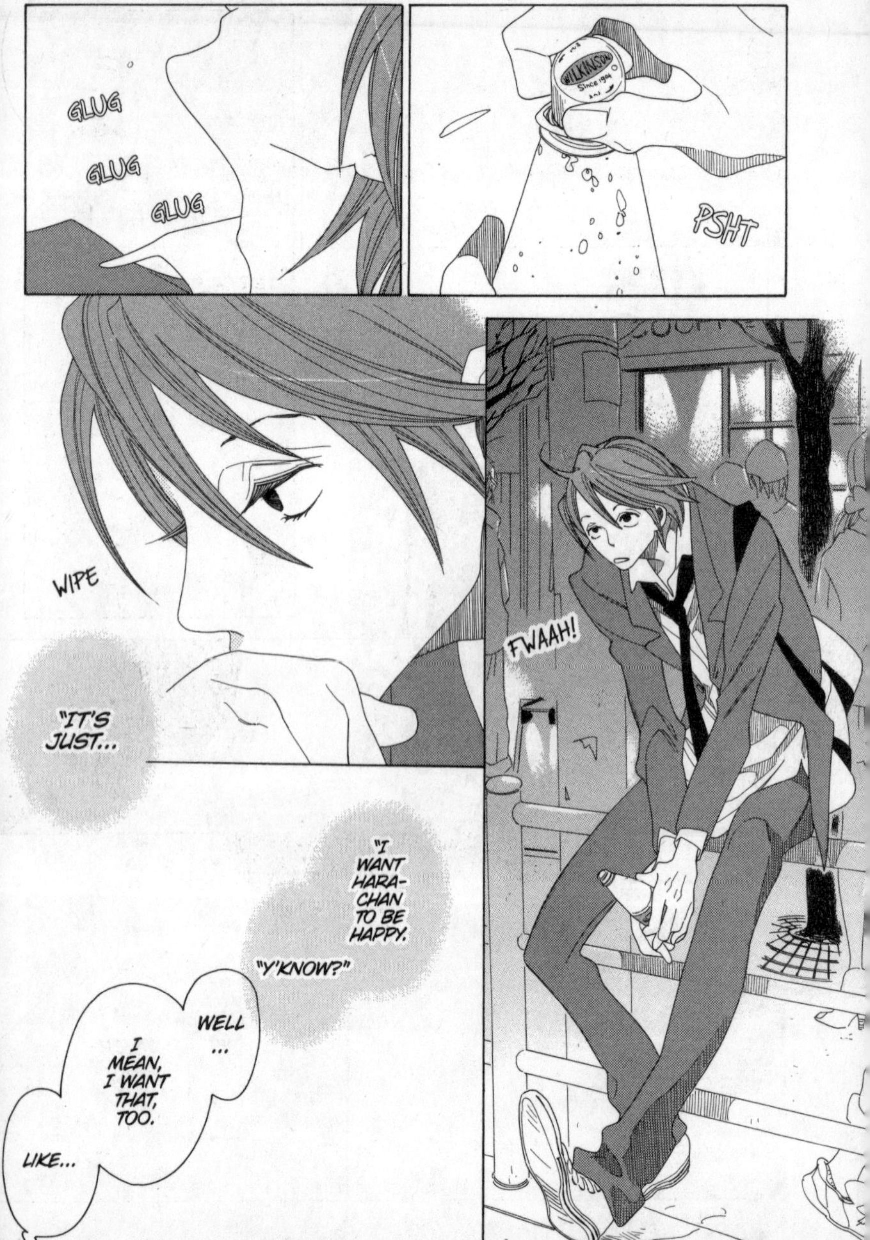
WILKINSON
Since 1904
PSHT
GLUG
GLUG
GLUG
FWAAH!
WIPE
"IT'S JUST...
"I WANT HARA-CHAN TO BE HAPPY.
"Y'KNOW?"
WELL...
I MEAN, I WANT THAT, TOO.
LIKE...

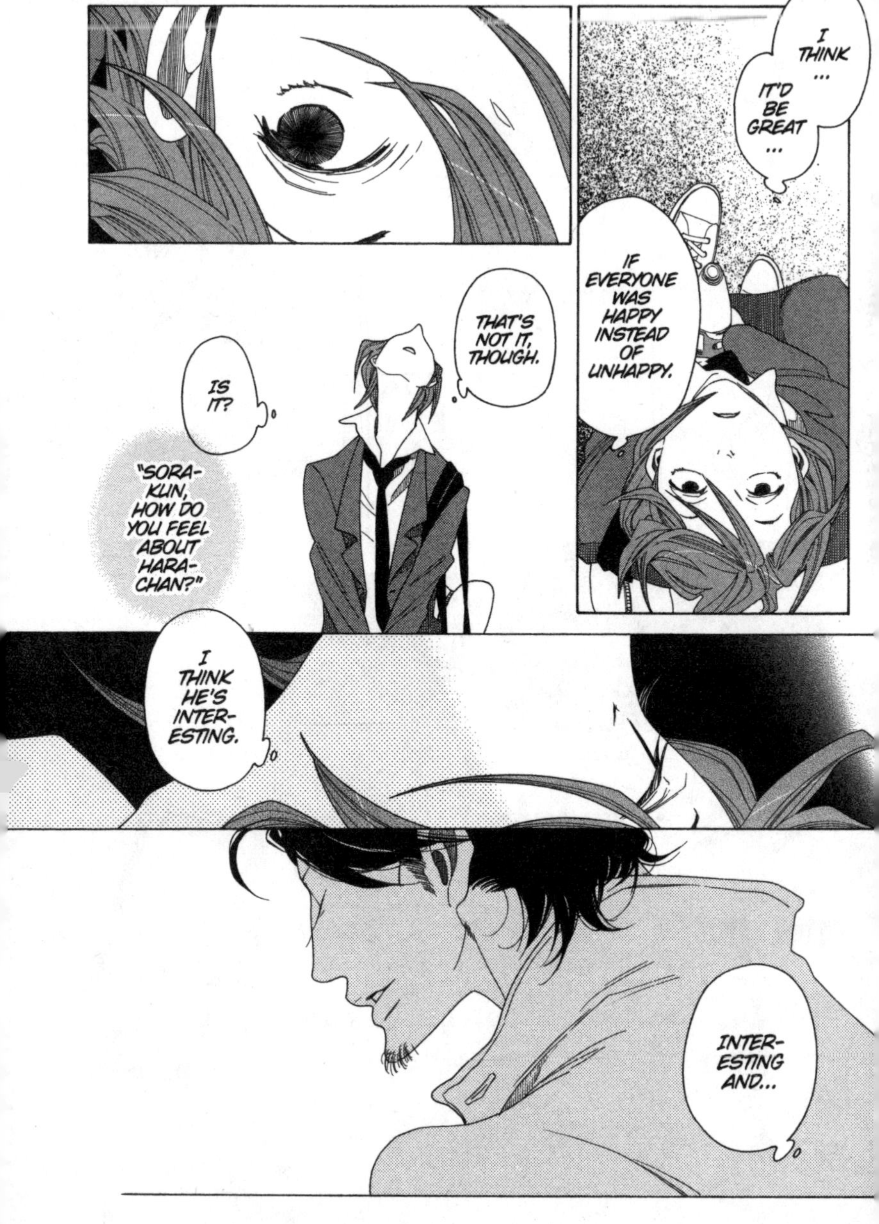
I THINK ...
IT'D BE GREAT ...
IF EVERYONE WAS HAPPY INSTEAD OF UNHAPPY.
THAT'S NOT IT, THOUGH.
IS IT?
"SORA-KUN, HOW DO YOU FEEL ABOUT HARA-CHAN?"
I THINK HE'S INTER-ESTING.
INTER-ESTING AND...

CLAP
NO. WAIT...
SNAP
NO. BUT ...
SNAP
CLAP
UNNNNNH.
FINE.
SNAP
BEEP
CALLING
SENSEI
RRRRRING
RRRRRING
VRZZ
VRZZ
VRZZ
VRZZ RRING
BEEP
HELLO?
OH!
YOU ANSWER-ED.

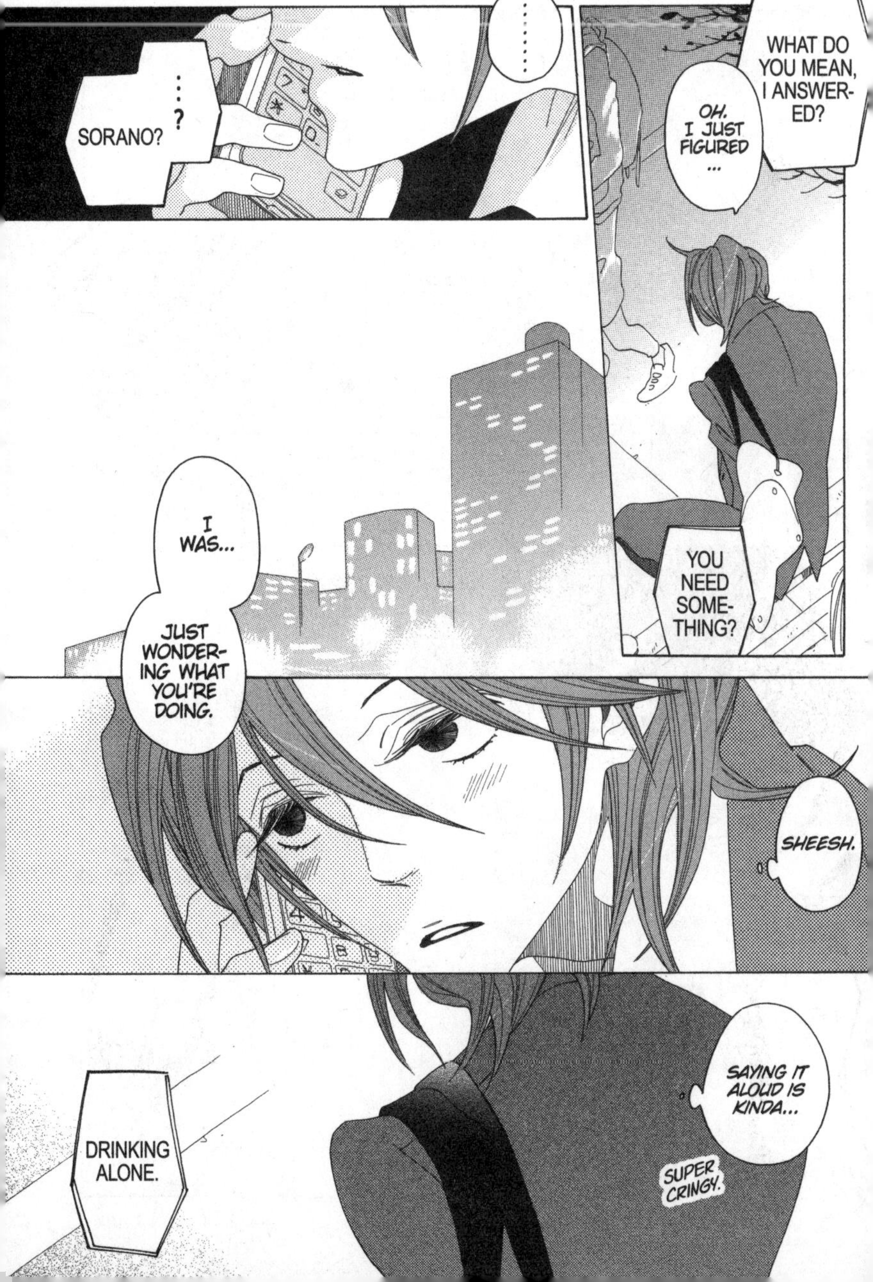
WHAT DO YOU MEAN, I ANSWERED?
OH. I JUST FIGURED ...
YOU NEED SOMETHING?
......
...? SORANO?
I WAS...
JUST WONDERING WHAT YOU'RE DOING.
SHEESH.
SAYING IT ALOUD IS KINDA...
SUPER CRINGY.
DRINKING ALONE.

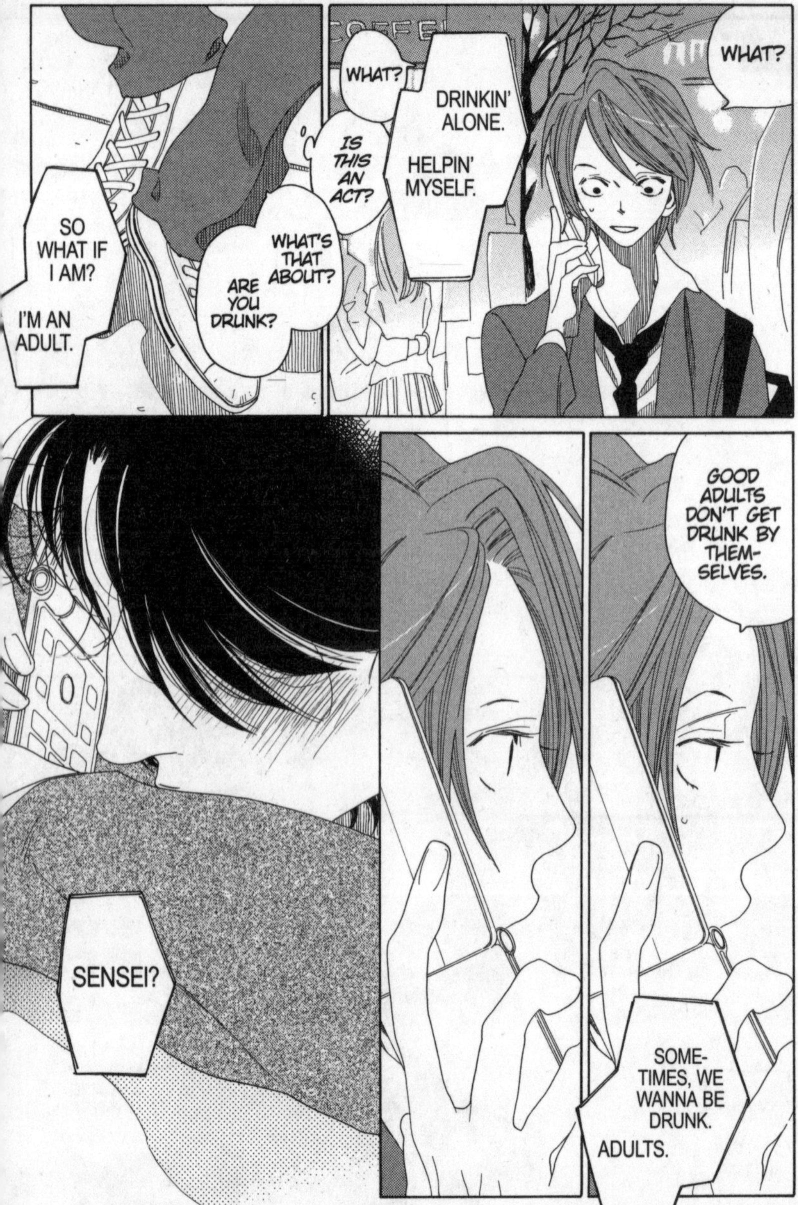
WHAT?
DRINKIN' ALONE.
HELPIN' MYSELF.
WHAT?
IS THIS AN ACT?
WHAT'S THAT ABOUT?
ARE YOU DRUNK?
SO WHAT IF I AM?
I'M AN ADULT.
GOOD ADULTS DON'T GET DRUNK BY THEM-SELVES.
SOME-TIMES, WE WANNA BE DRUNK.
ADULTS.
SENSEI?

I'M A BIT TIPSY.

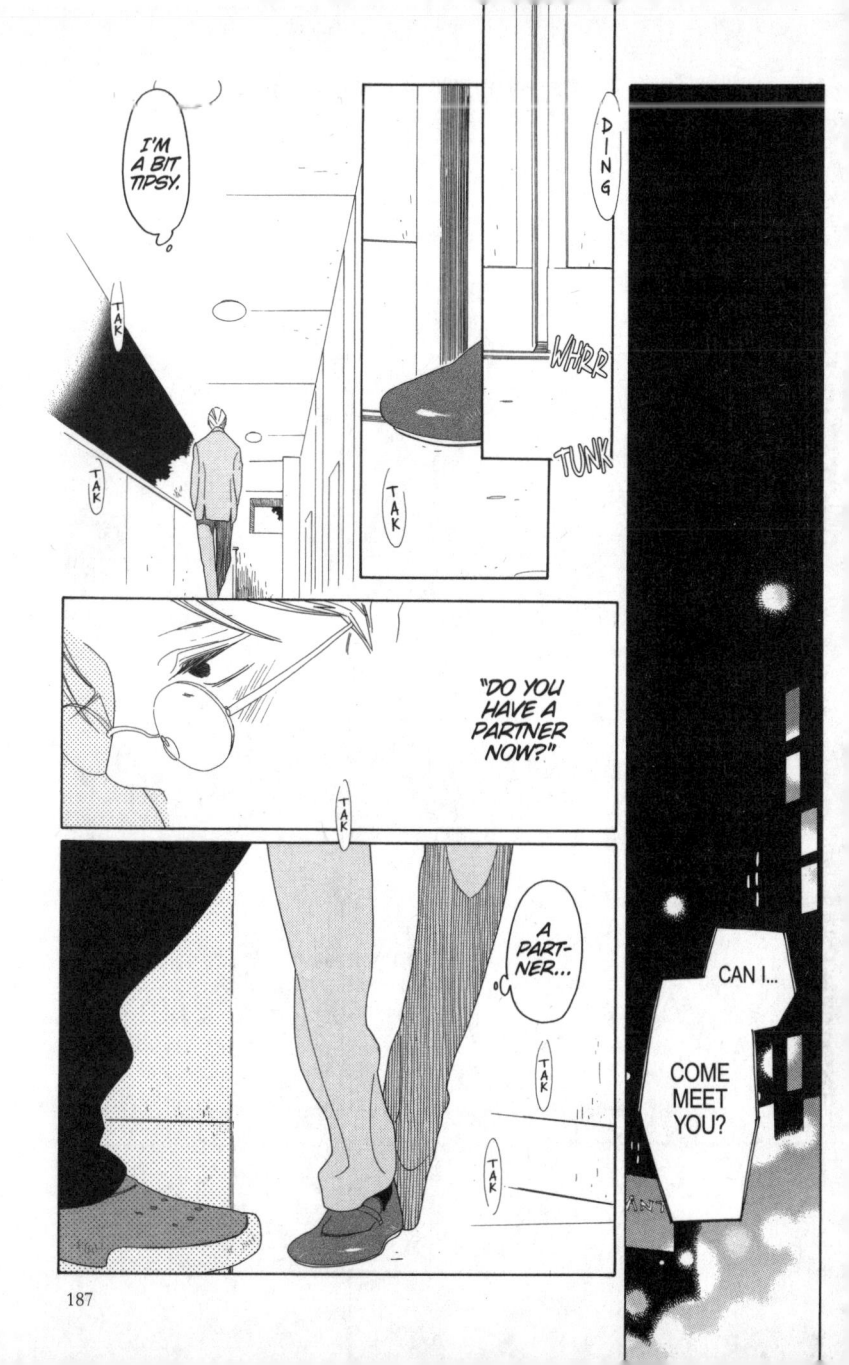

DING
WHRR
TUNK

TAK
TAK
TAK

"DO YOU HAVE A PARTNER NOW?"

A PARTNER...

TAK
TAK
TAK

CAN I...

COME MEET YOU?

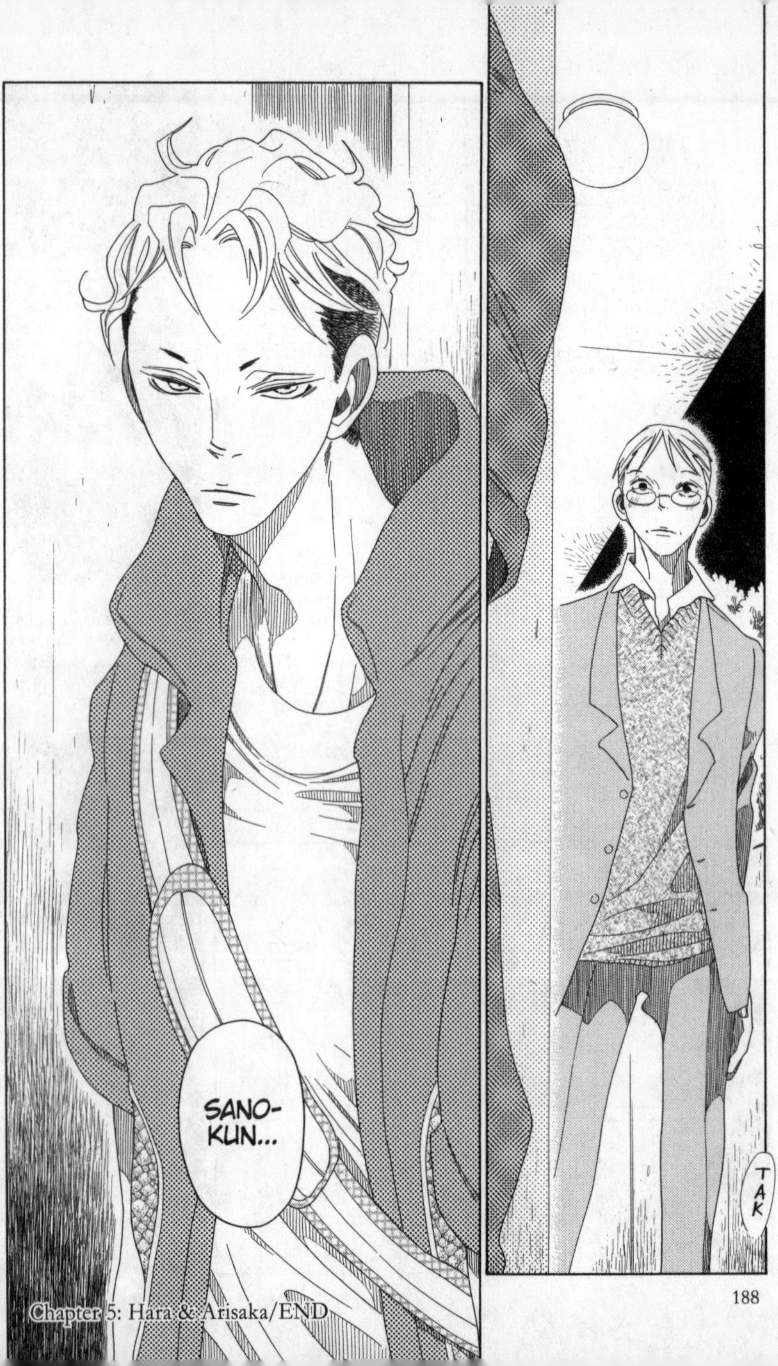
TAK
SANO-KUN...

Chapter 5: Hara & Arisaka/END

[Chapter 6: Sora and the Drunk]

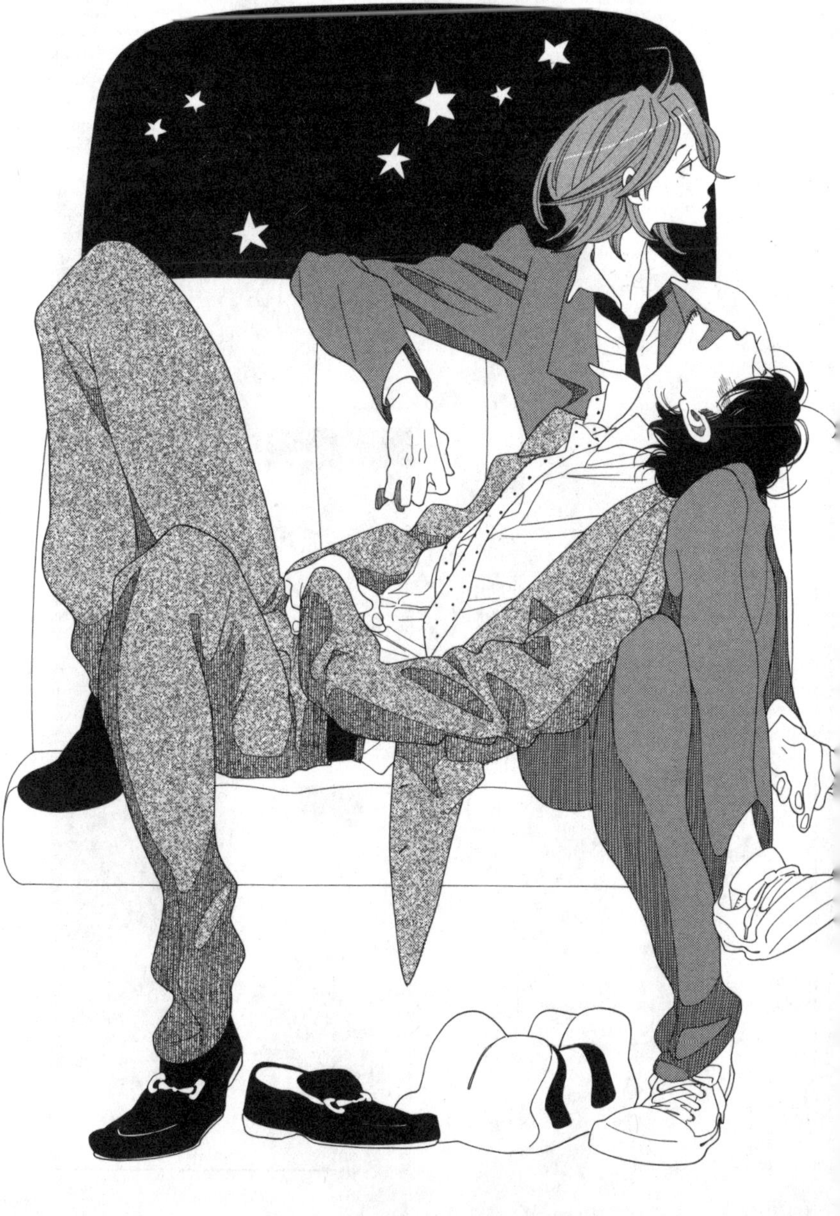

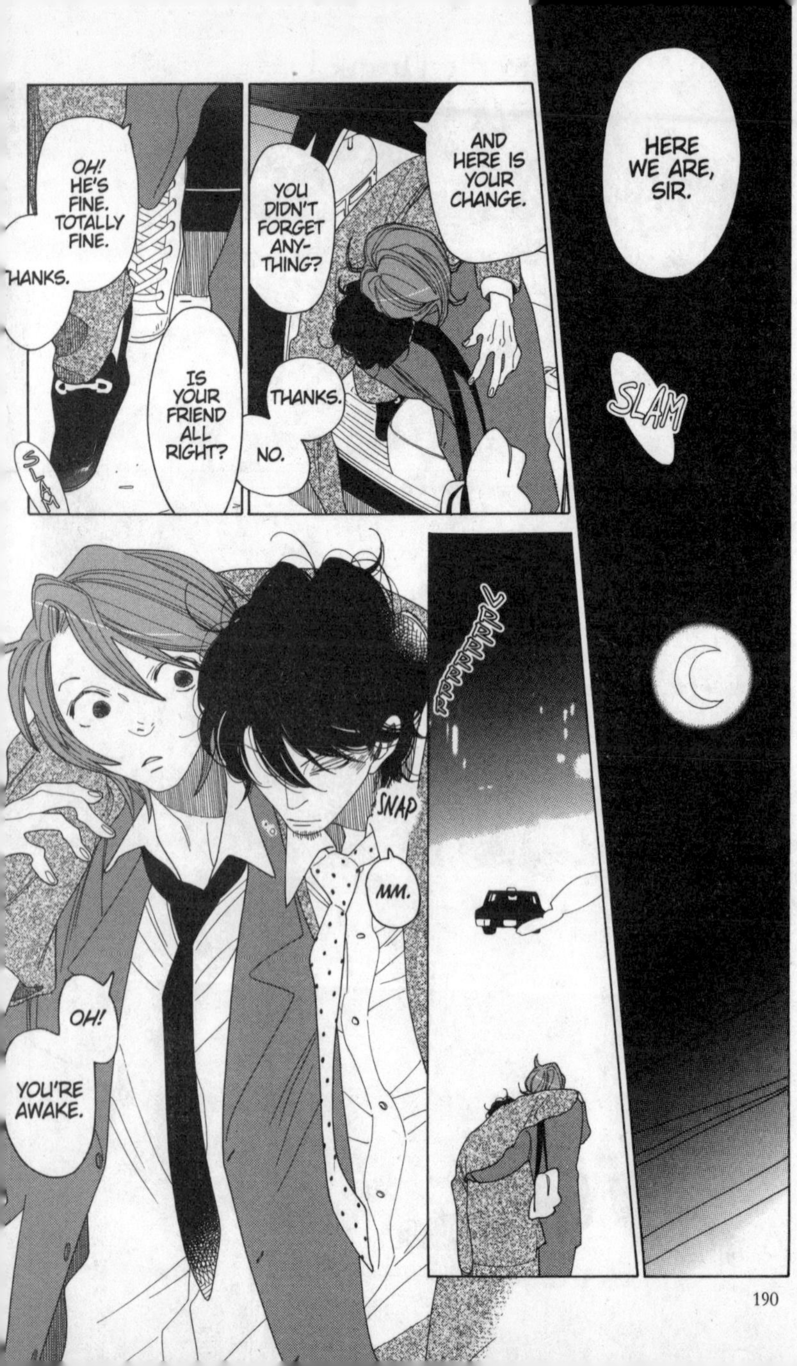
HERE WE ARE, SIR.
SLAM
AND HERE IS YOUR CHANGE.
YOU DIDN'T FORGET ANY-THING?
THANKS.
NO.
IS YOUR FRIEND ALL RIGHT?
OH! HE'S FINE. TOTALLY FINE.
THANKS.
SLAM
VRRRRRRRRR
SNAP
MM.
OH!
YOU'RE AWAKE.

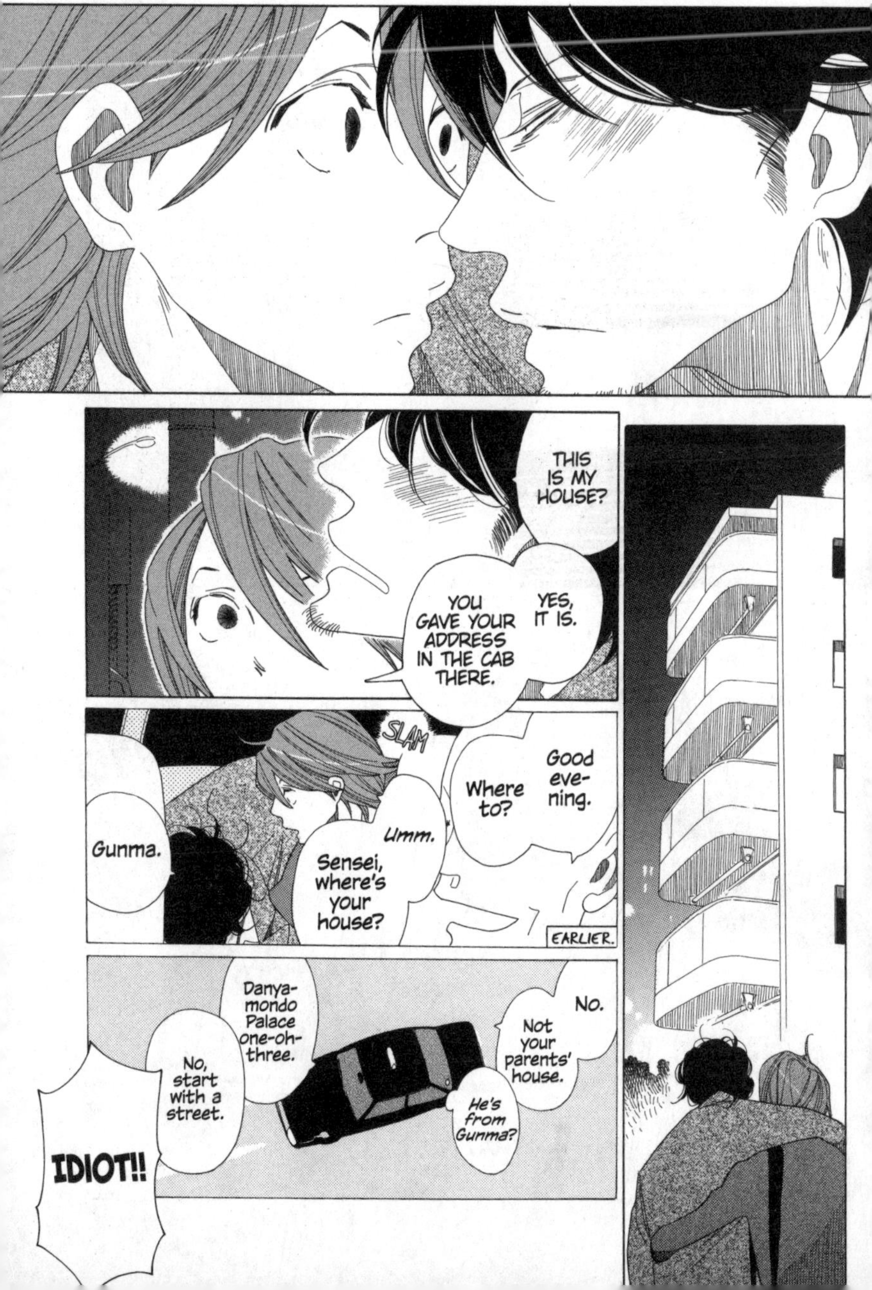
THIS IS MY HOUSE?
YES, IT IS.
YOU GAVE YOUR ADDRESS IN THE CAB THERE.
EARLIER.
Good eve-ning.
Where to?
SLAM
Umm.
Sensei, where's your house?
Gunma.
No.
Not your parents' house.
He's from Gunma?
Danya-mondo Palace one-oh-three.
No, start with a street.
IDIOT!!

A STUDENT!
AT HIS TEACHER'S HOUSE!
DOES NOT COMPU-UUUUTE!
SHAKE
SHAKE
ACK!
HEY!
SHAKE
SHAKE
SEN-SEI...!
SHAKE
FREEZE
SHFF
FLING
HUH...?!
WHAT?!
DASH
HEY!
WHOA!!
YOU CAN'T JUST--!

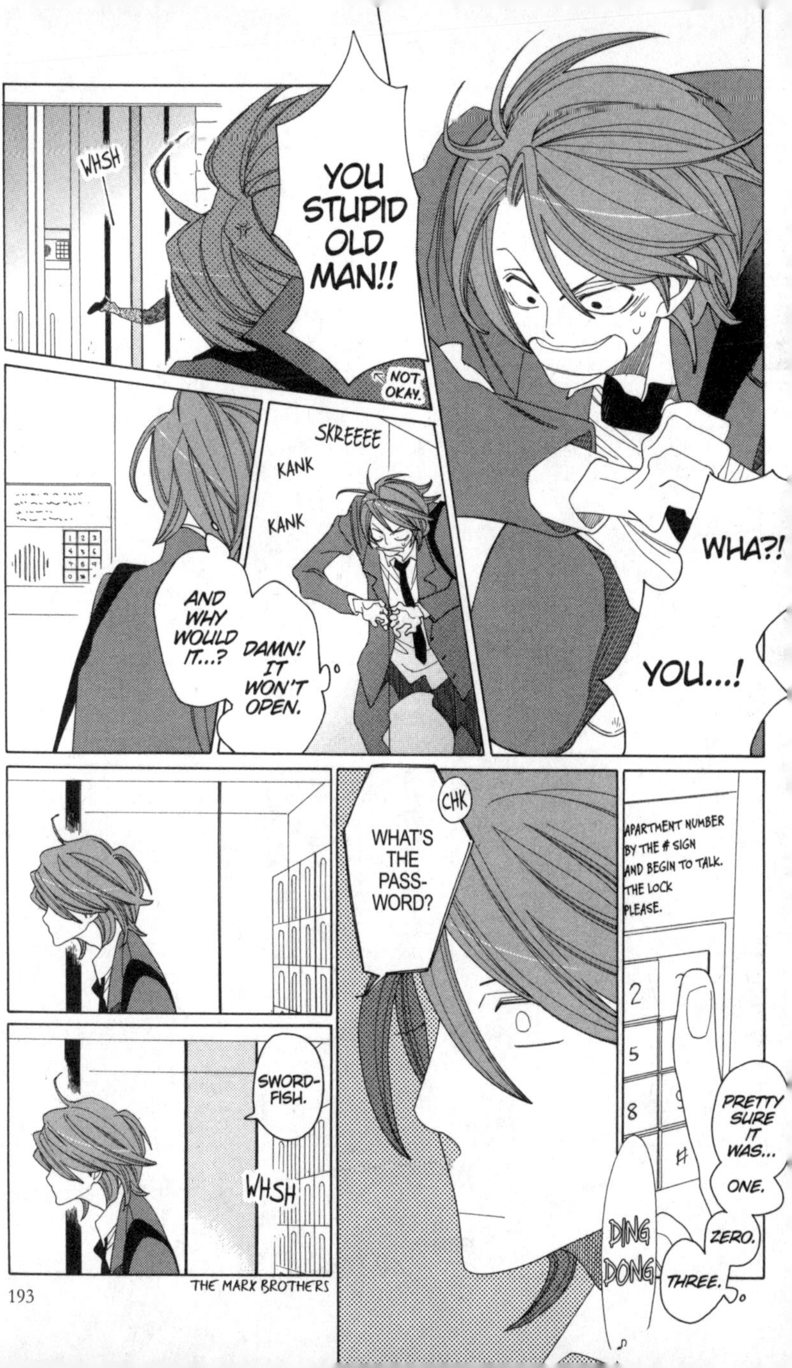
SKREEEE
KANK
KANK
DAMN! IT WON'T OPEN.
AND WHY WOULD IT...?
WHA?!
YOU...!
YOU STUPID OLD MAN!!
WHSH
NOT OKAY.
APARTMENT NUMBER
BY THE # SIGN
AND BEGIN TO TALK.
THE LOCK
PLEASE.
PRETTY SURE IT WAS...
ONE.
ZERO.
THREE.
DING DONG
CHK
WHAT'S THE PASS-WORD?
SWORD-FISH.
WHSH

THE MARX BROTHERS

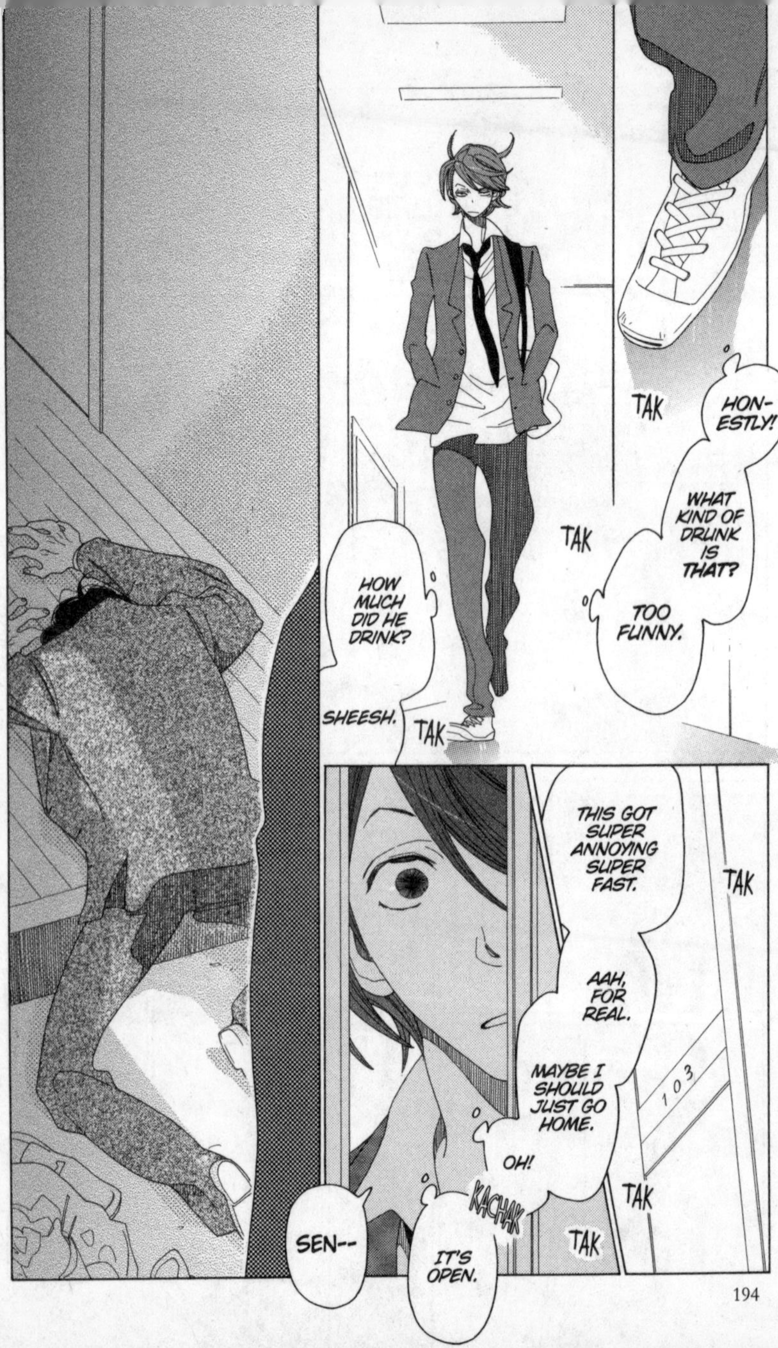

TAK
HON-ESTLY!
WHAT KIND OF DRUNK IS THAT?
TOO FUNNY.
TAK
HOW MUCH DID HE DRINK?
SHEESH.
TAK
TAK
THIS GOT SUPER ANNOYING SUPER FAST.
AAH, FOR REAL.
MAYBE I SHOULD JUST GO HOME.
103
TAK
TAK
OH!
KACHAK
IT'S OPEN.
SEN--

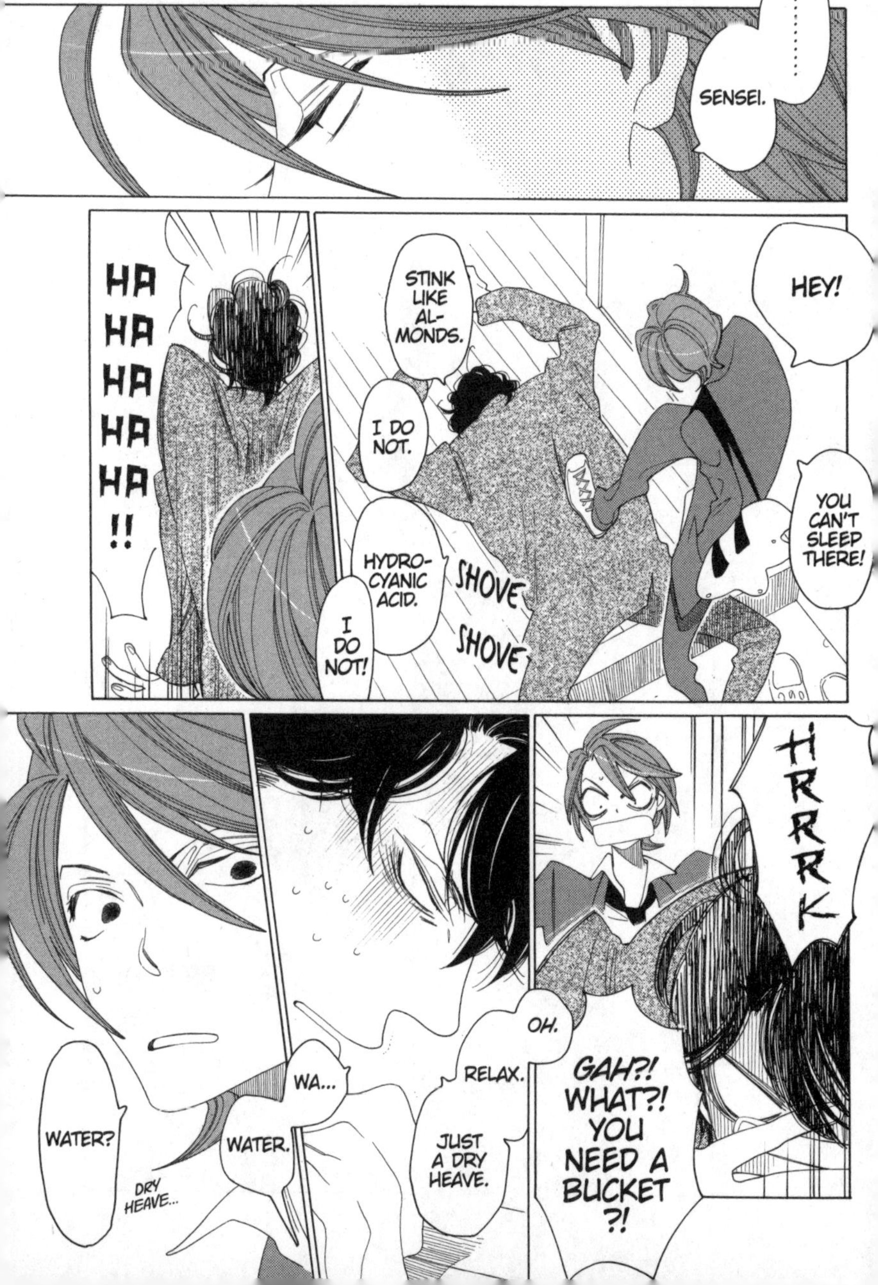
......
SENSEI.
HEY!
YOU CAN'T SLEEP THERE!
STINK LIKE AL-MONDS.
I DO NOT.
HYDRO-CYANIC ACID.
SHOVE
SHOVE
I DO NOT!
HA HA HA HA HA!!
HRRRK
GAH?! WHAT?! YOU NEED A BUCKET?!
OH.
RELAX.
JUST A DRY HEAVE.
WA...
WATER.
WATER?
DRY HEAVE...

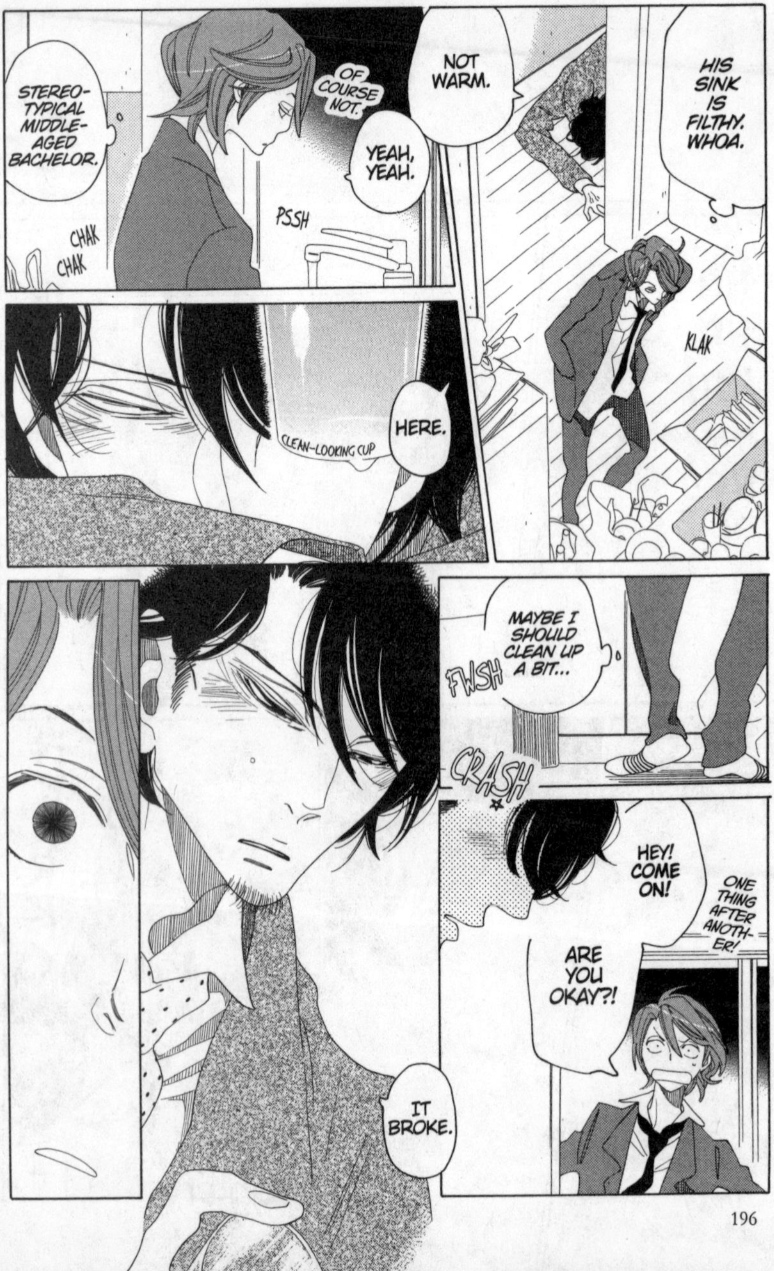
HIS SINK IS FILTHY. WHOA.
NOT WARM.
KLAK
OF COURSE NOT.
YEAH, YEAH.
PSSH
STEREO-TYPICAL MIDDLE-AGED BACHELOR.
CHAK CHAK
HERE.
CLEAN-LOOKING CUP
MAYBE I SHOULD CLEAN UP A BIT...
FWSH
CRASH
ONE THING AFTER ANOTH-ER!
HEY! COME ON!
ARE YOU OKAY?!
IT BROKE.

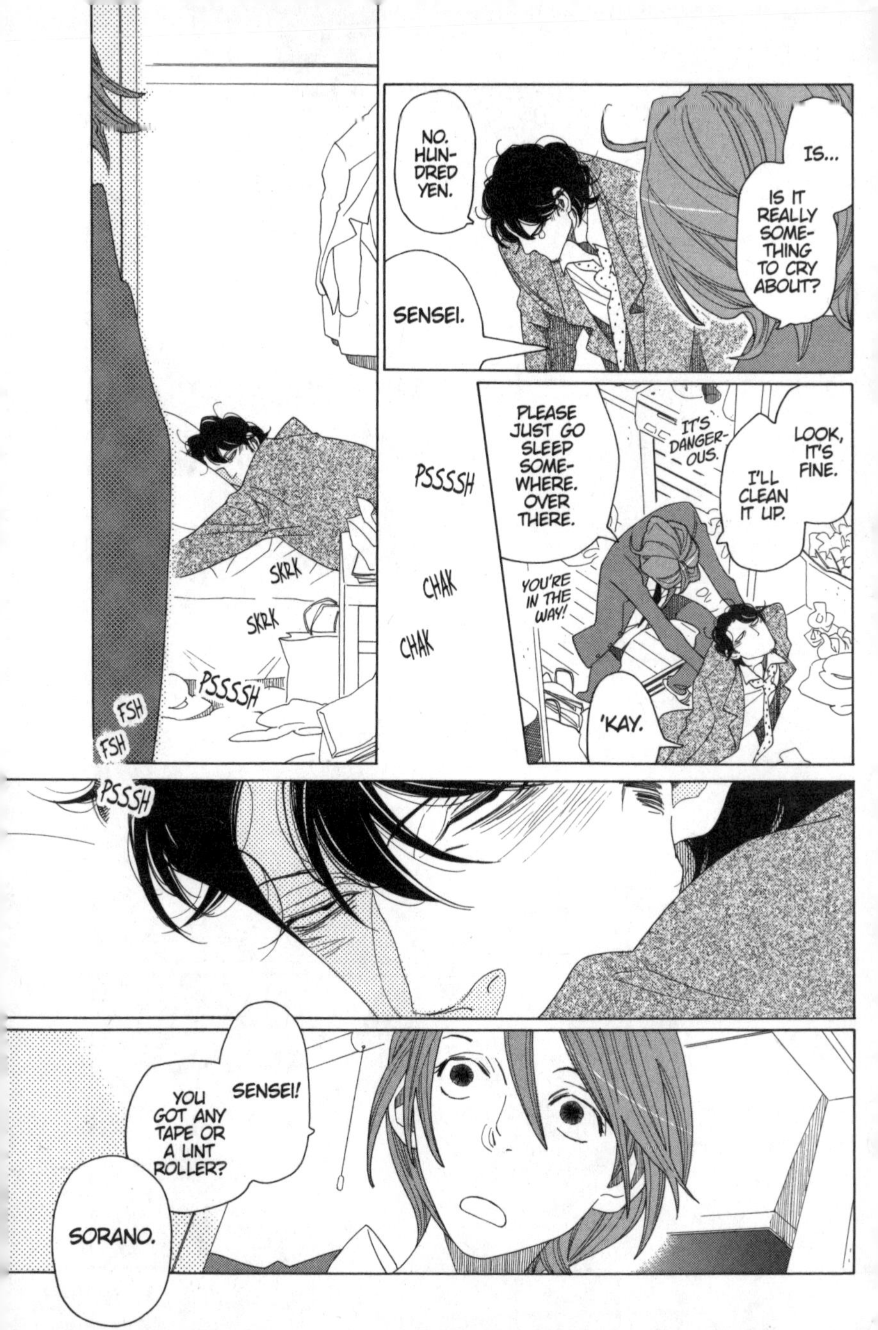
IS...
IS IT REALLY SOMETHING TO CRY ABOUT?
NO. HUNDRED YEN.
SENSEI.
LOOK, IT'S FINE.
I'LL CLEAN IT UP.
IT'S DANGEROUS.
PLEASE JUST GO SLEEP SOMEWHERE. OVER THERE.
YOU'RE IN THE WAY!
PSSSSH
CHAK
CHAK
'KAY.
SKRK
SKRK
PSSSSH
FSH
FSH
PSSSH
SENSEI!
YOU GOT ANY TAPE OR A LINT ROLLER?
SORANO.

WHY ARE YOU HERE...?
BE-CAUSE YOU...
WAIT.
IT'S NOT LIKE HE CALLED ME.
YOU WERE SUPER DRUNK.
OUT DRINKING BY YOUR-SELF.
AND I WAS WORRIED.
SO...
I JUST...
I...

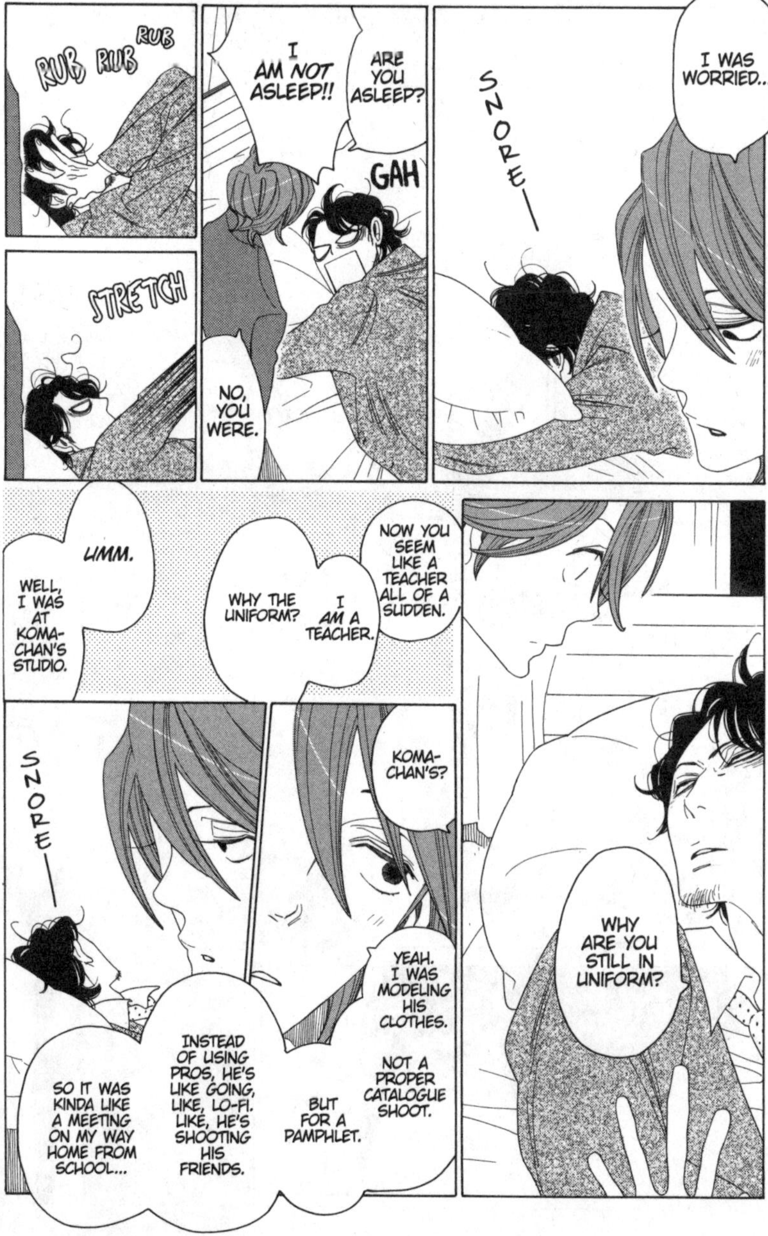
I WAS WORRIED...
SNORE—
ARE YOU ASLEEP?
I AM *NOT* ASLEEP!!
GAH
NO, YOU WERE.
RUB RUB RUB
STRETCH
WHY ARE YOU STILL IN UNIFORM?
NOW YOU SEEM LIKE A TEACHER ALL OF A SUDDEN.
I *AM* A TEACHER.
WHY THE UNIFORM?
UMM.
WELL, I WAS AT KOMA-CHAN'S STUDIO.
KOMA-CHAN'S?
YEAH. I WAS MODELING HIS CLOTHES.
NOT A PROPER CATALOGUE SHOOT.
BUT FOR A PAMPHLET.
INSTEAD OF USING PROS, HE'S LIKE GOING, LIKE, LO-FI. LIKE, HE'S SHOOTING HIS FRIENDS.
SO IT WAS KINDA LIKE A MEETING ON MY WAY HOME FROM SCHOOL...
SNORE—

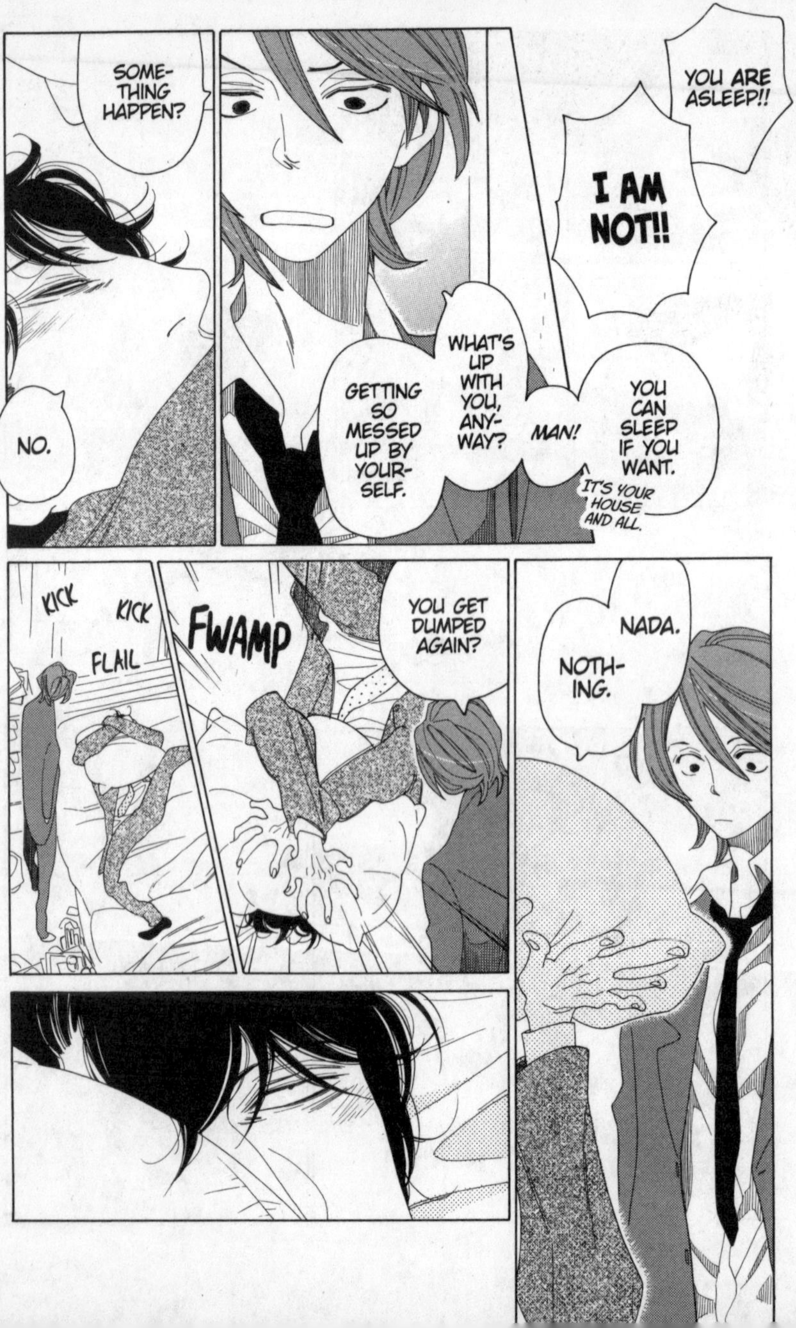
YOU ARE ASLEEP!!
I AM NOT!!
YOU CAN SLEEP IF YOU WANT.
IT'S YOUR HOUSE AND ALL.
MAN!
WHAT'S UP WITH YOU, ANYWAY?
GETTING SO MESSED UP BY YOURSELF.
SOME-THING HAPPEN?
NO.
NADA.
NOTH-ING.
YOU GET DUMPED AGAIN?
FWAMP
KICK
KICK
FLAIL

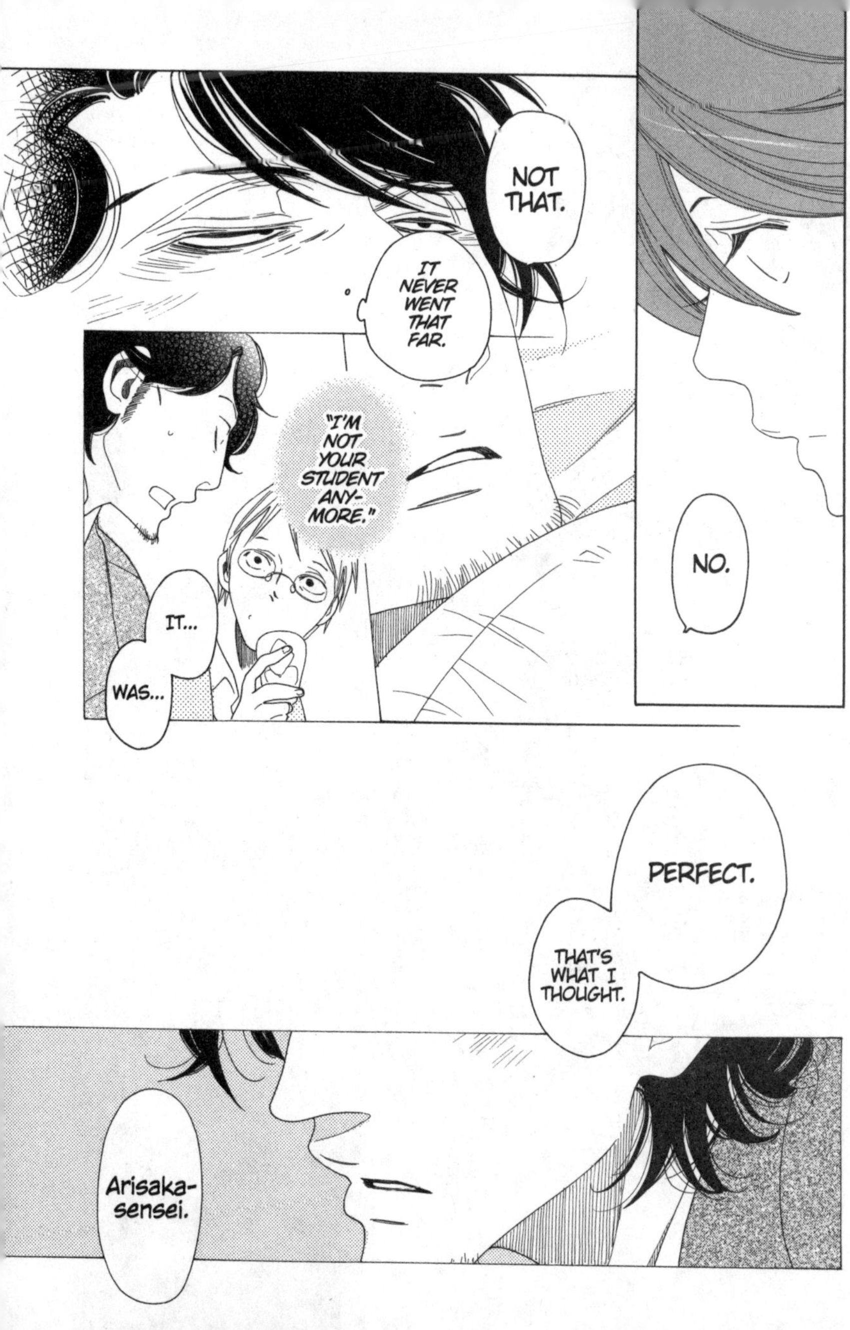
NO.
NOT THAT.
IT NEVER WENT THAT FAR.
"I'M NOT YOUR STUDENT ANYMORE."
IT...
WAS...
PERFECT.
THAT'S WHAT I THOUGHT.
Arisaka-sensei.

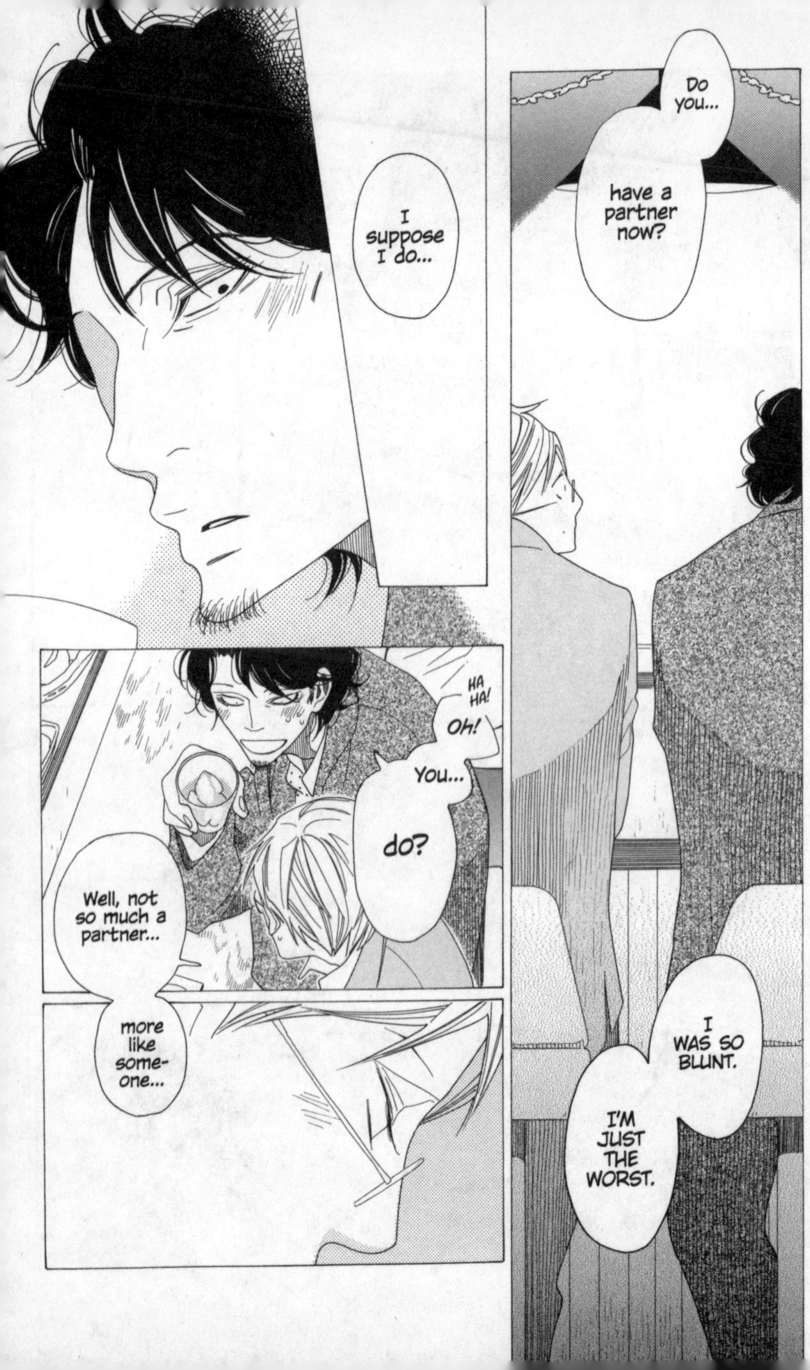
Do you...
have a partner now?
I WAS SO BLUNT.
I'M JUST THE WORST.
I suppose I do...
HA HA!
Oh!
You...
do?
Well, not so much a partner...
more like some-one...

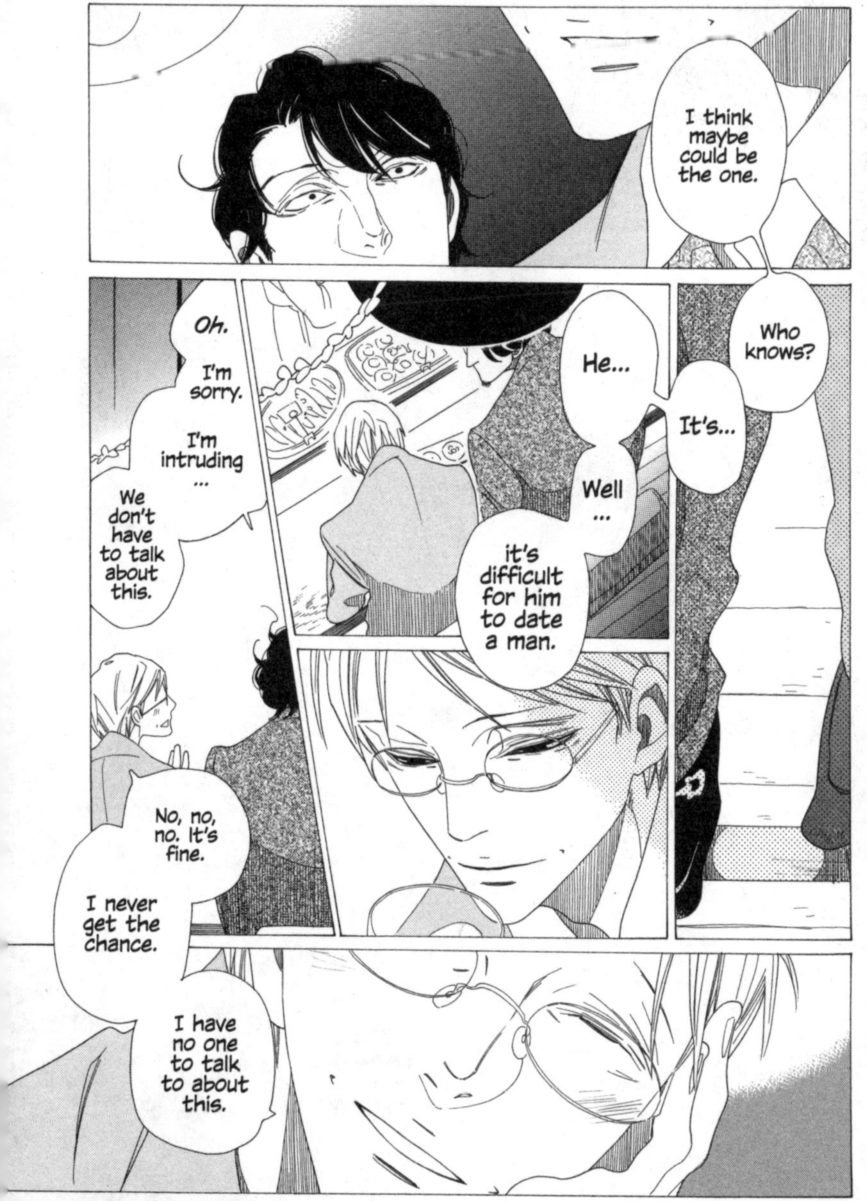
I think maybe could be the one.
Who knows?
It's...
He...
Well...
it's difficult for him to date a man.
Oh.
I'm sorry.
I'm intruding...
We don't have to talk about this.
No, no, no. It's fine.
I never get the chance.
I have no one to talk to about this.

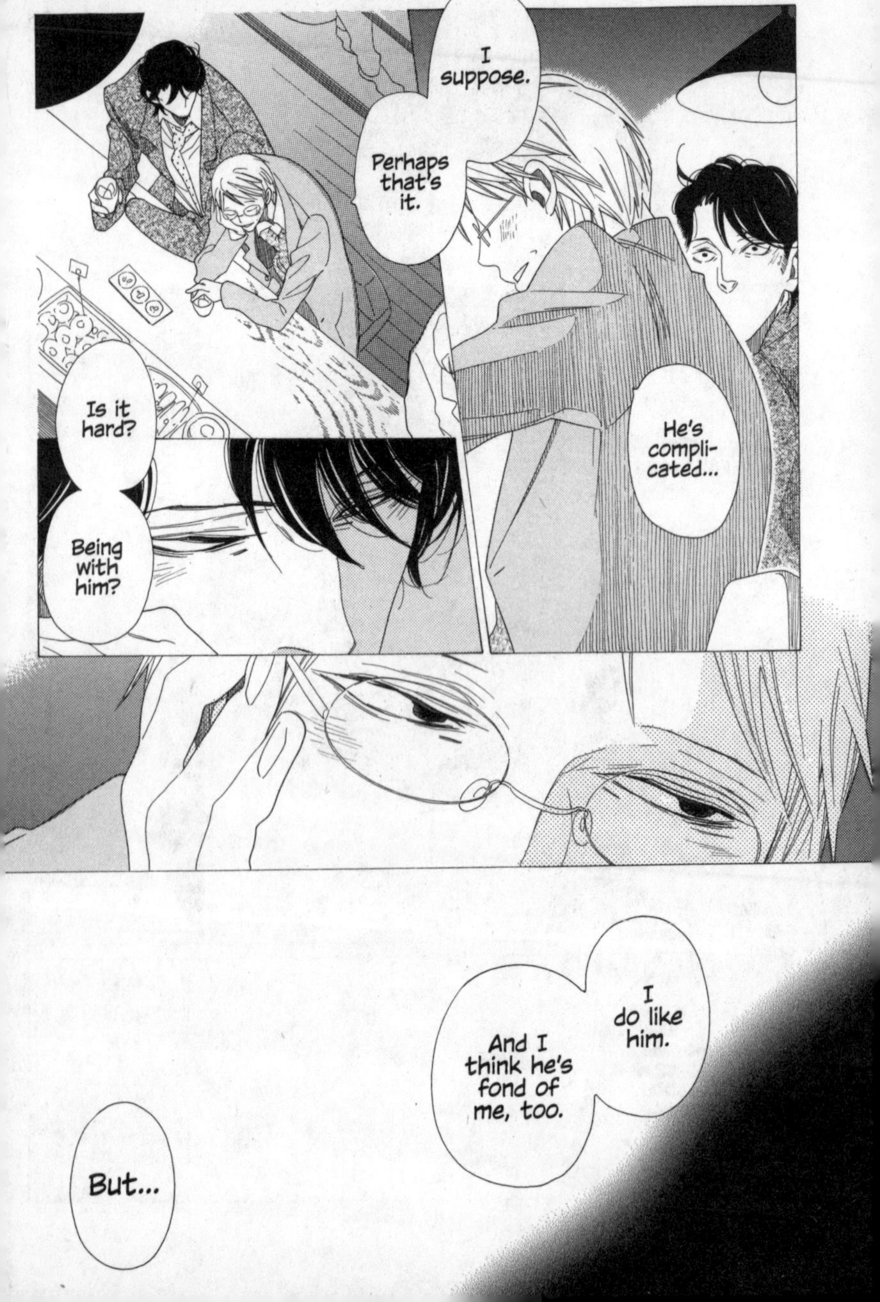
Is it hard?
Being with him?
He's complicated...
I suppose.
Perhaps that's it.
I do like him.
And I think he's fond of me, too.
But...

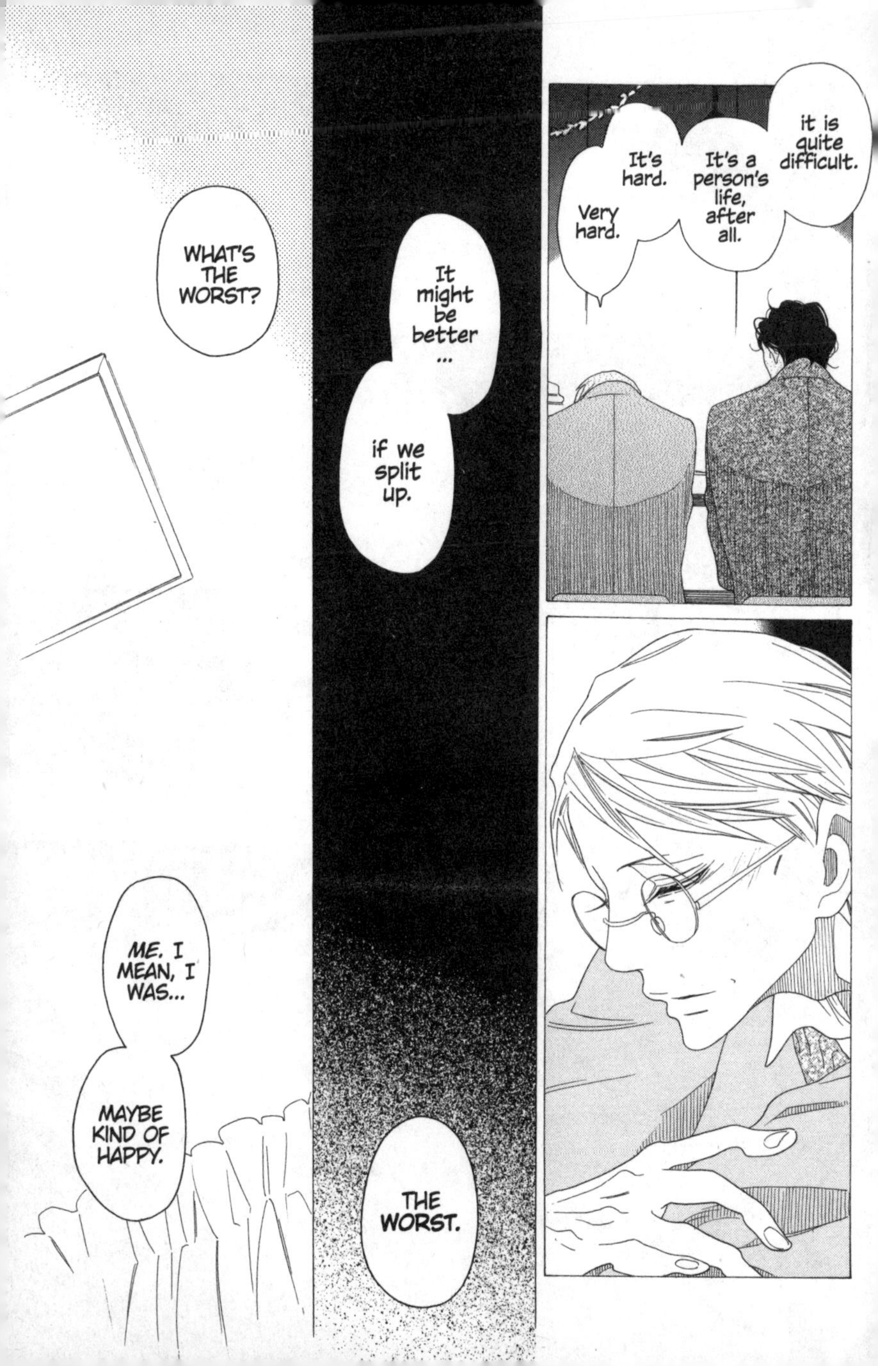
it is quite difficult.
It's a person's life, after all.
It's hard.
Very hard.
It might be better...
if we split up.
THE WORST.
WHAT'S THE WORST?
ME. I MEAN, I WAS...
MAYBE KIND OF HAPPY.

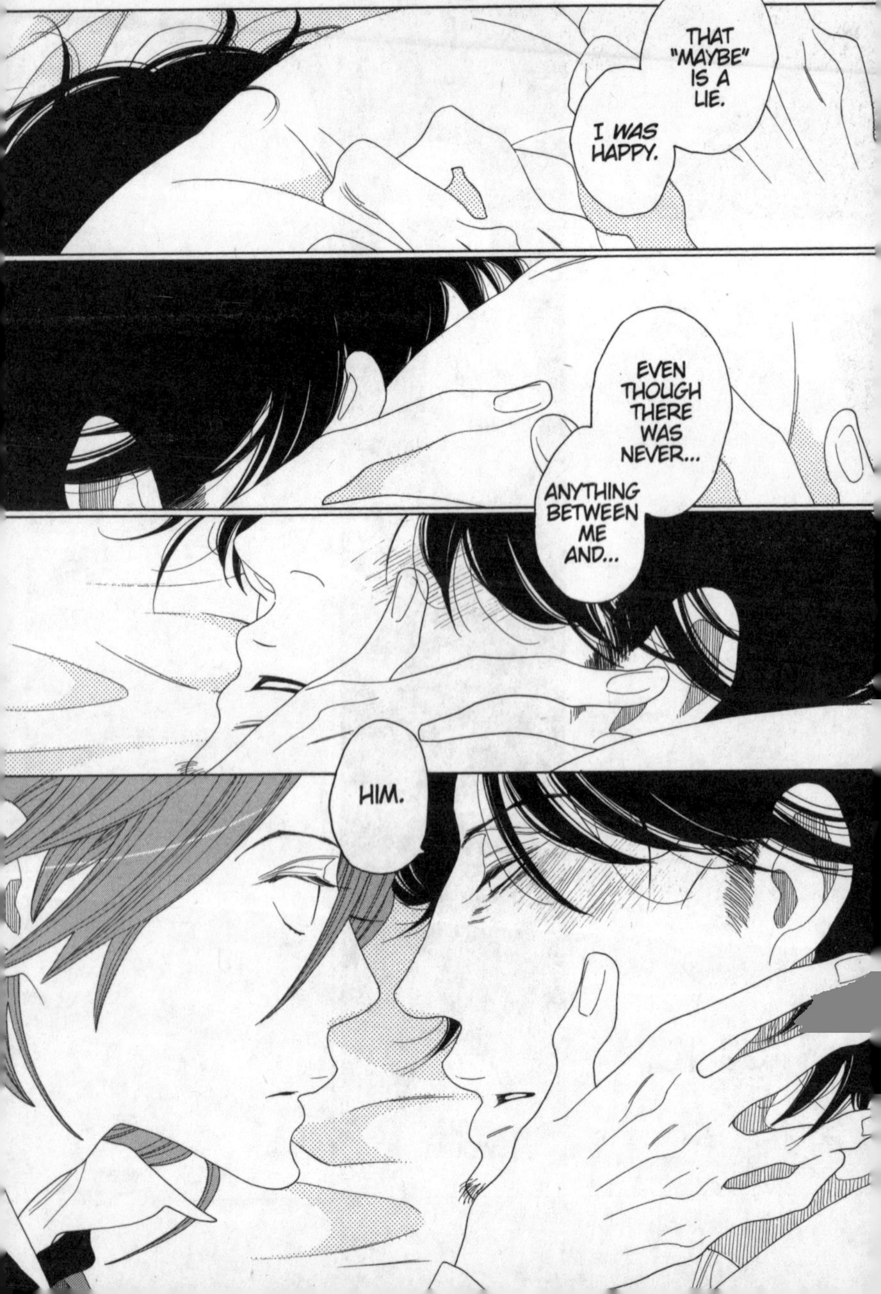
THAT "MAYBE" IS A LIE.
I *WAS* HAPPY.
EVEN THOUGH THERE WAS NEVER...
ANYTHING BETWEEN ME AND...
HIM.

WHAT?
I THOUGHT YOU WERE MAYBE CRYING.
CRYING?
DON'T BE AN IDIOT.
THIS KID...
YOU CRIED WHEN YOU BROKE THE GLASS.
HE'S GOT SUPER-THICK LASHES.
WHAT AN UNRELIABLE TEACHER.
THAT...
WAS DIFFER-ENT.
HIS SKIN'S SO BRIGHT AND CLEAR.
HAAH.
HE REALLY IS A TEEN-AGER.

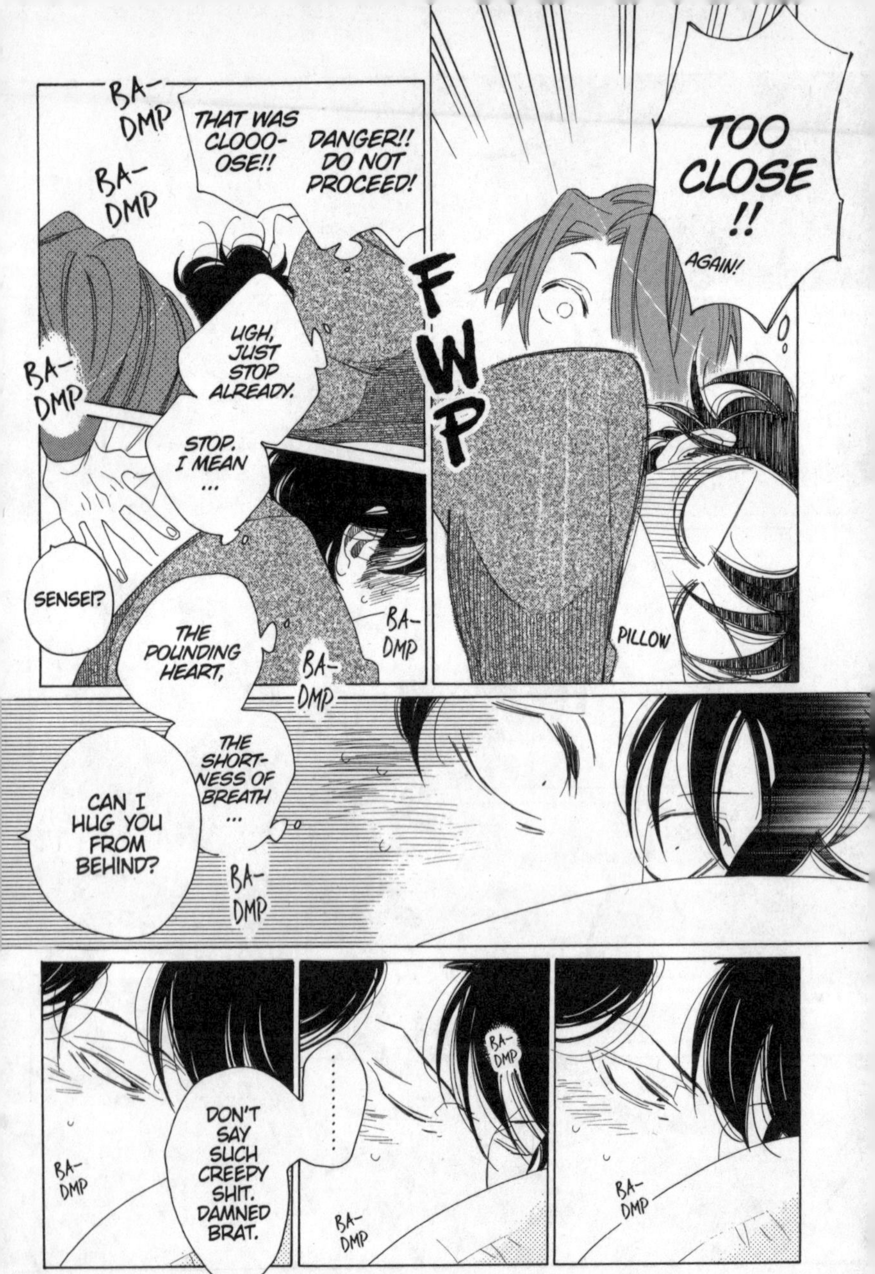
TOO CLOSE!!
AGAIN!
FWP
PILLOW
BA-DMP
DANGER!! DO NOT PROCEED!
THAT WAS CLOOOOSE!!
BA-DMP
UGH, JUST STOP ALREADY.
BA-DMP
STOP. I MEAN ...
SENSEI?
BA-DMP
THE POUNDING HEART,
BA-DMP
THE SHORTNESS OF BREATH ...
BA-DMP
CAN I HUG YOU FROM BEHIND?
BA-DMP
BA-DMP
......
BA-DMP
DON'T SAY SUCH CREEPY SHIT. DAMNED BRAT.
BA-DMP

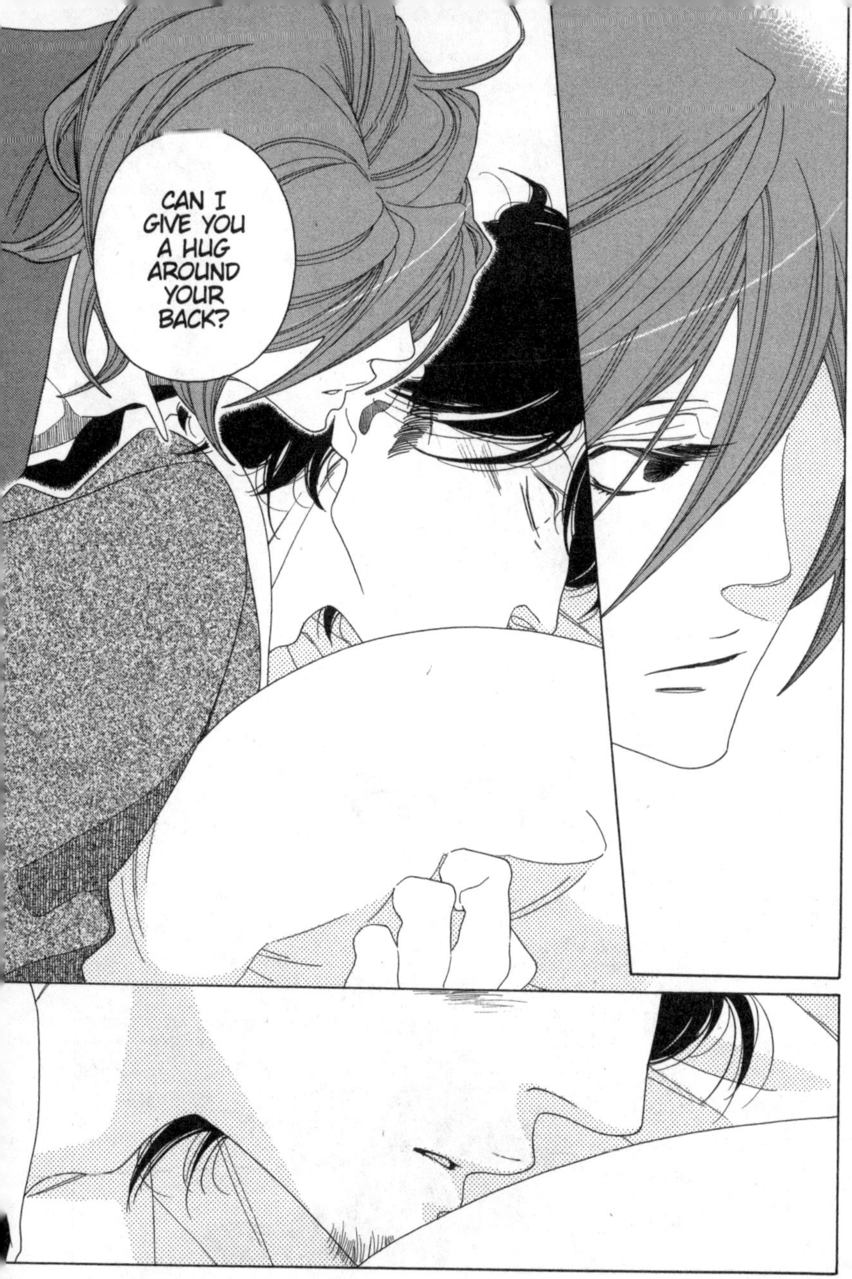
CAN I GIVE YOU A HUG AROUND YOUR BACK?

SHUDDER
SHUDDER
CLUTCH
SO SERI-OUS.
YOU'RE OVER-THINK-ING.
THAT'S IT.
PHYSICAL CONTACT ...
FINE.

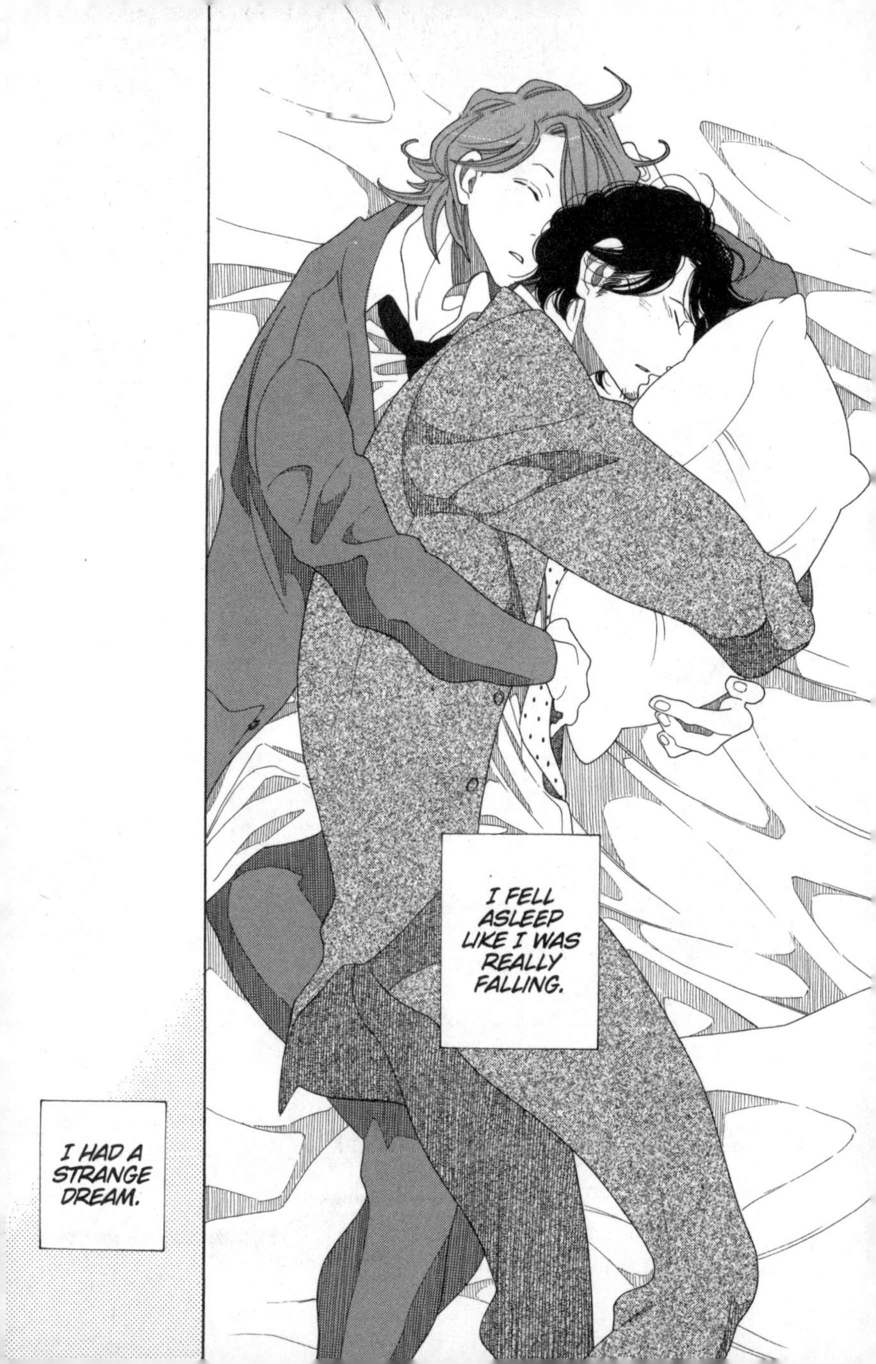
I FELL ASLEEP LIKE I WAS REALLY FALLING.
I HAD A STRANGE DREAM.

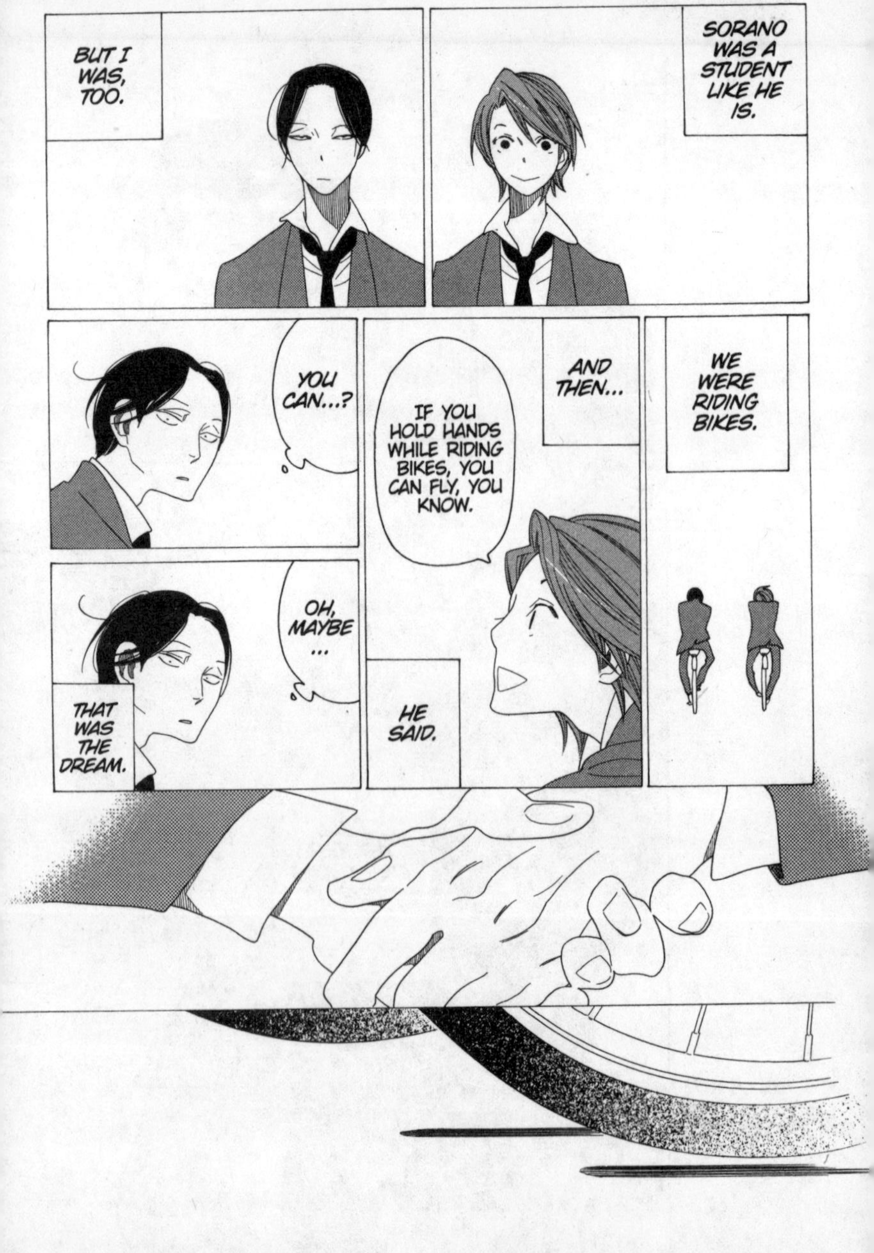
SORANO WAS A STUDENT LIKE HE IS.
BUT I WAS, TOO.
WE WERE RIDING BIKES.
AND THEN...
IF YOU HOLD HANDS WHILE RIDING BIKES, YOU CAN FLY, YOU KNOW.
HE SAID.
YOU CAN...?
OH, MAYBE ...
THAT WAS THE DREAM.

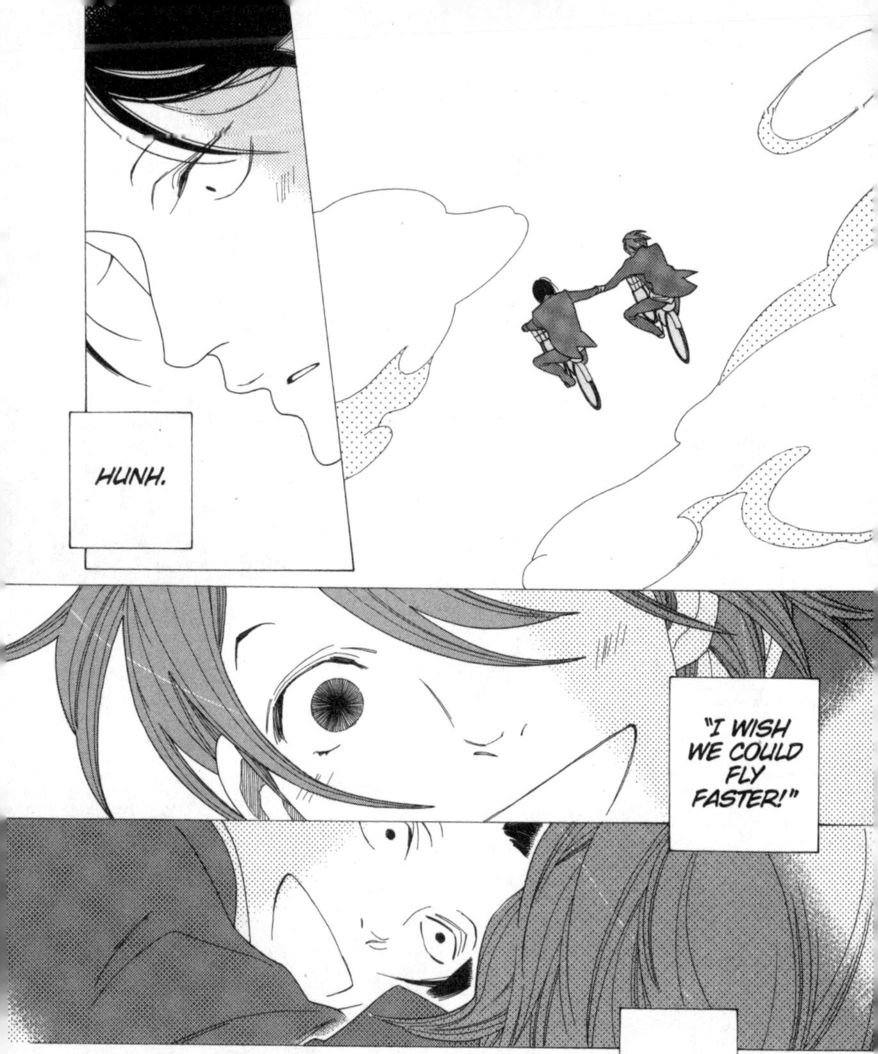
HUNH.
"I WISH WE COULD FLY FASTER!"
I THOUGHT.

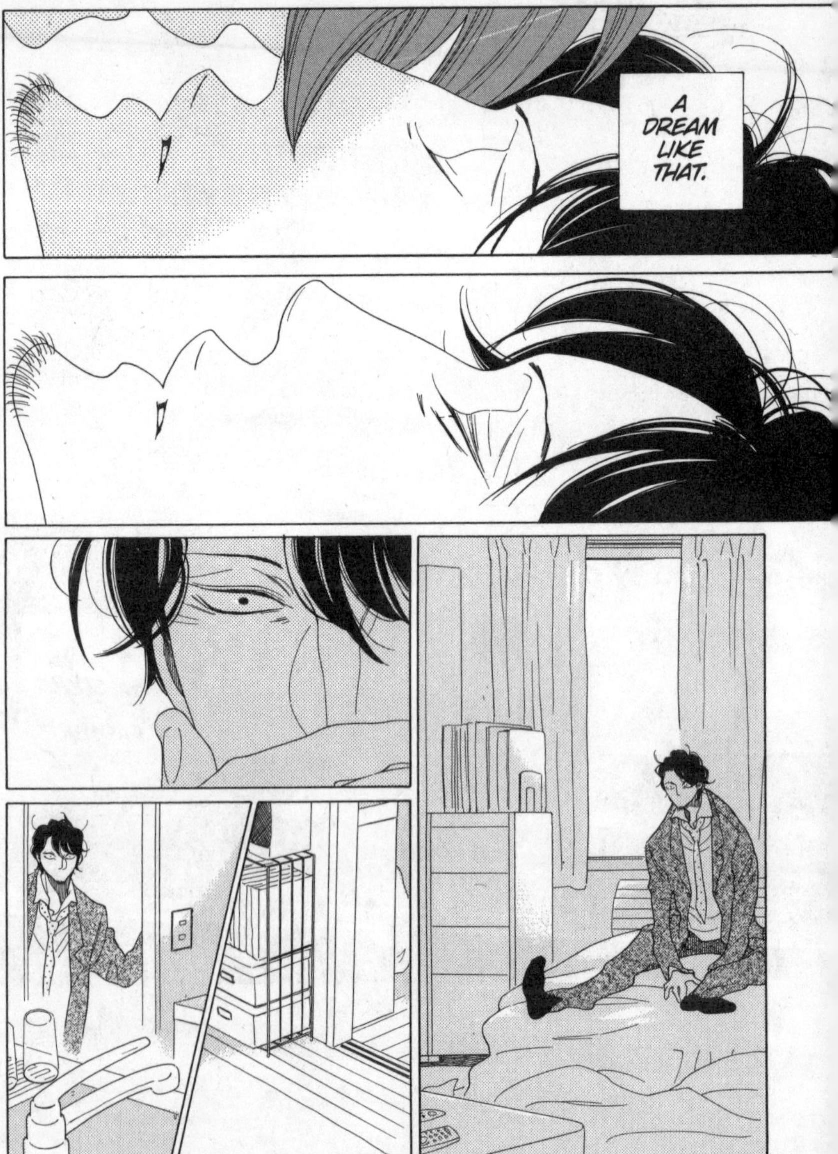
A DREAM LIKE THAT.

WOW
LIKE A BRAND-NEW GIRLFRIEND.
NOT THAT I'D KNOW.
HM?
FWP
Morning!
Might be glass around here
Bare feet are dangerous!
HA HA!
WHOA, WHOA. WHAT?
BUT I ALREADY WALKED OVER HERE TO PICK UP THE NOTE!
AAAAAAH...
I'M SO HUNGOVER.
YAWN

I'M TIRED.
MY BODY HURTS.
SO THIS IS THE PAIN OF BEING THE BIG SPOON.
SLRRP
I DON'T WANNA GO TO SCHOOL.
SLRP
AND...
LIKE...

HE WAS ASLEEP.
RIGHT?
PROBABLY.
SLRRP
SLRRRRRP
SLRRRP
I NEED HIM TO HAVE SLEPT THROUGH THAT.
PLEASE, GOD!
FOR REAL.
AAAH.
DO I MAYBE LIKE HIM?

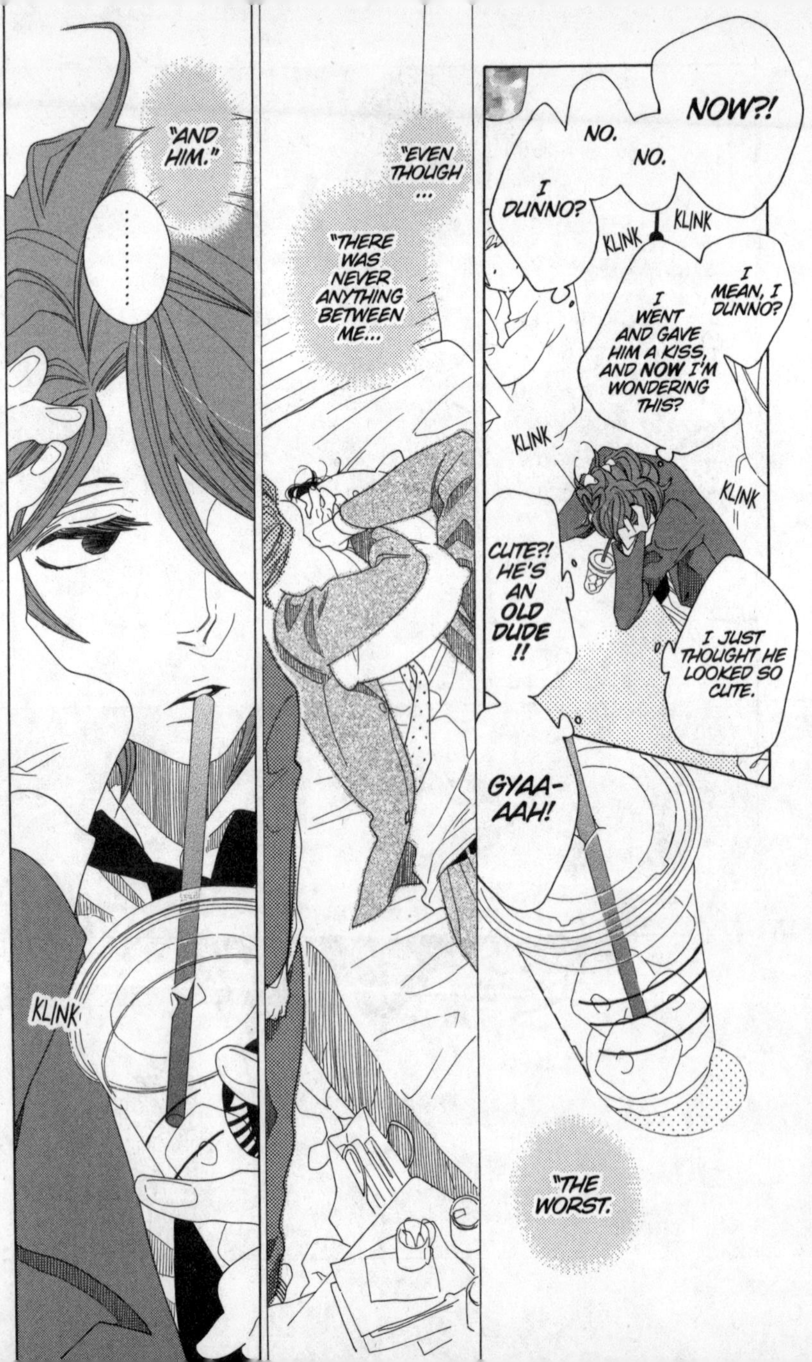
NOW?!
NO.
NO.
I DUNNO?
KLINK
KLINK
I MEAN, I DUNNO?
I WENT AND GAVE HIM A KISS, AND NOW I'M WONDERING THIS?
KLINK
KLINK
I JUST THOUGHT HE LOOKED SO CUTE.
CUTE?! HE'S AN OLD DUDE !!
GYAA-AAH!
"THE WORST.
"EVEN THOUGH ...
"THERE WAS NEVER ANYTHING BETWEEN ME...
"AND HIM."
......
KLINK

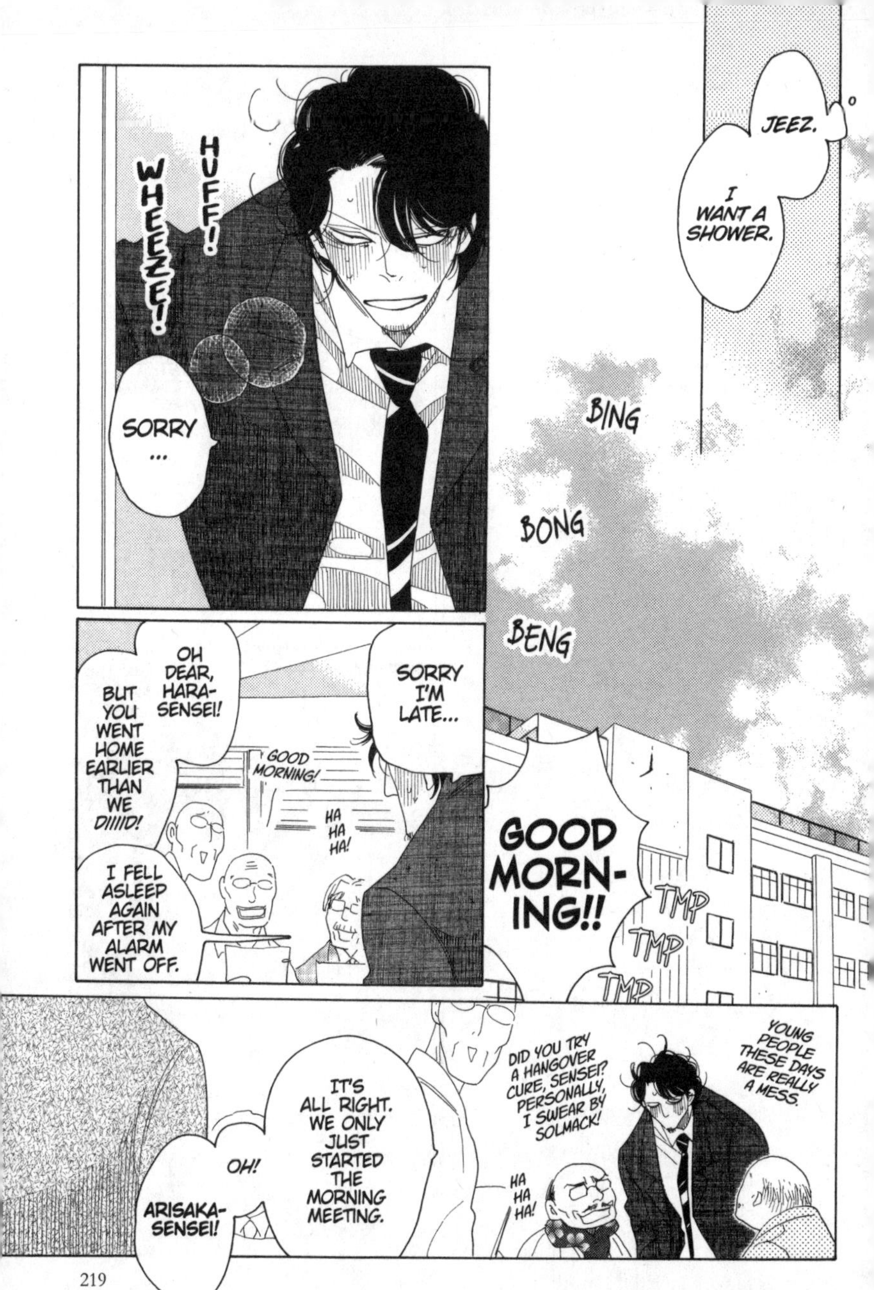
JEEZ.
I WANT A SHOWER.
BING
BONG
BENG
GOOD MORNING!!
TMP
TMP
TMP
HUFF!
WHEEZE!
SORRY ...
SORRY I'M LATE...
GOOD MORNING!
OH DEAR, HARA-SENSEI!
BUT YOU WENT HOME EARLIER THAN WE DIIIID!
HA HA HA!
I FELL ASLEEP AGAIN AFTER MY ALARM WENT OFF.
YOUNG PEOPLE THESE DAYS ARE REALLY A MESS.
DID YOU TRY A HANGOVER CURE, SENSEI? PERSONALLY, I SWEAR BY SOLMACK!
HA HA HA!
IT'S ALL RIGHT. WE ONLY JUST STARTED THE MORNING MEETING.
OH!
ARISAKA-SENSEI!

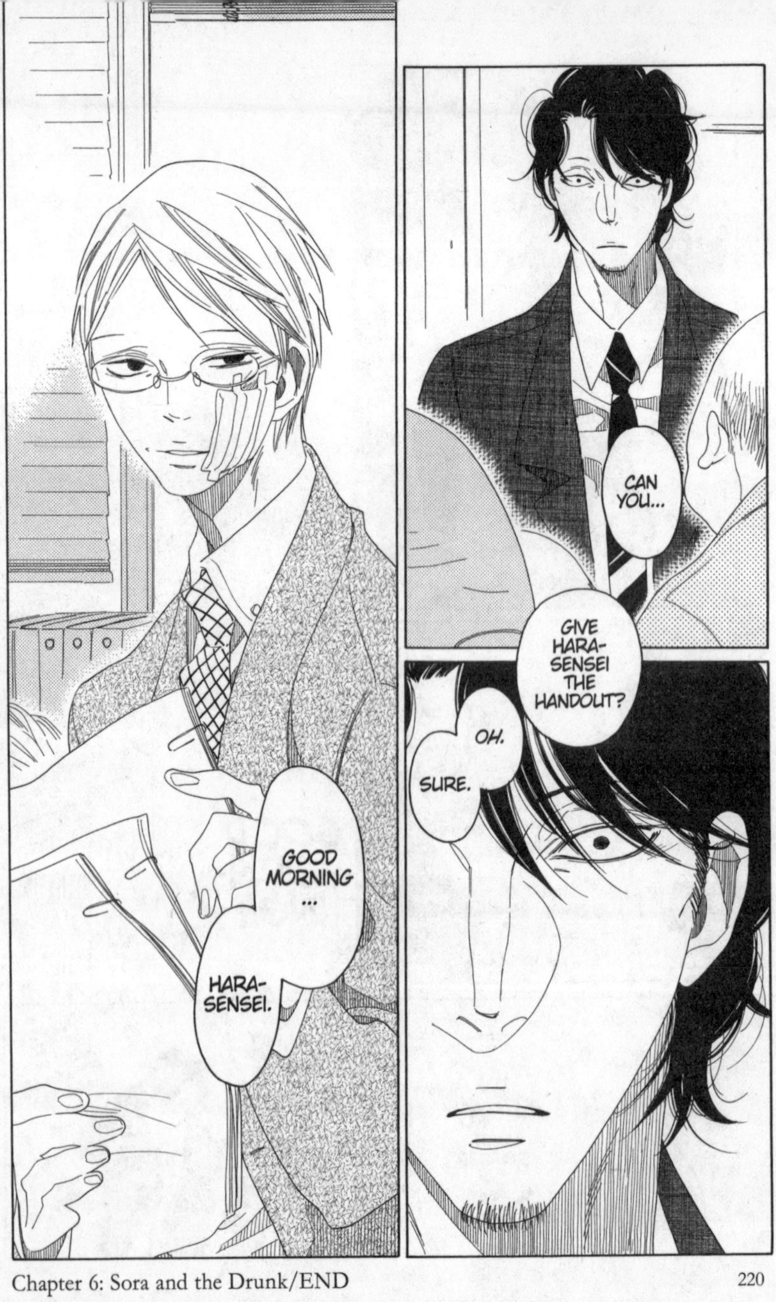
CAN YOU...
GIVE HARA-SENSEI THE HANDOUT?
OH.
SURE.
GOOD MORNING...
HARA-SENSEI.

[Final Chapter: Sora & Hara]

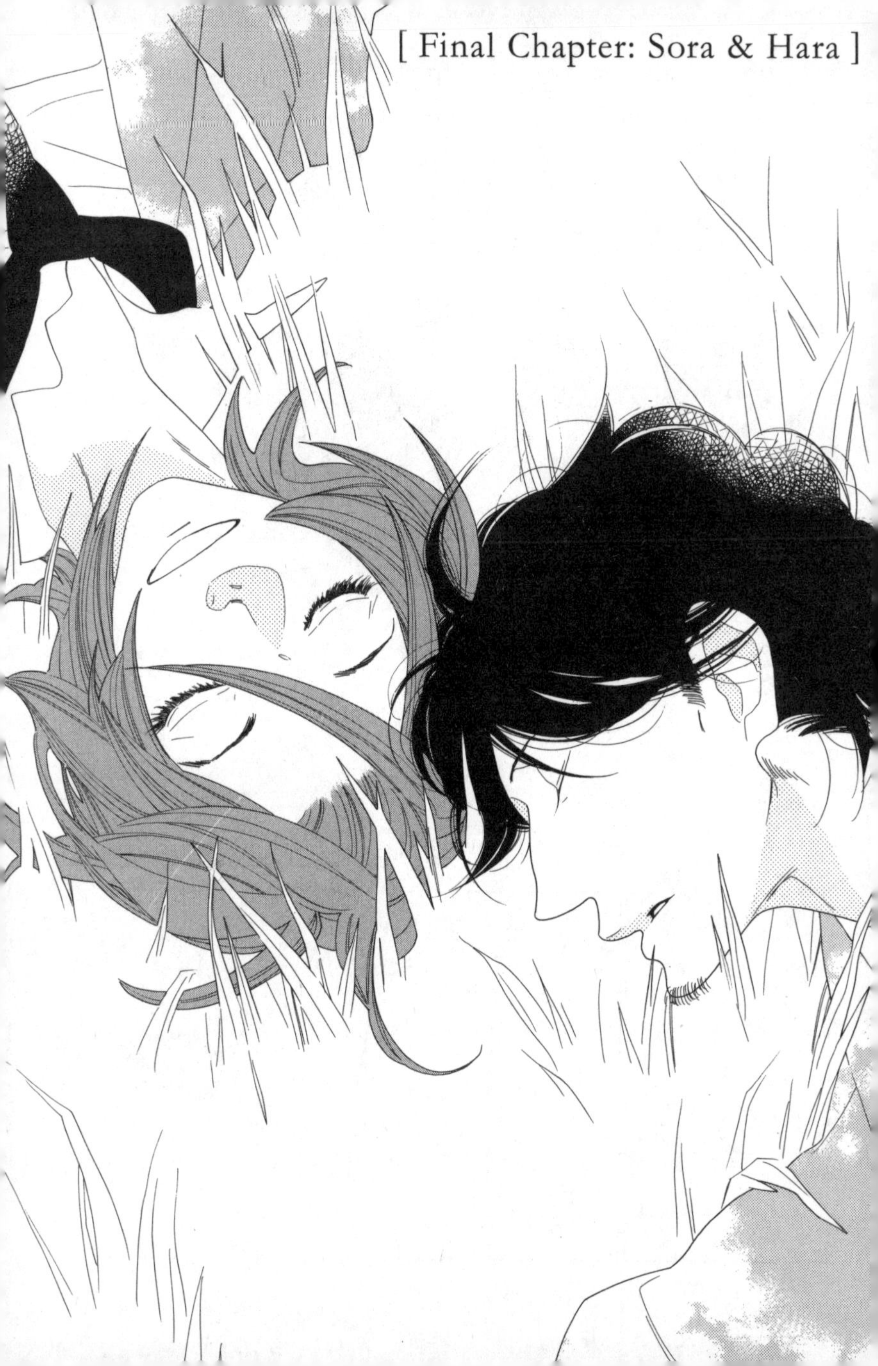

HE FELL AFTER DRINKING TOO MUCH.
APPAR-ENTLY.
RIGHT?
ARISAKA-SENSEI?
AAH, IT'S SO EMBAR-RASSING!
OH, THANK YOU.
HERE, HARA-SENSEI.
HONEST-LY!
YOUNG PEOPLE THESE DAYS TRULY ARE A MESS!
ONE OF THEM OVER-SLEEPS, ONE CAN'T STAY ON HIS FEET.
HA HA HA HA!
PSSSH
KEEP THE WASH-ROOMS CLEAN.
PSSSH

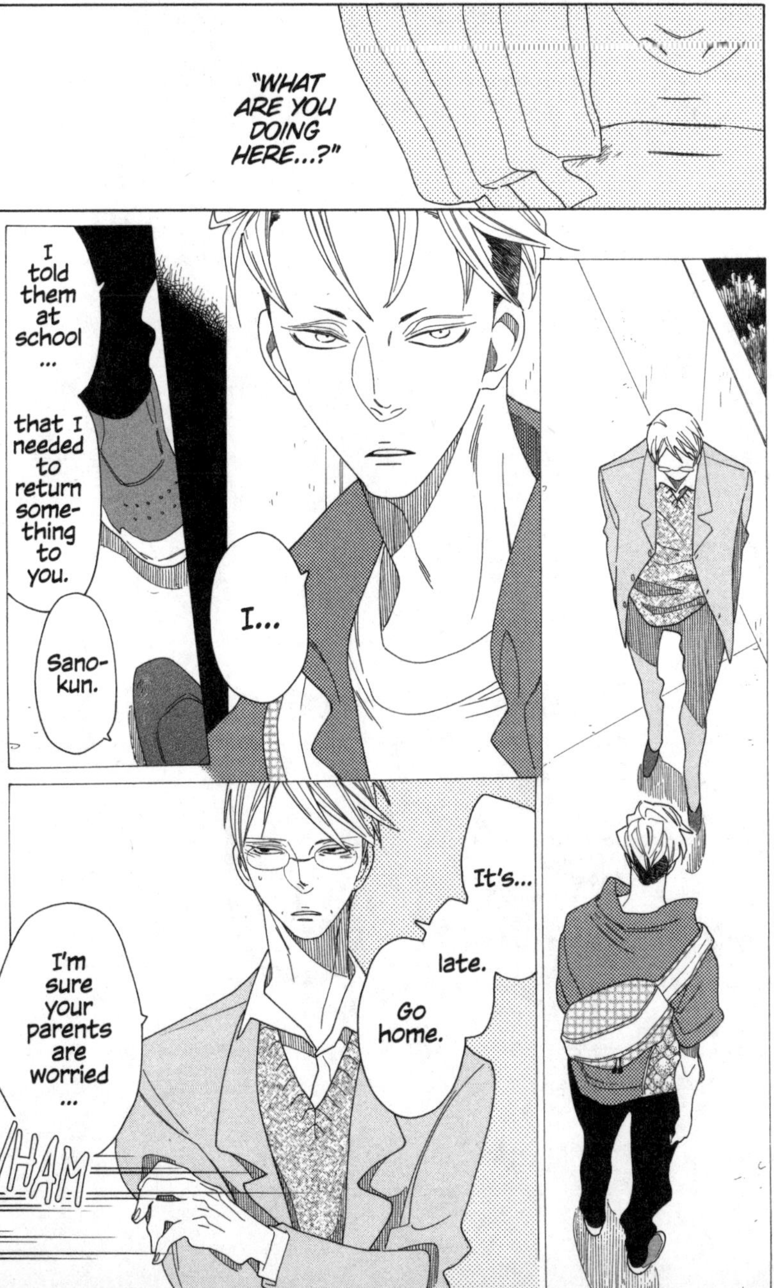
"WHAT ARE YOU DOING HERE...?"
I...
I told them at school... that I needed to return something to you.
Sano-kun.
It's... late.
Go home.
I'm sure your parents are worried...
WHAM

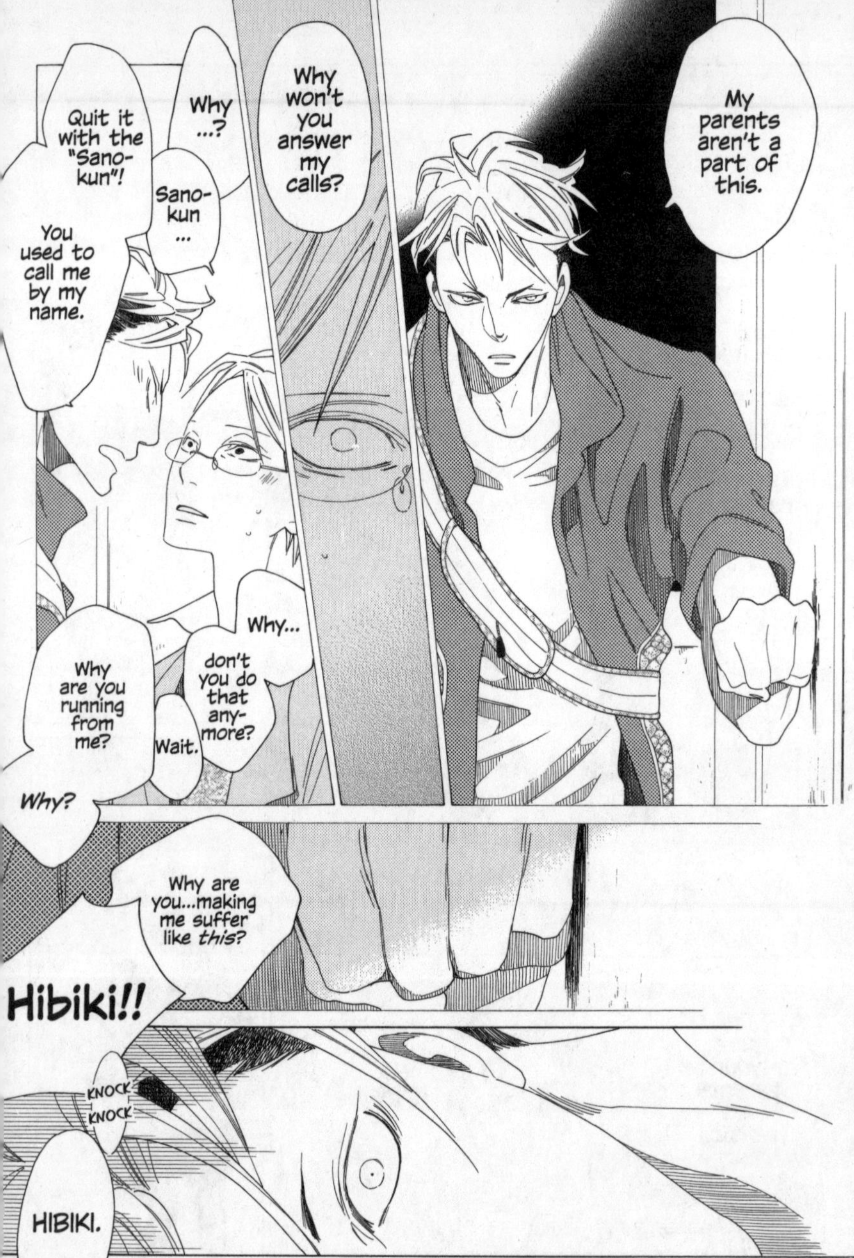

My parents aren't a part of this.
Why won't you answer my calls?
Why ...?
Quit it with the "Sano-kun"!
Sano-kun ...
You used to call me by my name.
Why...
don't you do that any-more?
Why are you running from me?
Wait.
Why?
Why are you...making me suffer like *this*?
Hibiki!!
KNOCK KNOCK
HIBIKI.

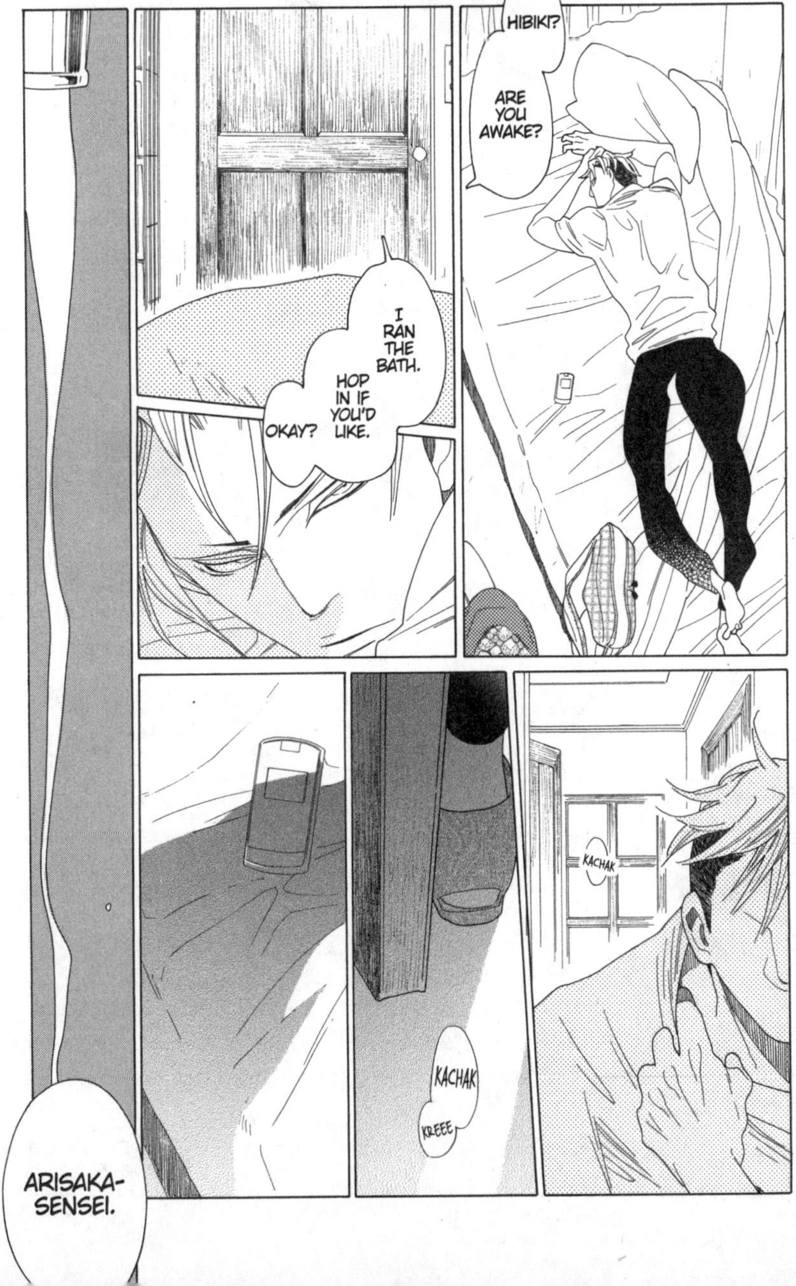
HIBIKI?
ARE YOU AWAKE?
I RAN THE BATH.
HOP IN IF YOU'D LIKE.
OKAY?
KACHAK
KACHAK
KREEE
ARISAKA-SENSEI.

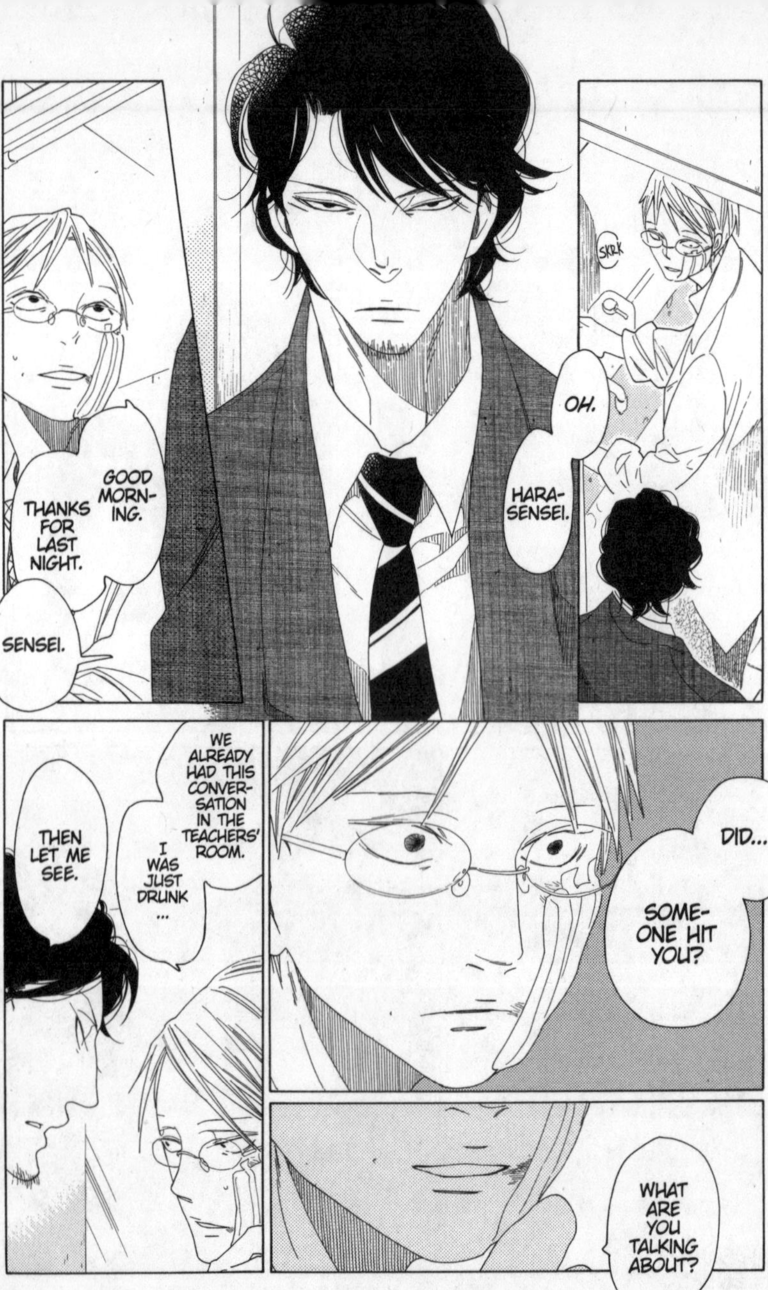
SKRK
OH.
HARA-SENSEI.
GOOD MORNING.
THANKS FOR LAST NIGHT.
SENSEI.
DID...
SOMEONE HIT YOU?
WHAT ARE YOU TALKING ABOUT?
WE ALREADY HAD THIS CONVERSATION IN THE TEACHERS' ROOM.
I WAS JUST DRUNK...
THEN LET ME SEE.

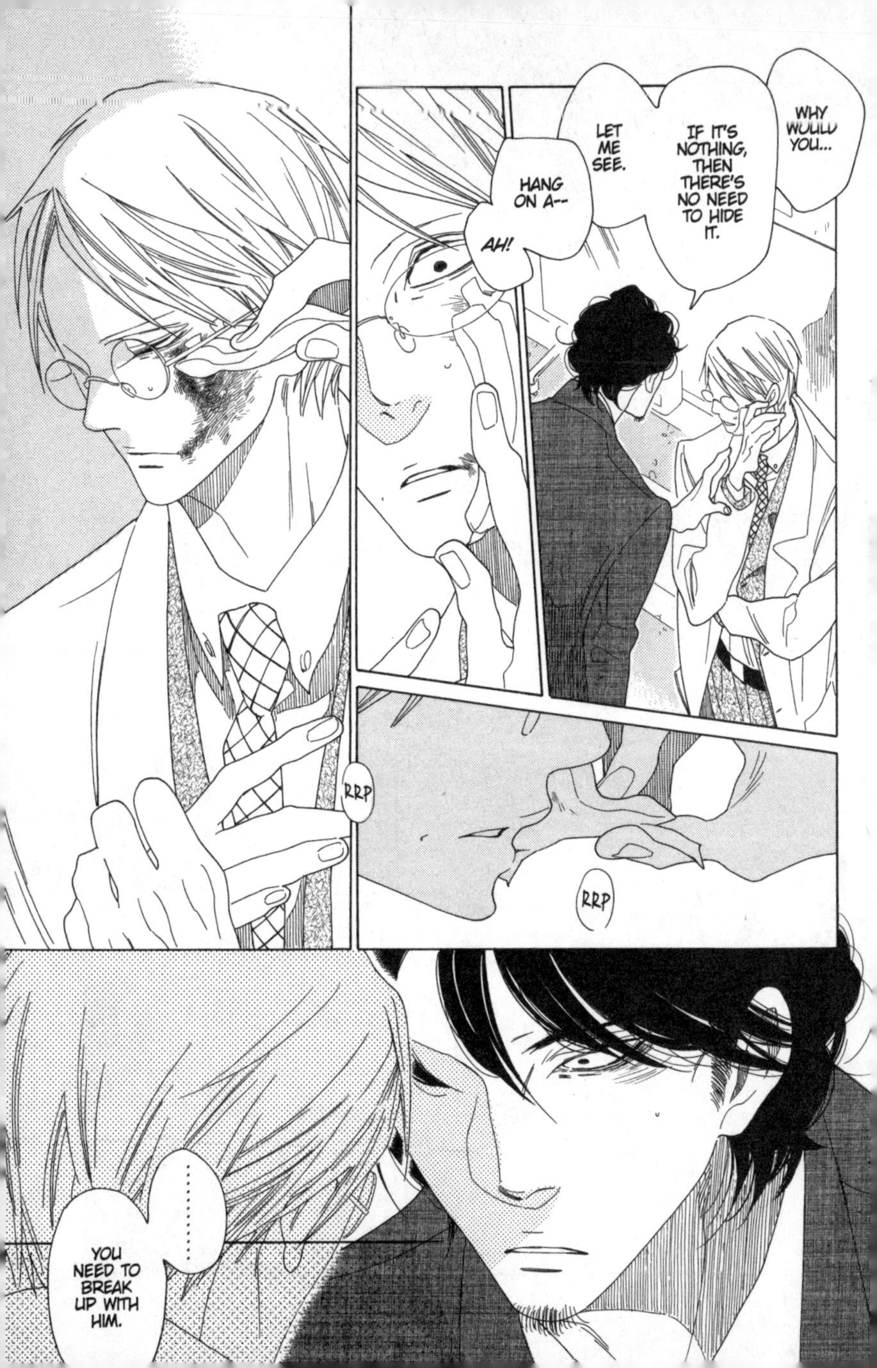

WHY WOULD YOU...
IF IT'S NOTHING, THEN THERE'S NO NEED TO HIDE IT.
LET ME SEE.
HANG ON A--
AH!
RRP
RRP
......
YOU NEED TO BREAK UP WITH HIM.

THIS...!
YOU CAN'T STAY WITH SOMEONE WHO'D DO THIS TO YOU!
HARA-KUN.
THIS ISN'T RIGHT.
PLEASE, LISTEN TO ME.
I JUST WANT YOU...
TO BE HAPPY.
SO...
HARA-KUN!
YOU'VE GOT IT ALL WRO--
VRZZ
VRZZ
VRZZ
VRZZ
GO AHEAD. ANSWER IT.
OH.
RIGHT.
VRZZ
VRZZ
VRZZ
VRZZ

BEEP
HELLO?
HIBIKI?
SHUDDER
OH...
OH... NO.
LAST NIGHT WAS...
LOOK.
I WANTED TO--
BAM!!
WAIT! HEY!
WHAT ARE YOU--?!
KLIK
BEEP BEEP
WHAT IS IT?
HELLO?
HELLO?!
BEEP
BEEP
BEEP
BEEP
BEEP
BEEP
....
KACHAK
I HAVE TO...
HUH?

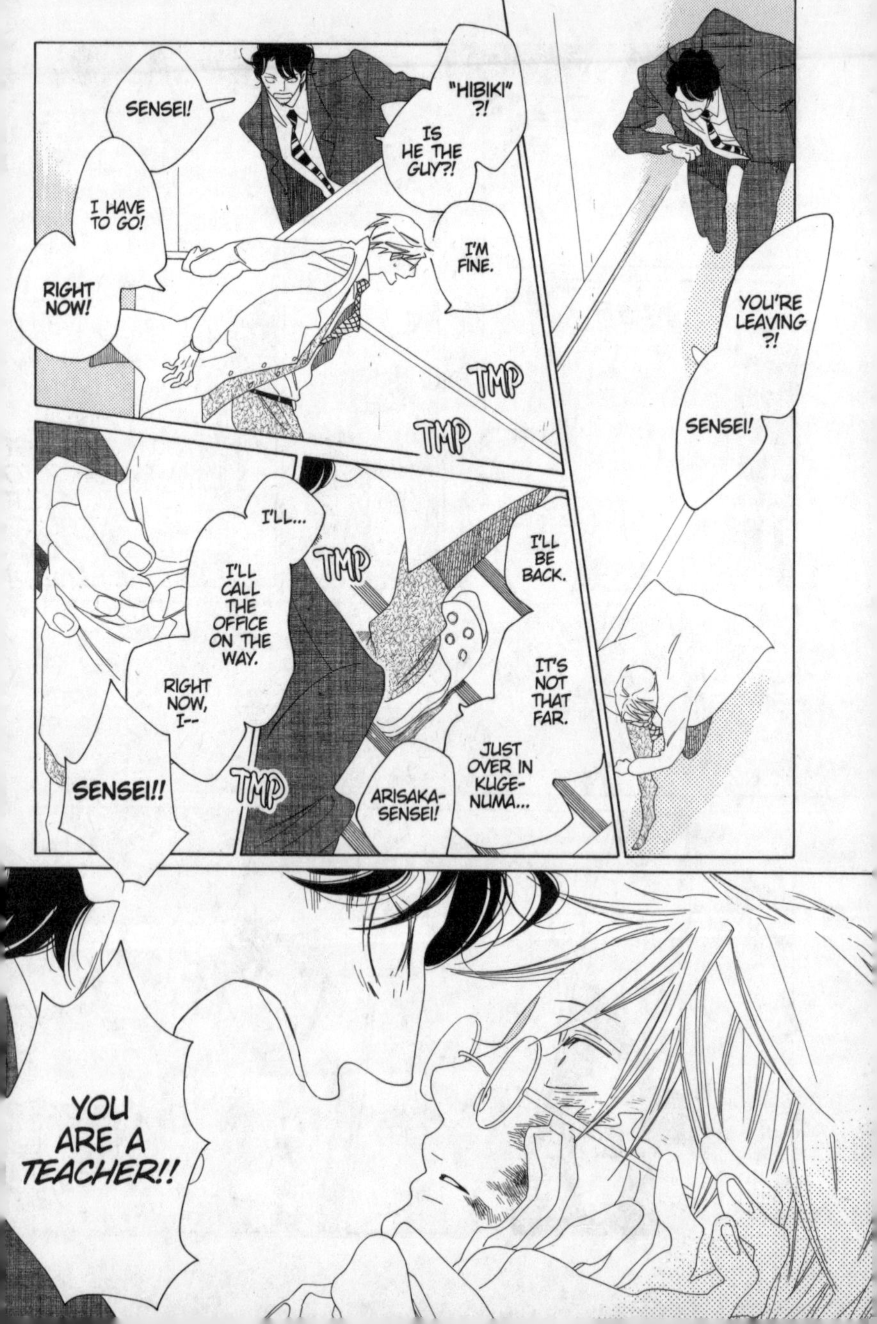
YOU'RE LEAVING ?!
SENSEI!
"HIBIKI" ?!
IS HE THE GUY?!
I'M FINE.
SENSEI!
I HAVE TO GO!
RIGHT NOW!
TMP
TMP
I'LL BE BACK.
IT'S NOT THAT FAR.
JUST OVER IN KUGE-NUMA...
ARISAKA-SENSEI!
TMP
TMP
I'LL...
I'LL CALL THE OFFICE ON THE WAY.
RIGHT NOW, I--
SENSEI!!
YOU ARE A TEACHER!!

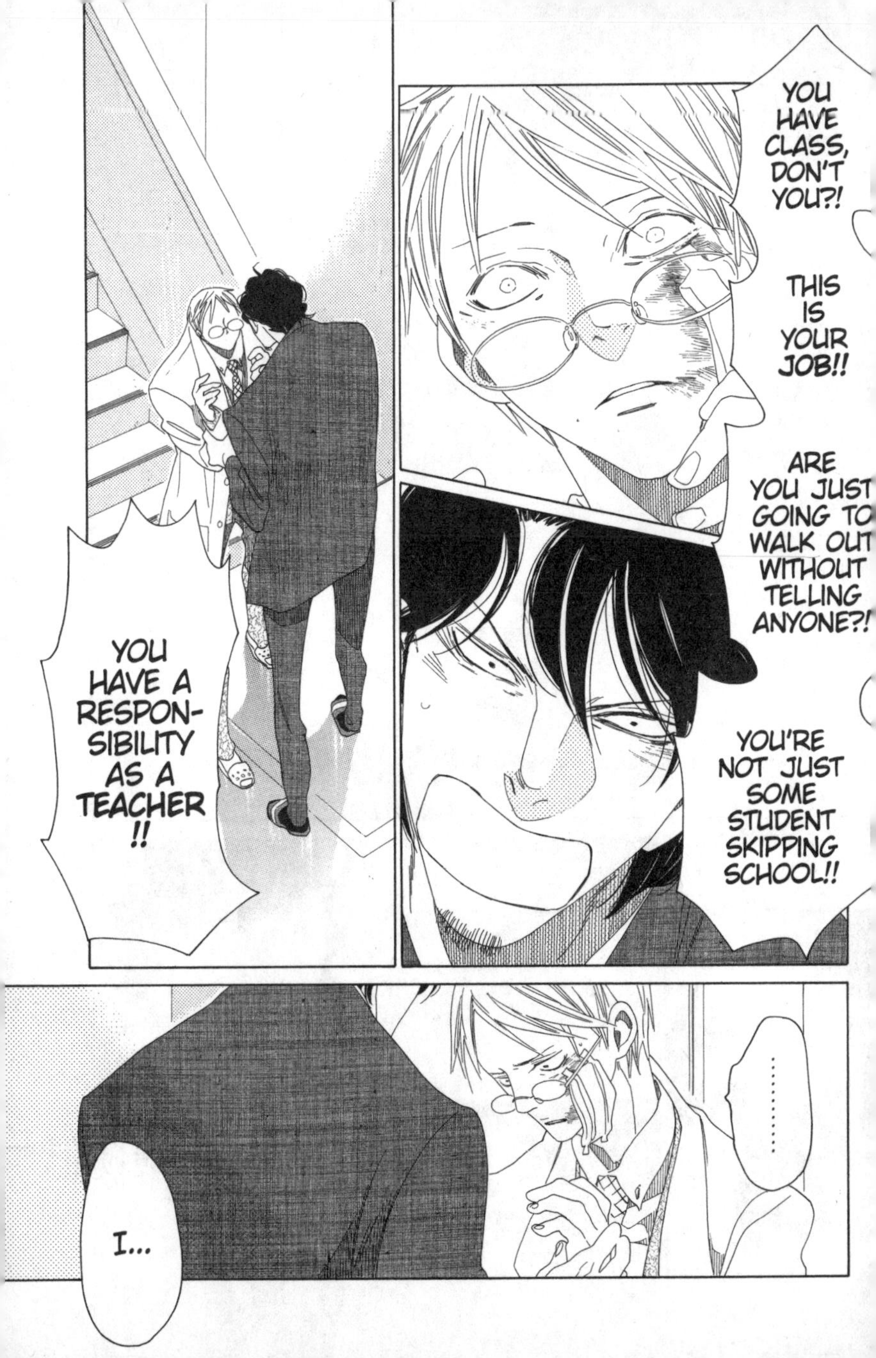
YOU HAVE CLASS, DON'T YOU?!
THIS IS YOUR JOB!!
ARE YOU JUST GOING TO WALK OUT WITHOUT TELLING ANYONE?!
YOU'RE NOT JUST SOME STUDENT SKIPPING SCHOOL!!
YOU HAVE A RESPON-SIBILITY AS A TEACHER!!
....
I...

I'LL GO FILL OUT THE FORMS, SO PLEASE WAIT IN THE PARKING LOT.
I'LL DRIVE YOU.
BAM
DASH
OH! HARA-CHAN!
YOU'RE LATE!
WHAT'S GOING ON?
OOOH!
DASH
SKRK SKRK
STUDY PERIOD
自習

HUFF! HUFF! HUFF! HUFF!

DASH

STUDY PERIOD

OOOH!

WHY'S HARASEN HERE?

HUH? THIS IS CHEMISTRY, RIGHT?

TAK

HOW LONG... HAS IT BEEN SINCE I RAN LIKE THIS?

OH! HARA-SENSEI!

	Oishi	3-B
	Ikuda	3-A
	Oyamada	Home Ec
	Oishi	Library
	Hashimoto	1-A
	Nakao	2-B
	Hara	OUT
	Arisaka	OUT

DASH

HUFF!

HUFF!

HUFF!

HUFF!

AH!

IT DOESN'T ACTUALLY MATTER.

BUT...

WAIT. I HAVE RECENTLY.

PRETTY SURE.

WHEN HE GOT TANGLED UP WITH THAT WEIRDO...

HUFF!

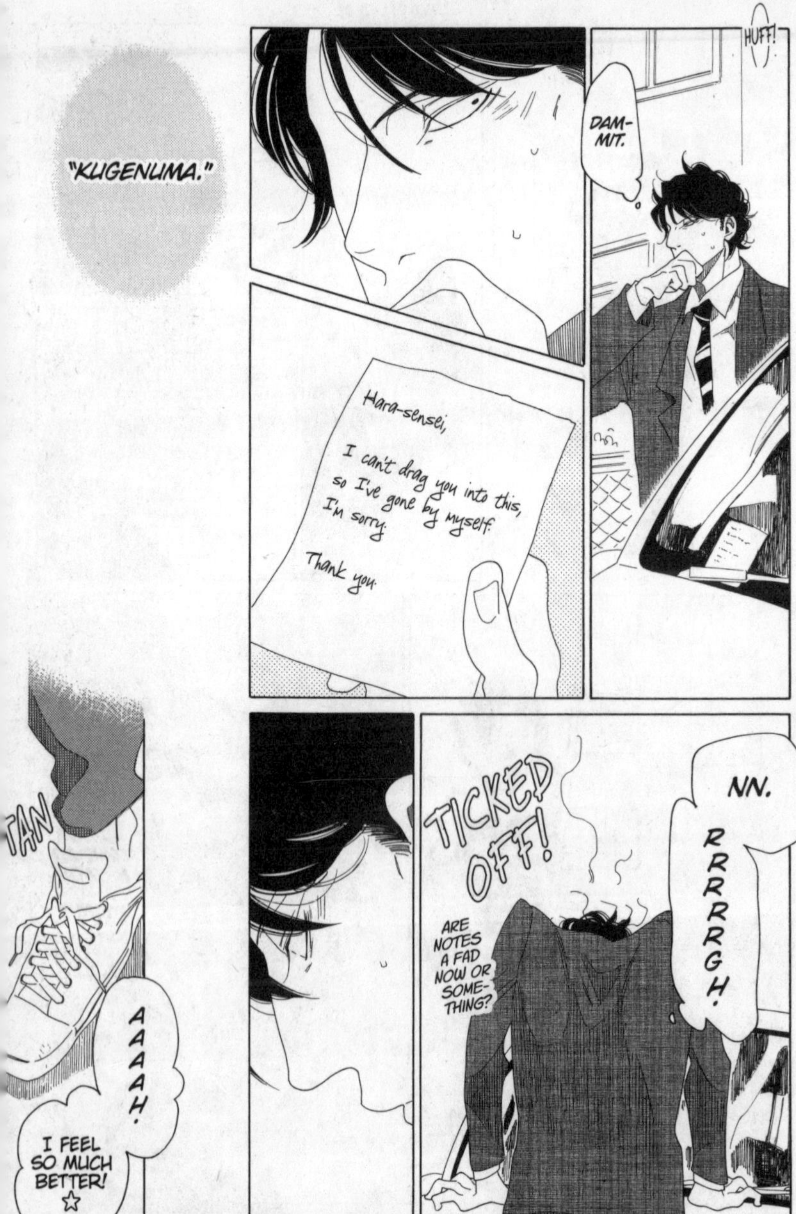
HUFF!
DAM-MIT.
Hara-sensei,
I can't drag you into this, so I've gone by myself. I'm sorry.
Thank you.
NN.
RRRRRGH.
TICKED OFF!
ARE NOTES A FAD NOW OR SOME-THING?
"KUGENUMA."
TAN
AAAAAH.
I FEEL SO MUCH BETTER! ☆

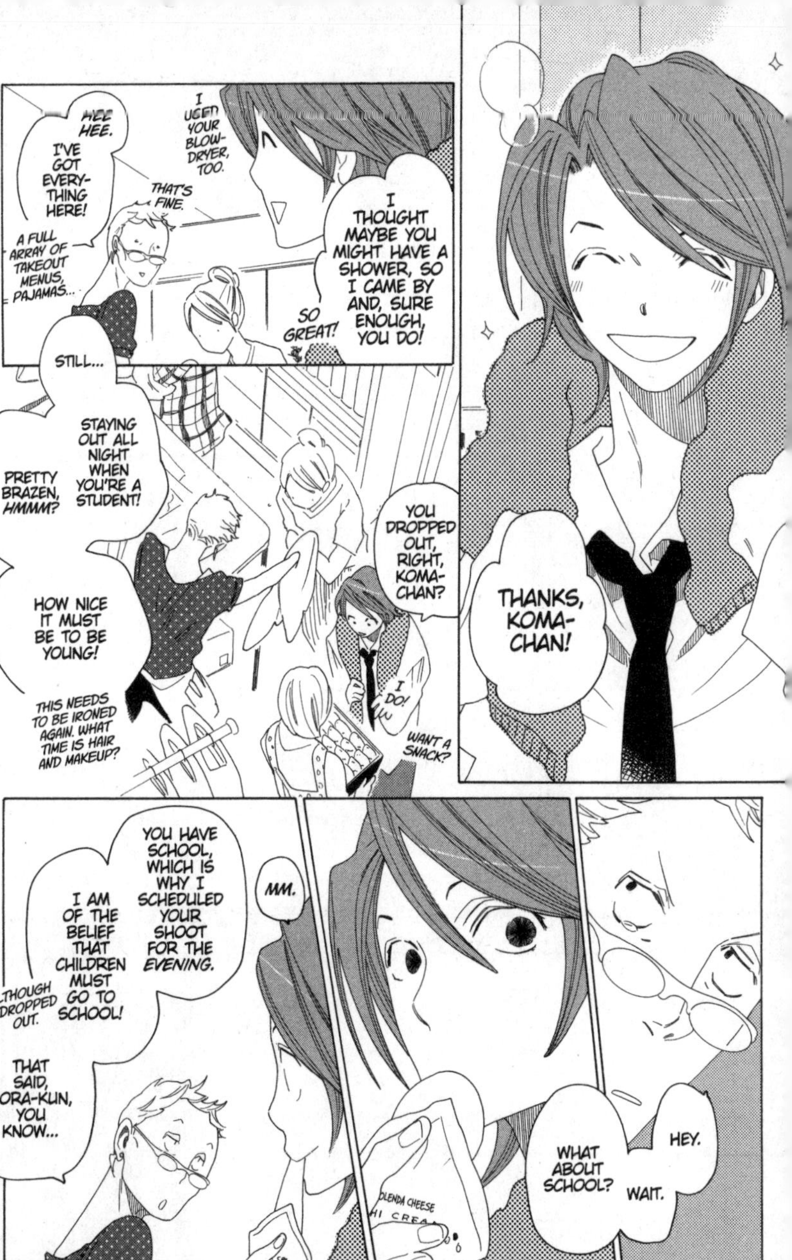
THANKS, KOMA-CHAN!
I THOUGHT MAYBE YOU MIGHT HAVE A SHOWER, SO I CAME BY AND, SURE ENOUGH, YOU DO!
I USED YOUR BLOW-DRYER, TOO.
SO GREAT!
THAT'S FINE.
HEE HEE. I'VE GOT EVERYTHING HERE!
A FULL ARRAY OF TAKEOUT MENUS, PAJAMAS...
YOU DROPPED OUT, RIGHT, KOMA-CHAN?
I DO!
WANT A SNACK?
STILL...
STAYING OUT ALL NIGHT WHEN YOU'RE A STUDENT!
PRETTY BRAZEN, *HMMM?*
HOW NICE IT MUST BE TO BE YOUNG!
THIS NEEDS TO BE IRONED AGAIN. WHAT TIME IS HAIR AND MAKEUP?
HEY.
WAIT.
WHAT ABOUT SCHOOL?
MM.
YOU HAVE SCHOOL, WHICH IS WHY I SCHEDULED YOUR SHOOT FOR THE *EVENING.*
I AM OF THE BELIEF THAT CHILDREN MUST GO TO SCHOOL!
ALTHOUGH I DROPPED OUT.
THAT SAID, SORA-KUN, YOU KNOW...

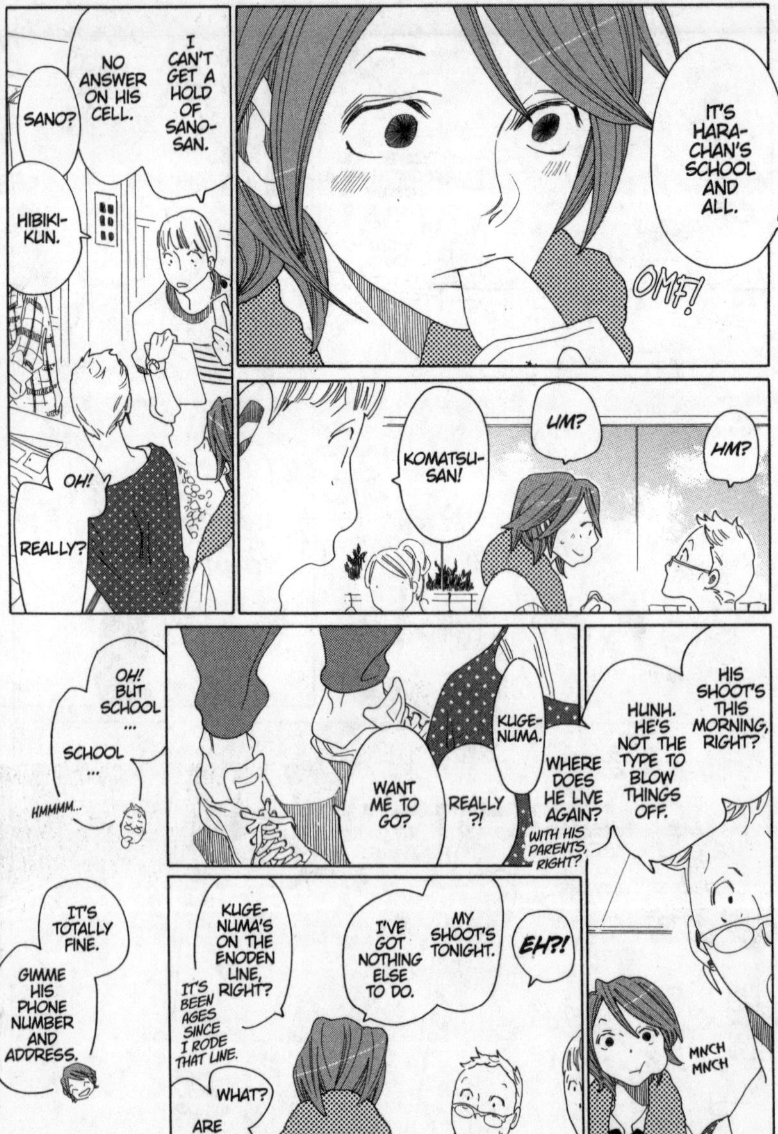
IT'S HARA-CHAN'S SCHOOL AND ALL.
OMF!
HM?
UM?
KOMATSU-SAN!
I CAN'T GET A HOLD OF SANO-SAN.
NO ANSWER ON HIS CELL.
SANO?
HIBIKI-KUN.
OH!
REALLY?
HIS SHOOT'S THIS MORNING, RIGHT?
HUNH. HE'S NOT THE TYPE TO BLOW THINGS OFF.
WHERE DOES HE LIVE AGAIN?
WITH HIS PARENTS, RIGHT?
KUGE-NUMA.
REALLY?!
WANT ME TO GO?
OH! BUT SCHOOL...
SCHOOL...
HMMMM...
MNCH MNCH
EH?!
MY SHOOT'S TONIGHT.
I'VE GOT NOTHING ELSE TO DO.
KUGE-NUMA'S ON THE ENODEN LINE, RIGHT?
IT'S BEEN AGES SINCE I RODE THAT LINE.
WHAT?
ARE YOU SURE?
IT'S TOTALLY FINE.
GIMME HIS PHONE NUMBER AND ADDRESS.

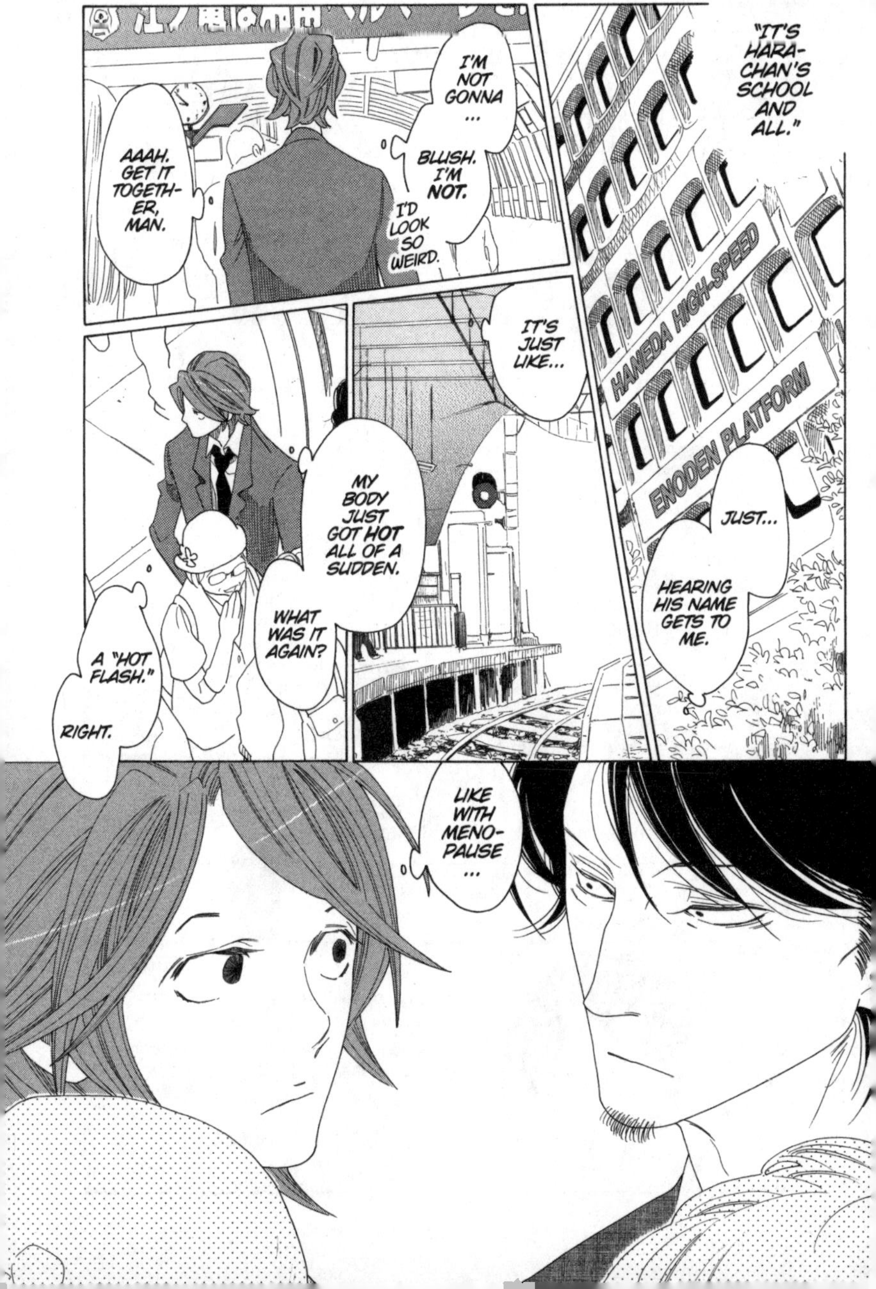
"IT'S HARA-CHAN'S SCHOOL AND ALL."
HANEDA HIGH-SPEED
ENODEN PLATFORM
JUST...
HEARING HIS NAME GETS TO ME.
I'M NOT GONNA...
BLUSH. I'M NOT.
I'D LOOK SO WEIRD.
AAAH. GET IT TOGETHER, MAN.
IT'S JUST LIKE...
MY BODY JUST GOT HOT ALL OF A SUDDEN.
WHAT WAS IT AGAIN?
A "HOT FLASH."
RIGHT.
LIKE WITH MENOPAUSE...

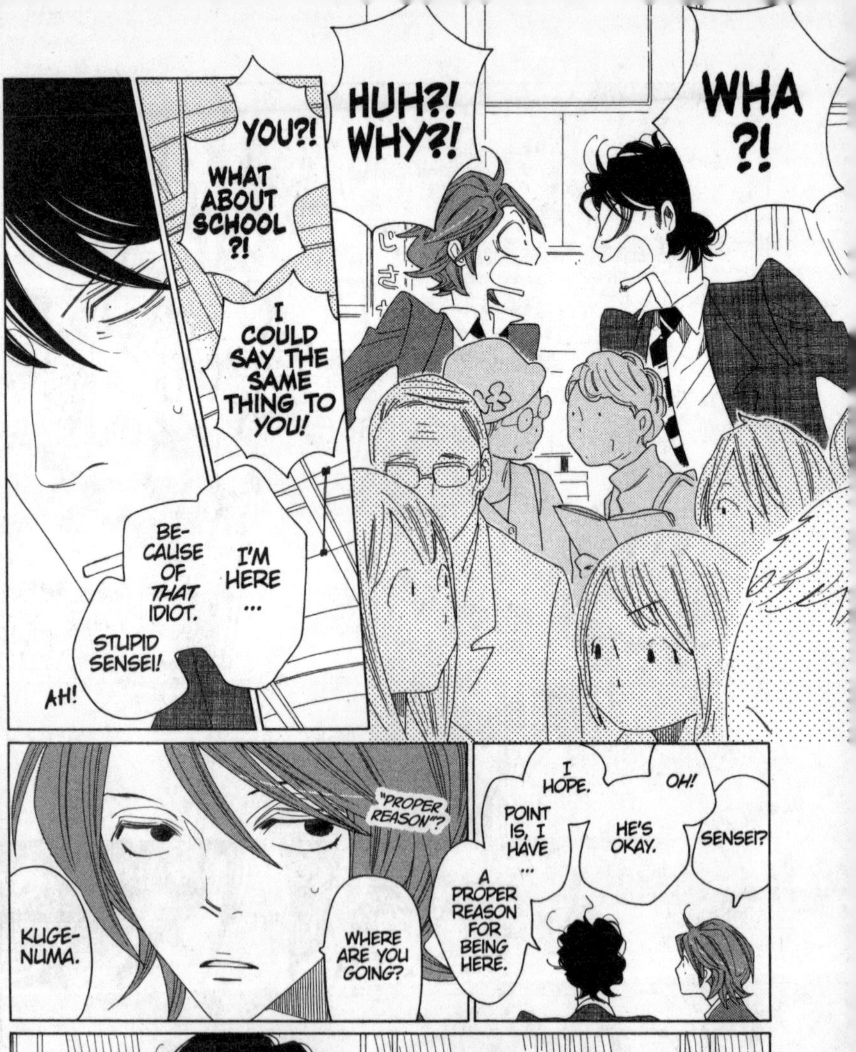
WHA ?!
HUH?! WHY?!
YOU?!
WHAT ABOUT SCHOOL ?!
I COULD SAY THE SAME THING TO YOU!
I'M HERE ...
BE-CAUSE OF *THAT* IDIOT.
STUPID SENSEI!
AH!
SENSEI?
OH!
HE'S OKAY.
I HOPE.
POINT IS, I HAVE ...
A PROPER REASON FOR BEING HERE.
"PROPER REASON"?
WHERE ARE YOU GOING?
KUGE-NUMA.
HUH? KUGE-NUMA?
THAT'S WHERE *I'M* GOING.
WHAT? YOU'RE GOING TO KUGENUMA?

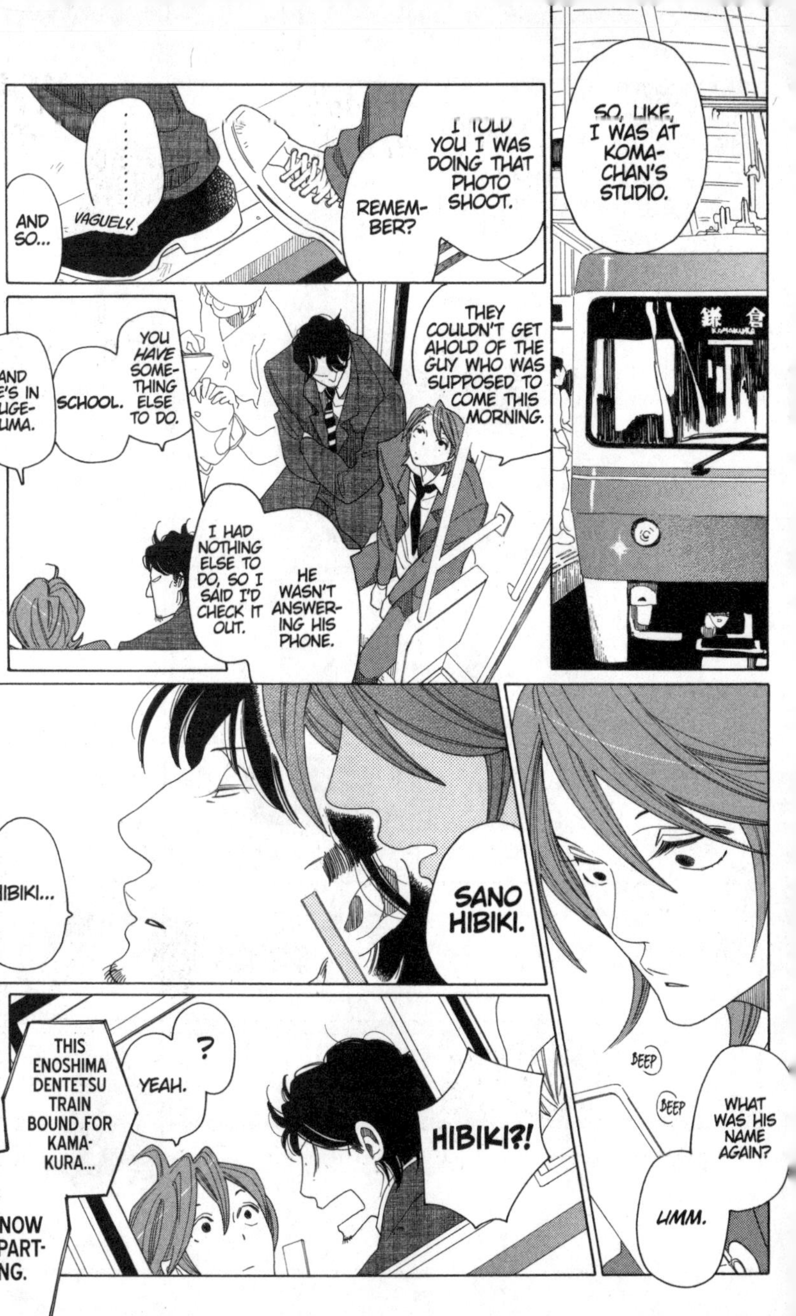
SO, LIKE, I WAS AT KOMA-CHAN'S STUDIO.
鎌倉
I TOLD YOU I WAS DOING THAT PHOTO SHOOT.
REMEMBER?
......
VAGUELY.
AND SO...
THEY COULDN'T GET AHOLD OF THE GUY WHO WAS SUPPOSED TO COME THIS MORNING.
HE WASN'T ANSWERING HIS PHONE.
I HAD NOTHING ELSE TO DO, SO I SAID I'D CHECK IT OUT.
YOU HAVE SOMETHING ELSE TO DO.
SCHOOL.
AND HE'S IN KUGENUMA.
BEEP
BEEP
WHAT WAS HIS NAME AGAIN?
UMM.
SANO HIBIKI.
HIBIKI...
HIBIKI?!
?
YEAH.
THIS ENOSHIMA DENTETSU TRAIN BOUND FOR KAMAKURA...
IS NOW DEPARTING.

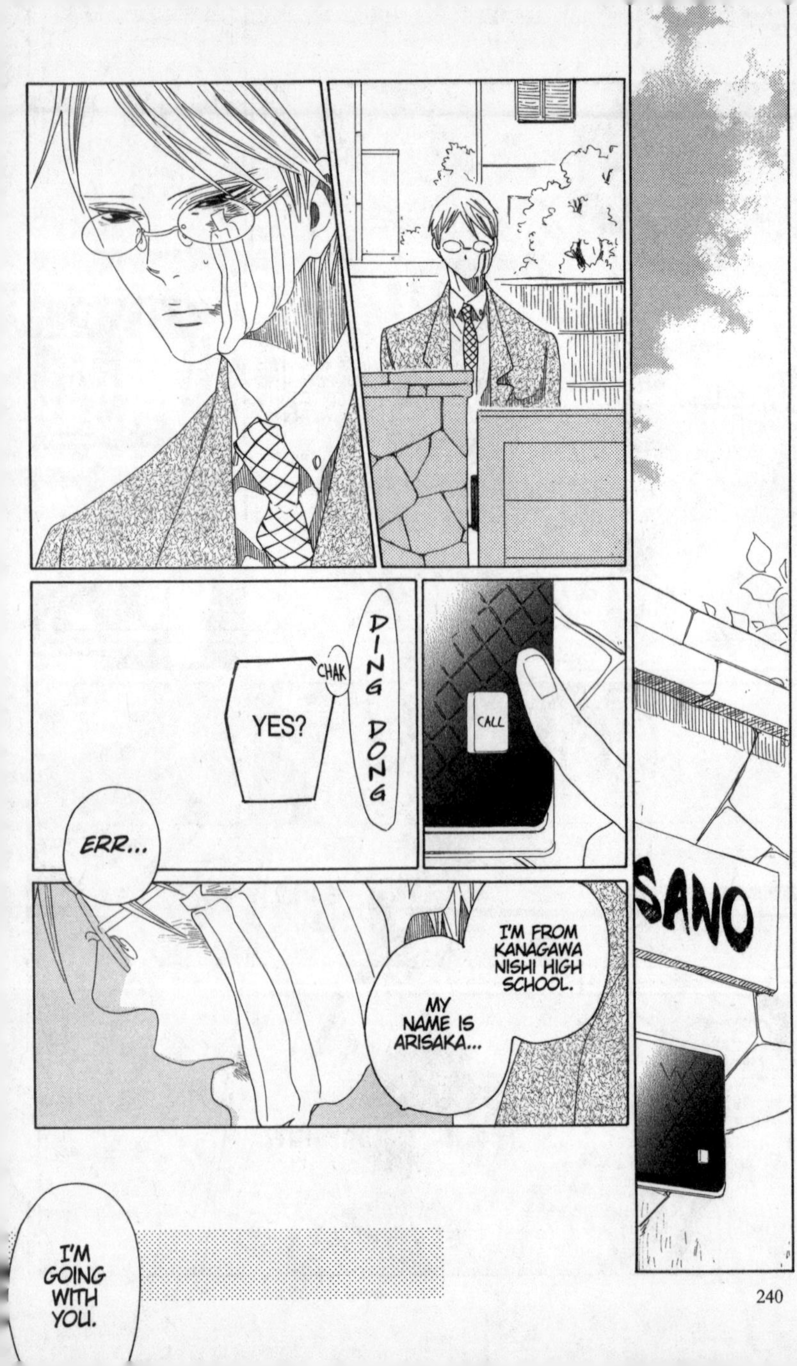
SANO
CALL
DING DONG
CHAK
YES?
ERR...
I'M FROM KANAGAWA NISHI HIGH SCHOOL.
MY NAME IS ARISAKA...
I'M GOING WITH YOU.

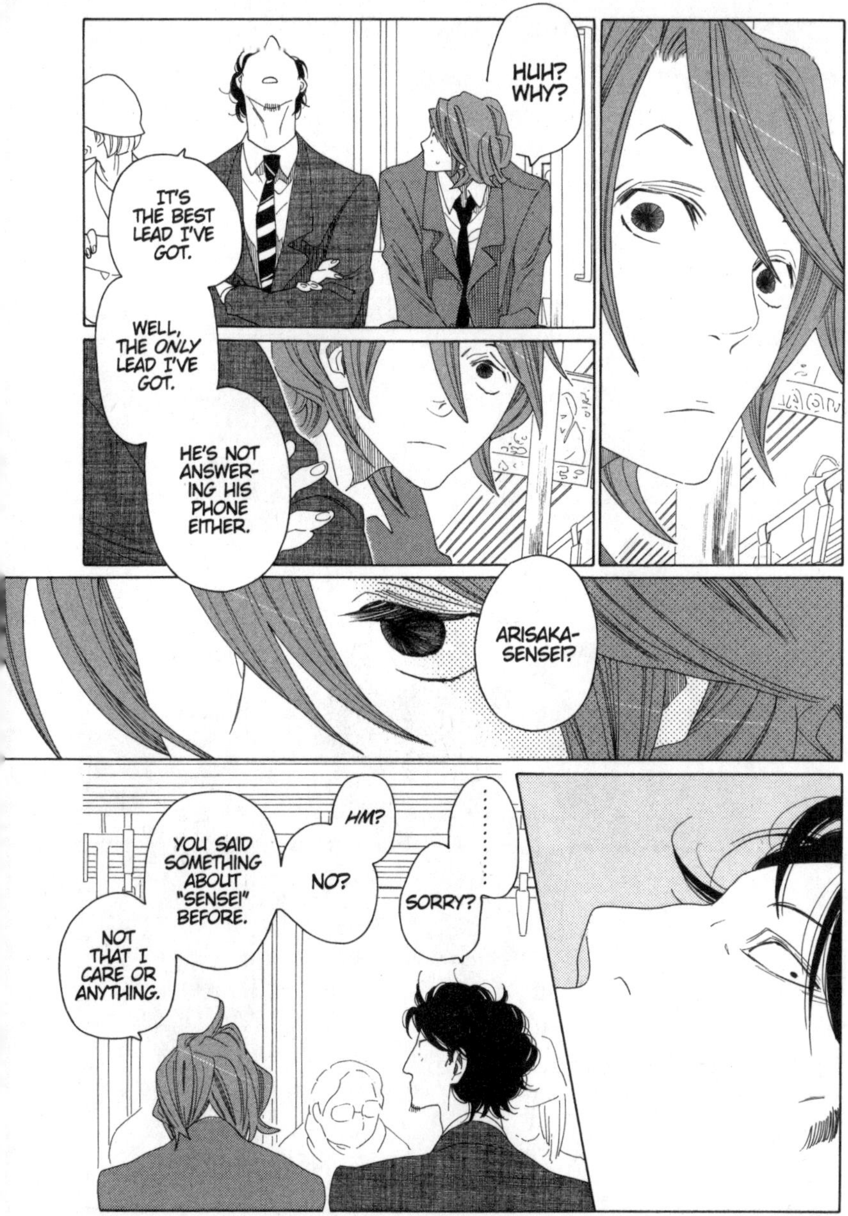
HUH? WHY?
IT'S THE BEST LEAD I'VE GOT.
WELL, THE *ONLY* LEAD I'VE GOT.
HE'S NOT ANSWERING HIS PHONE EITHER.
ARISAKA-SENSEI?
......
SORRY?
HM?
NO?
YOU SAID SOMETHING ABOUT "SENSEI" BEFORE.
NOT THAT I CARE OR ANYTHING.

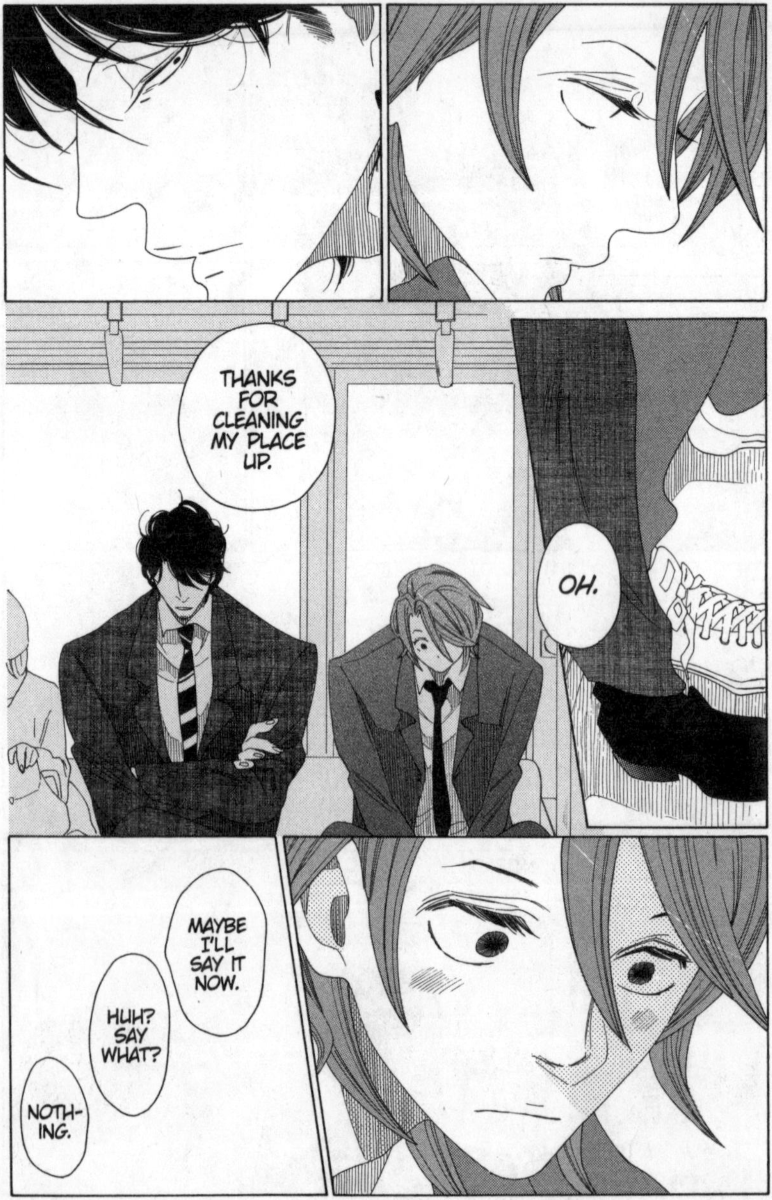
OH.
THANKS FOR CLEANING MY PLACE UP.
MAYBE I'LL SAY IT NOW.
HUH? SAY WHAT?
NOTH-ING.

くげぬま
鵠沼
KUGENUMA
EN 04
EN 03
やなぎこうじ
PROB-ABLY AROUND HERE--
JUST LEAVE!
WHAP

PLEASE!
I JUST WANT TO TALK!
PLEASE LOWER YOUR VOICE.
YOU ALREADY TALKED LAST NIGHT, DIDN'T YOU?
YOU HAVE NOTHING LEFT TO TALK ABOUT.
PLEASE STAY AWAY FROM US.
IT'S YOUR PROBLEM NOW.
BUT!
HE STILL WON'T ACCEPT IT.
IF WE COULD JUST TALK--
GO AWAY!

IF YOU KEEP THIS UP, I'LL CALL THE POLICE!
SENSEI!
HA... HARA-KUN.
WHAT ARE YOU...?
H-HEY.
ARE YOU ALL RIGHT?
WHO ARE YOU?
WHAT IS THIS?
MARCHING IN HERE...!
WHAT ARE THE NEIGHBORS GOING TO SAY--
I'M SORRY FOR ALL THE FUSS.
I'M A COLLEAGUE OF ARISAKA'S.
MY NAME IS HARA.

WHAT DID ARISAKA--
IF YOU'RE HIS COLLEAGUE, THEN YOU *KNOW*, DON'T YOU?!
YOU HAVE TO DO SOMETHING ABOUT HIM!
THE FACT HE'S...
STILL TEACHING IS *RIDICULOUS!*
WE'RE HAPPY TO TAKE YOU TO COURT, YOU KNOW.
PLEASE. LET'S NOT BE RASH.
WHAT EXACTLY...
YOU REALLY DON'T KNOW?!
ARE YOU GOING TO MAKE ME SAY IT?!
THIS MAN, HE...
HE TOUCHED ...!
OUR SON, HIS OWN STUDENT ...!!
I DID *NOT!*

I SWEAR I DIDN'T!
MRS. SANO!
I...!
STOP IT! YOU'RE REPULSIVE!
HOW DARE YOU COME HERE AND SHOUT AT ME?!
A TEACHER, DOING SOMETHING LIKE *THAT*!
AND...
WITH A MALE STUDENT!!
CLANK
PERVERT!!
FREAK!
JUST GO!
GO ALREADY!!
CLANG
SEN-SEI!!

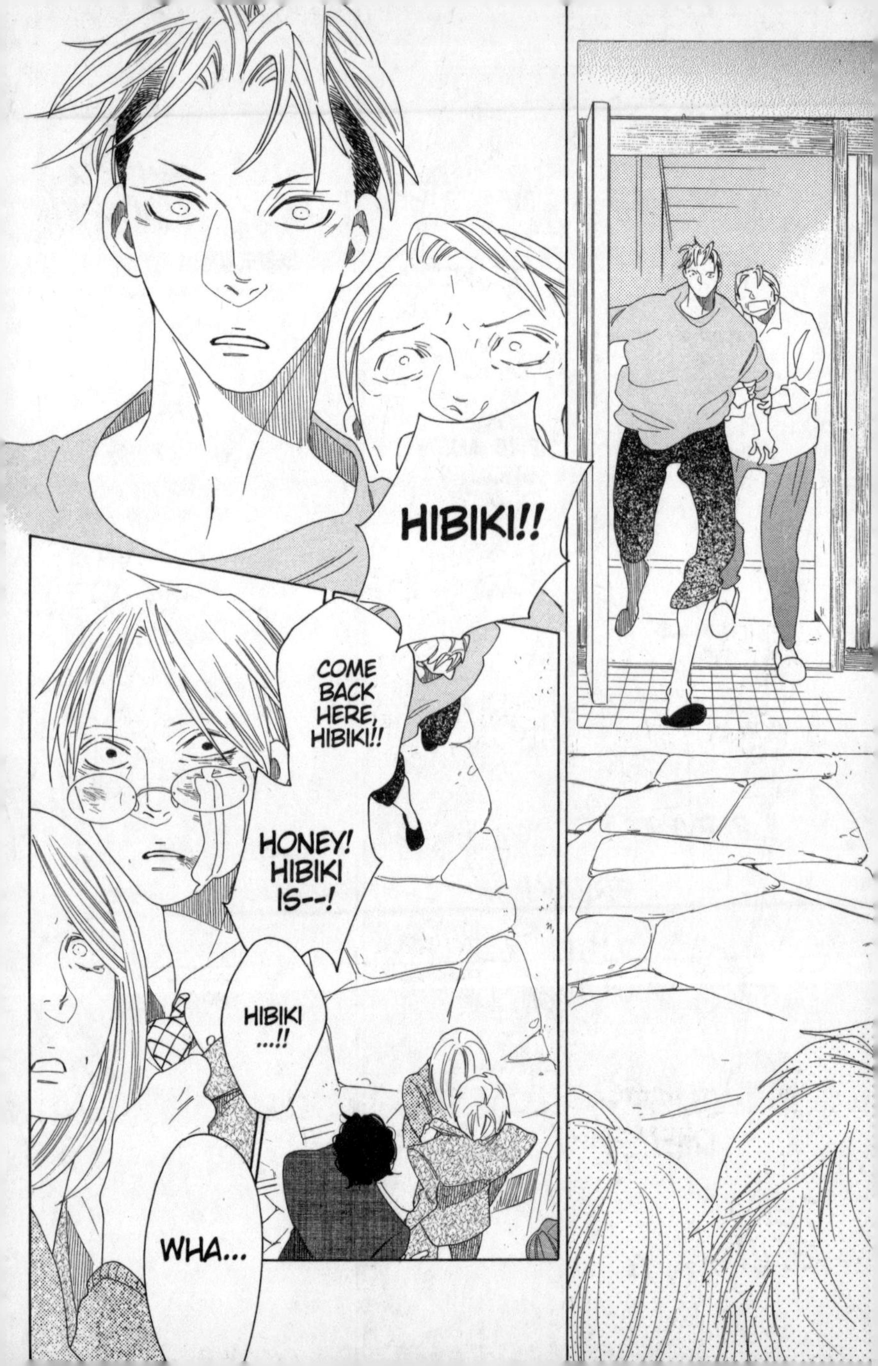
HIBIKI!!
COME BACK HERE, HIBIKI!!
HONEY! HIBIKI IS--!
HIBIKI ...!!
WHA...

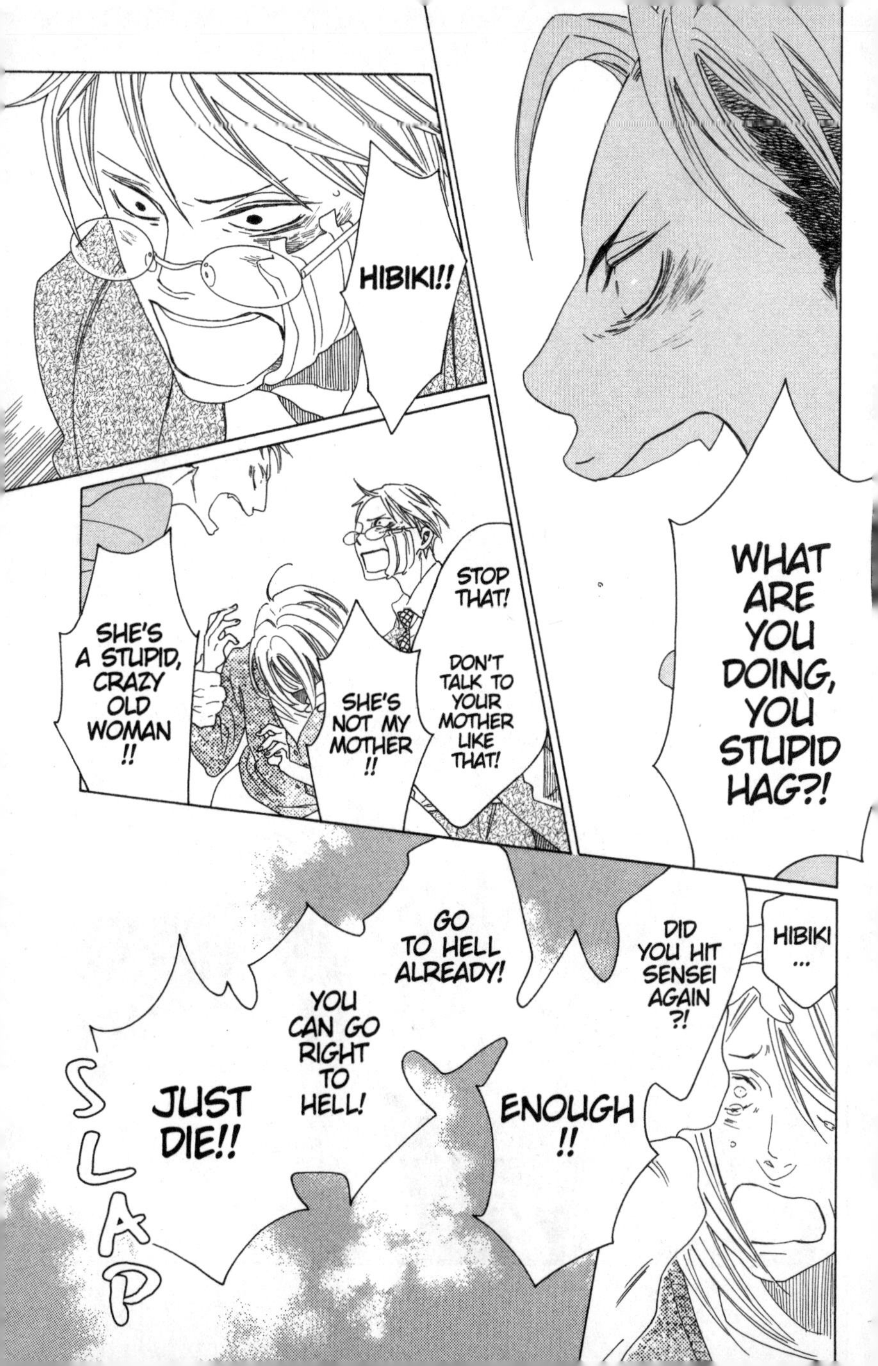
WHAT ARE YOU DOING, YOU STUPID HAG?!
HIBIKI!!
STOP THAT!
DON'T TALK TO YOUR MOTHER LIKE THAT!
SHE'S NOT MY MOTHER!!
SHE'S A STUPID, CRAZY OLD WOMAN!!
HIBIKI...
DID YOU HIT SENSEI AGAIN?!
ENOUGH!!
GO TO HELL ALREADY!
YOU CAN GO RIGHT TO HELL!
JUST DIE!!
SLAP

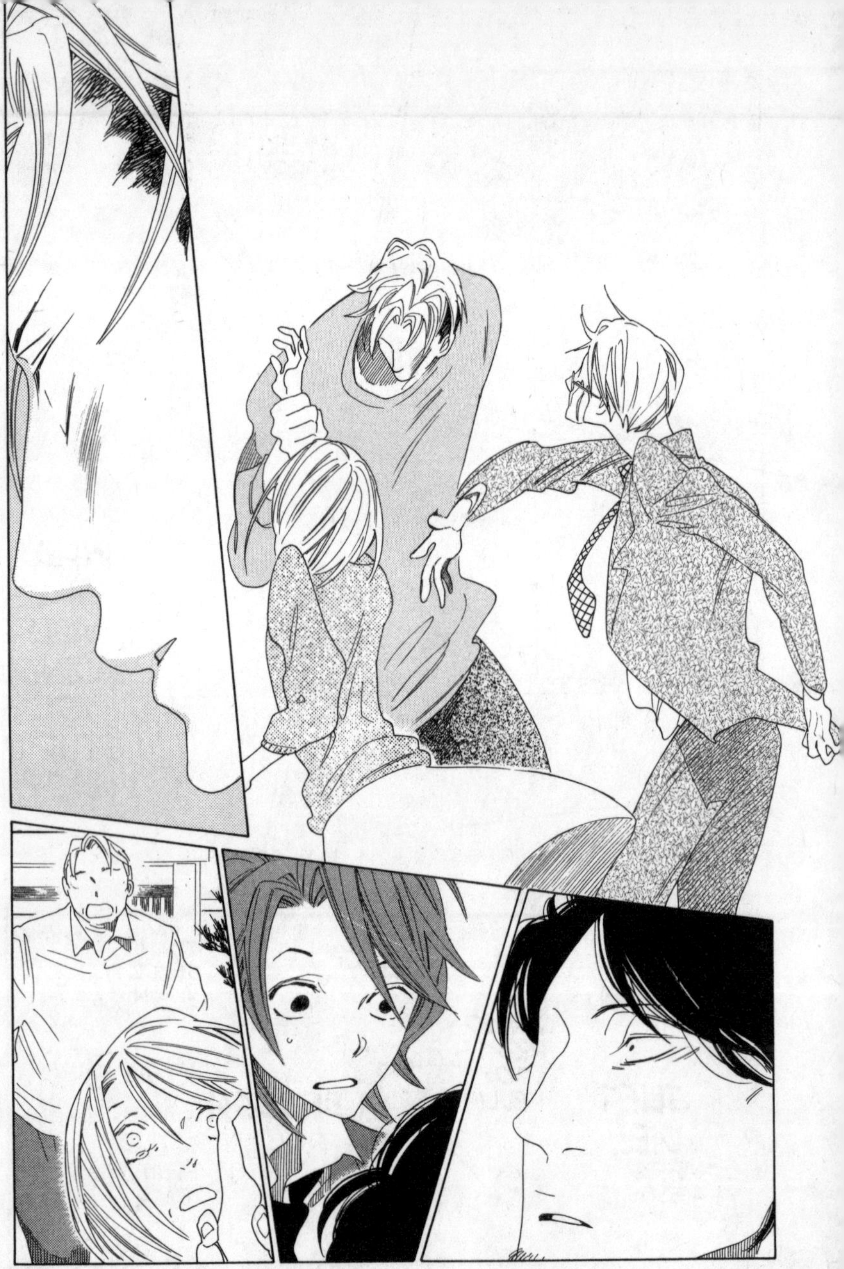

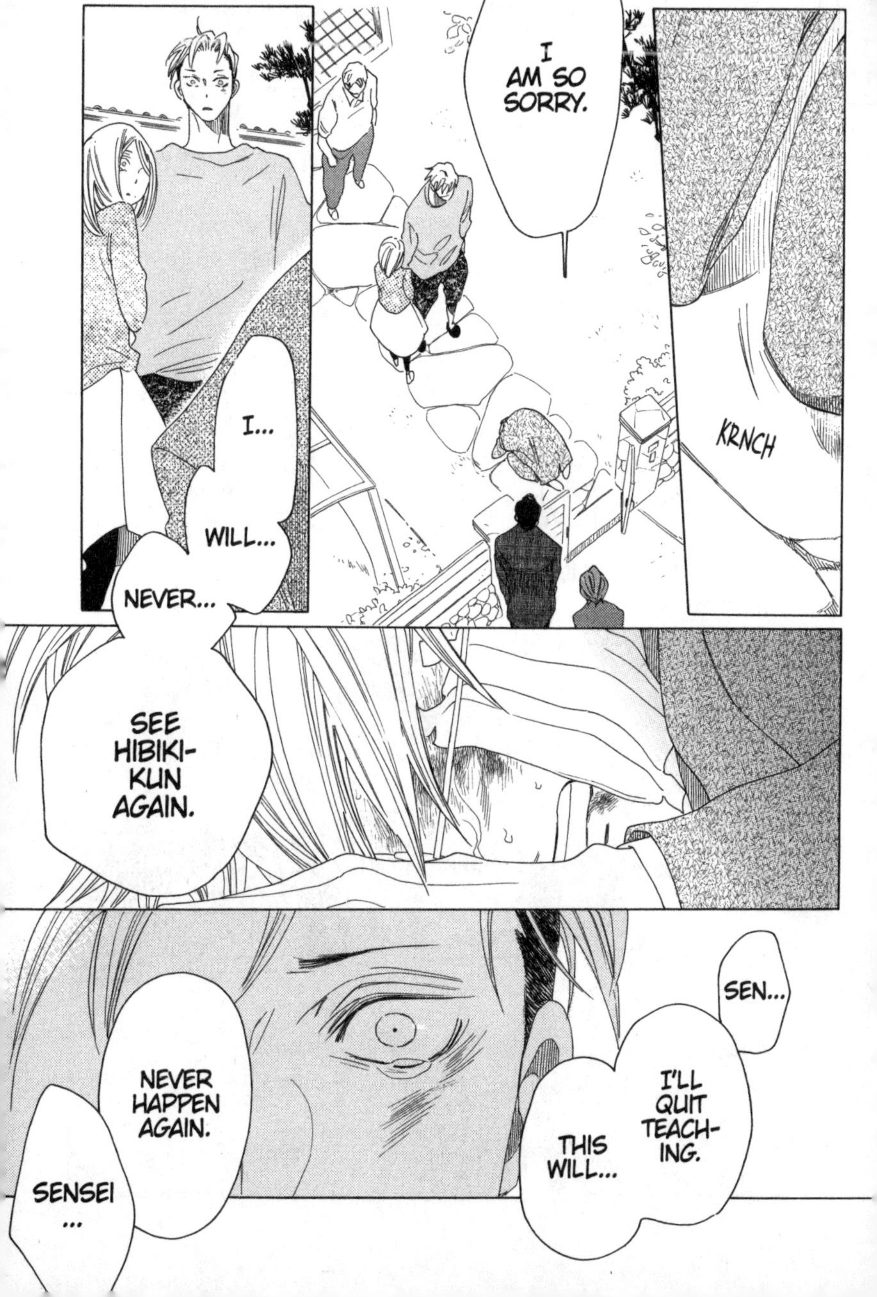
KRNCH
I AM SO SORRY.
I...
WILL...
NEVER...
SEE HIBIKI-KUN AGAIN.
SEN...
I'LL QUIT TEACHING.
THIS WILL...
NEVER HAPPEN AGAIN.
SENSEI...

NO. SENSEI ...
NO!
HIBIKI ...
WHY WOULD YOU SAY THAT?!
YOU SAID...
YOU SAID WE COULD BE TOGETHER WHEN I GRADUATED!
THAT YOU'D LOVE ME THEN!
YOU SAID SO, DIDN'T YOU?!
SO WHY WOULD YOU...
STOP IT, HIBIKI.
HIBIKI !!
WAS IT ALL A LIE?!
SENSEI?
SENSEI!
I DOUBT THAT.

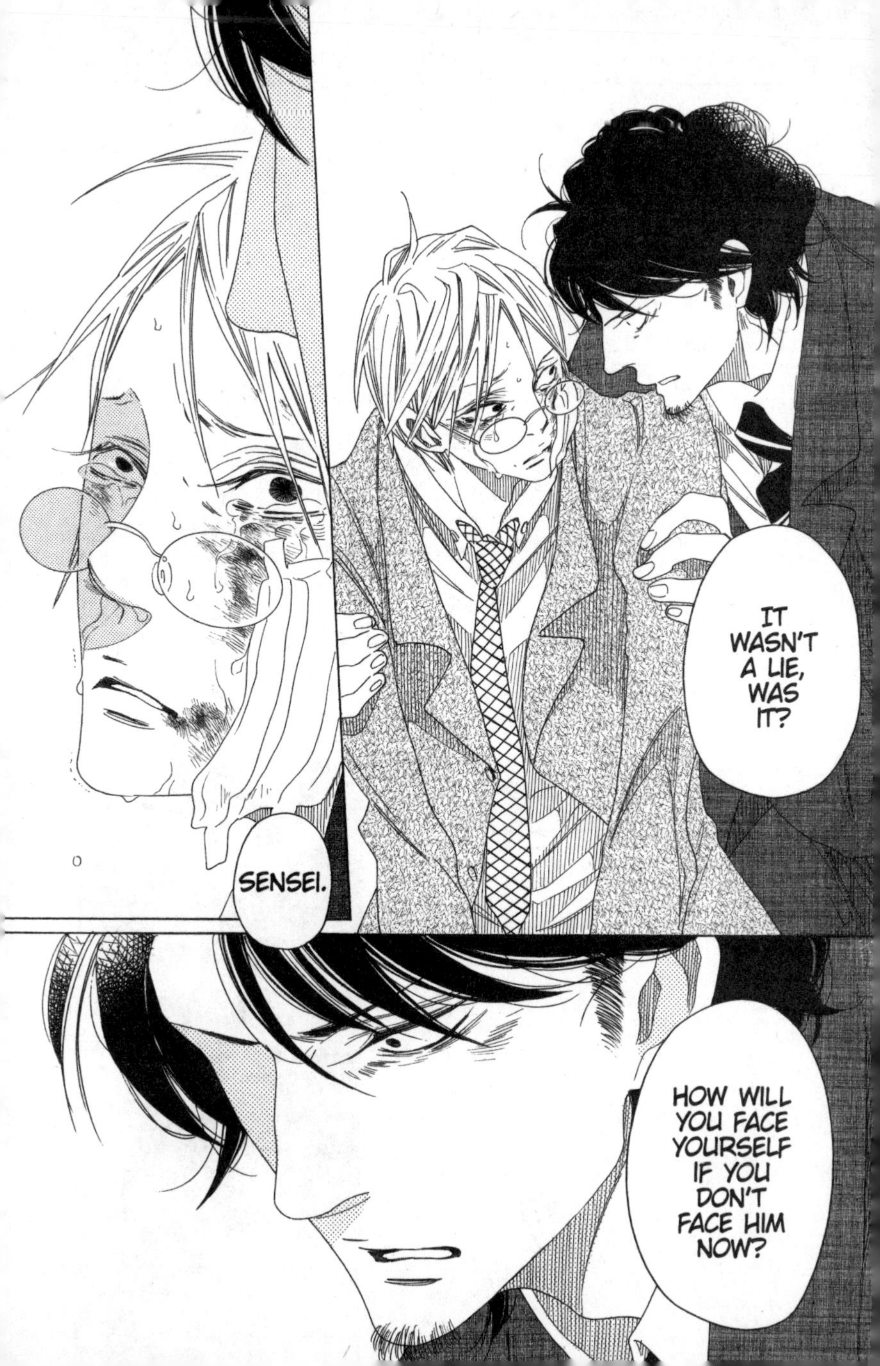
IT WASN'T A LIE, WAS IT?
SENSEI.
HOW WILL YOU FACE YOURSELF IF YOU DON'T FACE HIM NOW?

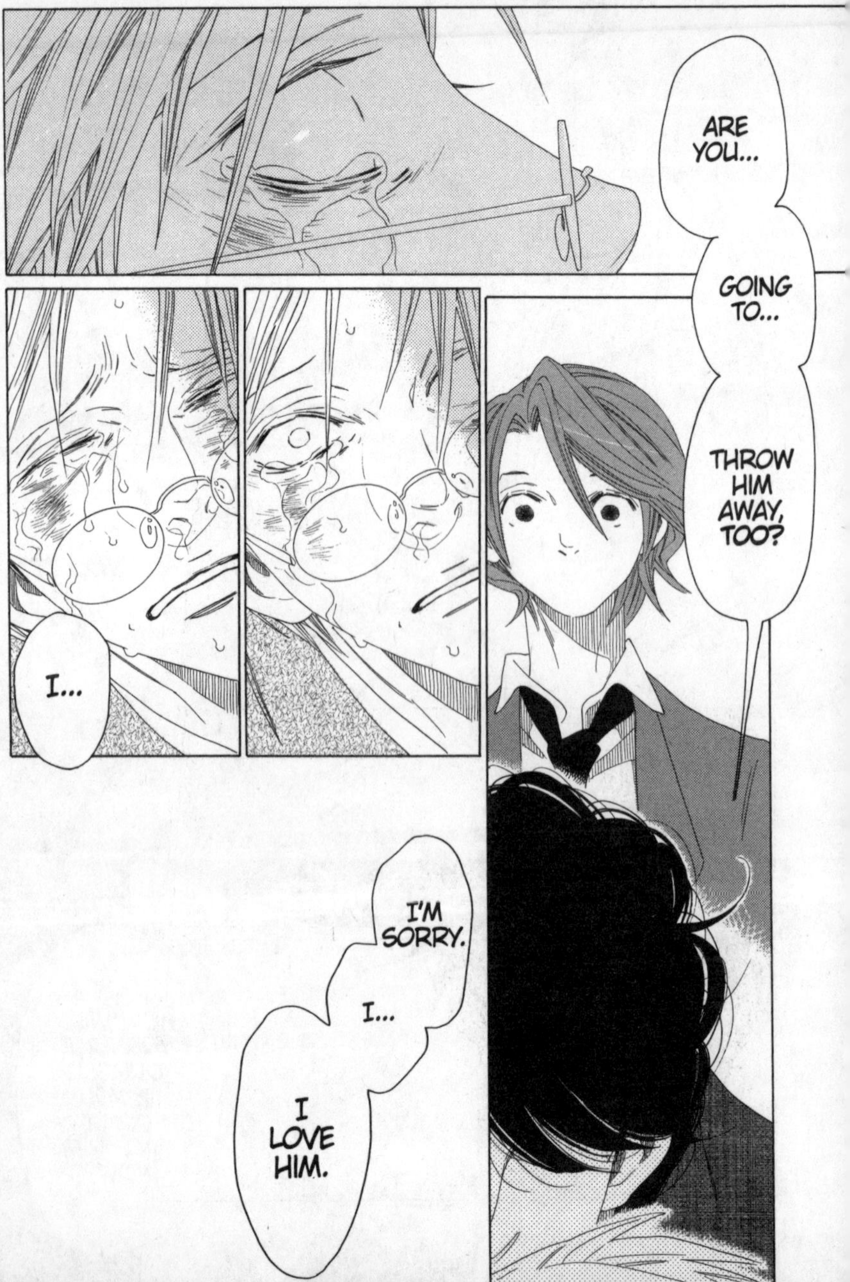
ARE YOU...
GOING TO...
THROW HIM AWAY, TOO?
I...
I'M SORRY.
I...
I LOVE HIM.

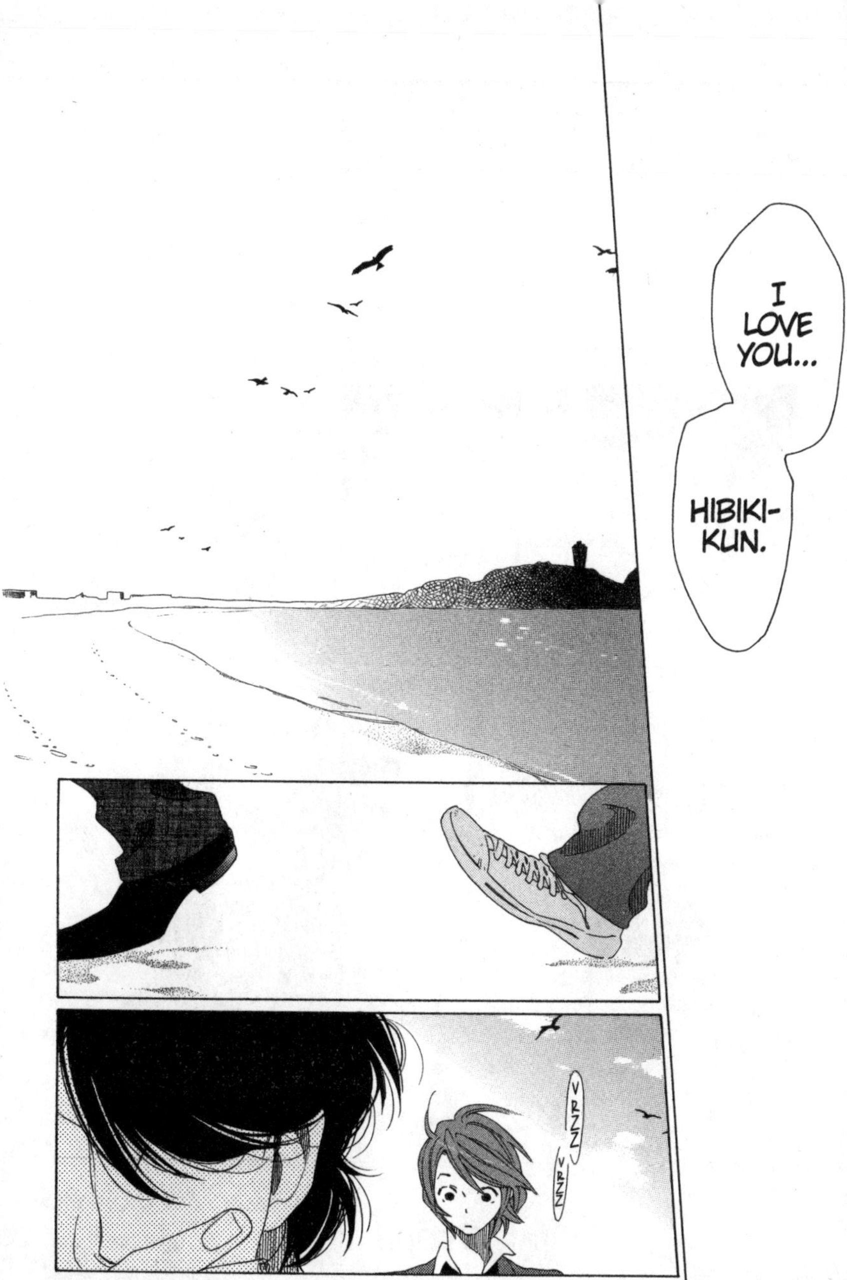
I LOVE YOU...
HIBIKI-KUN.
VRZZ
VRZZ

	HM?
	MAIL. A MESSAGE FROM KOMA-CHAN.
	HE'LL MOVE HIBIKI'S SHOOT TO NEXT WEEK.
	OH.
YOU OKAY?	

IN WHAT WAY?

SHE REALLY LET LOOSE ON YOU WITH SOME BODY BLOWS THERE.

Stop it!

Stop!

THUMP

Ma'am.

No one asked you!!

I'm sick of this!

Enough!

Stop!

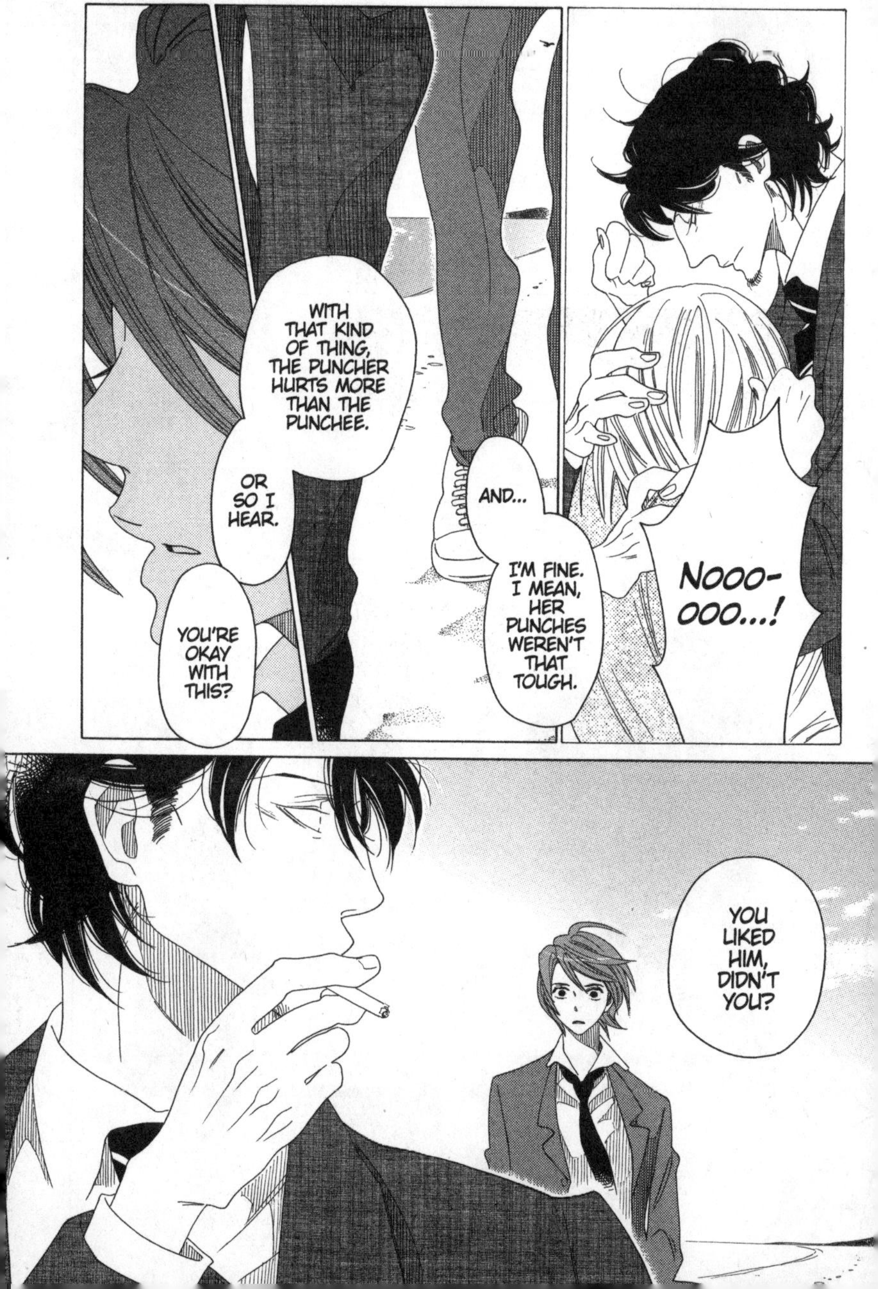
NOOO-OOO...!
WITH THAT KIND OF THING, THE PUNCHER HURTS MORE THAN THE PUNCHEE.
OR SO I HEAR.
AND...
I'M FINE. I MEAN, HER PUNCHES WEREN'T THAT TOUGH.
YOU'RE OKAY WITH THIS?
YOU LIKED HIM, DIDN'T YOU?

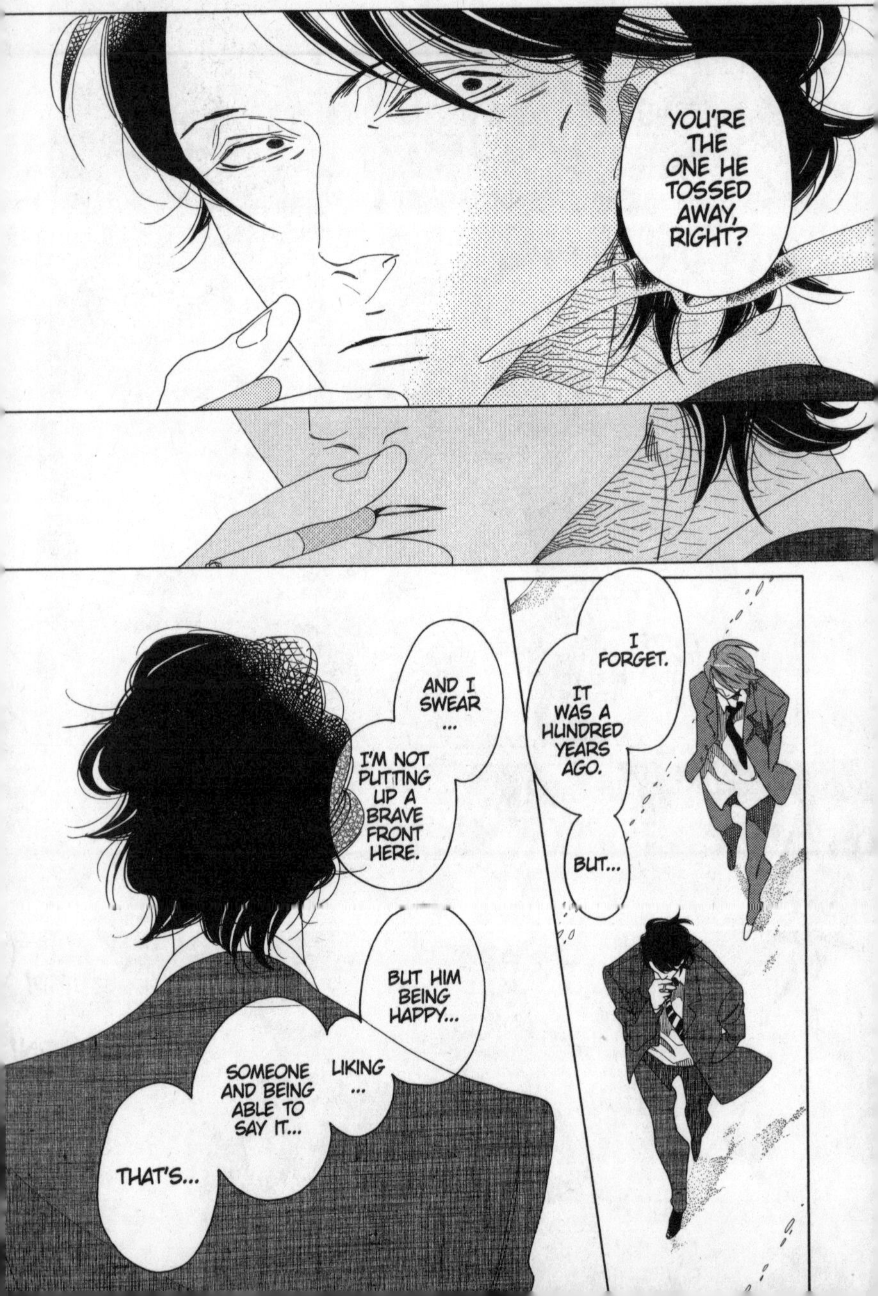
YOU'RE THE ONE HE TOSSED AWAY, RIGHT?
I FORGET.
IT WAS A HUNDRED YEARS AGO.
BUT...
AND I SWEAR...
I'M NOT PUTTING UP A BRAVE FRONT HERE.
BUT HIM BEING HAPPY...
LIKING...
SOMEONE AND BEING ABLE TO SAY IT...
THAT'S...

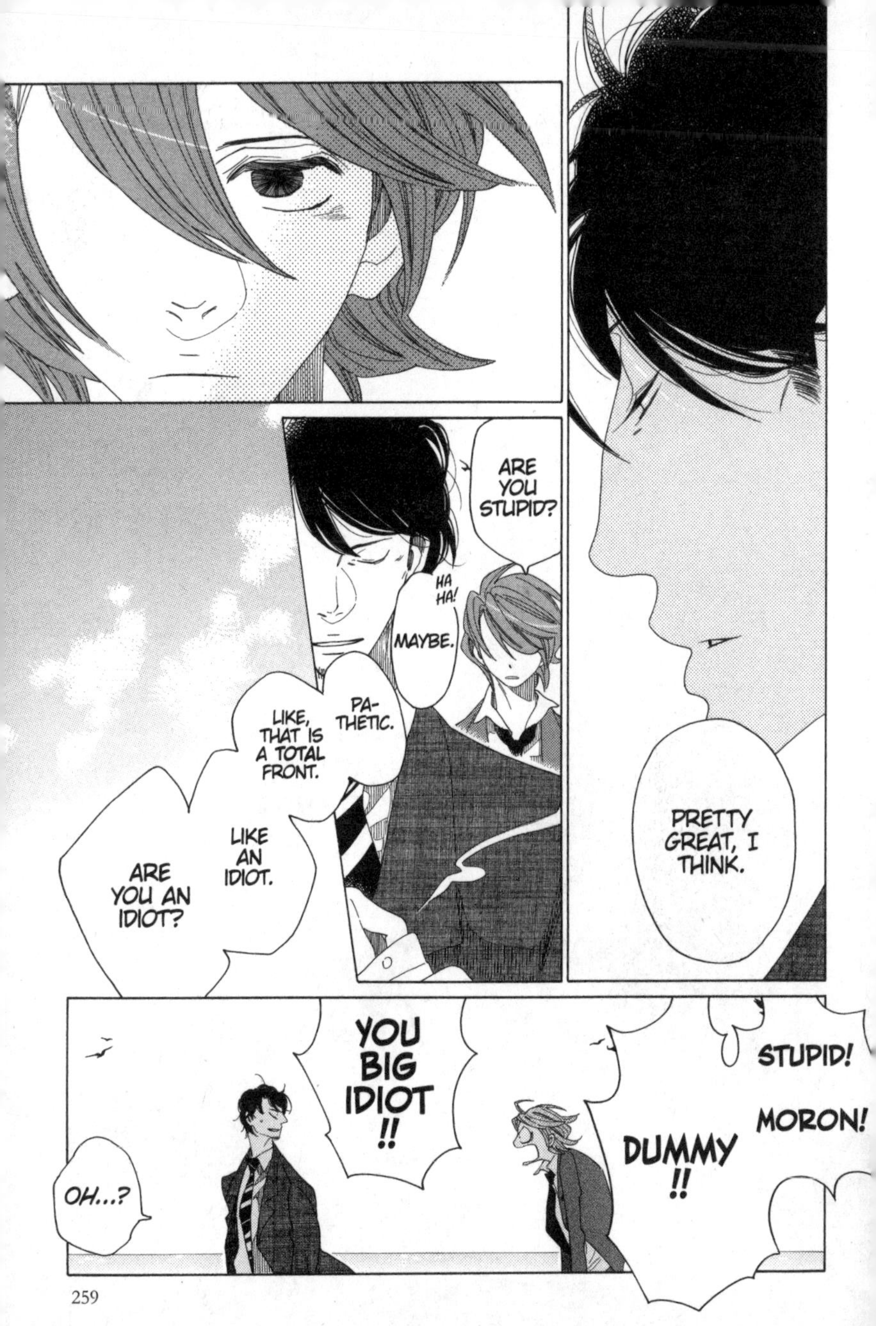
PRETTY GREAT, I THINK.
ARE YOU STUPID?
HA HA!
MAYBE.
PA-THETIC.
LIKE, THAT IS A TOTAL FRONT.
LIKE AN IDIOT.
ARE YOU AN IDIOT?
STUPID!
MORON!
DUMMY!!
YOU BIG IDIOT!!
OH...?

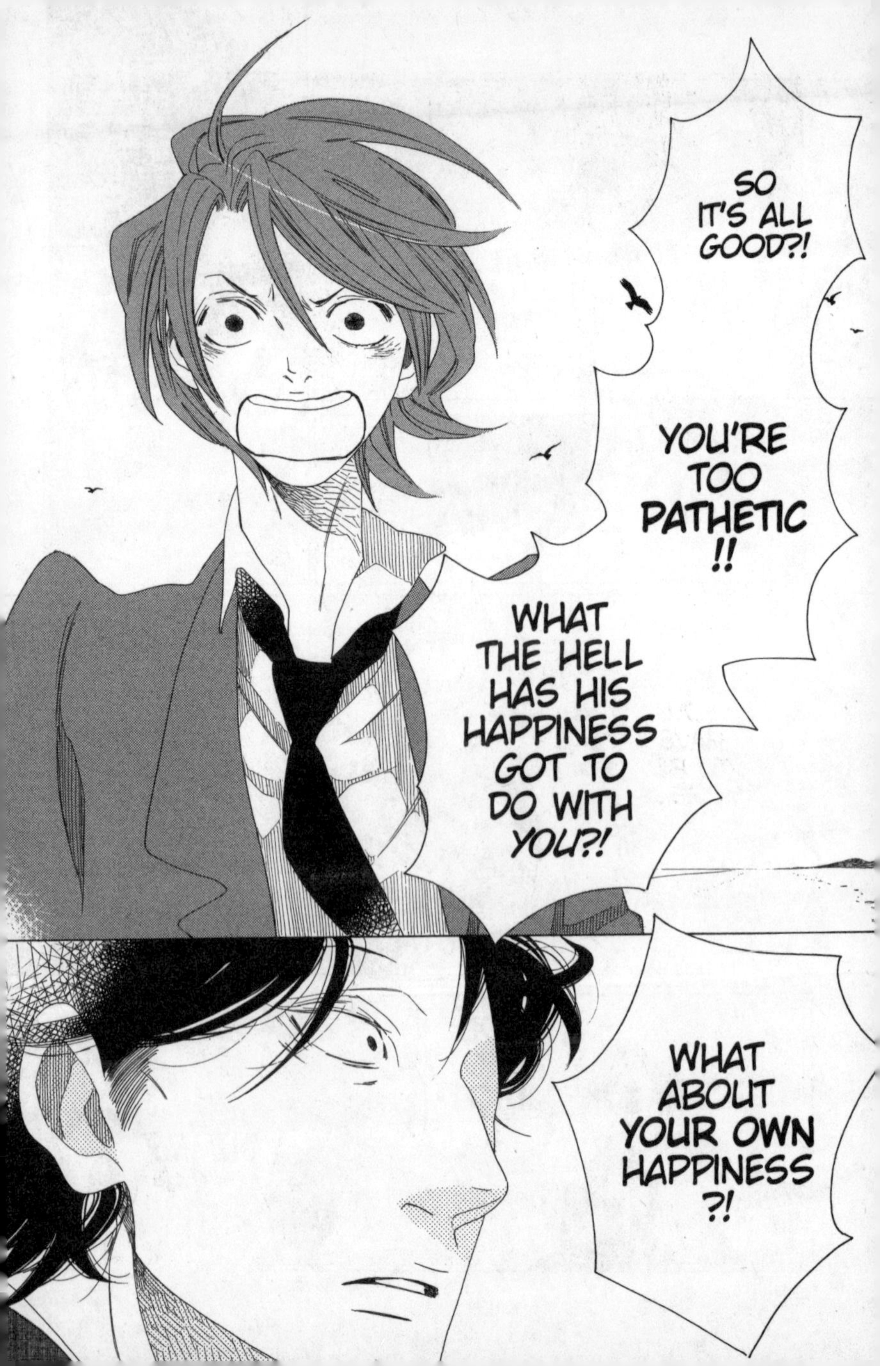
SO IT'S ALL GOOD?!
YOU'RE TOO PATHETIC !!
WHAT THE HELL HAS HIS HAPPINESS GOT TO DO WITH *YOU*?!
WHAT ABOUT YOUR OWN HAPPINESS ?!

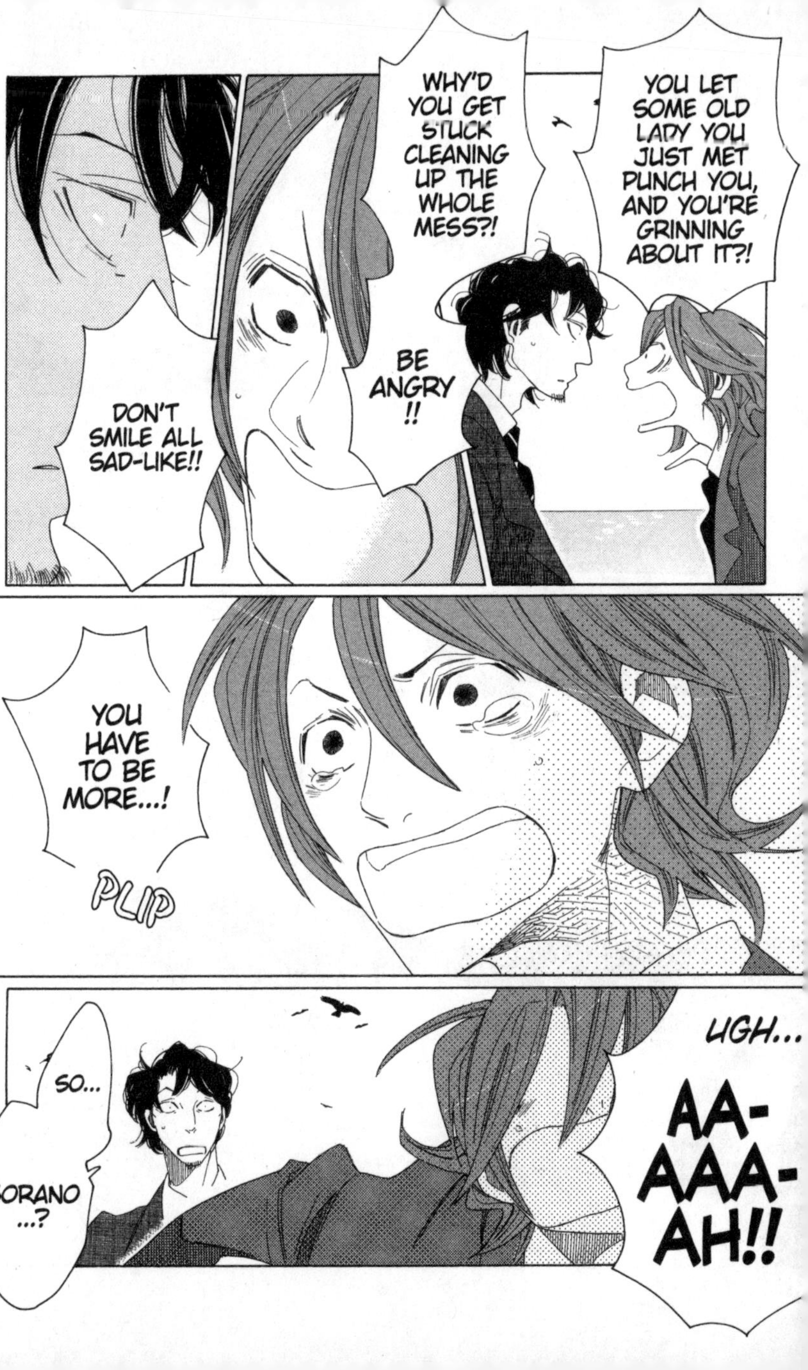
YOU LET SOME OLD LADY YOU JUST MET PUNCH YOU, AND YOU'RE GRINNING ABOUT IT?!
WHY'D YOU GET STUCK CLEANING UP THE WHOLE MESS?!
BE ANGRY !!
DON'T SMILE ALL SAD-LIKE!!
YOU HAVE TO BE MORE...!
PLIP
UGH...
AA-AAAA-AH!!
SO...
SORANO ...?

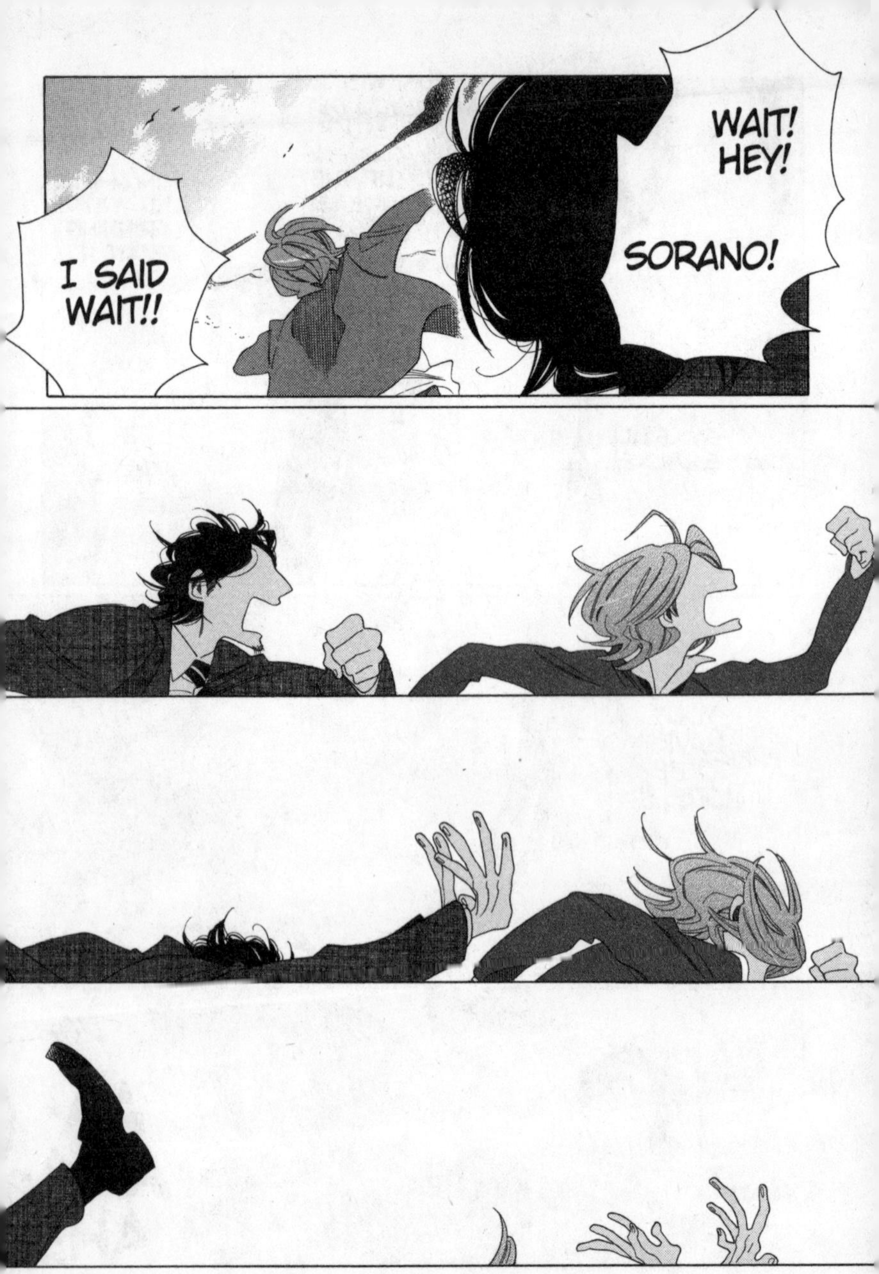
WAIT! HEY! SORANO!
I SAID WAIT!!

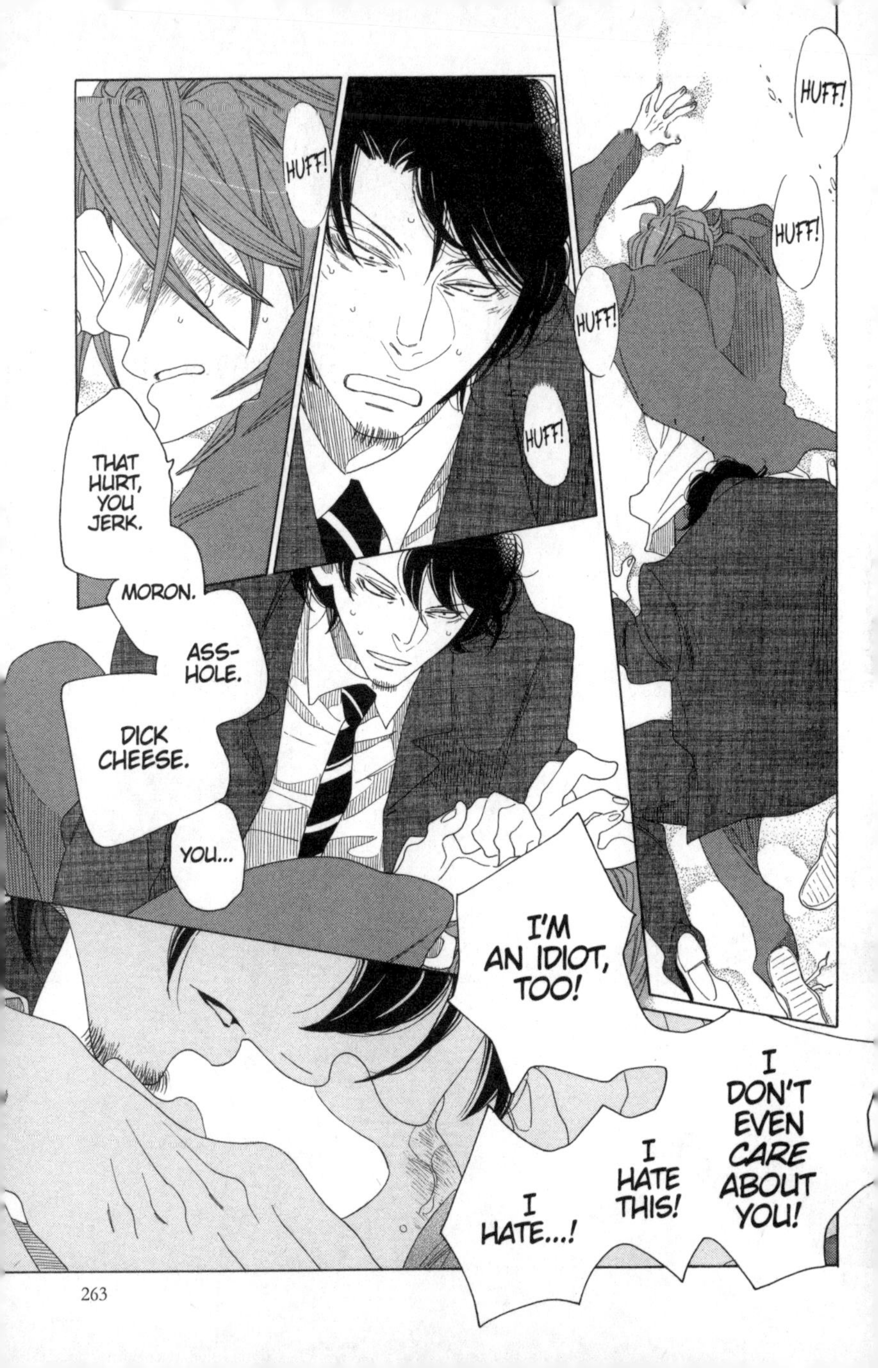
HUFF!
HUFF!
HUFF!
HUFF!
HUFF!
THAT HURT, YOU JERK.
MORON.
ASS-HOLE.
DICK CHEESE.
YOU...
I'M AN IDIOT, TOO!
I DON'T EVEN CARE ABOUT YOU!
I HATE THIS!
I HATE...!

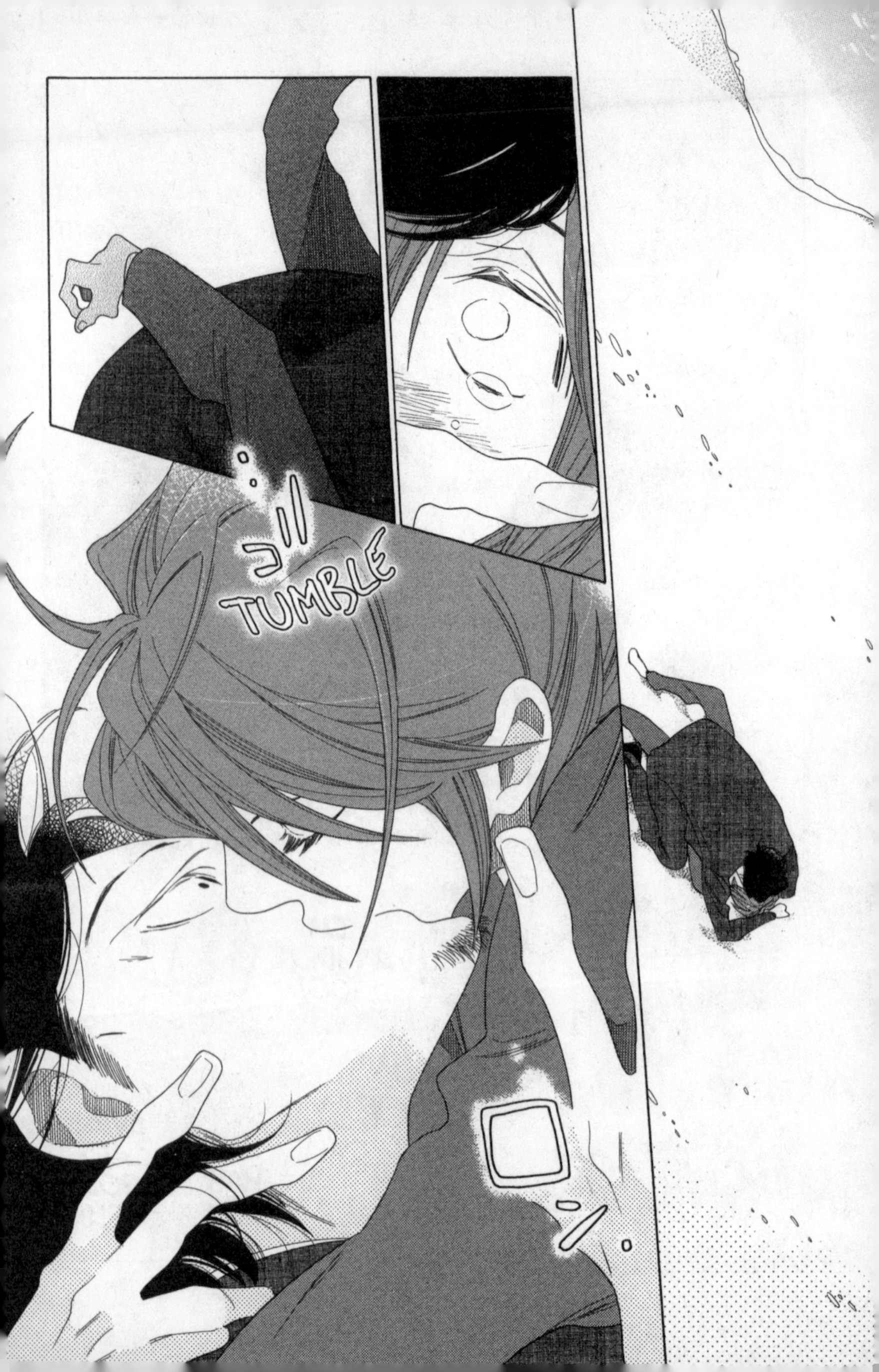
TUMBLE

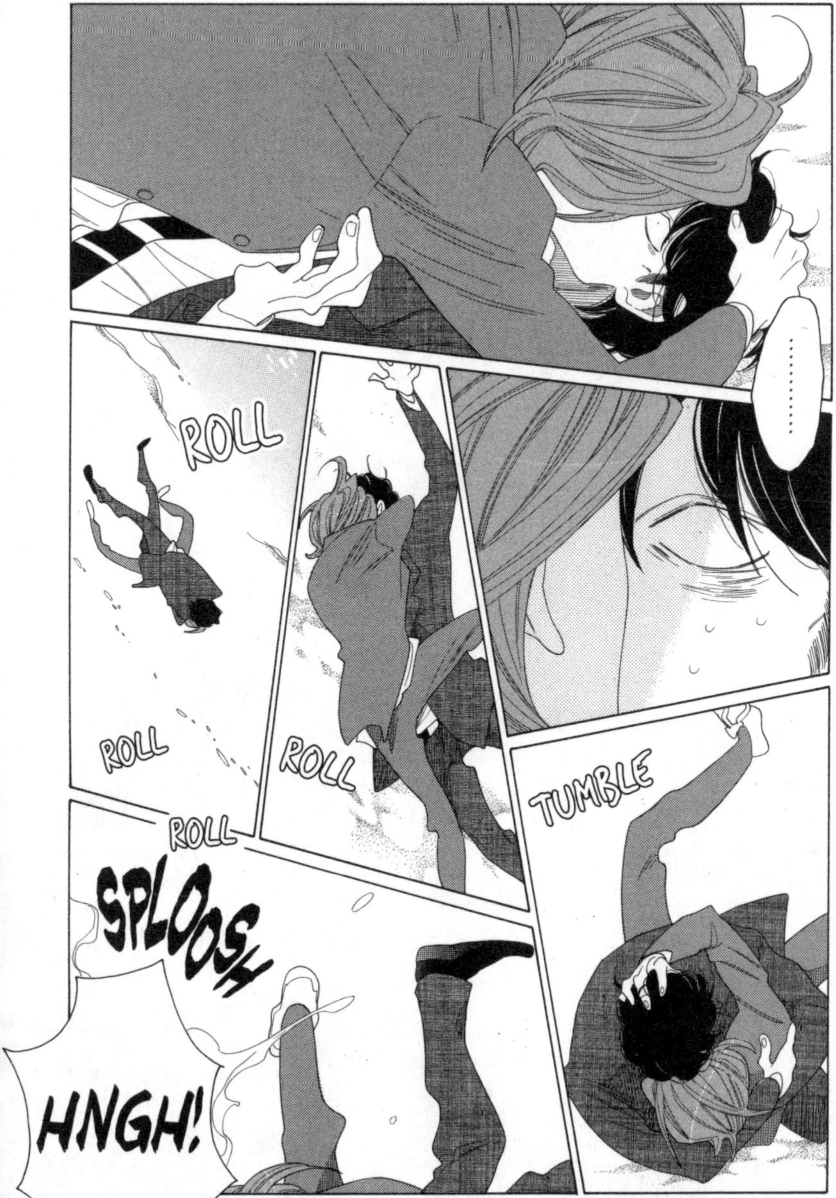
……
ROLL
ROLL
ROLL
TUMBLE
ROLL
SPLOOSH
HNGH!

COLD! COLD!!
HA HA HA HA HA!
DON'T SIT THERE LAUGHING!
IDIOT!
YOU'RE SOAKED, TOO!
PFT!
HEH HEH.
BWAH HA HA HA HA!
AH HA HA HA HA!
YOU GOT A CASE OF THE GIGGLES NOW?
AAH, IT'S HOPELESS.
I LIKE YOU, SENSEI.

I'M GONNA MAKE YOU HAPPY.
LET'S BE HAPPY TOGETH-ER.

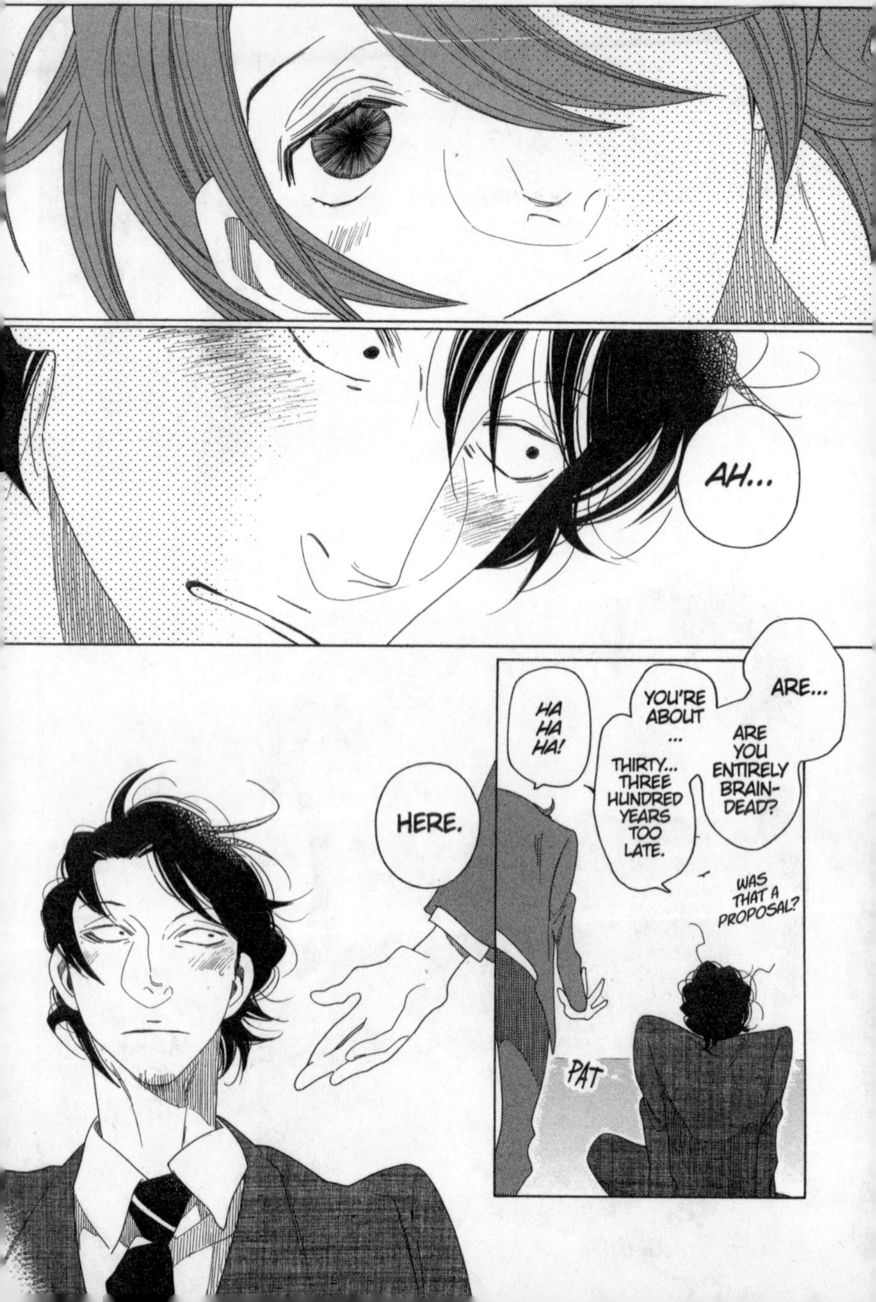
AH...
ARE...
ARE YOU ENTIRELY BRAIN-DEAD?
YOU'RE ABOUT ...
THIRTY... THREE HUNDRED YEARS TOO LATE.
HA HA HA!
WAS THAT A PROPOSAL?
PAT
HERE.

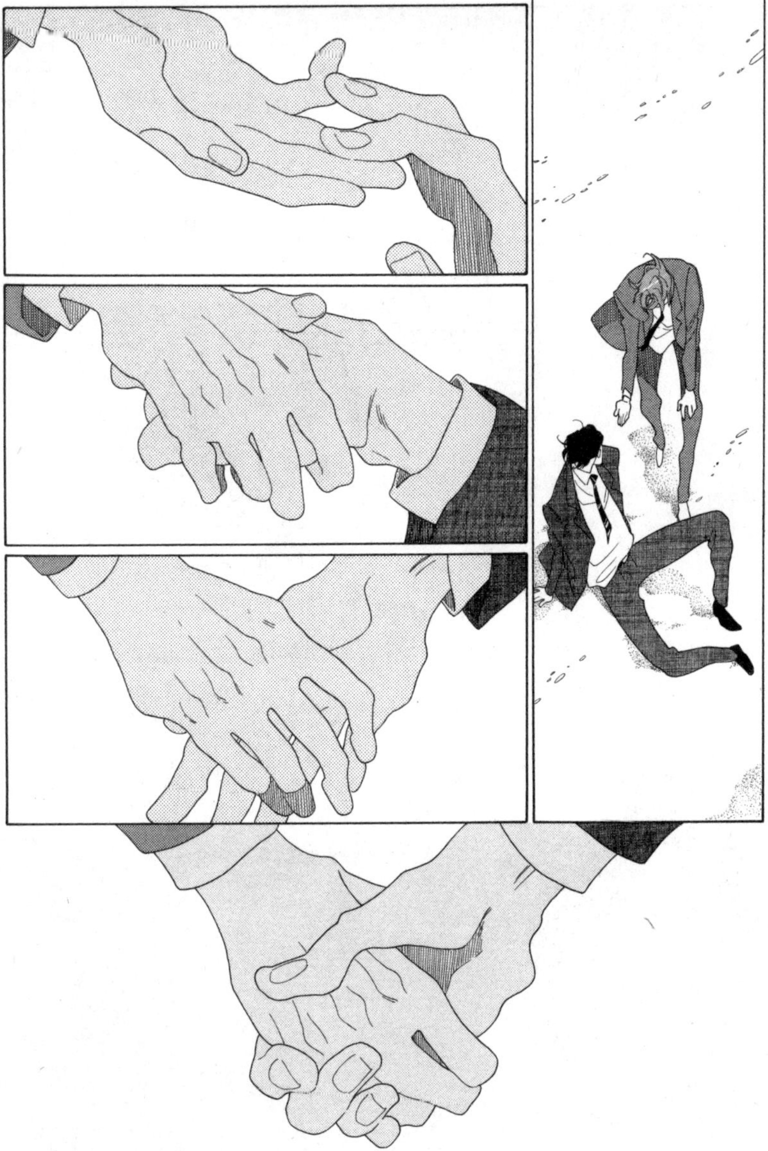

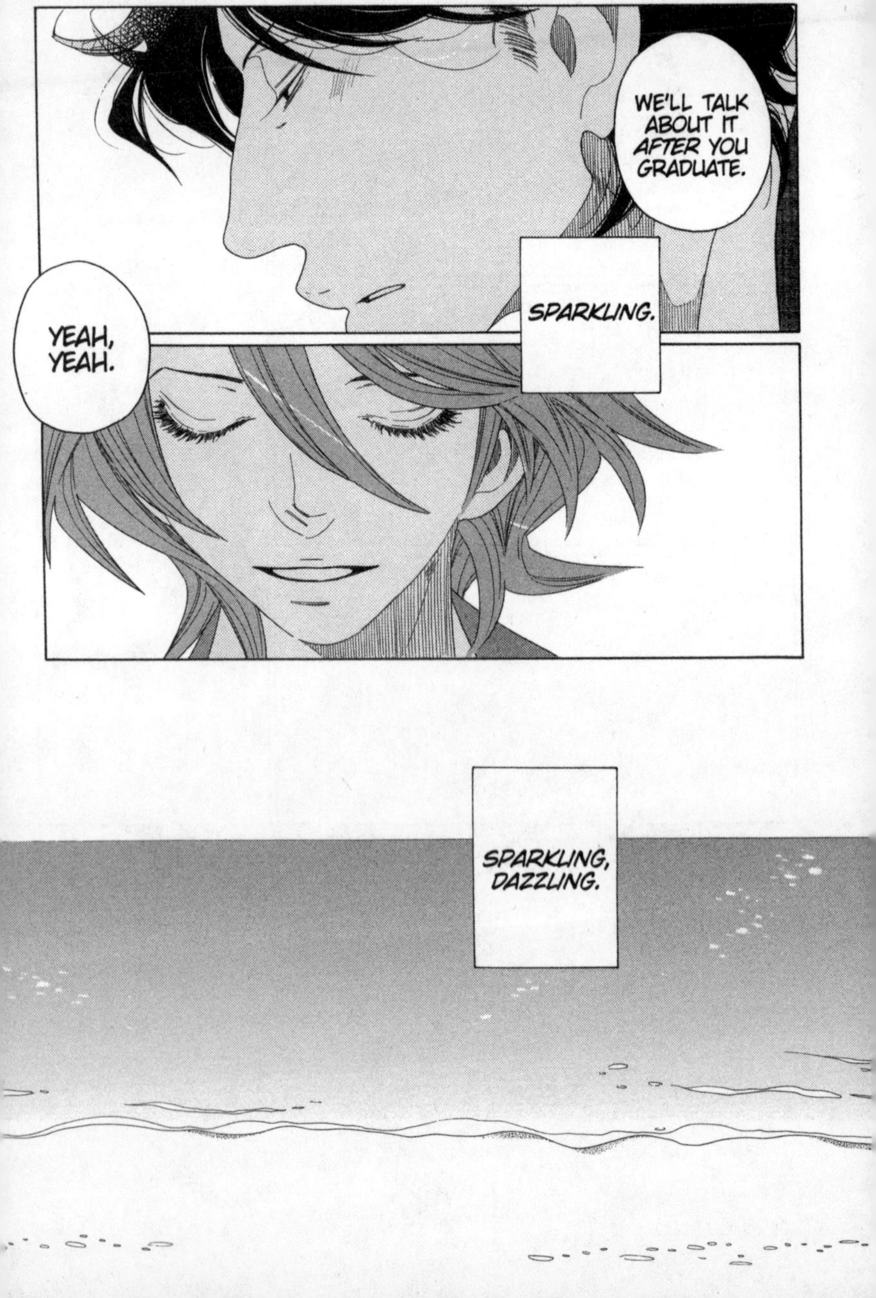

WE'LL TALK ABOUT IT AFTER YOU GRADUATE.
SPARKLING.
YEAH, YEAH.
SPARKLING, DAZZLING.

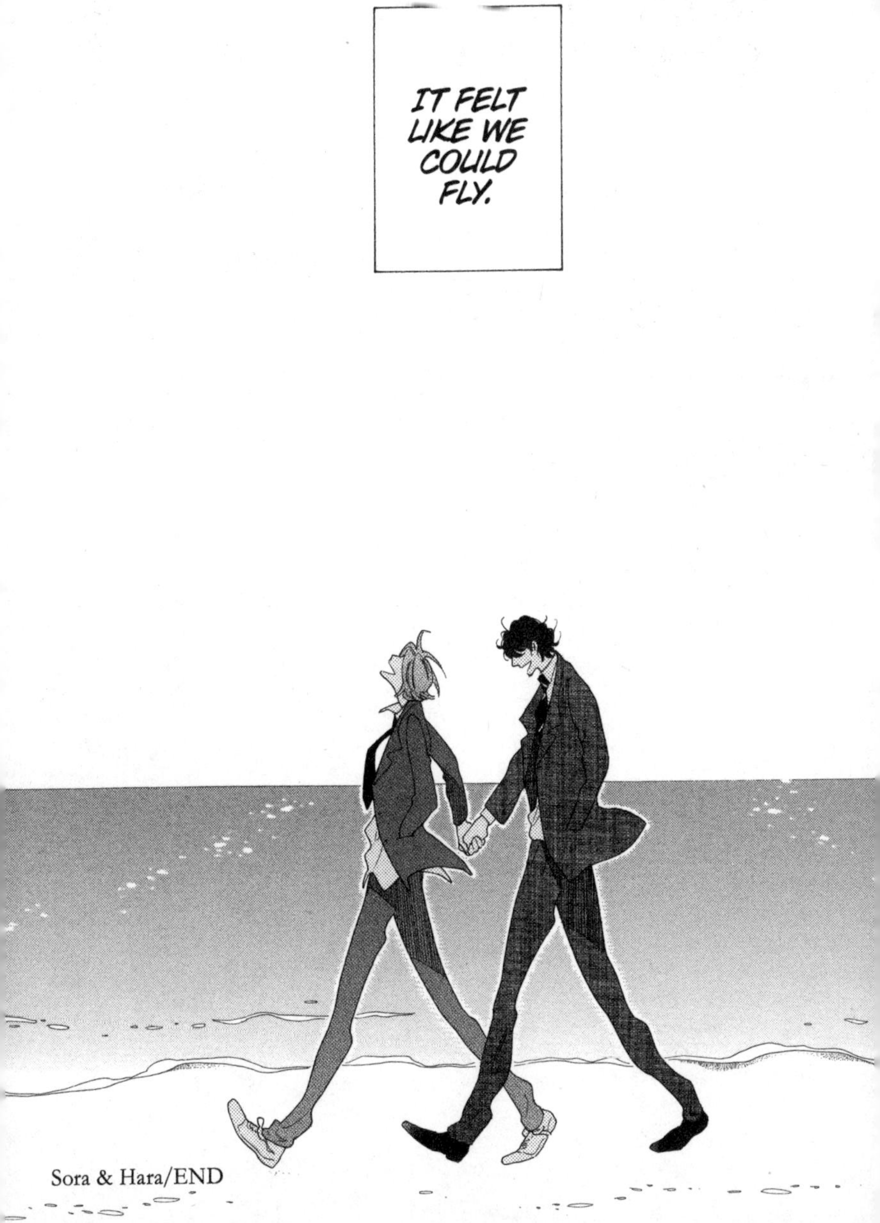
IT FELT LIKE WE COULD FLY.
Sora & Hara/END

"PLEASE MAKE HARA-SENSEI HAPPY."

I GOT SO MANY MESSAGES LIKE THIS AFTER THE EARLIER VOLUMES OF CLASSMATES.

AND THEN...

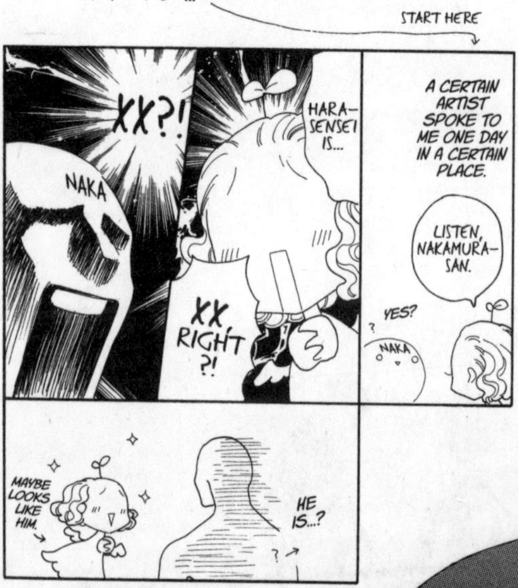
START HERE
A CERTAIN ARTIST SPOKE TO ME ONE DAY IN A CERTAIN PLACE.
LISTEN, NAKAMURA-SAN.
YES?
?
NAKA
HARA-SENSEI IS...
XX RIGHT?!
XX?!
NAKA
HE IS...?
?
MAYBE LOOKS LIKE HIM.

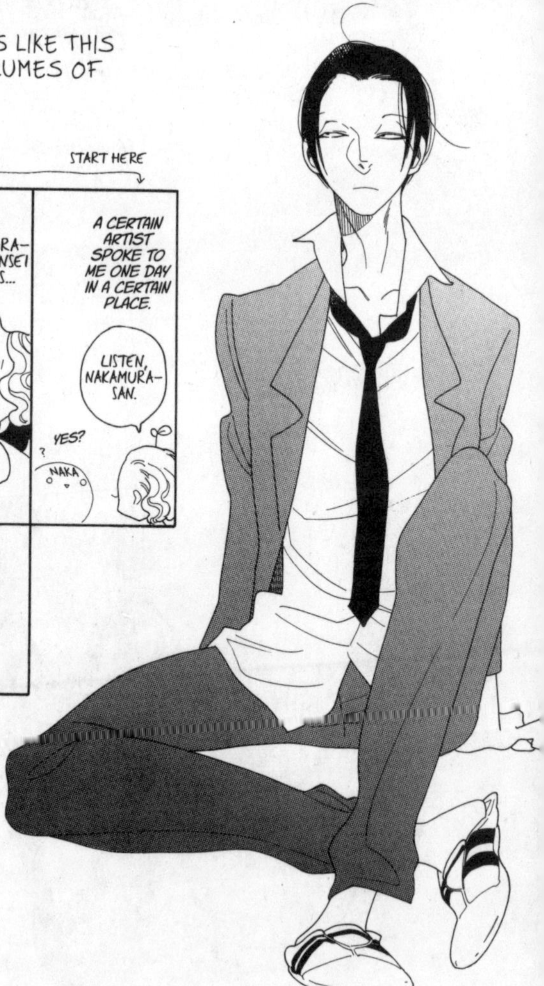

WHAT IS XX THEN? ANYTHING WORKS, ACTUALLY. I HAD A LOT OF PEOPLE SAYING THIS TO ME, AND PERSONALLY, I WOULD AGREE OR DISAGREE, THINKING "HE IS...?". ANYTHING WORKS, THOUGH.

SORANO

THE ACTUAL AGE DIFFERENCE BETWEEN THE TWO OF THEM IS TWENTY-TWO YEARS, SO WHEN HARA-SENSEI WAS IN JUNIOR HIGH, SORANO WASN'T EVEN BORN.

HE'S THE TYPE TO MAKE HIS MOTHER SIGH, "BUT HE WAS SO CUTE WHEN HE WAS LITTLE..."

— IT'S IMPORTANT TO WANT TO BE HAPPY, BUT IT'S MAYBE ALSO IMPORTANT TO WANT SOMEONE TO MAKE YOU HAPPY. MAYBE THAT'S WHAT IT MEANS TO GET CLOSE TO A PERSON. TO TRY LEANING ON THEM, PHYSICALLY, EMOTIONALLY. THIS IS THAT KIND OF STORY.

— I'M SURE HE'LL BE ABLE TO BE HAPPY. BECAUSE HE IS LOVED.

— SO MANY PEOPLE HELPED ME IN THE CREATION OF THIS BOOK. TO MY FAMILY, MY FRIENDS, MY EDITOR E-MOTO-SAN, THE DESIGNER U-GAWA-SAN, AND EVERYONE WHO PICKED UP THIS BOOK AND YOUR FAMILIES, I WILL PRAY FOR YOUR GREAT HAPPINESS.

ASUMIKO NAKAMURA

MARCH 2012

Classmates

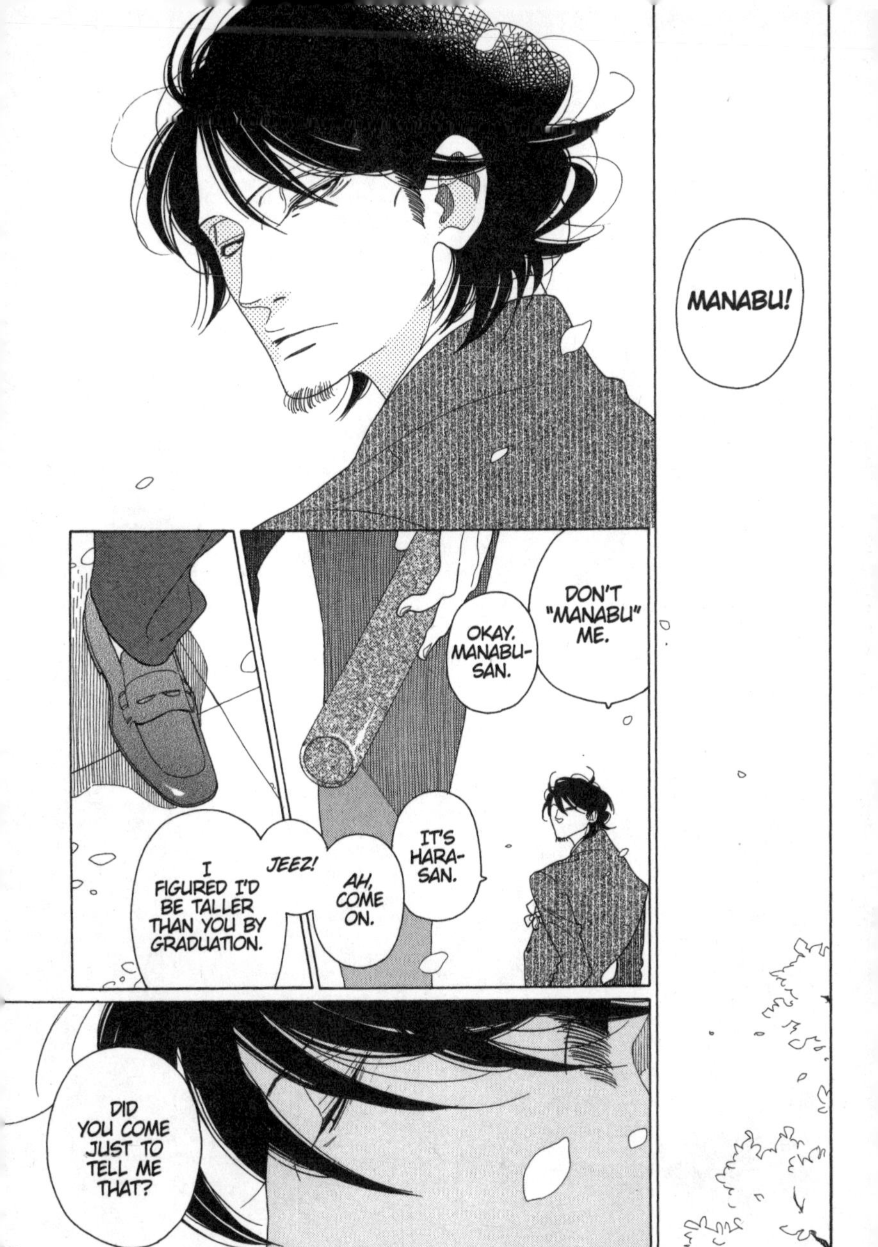
MANABU!
DON'T "MANABU" ME.
OKAY. MANABU-SAN.
IT'S HARA-SAN.
AH, COME ON.
JEEZ!
I FIGURED I'D BE TALLER THAN YOU BY GRADUATION.
DID YOU COME JUST TO TELL ME THAT?

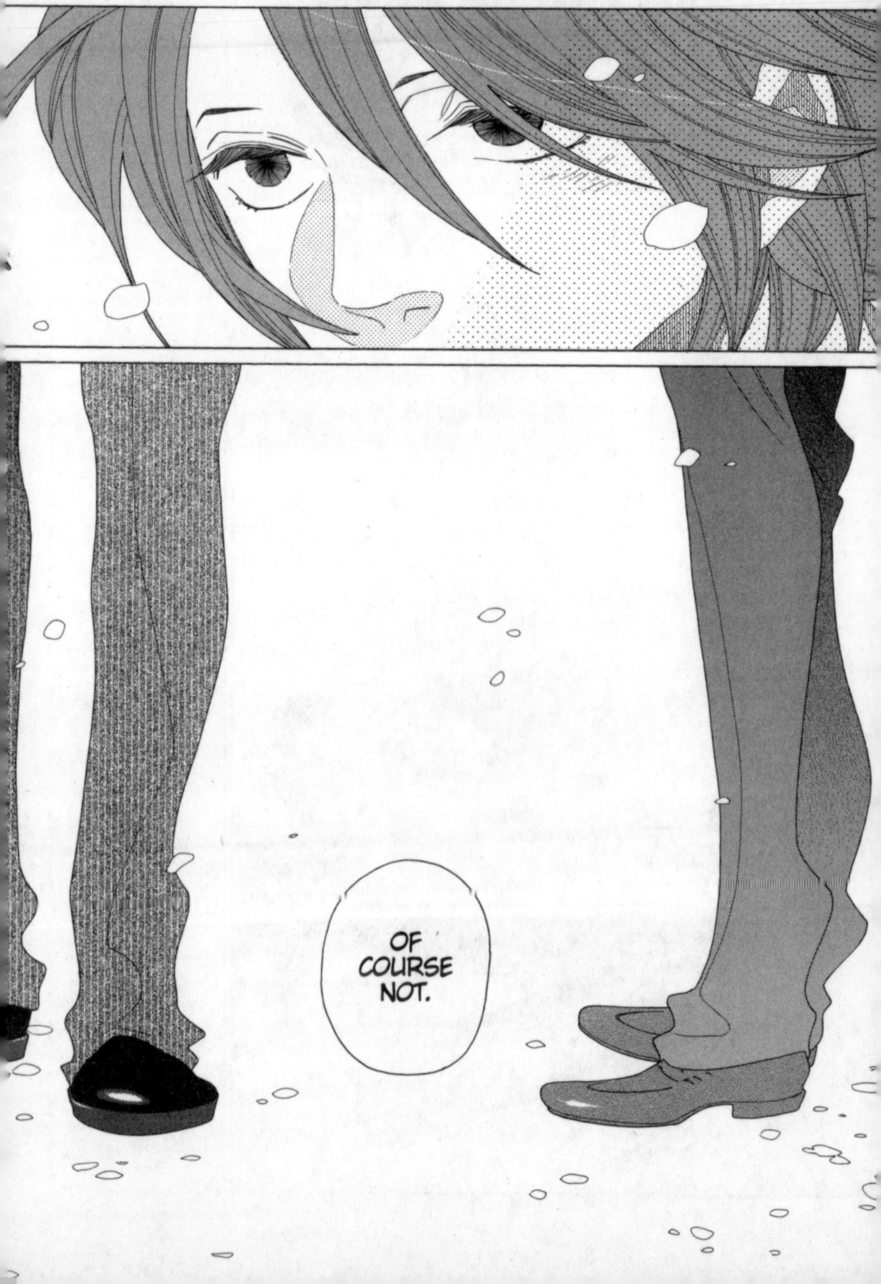
OF COURSE NOT.

Classmates

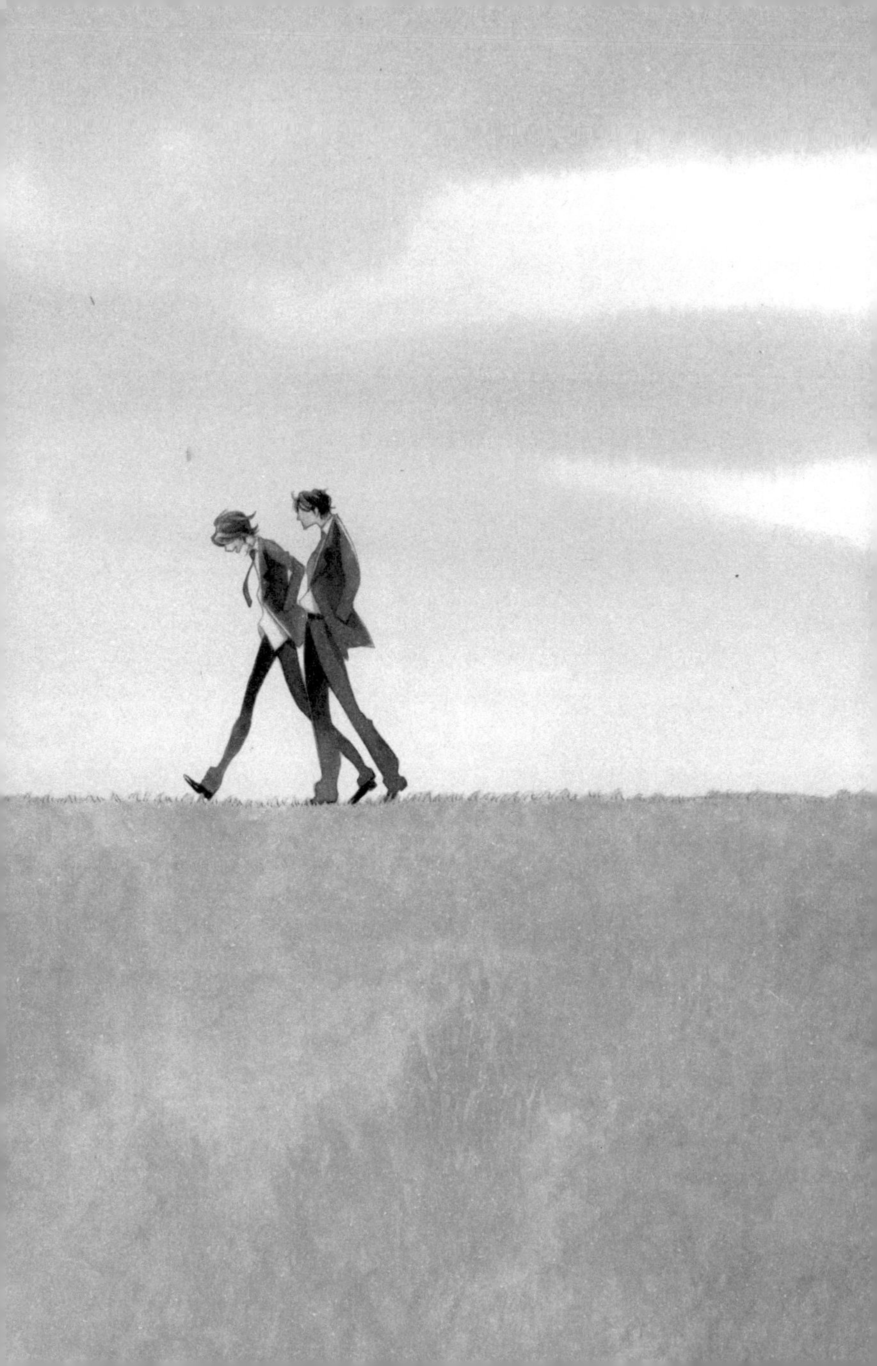

Classmates

Experience all that SEVEN SEAS has to offer!

SEVENSEASENTERTAINMENT.COM
Visit and follow us on Twitter at twitter.com/gomanga/

SEVEN SEAS ENTERTAINMENT PRESENTS

Classmates

story and art by **ASUMIKO NAKAMURA**   VOL. 4 Sora & Hara

TRANSLATION
Jocelyne Allen

LETTERING
Ray Steeves

COVER DESIGN
Hanase Qi

PROOFREADER
Peter Adrian Behravesh
Danielle King

EDITOR
Shannon Fay

PRODUCTION ASSOCIATE
Christa Miesner

PRODUCTION MANAGER
Lissa Pattillo

MANAGING EDITOR
Julie Davis

ASSOCIATE PUBLISHER
Adam Arnold

PUBLISHER
Jason DeAngelis

Sora & Hara
©Asumiko Nakmura 2012
Originally published in Japan in 2012 by AKANESHINSHA, Tokyo.
English translation rights arranged with COMIC HOUSE, Tokyo,
Original Design: Takuya Uchikawa Design Office

No portion of this book may be reproduced or transmitted in any form without written permission from the copyright holders. This is a work of fiction. Names, characters, places, and incidents are the products of the author's imagination or are used fictitiously. Any resemblance to actual events, locales, or persons, living or dead, is entirely coincidental.

Seven Seas press and purchase enquiries can be sent to Marketing Manager Lianne Sentar at press@gomanga.com. Information regarding the distribution and purchase of digital editions is available from Digital Manager CK Russell at digital@gomanga.com.

Seven Seas and the Seven Seas logo are trademarks of Seven Seas Entertainment. All rights reserved.

ISBN: 978-1-64827-653-8

Printed in Canada

First Printing: November 2021

10 9 8 7 6 5 4 3 2 1

FOLLOW US ONLINE: *www.sevenseasentertainment.com*

READING DIRECTIONS

This book reads from ***right to left***, Japanese style. If this is your first time reading manga, you start reading from the top right panel on each page and take it from there. If you get lost, just follow the numbered diagram here. It may seem backwards at first, but you'll get the hang of it! Have fun!!

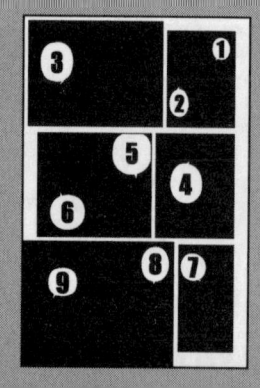